W9-BPK-790

Extraordinary acclaim for David Morrell's

Murder as a Fine Art

"Morrell's masterful blend of fact and fiction reads like a nineteenth-century novel, evoking 1854 London with such finesse that you'll hear the hooves clattering on cobblestones, the racket of dustmen, and the shrill call of vendors." — Tina Jordan, *Entertainment Weekly*

"Phenomenal.... Morrell invokes 1850s London in this tense and gritty historical mystery." — *Library Journal* (Best Books of 2013)

"Good, gory fun.... One of David Morrell's best.... Highly entertaining.... An inspired blend of innovation, history and gore. Murder is rarely this much fun." — Patrick Anderson, *Washington Post*

"Hot-blooded.... David Morrell writes action scenes like nobody's business." — Marilyn Stasio, *New York Times Book Review*

"A brilliant crime thriller. Everything works—the horrifying depiction of the murders, the asides explaining the impact of train travel on English society, nail-biting action sequences—making this book an epitome of the intelligent page-turner." — *Publishers Weekly*

"Stunning.... The drama feels shockingly real because Morrell's thorough and erudite research of the people and culture of the British Empire's heyday informs every page of the novel. Morrell takes the genre into new artistic territory with *Murder as a Fine Art,* a literary thriller that pushes the envelope of fear." — Waka Tsunoda, Associated Press

"David Morrell fans—and they are legion—can look forward to celebrating *Murder as a Fine Art* as one of their favorite author's strongest and boldest books in years." — Dan Simmons, author of *Drood*

Murder as a Fine Art

Also by David Morrell

Novels

First Blood

Testament

Last Reveille

The Totem

Blood Oath

The Brotherhood of the Rose

The Fraternity of the Stone

Rambo (First Blood Part II)

The League of Night and Fog

Rambo III

The Fifth Profession

The Covenant of the Flame

Assumed Identity

Desperate Measures

The Totem (Complete and Unaltered)

Extreme Denial

Double Image

Burnt Sienna

Long Lost

The Protector

Creepers

Scavenger

The Spy Who Came for Christmas

The Shimmer

The Naked Edge

Short Fiction

The Hundred-Year Christmas

Black Evening

Nightscape

Illustrated Fiction

Captain America: The Chosen

Nonfiction

John Barth: An Introduction

Fireflies: A Father's Tale of Love and Loss

The Successful Novelist: A Lifetime of Lessons about
Writing and Publishing

Edited By

American Fiction, American Myth: Essays by Philip Young
edited by David Morrell and Sandra Spanier

Tesseracts Thirteen: Chilling Tales of the Great White North
edited by Nancy Kilpatrick and David Morrell

Thrillers: 100 Must-Reads
edited by David Morrell and Hank Wagner

Murder as a Fine Art

David Morrell

MULHOLLAND BOOKS

LITTLE, BROWN AND COMPANY

NEW YORK   BOSTON   LONDON

Copyright © 2013 by Morrell Enterprises, Inc.
Reading group guide copyright © 2014 by Morrell Enterprises, Inc., and Little, Brown and Company.

Mulholland Books / Little, Brown and Company
Hachette Book Group
237 Park Avenue, New York, NY 10017
mulhollandbooks.com

Originally published in hardcover by Mulholland Books / Little, Brown and Company, May 2013
First Mulholland Books paperback edition, June 2014

Mulholland Books is an imprint of Little, Brown and Company, a division of Hachette Book Group, Inc. The Mulholland Books name and logo are trademarks of Hachette Book Group, Inc.

The publisher is not responsible for websites (or their content) that are not owned by the publisher.

The Hachette Speakers Bureau provides a wide range of authors for speaking events. To find out more, go to hachettespeakersbureau.com or call (866) 376-6591.

Library of Congress Cataloging-in-Publication Data

Morrell, David.
    Murder as a fine art / David Morrell. — 1st ed.
        p. cm.
    ISBN 978-0-316-21679-1 (hc) / 978-0-316-21678-4 (pb)
    1. De Quincey, Thomas, 1785–1859 — Fiction.   2. Fathers and daughters — Fiction.   3. Serial murderers — Fiction.   4. London (England) — Social life and customs — 19th century — Fiction.   I. Title.
    PR9199.3.M65M87 2013
    813'.54 — dc23   2012020034

10   9   8   7   6   5   4   3   2   1

RRD-C

Printed in the United States of America

To Robert Morrison and Grevel Lindop
For guiding my journey into all things Thomas De Quincey

CONTENTS

Murder as a
Fine Art

INTRODUCTION

At FIRST GLANCE, it seems odd that mid-Victorian England, known for its tightly controlled emotions, became obsessed with a new type of fiction called the novel of sensation. When Wilkie Collins published *The Woman in White* in 1860, he set off what Victorian critics called a Sensation Mania that satisfied the "cravings of a diseased appetite," "a virus...spreading in all directions." This shocking new fiction had its roots in Gothic novels of the previous century, with the difference that sensation novelists set their stories not in ancient, brooding castles but instead in the very real homes and neighborhoods of Victorian England. Darkness didn't come from the supernatural. Rather, it festered in the hearts of supposedly respectable public figures whose private lives hid dismaying secrets. Insanity, incest, rape, blackmail, infanticide, arson, drug abuse, poison, sadomasochism, and necrophilia — these were some of what sensation novelists insisted were concealed behind the Victorian veneer of decorum and reserve.

Upon closer inspection, the mid-Victorian mania for sensation makes sense as a reaction to the rigidly controlled emotions of that era. It's difficult to exaggerate the degree to which middle- and upper-class Victorians separated their personal and public lives, concealing their true feelings from outsiders. The common practice of always keeping draperies closed perfectly represents the Victorian attitude that one's home and private life were sacred domains to be looked out from but not seen into. Secrets not only abounded in each household but also were taken for granted and respected as being no one else's business.

Thomas De Quincey, a controversial Victorian author whose theories about the subconscious anticipated those of Freud by seventy years, had this to say about repression and secrets: "There is no such thing as forgetting. The inscriptions on the mind remain forever, to be revealed when the night returns." De Quincey became famous when he did the unthinkable, exposing his private life in a notorious best seller, *Confessions of an English Opium-Eater,* which William S. Burroughs later described as "the first, and still the best, book about drug addiction."

De Quincey's lurid writing, especially "On Murder Considered as One of the Fine Arts," qualifies him as an originator of the novel of sensation. That disturbing essay dramatizes the infamous Ratcliffe Highway killings that terrorized both London and all of England in 1811. It's tempting to compare the effect of those killings to the fear that engulfed London's East End during Jack the Ripper's blood spree at the opposite end of the century, in 1888. But in fact the panic that resulted from the Ratcliffe Highway killings was far worse and more widespread because those multiple murders were the first of their kind to become common knowledge throughout England, thanks to the growing importance of newspapers (fifty-two in London alone in 1811) and a recently perfected system of mail coaches that crossed the country at a relentless ten-mile-an-hour pace.

Moreover, Jack the Ripper's victims were all prostitutes whereas the Ratcliffe Highway victims were business owners and their families. Streetwalkers feared Jack the Ripper while literally everyone had reason to fear the Ratcliffe Highway killer. What happened to his victims is mirrored in this novel's first chapter, which some might find shocking but which is based on the historical record.

It is long since we read Thomas De Quincey, but his bloody horrors are still fresh and, to this day, terrible in their power. For long after we read him, every night brought a renewal of the most real shuddering, the palsying dread, and the nightmares with which our first reading of him cursed us.

British Quarterly Review, 1863

I

The Artist of Death

Something more goes to the composition of a fine murder than two blockheads to kill and be killed, a knife, a purse, and a dark lane. Design, grouping, light and shade, poetry, and sentiment are indispensable to the ideal murder. Like Aeschylus or Milton in poetry, like Michelangelo in painting, a great murderer carries his art to a colossal sublimity.

> Thomas De Quincey
> "On Murder Considered as One of the Fine Arts"

London, 1854

TITIAN, RUBENS, AND VAN DYKE, it is said, always practiced their art in full dress. Prior to immortalizing their visions on canvas, they bathed, symbolically cleansing their minds of any distractions. They put on their finest clothes, their best wigs, and in one case even a diamond-hilted sword.

The artist of death had similarly prepared himself. Dressed in evening clothes, he sat for two hours staring at a wall, focusing his sensations. When darkness cast shadows through a curtained window, he lit an oil lamp and put the equivalent of brushes, paint, and canvas into a black leather bag. Mindful of Rubens, he included a wig, which was yellow in contrast with the light brown of his own hair. A matching actor's beard was added to the bag. Ten years earlier, a beard would have drawn attention, but a recent trend made beards almost to be expected, as opposed to his increasingly unusual clean-shaven features. He set a heavy ship carpenter's mallet among the other items in the bag. The mallet was aged and had the initials J. P. stamped into its head. In place of the diamond-hilted sword that one artist had worn as he painted, the artist placed a folded, ivory-handled razor in his pocket.

He stepped from his refuge and walked awhile until he reached a busy intersection, where he waited at a cab stand. After two minutes, an empty hansom finally came along, its driver seated prominently behind the sleek vehicle. The artist of death didn't mind standing in plain view, despite the cold December night. In fact, at this point he wanted to be seen, although anyone observing him would soon find it difficult as fog drifted in from the Thames, casting a halo around gas lamps.

The artist paid eightpence for the driver to take him to the Adelphi theater in the Strand. Amid the bustle of carriages and the clop of hooves, he made his way toward a well-dressed crowd waiting to go inside. The Adelphi's gas-lit marquee indicated that the sensational melodrama *The Corsican Brothers* was being performed. The artist of death was familiar with the play and could answer any questions about it, especially its unusual device of two first acts, which occurred in sequence but were meant to be imagined as taking place simultaneously. In the first part, a brother saw the ghost of his twin. The next part dramatized how the twin was killed at the same time the brother saw his ghost. The revenge in the final part was so violent, with such copious amounts of stage blood, that many members of the audience claimed to be shocked, their outrage promoting ticket sales.

The artist of death joined the excited crowd as they entered the theater. His pocket watch showed him that the time was seven twenty. The curtain was scheduled to rise in ten minutes. In the confusion of the lobby, he passed a vendor selling sheet music of the "Ghost Melody" featured in the play. He exited through a side door, walked along a fog-shrouded alley, concealed himself behind shadowy boxes, and waited to determine if anyone followed him.

Feeling safe after ten minutes, he left the far end of the alley, walked across two streets, and hired another cab, no longer needing to wait inasmuch as numerous empty cabs were now departing from the theater. This time, he went to a less fashionable part of the city. He closed his eyes and listened to the cab's wheels shift from the large, smooth, granite paving stones on the main streets to the small, rough cobblestones of the older lanes in London's East End. When he descended into an area where evening clothes were hardly common, the driver no doubt believed that the artist intended to solicit a streetwalker.

Behind the closed door of a public privy, he took ordinary clothes from the leather bag, put them on, and folded his theater garments into the bag. As he continued along increasingly shabby streets, he found stoops, nooks, and alleys in which he dirtied the common clothes he now wore and smeared his leather bag with mud. He entered a filthy mews cleanshaven, with light brown hair, and left it wearing the yellow beard and wig. His collapsible top hat had long since been put in the bag, replaced by a weathered sailor's cap. The ship carpenter's mallet was now in a pocket of a tattered sailor's coat.

In this way, the artist occupied two hours. Far from being tedious, the attention to detail was pleasurable, as was the opportunity to reflect upon the great composition ahead. Through the concealing fog, he came within sight of his destination, a mediocre shop that sold clothing to merchant sailors who frequented this area near the London docks.

He paused on a corner and glanced at his pocket watch, taking care that no one saw it. A watch was so unusual in this impoverished area that anyone who glimpsed it would suspect that the artist wasn't the sailor he pretended to be. The hands on the watch showed almost ten. Everything was on schedule. His previous visits had revealed that the area's policeman passed along this street at ten fifteen. Punctuality was part of the job, each constable navigating his two-mile route every hour. The time it took for the constable to reach this point seldom varied.

The only person in view was a prostitute, whom the chill night had not encouraged to go back to whatever cranny she called home. When she started to approach, the artist gave her a sharp look that made her stop abruptly and disappear in the fog in the opposite direction.

He returned his attention to the shop, noting that its window had a film of dust that dimmed the glow of a lamp inside. A man's shadow stepped out and swung a shutter into place, closing as usual at ten.

The moment the shadow went back inside, the artist crossed the empty street and reached for the door. If it was already bolted shut, he would knock, with the expectation that the merchant wouldn't begrudge the further five minutes necessary for a final sale.

But the door wasn't locked. It creaked as the artist pushed it open and stepped into a shop that was only slightly warmer than the street.

A man turned from lowering an overhead lantern. He was perhaps thirty — thin, pale, and weary-eyed. He wore a black shirt with a band collar. One of the shirt's buttons didn't match the others. The cuffs of his trousers were frayed.

Does a great work of art require a great subject? Does the murder of a queen create a grander impact than that of a commoner? No. The goal of the art of murder is pity and terror. No one pities a murdered queen or prime minister or man of wealth. The immediate emotion is one of disbelief that even the powerful are not immune to mortal blows. But shock does not linger whereas the sorrow of pity does.

On the contrary, the subject should be young, hardworking, of low means, with hope and ambition, with sights on far goals despite the discouragement that wearies him. The subject should have a loving wife and devoted children dependent on his never-ending exertions. Pity. Tears. Those were the requirements for fine art.

"Just about to lock up? Lucky I caught you," the artist said as he closed the door.

"The missus is getting dinner ready, but there's always time for one more. How can I help?" The lean shopkeeper gave no indication that the artist's beard didn't appear genuine or that he recognized the man, who in another disguise had visited the shop a week earlier.

"I need four pairs of socks." The artist glanced behind the counter and pointed. "Thick. Like the kind you have on that shelf up there."

"Four pairs?" The shopkeeper's tone suggested that today they would be a sizable purchase. "A shilling each."

"Too much. I hoped to get a better price buying so many. Perhaps I should go somewhere else."

Behind a closed door, a child cried in a back room.

"Sounds like somebody's hungry," the artist remarked.

"Laura. When *isn't* she hungry?" The shopkeeper sighed. "I'll add an extra pair. Five for four shillings."

"Done."

When the shopkeeper walked toward the counter, the artist reached back and secured the bolt on the door. He coughed loudly to conceal the noise, aided by the hollow rumble of the shopkeeper's footsteps. Following, he removed the mallet from his coat pocket.

The shopkeeper stepped behind the counter and reached for the socks on an upper shelf, where the artist had noticed them a week earlier. "These?"

"Yes, the unbleached ones." The artist swung the mallet. His arm was muscular. The mallet had a broad striking surface. It rushed through the air and struck the shopkeeper's skull. The force of the blow made a dull cracking sound, comparable to when a pane of ice is broken.

As the shopkeeper groaned and sank, the artist struck again, this time aiming downward toward the slumping body, the mallet hitting the top of his head. Now the sound was liquid.

The artist removed a smock from his bag and put it over his clothes. After stepping behind the counter, he drew the razor from his pocket, opened it, pulled back the shopkeeper's now misshapen head, and sliced his throat. The finely sharpened edge slid easily. Blood sprayed across garments on shelves.

The overhead lantern seemed to brighten.

A fine art.

Again, the child cried behind the door.

The artist released the body, which made almost no sound as it settled onto the floor. He closed the razor, returned it to his pocket, then picked up the mallet next to the bag and reached for the second door, behind which he heard a woman's voice.

"Jonathan, supper's ready!"

When the artist pushed the door inward, he encountered a short, thin woman on the verge of opening it. She had weary eyes similar to the shopkeeper's. Those eyes enlarged, surprised by both the artist's presence and the smock he wore. "Who the devil are *you?*"

The passage was narrow, with a low ceiling. The artist had seen it briefly when pretending to be a customer a week earlier. In the cramped area, to get a full swing, he needed to hold the mallet beside his leg and thrust upward, striking the woman under her chin. The force knocked her head backward. As she groaned, he shoved her to the floor. He dropped to one knee and now had space to raise his arm, delivering a second, third, and fourth blow to her face.

To the right was a doorway into a kitchen. Amid the smell of boiled mutton, a dish crashed. The artist straightened, charged through the doorway, and found a servant girl — someone he had seen leave the shop on an errand a week earlier. She opened her mouth to scream. In the larger space of the kitchen, he was able to use a sideways blow that stopped the scream, shattering her jaw.

"Mama?" a child whimpered.

Pivoting toward the doorway, the artist saw a girl of approximately seven in the corridor. Her hair was in pigtails. She held a ragdoll and gaped at her mother's body on the floor.

"You must be Laura," the artist said.

He whacked her skull in.

Behind him, the servant moaned. He slit her throat.

He slit the mother's throat.

He slit the child's throat.

The coppery smell of blood mingled with that of boiled mutton as the artist surveyed his tableau. The rush of his heart made him breathless.

He closed his eyes.

And jerked them open when he again heard a child's cry.

It came from farther down the corridor. Investigating, he reached a second open door. This one led into a crowded, musty-smelling bedroom, where a candle revealed a baby's cradle, its wicker hood pulled up. The cries came from beneath the hood.

The artist returned to the kitchen, retrieved the mallet, proceeded to the bedroom, smashed the cradle into pieces, pounded at a bundle in the wreckage, and slit its throat.

He rewrapped the bundle and put it under a remnant of the cradle's hood.

The candle appeared to become stunningly bright. In absolute clarity, the artist noted that his hands were covered with blood. His smock was red with it, as were his boots. Finding a cracked mirror on a drab bureau in the bedroom, he determined that his beard, wig, and cap were unmarked, however.

He went to the kitchen, filled a basin from a pitcher of water, and washed his hands. He took off his boots and washed them also. He removed the smock, folded it, and set it on a chair.

After leaving the mallet on the kitchen table, he stepped into the passageway, admired the servant's corpse on the kitchen floor, and closed the door. He shut the door to the bedroom also. He walked to the front of the shop and considered the artistry of the mother and the seven-year-old girl in the blood-covered passageway.

He closed that door also. The shopkeeper's body could be seen only if someone looked behind the counter. The next person to enter the shop would encounter a series of surprises.

Terror and pity.

A fine art.

Abruptly someone knocked on the door, making the artist whirl.

The knock was repeated. Someone lifted the latch, but the artist had made certain that the bolt was secured.

The front door did not have a window. With the shutter closed on the main window, whoever knocked on the door could not see inside, although the lamplight was evidently still detectable through cracks around the door.

"Jonathan, it's Richard!" a man shouted. "I brought the blanket for Laura!" More knocking. "Jonathan!"

"Hey, what's the trouble there?" an authoritative voice asked.

"Constable, I'm glad to see you."

"Tell me what you're doing."

"This is my brother's shop. He asked me to bring an extra blanket for his baby girl. She has a cold."

"But why are you pounding?"

"He won't open the door. He expects me, but he doesn't open the door."

"Knock louder."

The door shook.

"How many people live here?" the policeman's voice asked.

"My brother, his wife, a servant girl, and two daughters."

"Surely *one* of them would hear you knocking. Is there a back entrance?"

"Down that alley. Over the wall."

"Wait here while I look."

After grabbing his bag, the artist opened the door to the passage, stepped through, and remembered to close the door. The risk made his heart pound. He hurried past the bodies of the mother and child, almost lost his balance on the slippery floor, and unlocked a back door. Stepping into a small outside area, he again took the precious time to close the door.

The fog smelled of chimney ashes. In the gloom, he glimpsed the shadow of what he assumed was a privy and ducked behind it, just before a grunting man pulled himself over a wall and scanned his lantern.

"Hello?" The man's voice was gruff. He approached the back door and knocked. "I'm a policeman! Constable Becker! Is everything all right in there?"

The constable opened the door and stepped inside. As the artist heard a gasp, he turned toward a murky wall behind the privy.

"God in heaven," the constable murmured, evidently seeing the bodies of the mother and the girl in the passageway. The floor creaked as the constable stepped toward them.

The artist took advantage of the distraction, set his bag on top of the wall, squirmed up, grabbed his bag, and dropped over. He landed on a muddy slope and slid to the bottom, nearly falling in slop. The noise when he hit seemed so loud that he worried the constable must have heard him. The legs of his trousers were soaked. Turning to the right, he groped along the wall in the foggy darkness. Rats skittered.

Behind him, he heard a distinctive alarm. Every constable carried a wooden clacker, which had a handle and a weighted blade that made a rapid snapping sound when it was spun. The constable now used his, its noise so loud that it couldn't fail to be heard by other patrolmen on their nearby routes.

The artist reached a fog-bound alley, guided by a dim streetlamp at the far end.

"Help! Murder!" the policeman shouted.

"Murder? Where?" a voice yelled.

"My brother's shop!" another voice answered. "Here! For heaven's sake, help!"

Windows slid up. Doors banged open. Footsteps rushed through the darkness.

Nearing the light at the end of the alley, the artist could see enough to hide the razor behind a pile of rubbish. A crowd rushed past in the fog, attracted by the din of the constable's clacker.

When the crowd was gone, the artist stepped from the alley and went in the opposite direction, staying close to the obscured buildings, prepared to vanish into an alcove if he heard anyone running toward him. The babble of the mob became a faint echo behind him.

He found a public privy, pulled off the yellow wig, and dropped it down the hole, then did the same with the beard. Five minutes later, in an alley near the edge of a better district, he removed his sailor's clothes and put on the theater clothes that he'd folded into the bag. He tossed the sailor's clothes, including the cap, into a corner, where someone would gladly take them in the morning. The mud-smeared leather bag he dropped among garbage a little farther on. It too would readily find a new owner.

In the better district, he followed the noise of hooves through the fog until he arrived at a main street. An empty cab waited at a stand near a restaurant. The driver looked down from his perch and assessed the artist's evening clothes, deciding that he was a safe passenger at this late hour.

As the driver took him to a music hall in the West End, the artist used a handkerchief to wipe mud from his shoes. He established a presence at the music hall, pretending to be just another theatergoer who wanted mellower entertainment after the bloody climax of *The Corsican Brothers*. Then he hired a final cab and went home, wondering if Titian, Rubens, and Van Dyke had ever felt as satisfied by their fine art as *he* did.

2

The Man Who Concealed His Red Hair

LONDON'S POLICE FORCE was established in 1829, the first organized law enforcement in England. Earlier, the city's security had depended on elderly night watchmen who were given a clacker along with a dusky lantern and told to call out each half hour as they made their rounds. Frequently, however, the old men passed the night sleeping in tiny watch-boxes. As London's population swelled to one and a half million, the city authorized Sir Robert Peel to create the Metropolitan Police, whose initial thirty-five hundred members were known as "bobbies" or "peelers," in allusions to his name.

By 1854, London had a population of almost three million, making it the largest city on the planet. Meanwhile, the police force had merely doubled, to seven thousand, with hardly enough personnel to control the city's seven hundred square miles. To supplement the regular force, a detective bureau had been created—eight plainclothes officers who roamed the city in disguise. Their anonymous existence unnerved many Victorians whose obsession with privacy gave them a morbid suspicion of being spied upon.

These detectives were chosen from the ranks of regular police officers. They already knew the streets, but what distinguished them was an extraordinary attention to detail, the ability to scan a busy hotel lobby or a crowded railway station and identify behavior that didn't fit: a possible robbery lookout who stood still while everyone else was moving, a possible pickpocket who surveyed the crowd before focusing on an individual within it, a possible pimp whose features were calculating while everyone else was merry.

The Metropolitan Police and its detective bureau were headquartered in London's Whitehall district, the site of numerous government buildings. Because the entrance was on a street called Great Scotland Yard, newspaper reporters referred to the police force by an abbreviated version of that street's name. Unmarried detectives and constables could live in a dormitory near headquarters, and it was there, at twenty-five minutes past midnight on Sunday, 10 December 1854, that Detective Inspector Sean Ryan, forty years old, was wakened by a constable who informed him that a multiple murder had occurred in the East End's Wapping district. While violence in the East End was common, murders themselves were rare. That year, only five murderers had been hanged in London, and those crimes had each involved a single victim. Even in the largest city in the world, a multiple murder was shocking.

Ryan, who had eaten a dinner of boiled beef and dumplings and slept poorly as a consequence, took only five minutes to dress, making sure that his gloves were in his shapeless jacket. Along with ten constables with whom he lived he stepped outside, noted that the cold air frosted his breath, and climbed onto a police wagon that he had ordered to be waiting for them. The chill, fog-laden streets had almost no traffic, allowing the group to reach the murder scene within forty minutes.

A crowd had gathered, as if at a public hanging, forcing the driver to stop the horses a distance away. Ryan and the constables stepped onto grimy cobblestones and followed the din of voices until a wall of bystanders prevented them from proceeding farther.

"It's Spring-Heeled Jack what did it, I tell you!" someone shouted, referring to a fire-breathing man with claws and springs attached to his boots, who had allegedly attacked a handful of Londoners seventeen years earlier and became a figure of local folklore.

"Naw, it's the Irish! Everywhere I turn there's a damned mick beggin' money! That famine was a crock! There weren't no famine!"

"Damned straight! The micks just lied to come here and steal our jobs! Ship 'em back home!"

"Hell, no. They're all thieves. Hang 'em!"

Ryan, whose parents had emigrated from Ireland when he was a child, had tried hard to replace his Irish accent with a London one. His clothes were equally anonymous. Accustomed to working undercover, he wore a newspaperboy's cap that was pulled down so that his red hair wouldn't be noticed.

"Constable," he told a man who accompanied him, "make a path."

"Right, Inspector."

The so-called bull's-eye lantern that each policeman carried had an interior reflector and a magnifying lens over the single aperture. The numerous harsh beams emphasized their gruff voices as the ten policemen pushed through, bellowing, "Step aside! Police! Clear the street!"

Ryan followed, hoping that the sight of so many police officers would distract the crowd's attention from him and preserve his anonymity. They came to one of many small shops in the area that catered to merchant sailors from the nearby London docks. This close to the Thames, the smell of excrement was strong. Without a sewage system, all the city's body wastes seeped into the river or were dumped there.

A constable stood guard outside the shop, the windows of which were shuttered, concealing the interior.

Like all uniformed officers, the constable was tall, with a hefty physical presence intended to discourage criminals from forcing him to pull out his truncheon. His helmet and wide belt displayed his police badge and the gold initials VR, which stood for *Victoria Regina*.

Ryan recognized the constable, particularly a scar on his broad chin that he'd acquired while subduing a lookout during a burglary case that he and Ryan had worked on a month earlier. "Is it you, Becker?"

"Yes, Inspector. Good to see you again, although I wish it was under better circumstances."

"What did you find?"

"Five bodies."

"*Five?* The constable who woke me said there were four."

"That's what I thought at first. Three adults and a young daughter. The neighbors say she was seven years old."

Seven years old? With effort, Ryan didn't show a reaction.

"But then I looked closer," Becker said. "In the bedroom, there was a lot of clutter from something that had been smashed. I didn't recognize at first that the pieces belonged to a cradle. A baby was under a chunk of the wicker hood."

"A baby," Ryan murmured. Concealing his emotions, he turned toward the constables who'd come with him. "Ask the neighbors about anything that seemed unusual. Strangers. Anybody who didn't look right."

Although it seems an obvious thing to do, the procedure that Ryan set in motion had existed for only a few decades. The science of what became known as criminology originated in France, where a professional criminal, Eugène François Vidocq, went to work for the Paris police and in 1811 organized a plainclothes detective unit. His operatives pretended to be beggars and drunkards, infiltrating taverns that criminals favored. Vidocq eventually resigned from the Paris police and formed the world's first private detective agency. In 1843, one year after London's own detective bureau was created, a team of those detectives—Ryan among them—journeyed to Paris, where Vidocq taught them his methods. For the first time, an organized investigation of a crime scene became standard policy.

"Make sure the neighbors understand that even the slightest detail that seemed out of place can be important. One of you needs to guard the door while Constable Becker and I go inside. I don't want anyone else to enter. Ready?" he asked Becker.

"It's strong," Becker warned, opening the door.

"I'm sure it is."

RYAN ENTERED FIRST.

Behind him, he heard someone in the crowd yelling, "Let us in! Give *us* a look!"

"Yeah," someone else shouted, "it's cold out here!"

Ryan shut the door after Becker joined him. The coppery odor of blood hung in the air.

Gathering his thoughts, Ryan studied the shop. An overhead lantern, grimed with soot. A drab counter. Shelves upon which lay garments and socks of laborer quality. A closed door to the left of the counter.

"Was that door shut when you came in?" he asked Becker.

"I entered through the back, but yes, the door was shut. After I searched, I left everything how I'd found it, the way you wanted things done three months ago."

"Good. You came in through the back? That door wasn't locked?"

"I opened it easily."

"So the killer escaped through the back before you entered."

"That was my suspicion."

Ryan didn't say what he was thinking. Becker was perhaps fortunate that the killer had no longer been inside when the constable entered. He might have been taken by surprise and become another victim.

Noticing a splotch of blood on the counter, Ryan steadied himself, proceeded to the entrance behind the counter, and found the first body. Its throat gaped, almost a second mouth. Its battered skull was misshapen. It sprawled in an enormous amount of blood, some of which had spurted onto clothing on the shelves.

Ryan had seen only a few bodies in a more mutilated condition, the result of countless rat bites or a long time in the river. His training helped to control his emotions.

Five pairs of socks lay in the blood.

"The shopkeeper must have been reaching for them. Where's the cash box?"

"Under the counter."

Ryan reached for the box and opened it, studying a mixture of gold, silver, and copper coins. "One pound, eight shillings, and two pennies."

"Business must have been slow." Becker's voice had a trace of pity.

"But to some people, this is a fortune. Why didn't the killer take the coins?"

Ryan proceeded toward the door to the left of the counter and opened it, confronted by the sight of the woman and the child on the floor. Their faces were bashed in and their throats slit.

For a moment, Ryan couldn't speak.

Again, his training took charge. "Someone stepped in the blood and slid, moving toward the back door. Was that you, Becker?"

"Absolutely not, Inspector."

"The slide mark makes the print indistinct, but it doesn't look like the boot had hobnails in the sole."

"Suggesting that the killer isn't a laborer?"

"Very observant, Becker."

Ryan opened a door to the right and smelled boiled mutton in addition to the blood. Breathing shallowly in the sickening atmosphere, he stared down at the corpse of a servant girl on the kitchen floor. Despite the anguish on her battered face, he noticed freckles, making him think that she might have been Irish like himself.

His revulsion made him turn away. He noticed a large mallet next to a plate on the kitchen table. His pulse intensified when he saw that the mallet's striking surface was covered with gore.

He'd never seen so much death together in one place. His voice became thick. "Did the shopkeeper's wife interrupt the killer before he could open the cash box under the counter? Is that why he came back here and killed them all? So there wouldn't be any witnesses? Then somebody knocked on the front door, and he fled before he had time to take the money?"

Ryan considered what he had just said. "No, that doesn't work. If he didn't have time to steal the money, why would he waste precious seconds closing the door behind him before he ran down the passage?"

"Perhaps he didn't know about the cash box," Becker suggested.

"Then why did he kill the owner?"

Stepping into the passage again, Ryan noted that a door farther along was closed as well. Inside, he found a small bedroom, the clutter of which suggested that many people slept in it. Jagged remnants of a cradle lay in several places. Becker had warned him that there was a dead baby. Even so, Ryan wasn't prepared when he discovered the tiny corpse wrapped in a blanket and shoved under a portion of the wicker cradle's shattered hood.

"Dear God." Ryan had been a detective for twelve years. Before that, he'd been a constable for eight years. Walking the streets of the largest city in the world, he'd seen what until now he'd believed was the worst that one human being could do to another. Now he realized how innocent he'd been, a word that he had never expected to apply to himself.

"A baby. The mallet blows would have..." Ryan paused in an effort to control his emotions. "A girl, you said?"

"Yes," Becker answered faintly.

"The blows would have killed her, but he slit her throat anyhow." A flash of anger escaped him. "Damn it, *why?* She couldn't possibly have identified him. There wasn't any reason to kill her. He didn't take the money. He closed all the doors. He left the mallet. Why? I don't understand."

Leaving the bedroom, Ryan walked angrily along the remainder of the passage and opened the back door.

A constable stood straighter. "You're not allowed back here."

"It's all right, Harry," Becker assured him, coming out. "This is Detective Inspector Ryan."

"Sorry, Inspector. Just being careful."

"Careful is good." Ryan stepped into the night. He'd hoped that the cold air would calm him, but the odor of the fog added to the nauseating smells that remained in his nostrils. "What's back here?"

The constable directed his lantern at a privy. He lowered the light toward compacted ground. "I looked, but the ground's too hard for footprints."

"Did you come through the house to get here?"

"No. Constable Becker said the fewer people inside, the better. He asked me to crawl over the wall where *he* did. Over there to the right."

"Use your lantern and show me."

London's notoriously thick fogs, known as particulars because they were unique or particular to London, were composed of coal smoke from a half million chimneys to which mist from the Thames attached itself. The city's walls had a permanent layer of soot. Now the lantern's beam revealed streaks in the grime where the two constables had rubbed against the wall's bricks as they squirmed over.

"Show me the rest of the wall."

Behind the privy, at the rear of the small back area, that portion of the wall also had streaks in the soot at the top.

"That's where the killer went over," Ryan decided.

The mob in front of the house sounded more unruly.

"Let us in, so we can see what the bastard did!" someone shouted. "Strangers is what done it! Anybody who knew Jonathan wouldn't've hurt him!"

Ryan told the policeman who'd been watching the back door, "Sounds like the other constables can use you out front. Take a position in the alley. Block anyone from coming toward the back. Don't be afraid to cause lumps if you need to."

"Right, Inspector. Anybody who tries to pass me will have a headache."

The constable stepped into the fog, heading toward the adjacent wall. The light from his lantern dimmed, then disappeared.

Ryan listened to the scrape of the constable's boots as he climbed over. Then he directed his attention toward Becker. "I need you to come with me."

"Right, Inspector."

Ryan pulled himself to the top of the wall and considered the fogbound darkness on the other side. "Hand me your lantern while you climb up. Be careful not to go over at the same place the killer did. We want to come down next to where he landed."

When he dropped to the bottom of the wall, Ryan's feet sank alarmingly into mud. He let out a sharp breath and almost slid down an incline, stopping himself by grabbing Becker.

"It hasn't rained. Why is mud here?" Ryan asked in confusion.

"Yes, the ground behind the shop is as dry as stone." Sounding equally confused, Becker took cautious steps down the slope and aimed his lantern. Its beam pierced the fog enough to reveal the source of the stronger-than-usual odor: a drainage ditch filled with murky, greasy liquid. "God help us, this is where the neighborhood's privies drain."

A carcass floated in the filth, possibly a dead dog.

Ryan almost gagged on the stench. "Do you believe cholera is caused by breathing miasma?"

"That's what my mother always warned me." Becker's words were forced, as if he held his breath.

"Have you heard of Dr. John Snow?"

"No." Becker spoke through tight lips.

"I worked with him during the cholera epidemic three months ago. Snow is confident that the disease comes from drinking bad water, not inhaling foul air from it."

"I hope he's right."

"Believe me, so do I. Let's make this quick. Lower the lantern toward the mud. There'll be footprints."

"There." Becker pointed. "Deep ones."

"Beauties. Lower the lantern a little more. See, these don't have hobnails in the soles, either. The prints are clear enough. I can make plaster casts."

"Heard about that. Never seen it done."

"You mix water with plaster of Paris until —"

An animal grunted.

Ryan tensed.

The next time the animal grunted, the sound was louder and closer. To the left.

"A pig," Becker said.

"Yes," Ryan agreed, uneasy.

"Sounds like a large one," Becker decided.

London had all kinds of livestock scattered through it. Farmers moving to the city or else laborers doing their best to survive often found a small space in a courtyard in which to keep an animal for food. Cows, pigs, goats, lambs, chickens — their sounds were as much a part of the city as the rattle of coaches and the clop of hooves.

But pigs served a double purpose. Not only did they provide meat; they also were rubbish eaters. Like the ever-present ravens, they were important in London's fight against being buried in its slops.

The pig grunted again, the sound on a level that was even with Ryan's groin.

"If they're hungry enough, they'll attack people." Becker held his lantern with one hand and pulled out his truncheon with the other. "I saw it happen once."

The lantern revealed a metal bracket in the brick wall. Becker hammered his truncheon against the bracket. The truncheon had a steel tip that made a ringing sound. "If that pig comes any nearer, it'll foul these footprints. You won't be able to make casts of them. But while we're standing here, the killer's getting farther away."

"What are you thinking?" Ryan asked.

"Someone needs to follow his tracks," Becker told him. "Someone else needs to protect these footprints. Go. You know what to look for. I'll stay and keep the pig away from the footprints."

"Are you sure you want to do that?" Ryan looked doubtfully toward the smothering darkness.

"Anything to catch the bugger who did this, Inspector. Go. Take the lantern."

"And leave you in the dark?"

"The alternative is *you'd* be in the dark. Without the lantern, how could you follow the tracks? Catch him."

"And if I *don't* catch him, maybe the prints you're guarding will help identify him? Very well." Ryan reluctantly took the lantern. "Thank you."

"Can I ask a question, Inspector?"

"Of course."

"What would I need to do to become a detective?"

"You're making a good start." Ryan assessed where the footprints led to the right, opposite where the pig was. "I'll bring back the lantern as quickly as I can."

He twisted its metal top, allowing more air to reach the burning wick. The light increased. Aiming it, he proceeded along the muddy slope. He heard the pig grunt yet again and the steel tip of Becker's truncheon hitting the bracket, ringing in the darkness.

Ryan stayed close to the wall and followed the footprints. He moved warily, mindful that the killer could have remained in the area. As tendrils of fog wrapped around him, he heard rats, their claws scraping across stones. After five minutes, he reached the rough pavement of a rubbish-strewn alley on his right and saw where the footprints left a track of mud. A cat raced in front of him, howling at something.

The remnants of mud lessened, but before they stopped, Ryan came to a hazy gas lamp at the end of the alley. Puzzled, he noticed that the last traces of muddy footprints went toward the wall on his left and then proceeded into the street. The voices of the mob came from the right, from the direction of the shop.

Everyone would have been so distracted by the commotion that they wouldn't have noticed the killer step out of this alley, Ryan thought.

But why did he go toward the wall here?

Directing the lantern, Ryan kicked at the rubbish. Filthy rags flew, along with broken glass and urine-reeking remnants of wooden crates.

Something pale caught his attention. He kicked more rubbish away and stooped to inspect what he'd found, his chest tightening when he identified the ivory on the handle of a folded razor.

WHILE INSPECTOR RYAN STUDIED THE RAZOR, Constable Becker stood in total darkness, feeling the fog drift across his face. The wall muffled the noise of the crowd on the street outside the shop, so the only sounds seemed to be the hammering of his truncheon and the grunting of the pig. The noise the animal made was deep and guttural, like someone with consumption trying to cough up blood.

"Get the blazes away from me!" Becker shouted, hoping to scare the animal into leaving.

But the pig didn't retreat.

In fact, the sounds it made seemed closer. Becker imagined that he saw its indistinct shape in the fog. He'd been raised on a farm and knew that pigs could be as heavy as two hundredweight, but that was if they had plenty of food. Would the rubbish this one scavenged, and the animal corpses it came across, be enough for it to grow that large? Even if the pig weighed two-thirds of what he feared, that would be enough to knock him over if it charged in the darkness, especially when he had trouble holding his balance on the muddy slope. His father had once lost his balance and fallen while feeding pigs. Big, ugly, and nasty, they had attacked. Their sharp teeth had torn chunks from his father's legs and arms. Alerted by his father's screams, Becker had thrown rocks at the pigs, distracting them while his father struggled over the fence, blood streaming from him.

Becker strained to shut out the memory just as he strained to assure himself that it was only his imagination that made him think he could see the pig's shadow growing in the fog. His effort not to inhale the foul odor from the excrement-filled ditch made him dizzy. Had Ryan been telling the truth that cholera was caused by drinking foul water rather than breathing its miasma? The odor was so terrible that Becker felt nauseous.

The pig snuffled closer.

Becker wanted frantically to leap toward the top of the wall, climb over, and drop to the safety of the courtyard. But he kept thinking about the five corpses in the shop and his promise to protect the killer's footprints. He was determined not to be a constable all his life. He was twenty-five years old. He'd tried a variety of spirit-crushing jobs, working sixty hours a week in a brick factory before he realized that his height as well as his muscles would help to qualify him as a policeman. He'd been patrolling the London streets for five years, mostly in the worst areas of the city, putting in more hours than at the brick factory, walking twenty miles each night, with only one night of rest every two weeks.

Nonetheless, as much as he was repelled by what he encountered, he was proud that being a policeman allowed him to apply his mind as much as his strength. He had a chance to stop people from being brutalized. But someone like Inspector Ryan had a much greater chance to do so, not to mention that a detective's salary was £80 per year compared to the £55 that a constable earned. If stopping a vicious pig from trampling these footprints was what it took to make a better life for himself, then by God he would stand firm.

His resolve was tested as he heard a second pig grunt in the swirling fog.

The second pig was in the opposite direction. Flanked by the two animals, Becker kept hammering his truncheon against the wall.

"Get away from me, you sons of whores!"

He suddenly heard the first pig charge through the mud. Judging the distance of the sound, he swung his truncheon with all his might and felt a solid impact. In the darkness, the pig squealed so fiercely that it reminded Becker of the sound they'd made every market season when his father had slit their throats.

Straddling the footprints that he'd sworn to defend, he swung his truncheon again—and again!—repeatedly feeling a jolt. The pig wailed and knocked against him, as tall as his thigh. Its weight shoved him so force-fully that he almost toppled into the drainage ditch.

Protect the footprints!

Crouching for balance, Becker swung as the pig swept past him. Striking a haunch, he felt his weapon sink into flesh. The pig squealed. Becker reversed his position, careful that the footprints between his legs weren't damaged.

Both pigs were now on one side of him. He was no longer forced to divide his attention. But if they charged together, he had no hope of stop-ping them before they knocked him to the muck and tore at him.

"You want to fight? Here!"

Becker stepped forward, putting the footprints behind him, better pro-tecting them. He swung the truncheon with all his strength and was shocked by the unexpected impact. The resultant wail was a combination of pain and fury. But the animal's fury was greater. Again, the first pig attacked. Or maybe it was the second. Becker had no way of telling as he swung, missed, and was startled by teeth gripping his sleeve. The teeth yanked. He pulled in the opposite direction.

His sleeve ripped. He fell. *The footprints! Don't land on the footprints!* Twisting, he veered from them. With a groan, he collided against the wall. The muck gave way, causing him to slip down onto his side. His metal-lined helmet clattered away. The pigs charged. He kicked with both feet, striking snouts and teeth, his fear creating the hallucination that he was on a new contraption he'd recently seen, something called a bicycle, his feet pumping wildly, except that he was sideways and the thick soles of his boots weren't pressing against pedals but striking eyes and ears and mouths. He screamed and struck harder, squirming with his back along the wall. *No! Too close to the footprints!*

As DETECTIVE INSPECTOR RYAN studied the folded razor he'd found, the lantern began to dim. He twisted its top to allow more air to reach the wick, but the adjustment had no effect. If anything, the lantern became weaker. He shook it, didn't hear any coal oil splashing in it, and knew that he would soon be in darkness.

He had just enough remaining light to see that, when he opened the razor, there was blood on the hinge and the blade. After closing it, he placed the razor in a coat pocket.

The lantern went dark. If not for the gas lamp beyond the alley, he wouldn't have been able to see anything. To his right, he heard the noise of the crowd in front of the shop. He stepped from the alley and made his way over slippery cobblestones, going from one murky lamp to the next, following the voices. Near the crowd, dim lights from windows added to that of the streetlamps. Owners who lived in rooms behind their shops had been wakened by the commotion and struck a match to their lanterns, making it easier to see.

When he came to the backs of the mob, he shifted toward the shops on the right, trying to squeeze along them.

"Hey, watch who you're pushing!" a man complained.

"Police. I need to get through."

"You don't look like any peeler to me."

"Plainclothes detective."

"Right, and I'm Lord Palmerston. Ain't that right, Pete? I'm bloody Lord Palmerston."

"Yeah. Lord Cupid. That's you."

"And this bloke thinks he's Queen Victoria, the way he's pushing."

"Really, I need to get through. Please make room so I —"

"Piss off, mate."

Smelling gin on the man's breath, Ryan went toward the middle of the crowd and again tried to move forward. He showed the policeman's lantern in the hopes that it would give him some authority. "Make way. I need to reach the shop."

"Where'd you steal a bobby's lantern?"

"I'm with the police. I need to get through."

"Yeah, right. Where's your badge? Sod off."

Ryan suddenly felt a hand in his coat pocket. A dipper was trying to steal from him. He slammed the lantern against the pickpocket's arm.

The would-be thief shouted, "He's got a razor in his pocket!"

"Who? Where?"

"Him! He's got a razor!"

When Ryan tried to pull away, hands grabbed him, shoving him against a lamppost, jolting him.

His cap fell off.

"Red hair!"

"He's Irish! We found the killer!"

"Listen to me! I'm with the police!"

"Then what are you doing with a razor in your pocket? Anybody seen him around here before?"

"Not likely! I'd remember that red hair!"

Feeling naked without his cap, Ryan tried to pull away.

"You're not going anywhere!"

A fist slammed into his stomach.

Ryan doubled over. Gasping for air, he swung upward with the lantern. As a man groaned, Ryan shoved him toward several other men, one of whom fell to the street. A gap opened. Hurrying through it, Ryan kept swinging the lantern.

"Don't let the killer get away!" a man shouted.

With the crowd in pursuit, Ryan saw the alley he'd just left and raced into it. But away from the streetlight, the darkness would be so thick that he couldn't continue running for fear he'd crash into something and injure himself so severely that he couldn't escape. The dim streetlamp revealed a board from a crate near where he'd found the razor. He grabbed the board and stepped fully into the gloom. When the mob reached the alley, the first man charged into it, and Ryan whacked the side of his head.

Wailing, the man scurried back into the street.

"What are you stalling for?" someone yelled. "Get in there after him!"

"*You* get in there!" the first man shouted back, rubbing his bleeding head.

"What's the trouble?" a voice demanded.

"Constable, we found the killer! He's in this alley! He's got a razor!"

"Step back!"

A harsh light glared through the fog.

The glare came closer.

"Police!" the voice announced. "Identify yourself!"

Ryan recognized the voice. The constable behind the lantern was one of the men with whom he shared a dormitory room near Scotland Yard.

"Hello, Constable Raleigh."

"How do you know my name?"

"Is the blister on your left foot any better?"

"The blister on…? Good heavens, that red hair. You're Detective Inspector Ryan!"

"Pound him!" a man yelled from the street.

"Give me your truncheon," Ryan said.

The constable obeyed.

"Take out your clacker," Ryan told him.

The constable pulled his clacker from his belt and flipped open its handle. In the light from the lantern, the metal on the clacker's blade looked formidable.

Ryan's shapeless coat held all kinds of objects that came in handy. He removed four strands of wool.

"What are *they* for?" the constable asked.

"To save our hearing."

Ryan balled two of the strands and put one into each of the policeman's ears. He did the same for his own ears. The plugs of wool muffled noise without shutting it out.

"I learned something," the constable said.

"Aim your lantern and sound the clacker as loud as possible. We're going to clear a path back to the shop. Ready?"

"With pleasure."

"Then let's establish some order."

"Get that Irishman out of here!" a man bellowed from the crowd.

The policeman aimed the lantern. "Make way!" Gripping the clacker's handle, he swung the blade fiercely.

"Move!" Ryan bellowed, stepping forward. He held the truncheon in one hand and the board in the other. "Clear the street!"

The mob stumbled away.

"Go!" the constable boomed, swinging his clacker as hard as he could.

The tallest man hesitated. Ryan struck his arm, causing a howl and a quick retreat into the fog.

Another man lunged. Ryan pounded his knee, dropping him.

Suddenly other clackers added to the pandemonium, constables hurrying toward Ryan and forming a line. They pushed at the crowd, thrusting lanterns toward faces, sometimes striking with the lead weights on their clackers.

The mob ran.

"Keep searching! Keep asking questions!" Ryan urged the constables. "Somebody lend me a lantern!"

Becker, he thought. He hurried into the shop and along the passage into the back courtyard.

"Becker!"

He ran past the privy and squirmed to the top of the wall.

"Can you hear me, Becker?"

When he peered over the top and directed the lantern, he gaped.

The constable lay near the excrement-filled ditch. His uniform was covered with filth and blood. Next to him were two huge pigs, covered with blood also, apparently dead.

"Becker! Say something! Are you all right?"

The constable squinted toward the light. "The pigs didn't ruin the footprints. I promised they wouldn't. Now you can make the plaster casts."

3

The Opium-Eater

THE COLOR OF LAUDANUM IS RUBY. It is a liquid that consists of 90 percent alcohol and 10 percent opium. Its taste is bitter. A Swiss-German alchemist invented it in the 1500s when he discovered that opium dissolved more effectively in alcohol than in water. His version included crushed pearls and gold leaves. In the 1660s, an English physician refined the formula, removed impurities such as the crushed pearls and the gold leaves, and prescribed it as a medicine for headaches as well as stomach, bowel, and nervous disorders. By the Victorian era, laudanum was so widely used as a pain reducer that virtually every household owned a bottle. Considering that opium's derivatives include morphine and heroin, laudanum's reputation as a pain reducer was well founded. Toothache, gout, diarrhea, tuberculosis, and cancer were only some of the ailments that laudanum manufacturers such as Batley's Sedative Solution, McMunn's Elixir, and Mother Bailey's Quieting Syrup claimed to alleviate. Women used laudanum to relieve menstrual cramps. Colicky babies were given it.

The concept of physical addiction was unknown in the 1850s. While a few physicians noted that prolonged use of laudanum could possibly produce a dependency, most people viewed an overfondness for laudanum as merely a habit, a failure of willpower that could easily be overcome by the typical Victorian virtues of discipline and character. As a consequence, the distribution of laudanum was unregulated by the law. It could be purchased readily and cheaply from any neighborhood druggist. But since no medical prescription was required, it could also be purchased from grocers, butchers, tailors, street merchants, tavern keepers, and even rent collectors. The recommended dosage—only as necessary for symptoms—was twenty-five drops, a third of a teaspoon, not to be used for prolonged periods of time. But many Victorians exceeded these suggestions and were indeed physically dependent on it, although the constraints of Victorian society discouraged anyone from confessing to what was considered a failure of fortitude.

It's impossible to determine precisely how many Victorians were dependent on the drug, but since millions used it on a daily basis, the number must have been considerable. The pallor of many women in the middle and upper classes, their frequent lack of appetite, their tendency to faint and to spend considerable time alone in dark rooms, the ornate patterns of overupholstered and overfurnished rooms, the persistently closed, thick curtains—these are evidence of a national dependency that the restraints of Victorian society discouraged anyone from discussing.

Thomas De Quincey made no secret of *his* dependency, however. During the 1820s he became the most notorious author in England because he was brazen enough to document his habit in a scandalous, national best seller, *Confessions of an English Opium-Eater.* In it, De Quincey described an incident in 1804 when he went to a pharmacy to buy a small quantity of laudanum to subdue persistent "pains of the head and face"—his first experience with the drug. At that time, he was a nineteen-year-old student at Oxford University, and his facial pains were probably the consequence of the nervous pressure that he felt as a young man without finances amid well-to-do students in the intense university environment. For nine years, he gradually increased the amount and frequency of his laudanum intake until by 1813 he was able to control his compulsion only for brief periods and with great effort. At the height of his dependency, his daily consumption increased from a third of a teaspoon to an astonishing sixteen-ounce decanter. One ounce would be lethal to anyone not accustomed to the opiate.

In spite of laudanum, or perhaps because of it, De Quincey wrote some of the most brilliant essays of the 1800s, particularly "The English Mail-Coach" and "On the Knocking at the Gate in *Macbeth*," a staple of Shakespeare criticism. His recollections of Wordsworth, Coleridge, and other literary figures with whom he was friends are irreplaceable. But he was unable to write fast enough to support his wife and eight children. Constantly owing money, he often fled his lodgings, pursued by numerous bill collectors.

An irate landlord once held him prisoner in a lodging house for a year, forcing him to keep writing in order to pay his considerable debt. The room became "snowed up" with paper, as De Quincey put it. "Not a square inch on the table to set a cup upon, no track from the door to the fireplace." He finally managed to escape by asking his publisher to smuggle laxative salts to him among the writing materials that the publisher sent. So constipating are the effects of opium that De Quincey sometimes couldn't relieve his bowels for as long as five days. But not this time. Overdosing on the laxative salts, he spent several days in the single privy that served the lodging house in which he was imprisoned. The tenants complained so greatly that the landlord reluctantly allowed De Quincey to leave.

By 1854, De Quincey was sixty-nine years old. His wife was dead. So were three of his sons. His remaining children had dispersed to Ireland, India, and Brazil, with the exception of Emily, his last-born child. Twenty-one and the only daughter not yet attached, Emily assumed the responsibility of embarking on the unique adventure of watching over her brilliant, eccentric, and unpredictable father.

From the Journal of Emily De Quincey

Sunday, 10 December 1854

This morning, I discovered Father again pacing the back courtyard. Once more, he had wakened much earlier than I, probably before dawn. Last night, I am certain that I heard his footsteps creaking past the door to my room, descending the stairs so that he could roam the dark streets. He claims that this is the only way he can avoid indulging in laudanum—by distracting himself with the effort of walking as much as fifteen miles each day.

Father's short stature emphasizes how thin he has become. I worry that his obsessive exercise will harm him more than help. The way he talks also worries me. Before we left our home in Edinburgh to journey here to London and promote his newly collected writings, his practice was to waken groggily no earlier than noon. For a long time, he refused to make the trip at all. Then abruptly he called it essential and surprised me by filling his hours with walking to prepare himself. Soon he wakened at nine. In a matter of weeks, he backed to eight o'clock, to seven, to six. On the train bound for London, he walked in place, his cheeks red from exertion.

"To avoid the laudanum," he kept insisting, although I know that he hasn't abandoned it entirely. Two decanters of the wretched liquid are among the clothes and books that he packed.

I was especially troubled when he said, "As my waking hour retreats from five to four to three, I fear that I am backing into yesterday."

Yesterday, though, is what I am convinced he wants to back into. His journey to London seems about his past more than his collected writings—or perhaps the two are disturbingly intertwined.

Our income from Father's work is too little for us to afford the splendid townhouse in which we are staying. A middle-aged woman who serves as maid and cook has been supplied to us as well. Father claims that he doesn't know who pays the bills, and I believe him. Perhaps one of his old acquaintances secretly provided the means for us to make this journey, although I can't imagine who, since so many of those acquaintances, Wordsworth and Coleridge, for example, have passed over, or as Father says, "have joined the majority," since far more people died over the centuries than are currently alive.

Our lodging is near Russell Square, and after we arrived four days ago, Father puzzled me by asking me to walk with him before we unpacked. Shortly after, we reached the Square, where I was delighted to find a wonderful park in the middle of the tumultuous city. A breeze had chased the fog away. In what Father told me was rare December sunlight, he surveyed the grass and the bare trees, the intensity of his blue eyes indicating his memories.

"When I was seventeen," he said, "I lived on the streets of London."

I knew that, of course, because Father had included some of those terrible events in his Opium-Eater *book.*

"I lived on the streets for the entire winter," he continued.

I knew this, too, but I have learned to let Father say what is on his mind.

"In those days, cows wandered this square. Many nights, a companion and I slept here, a rag that could barely be called a blanket wrapped around us. I'd been lucky enough to find an old bucket. When the udders on the cows were full, I did my best to milk one of them. The warmth of the milk helped us not to shiver."

Father spoke without looking at me, his attention focused totally on his memories. "So much has changed. Coming from the train station, which didn't exist then, I hardly recognized much of the city. There are so many places I need to see."

His tone suggested that he didn't want *to see some of those places, even though he* needed *to.*

"Ann," *he murmured.*

My mother's name was Margaret. Mine is Emily.

"Ann," *he repeated.*

Remembering that conversation, I watched the intensity with which Father paced the back courtyard.

Our housekeeper, Mrs. Warden, stepped into the kitchen. She wore a solemn bonnet. A hymnbook was under her arm. Bread, butter, strawberry jam, and a pot of tea were on the table.

"I'll be leaving for church now, Miss De Quincey. I suppose that you and your father will soon be going there also."

Since our arrival, Mrs. Warden's manner toward my father has been guarded while her tone toward me has been sympathetic, as if she believes I have a great many burdens.

"Yes. Church," *I responded, hoping that I didn't sound as if I were lying.*

"He seems very religious," *Mrs. Warden continued with reluctant approval,* "which, if you don't mind me being honest, is not what I expected, given the 'book' he wrote."

Father wrote many books over the years, but Mrs. Warden's emphasis left no doubt which of them she meant.

"Yes, the book," I said.

"I haven't read it myself, of course."

"Of course."

Again, Father walked past the window, pacing the courtyard from corner to corner to corner to corner. His lean face was tense with exertion. His gaze was on something in his mind far beyond the courtyard wall. He fingered beads in his hands.

"I see how devoted he is to the rosary," Mrs. Warden said. "Praying while walking improves both the soul and the body."

The beads that Father clutched had sections of ten. One in each section was blue. The remaining nine were white.

"I haven't met many Romans." Mrs. Warden referred to Roman Catholics uncomfortably. "But I'm sure papists can be as religious as Church of Englanders."

Father, in fact, belongs to the Church of England and often writes about the knotted mysteries of religion. As for the beads, I didn't know how to explain them without rekindling her suspicions about him, so I merely nodded.

"Well, I'll be off," Mrs. Warden said.

"Thank you. Father says not to expect us until late."

As Mrs. Warden turned to leave, she gave me a look that suggested, if I was indeed going to church, she did not approve of my costume. She herself wore a hooped dress with flounces that made it so wide she had difficulty squeezing through the doorway. I do not exaggerate that she seemed to have a birdcage under her dress. My own preference is for the clothing that Amelia Bloomer recently advocated — long comfortable pants that cuff at my ankles and are hidden beneath my naturally hanging dress. I do not understand the ridicule with which the newspapers greet this way of dressing, referring to the undertrousers as "bloomers," but I would sooner be mocked for my clothing than be forced to restrict my movements for the sake of convention.

After Mrs. Warden closed the front door, Father came in from the courtyard, as if he had heard her depart. He set his beads on the table.

He hadn't worn a hat. His short brown hair—amazingly not grayed by age—glistened with perspiration, only some of which was from exercise. Much of it was no doubt caused by his need for laudanum.

"How far did you walk?" I asked.

"Only five miles."

The beads weren't at all a rosary but instead a system that Father uses to determine how far he proceeds in a small area. When we arrived at the house, he measured the distance along the courtyard's four walls, which became the equivalent of one white bead. After he walked through nine white beads and a blue bead, he began a new set of ten. In this way, all he needed to do was keep a count of the blue beads and multiply them by ten as well as the distance. He claims this is simple, but when I try to explain this, most people grimace as if they have a sudden headache.

"Father, it's time for tea," I said.

"My stomach couldn't possibly tolerate it, Emily. We must be going."

"Tea," I repeated.

"There are many places I need to visit."

"Bread, butter, and jam," I said.

Since we came to London, Father's schedule has been occupied by interviews, to which I accompany him to make certain that he remembers to eat and drink. An American version of his collected works is now available along with four volumes of an ongoing British edition, which is one reason Father journeyed here—so that he could speak with booksellers as well as the Fleet Street magazines and newspapers.

It is undignified, but in truth, we need the money. As much as Father is addicted to laudanum, he is addicted to acquiring books. Over the years, no sooner did he cram one cottage with books than he rented another and another. Debts have accumulated to the point that I fear we will end in paupers' court. This journey to London was indeed essential, although perhaps not in the sense that I believe Father secretly means.

His valiant attempt to earn income for us comes with its own cost. From his youth when one of his brothers bullied him, Father has endured painful difficulty relating to people. His stomach and other digestive organs are seldom at ease except when calmed by laudanum or when I am able to shield him. Now he is forced to greet the world and pretend to welcome it so that people will buy his writings and give him the means to retreat. His brave, humiliating efforts have been successful. Book buyers are eager to meet the infamous Opium-Eater, whose candid details about his drug habit are still a scandal thirty-three years after he first wrote about them.

Recently, Father also added a third installment to his horrid essay "On Murder Considered as One of the Fine Arts." Although I am grateful that the added material promoted sales, I confess that the gruesome descriptions of killings are too shocking for me to finish. People ask if I am afraid to live with Father, given how violent he must be. I tell them that Father is the gentlest man in God's creation, to which well-wishers give me skeptical looks, as if to say, "We know that you must lie because he is your father, but truly anyone who writes about murder so vividly and with so much blood must secretly be a violent man."

Today being Father's first day of leisure, he and I walked to the nearby British Museum. The area was deserted, everyone attending church, which is why Father chose this time to go onto the streets. The museum was closed, but Father would probably have been too preoccupied to go inside, regardless.

The cold breeze continued to chase the fog. Father stared at the museum's dramatic forecourt, his jaw muscles flexing with his need for laudanum.

"This didn't exist the last time I was in London," he told me. "For twenty-five years, it was the largest construction area in all of Europe, but I never saw it."

The enormous building made me feel small and vulnerable.

"The cuneiform tablets of Assyria are in there," Father continued, his tone mournful. "So is the Rosetta stone. Keys to translating the past. But who can translate the ruins in our memories?"

People say that Father has an odd way of speaking, but to me, it is the other way around. Most people are so boring that they lull me nearly to sleep. I do not always understand Father, but I have never found him other than stimulating, even when he exasperates me. Perhaps that is why, at the age of twenty-one, I have not yet found a gentleman with whom I can imagine spending as many years as I have spent with Father.

We hired a cab and went to all the landmarks that had been constructed in the decades since he was away: Buckingham Palace, Belgrave Square, Trafalgar Square, the National Gallery, and the new Houses of Parliament.

But we never stepped out of the cab, and we never lingered. Even though Father was seated, his feet moved as if he were nervously walking. I had the impression that he selected our destinations at random. Eventually I realized that all the places we had seen had been a postponement, that we were finally proceeding toward what Father needed to see and yet did not want to.

The cab let us off at Marble Arch, which Father told me is an imitation of the Arch of Constantine in Rome. It apparently was originally white but now is gray from the city's perpetual soot. As a carriage went through the large central opening, we entered a small pedestrian arch on the left. From a room, a policeman nodded to us.

"This, too, didn't exist," Father said.

Behind us was the expanse of Hyde Park. Church services having ended, carriages came and went. Families with warm coats strolled among the trees. But Father's attention was directed ahead of us toward Oxford Street.

"This street was a colder, harsher place back then," he recalled, leading me along it.

Shops and businesses filled each side. The commercial heart of the city, closed for Sunday, seemed unnaturally silent.

"When I was seventeen and lived on the streets," Father said.

He directed a long look toward steps in front of a shop.

"For five months, most of them in the winter."

He studied a bakery, as if seeing it from long ago.

"It was mostly here. On Oxford Street. Look at that bakery. When I was starving, how I dreamed about bakeries. Did I ever tell you about the skeleton?"

Coming from Father, the morbid question didn't seem unusual. "Skeleton?"

"At the Manchester Grammar School that I attended. A surgeon associated with it had a skeleton hanging in his room. The story was that it came from a notorious highwayman. In those days, before the railways, robbers along roads posed a constant menace. This one had been hanged, and the surgeon had paid the executioner to give him the body since executions were one of the few legal ways for medical students to acquire a corpse for dissection. But it turned out that in the haste with which the executioner cut the body from the scaffold, the highwayman hadn't quite expired. So the surgeon and his medical students slipped a scalpel into him, made sure that the highwayman had drawn his last breath, and then dissected him. Eventually what was left of the corpse was boiled in lye until only the skeleton remained."

Father's disturbing comments didn't surprise me, although I was grateful that no passerby was close enough to hear.

"The way I felt about that wretched skeleton was the way I felt about the school," Father continued. "The man who taught me Latin and Greek resented how quickly those subjects came to me compared to the difficulty with which he had learned them. His resentment eventually turned to anger and then to physical cruelty. In the end, I begged my guardians to release me from the horrors of that school."

Father's own father, a traveling merchant whom he almost never saw, had died from consumption when Father was seven. The will stipulated that four guardians would manage Father's life, but they fulfilled their duties so poorly that his education was infrequent and incompetent.

"One guardian in particular refused. He wanted absolute obedience from me, the same as the teacher did, and this I would not give. So I ran away. I couldn't go to my mother. She would merely have turned me over to the guardians. So I borrowed a little money from a family friend who sympathized with my desperation. For a time, I stayed at various farms in Wales, but eventually, as my meager funds lessened, I tried my luck here in London. It nearly killed me."

The breeze no longer chased the fog. A haze developed, limiting visibility to a few feet. The cold deepened, making me grateful that I wore a warm coat.

Father walked onward, gazing at the entrances and shuttered windows of various shops, seeming to know them extremely well.

"My few coins meant that I could eat only once a day—tea with bread and butter. Soon I didn't have money even for that. I begged, but the city has a great many beggars. If not for a man with a house nearby on Greek Street, I don't know which would have killed me first: the elements or starvation. The man was associated with money lending and shadier elements of the legal profession. His name was Brunell, but he also called himself Brown. He kept on the move to prevent his enemies from catching him. Every night, he slept in a different part of London. In the morning, he went to the house I mentioned, and in the afternoon, he went somewhere else. The house was unoccupied so much that it was at risk of being vandalized, so when I came to him in an effort to borrow money, something about me made him offer a bargain. He allowed me to find shelter there at night in exchange for causing considerable noise if someone tried to break in.

"The house was shabby. Except for the room in which he kept his papers, there wasn't a stick of furniture. At night, without candles, it was frightfully dark. I tried to sleep on the bare floor, shivering while I listened to the rats. Their numerous claws scratched across the floors. My illness and hunger, not to mention my festering dreams, allowed me only a kind of dog's sleep in which I could hear myself moaning. My nerves set my muscles to twitching and my legs kicking, constantly waking me.

"Fortunately Brunell or Brown or whatever his real name was enjoyed talking about Greek and Latin literature. Each morning, when he came to the house with pastries for his breakfast, he allowed me to eat crumbs while we discussed the Odyssey or the Aeneid. Otherwise, my only food consisted of scraps I begged during daylight from indifferent people on the busy streets. I would have perished if not for a girl who took pity on me, even though she herself deserved all the pity in the world.

"Her name was Ann."

The name came unexpectedly, as if a bell had rung at an unanticipated moment. The cold deepened. I gripped my coat closer around me and was grateful when Father resumed walking along Oxford Street. The fog crept nearer. Visibility was now even worse.

"Ann was sixteen years old," Father said. "She was what might be called a peripatetic woman."

"You have never shielded me," I replied. "Say what you mean."

Father nonetheless hesitated. "A streetwalker. Ann's poverty had been imposed upon her because of a legal disagreement regarding money that she inherited from her parents. But others found ways to intercept the bequest, and Ann never received the money. Throughout those winter months, she suffered from a cough, but she treated me as if I were more sickly. I often walked with her on Oxford Street or rested with her under the shelter of porticoes. She defended me against watchmen who attempted to drive me off steps where I tried to rest and regain my strength."

Father's eyes again assumed that far-away look. He stopped and pointed down at where we stood.

"Our only amusement was to wait for the organ grinder to wheel his instrument onto this corner. The player always pretended that the organ weighed three times more than it actually did. When he turned the crank, he strained his face and breathed with difficulty, making it seem that turning the crank was the hardest job in the world. Ann and I held hands while we listened to the music. People sometimes dropped coins in a cup attached to the organ, and from the way the player expressed his thanks, you'd have thought he'd been given a fortune instead of the smallest coins anyone could spare. For us, those meager coins would indeed have been a fortune. But without food, at least we had music, and I never fail to hear an organ that doesn't remind me of those evenings, standing near the old oil lamp that used to be here, putting my arm around Ann."

Father drew a breath, forcing himself to continue. "One evening when I felt more than usually faint, I asked Ann to take me onto a side street. There, as we sat on the steps of a house, I suddenly grew worse. I'd been leaning my head against her breast. At once I slipped from her arms and fell. Ann cried out in alarm and ran toward Oxford Street. In less time than I could imagine, she returned with a glass of seasoned wine. It was exactly the right thing to bring. My empty stomach could not have tolerated food. The stimulant gave me enough energy that I was able to sit up. Ann had no reason to expect that I would ever reimburse her, and yet she bought that wine when she barely had enough money to sustain her own needs.

"How often I think of the speed with which Fortune's wheel can turn. A few days after Ann brought me the wine, I was begging on Albemarle Street. A gentleman who knew my family happened to walk past and recognized me. At first, he thought he'd made a mistake, so shocked was he by my condition. I answered his many questions, explaining that if he told my mother, she would alert my guardians and they would force me back to that wretched school from which I would again escape. He heard the strain in my voice and promised not to betray my confidence. The next day he presented me with a ten-pound bank note, a sum that I could not imagine.

"When the man in whose house I took shelter at night learned about my ten pounds, he demanded three of them. I asked him to let Ann stay there also, but he warned that he'd throw me out if I brought a streetwalker inside. I used some of the remaining money—five shillings—to buy food for Ann and me. I spent fifteen shillings (I recall how it pained me to count it out) on clothes that would help me implement a plan that my benefactor had suggested. At the Manchester school, I'd made friends with a boy whose wealthy father admired students with a talent for Latin and Greek.

"I determined to go to my friend, who was now at Eton, and persuade him to take me to his father, in the hopes of receiving help. With that in mind, I gave Ann two pounds, not only for food but for medicines to treat her cough. At six o'clock on a dark winter evening, she and I walked hand in hand toward Piccadilly. It was my intention to catch the mail coach for Eton.

"We went through a part of London that no longer exists. I promised her that she would share in any good fortune I met, that I would never forsake her. I told her I loved her, that as much as I didn't wish to leave her I was filled with hope for our future. Ann, however, was overcome with sorrow. When I said good-bye and kissed her, she put her arms around my neck and wept.

"I expected to return in a week. The plan had been, in eight nights, at six o'clock, Ann would wait for me near the bottom of Great Titchfield

Street, our customary rendezvous. But my efforts at Eton turned out to be so frustrating and time-consuming that it was many months before I was able to return to London.

"At six o'clock, I rushed to the bottom of Great Titchfield Street. I waited and waited. Ann did not arrive. The next night, I waited. Ann still did not arrive. The next night and the night after were the same. During the day, I went to Ann's meager lodgings, but none of the streetwalkers who lived there had seen her. Somebody said that the landlord had treated her so badly that she'd been forced to go elsewhere. When I went to other lodgings where streetwalkers stayed, this new group didn't know me. They considered my recently purchased clothes and decided that I was a gentleman in search of a companion. They offered themselves in Ann's place. Others suspected that I might have something to do with the law or that I was searching for someone who had robbed me. They wouldn't talk to me.

"Day and night, I searched Oxford Street. I spread my search to all the neighboring streets. I waited at our favorite spot near the organ grinder. But with no success. After so many months, Ann had perhaps despaired of my promises and would never return to our rendezvous. Perhaps I passed within a few feet of her but never knew it in the crowded labyrinth of the streets where a few feet can be the equivalent of miles. Or perhaps, in my absence, Ann had succumbed to her dreadful cough. Although I grieved deeply at that possibility, I took comfort in knowing that if Ann had indeed been taken to her grave, at least she would no longer be a victim.

"In the end, my quest to improve my prospects required me to board another mail coach. Over the years, whenever I returned to London, I never failed to go to Great Titchfield Street at six o'clock. Ann was never there. I always looked for her on whatever other street I happened to be, but she was never there, either."

Father's voice echoed in the fog, the yellow of which had now thickened enough that I could see only five shops away from me.

"I need to ask you something," Father said.

"When haven't we been able to discuss any topic? What do you need to ask?" I wondered.

Father continued with difficulty. "Does it trouble you that, at one time, the closest person to me in the world was a streetwalker?"

I considered my answer. "If it is a choice between remaining alive and surrendering one's virtue, I can understand the path that Ann was forced to take."

"Does it trouble you that I speak about Ann as if she could have been your mother?"

"All of this happened fifty-two years ago. Mother has been dead for fifteen of those years. It is no dishonor to Mother that you cared for a woman long before you and she were married. What are you leading to?"

"Leading to?"

"For a month, you've been hiding something. Is Ann the reason you agreed to come to London?"

Father looked away.

I didn't relent. "Initially you were strong in your refusal to come here to promote your writings. Your laudanum and your reluctance to relate to strangers were a sufficient explanation. But then one day you abruptly changed your mind, reduced your laudanum intake, and said that it was essential for you to journey here."

"Yes. After the message I received in the mail."

"Message?"

The fog was now four shops away.

"You wondered how we came to have the benefit of the fine house where we're staying," Father told me.

"Yes, and you answered that you didn't know."

"That is true. I didn't — and still don't. The offer was part of the same message. The person who sent the letter didn't sign it. But the documents for the rental of the house and the hire of Mrs. Warden turned out to be authentic. I didn't tell you the rest of it because I couldn't bring myself to relive the darkness of those days. I make a habit of saying that no one can ever truly forget, but in fact, I deluded myself into trying to do just that — to forget."

"You said you didn't tell me the rest of it. Father, what do you mean?"

He drew a breath, then revealed what he'd been holding inside. "The message I received told me that if I came to London, I would learn what happened to Ann."

The statement was so surprising that for a moment I couldn't speak. I stepped closer. "Learn what happened to Ann? Have you? We've been in London four days. Has the person contacted you?"

"No. It remains as large a mystery as the day I received the letter. I thought perhaps that as I traveled throughout the city, speaking to book-sellers and newspaper writers, someone would approach me in the crowd and suggest that we have a private word."

"Why would someone go to the expense of leasing a house for us but not bother to contact you about his reasons for bringing you here?"

"I have no idea. Those days were the worst of my life. And the best. Because of Ann. If things had been different, she might have been your mother."

"And it was that difficult for you to tell me?"

"Perhaps we have not in fact been able to talk about every topic," Father replied.

"That will change."

"Yes," Father granted.

The fog swirled, its chill deepening. I held my coat tighter.

"Let's return to the house," Father decided.

"In this fog, how can we possibly find it?"

"The one street in the world I know without fail is Oxford Street. Don't worry, Emily. We shall make our way home."

As a carriage clattered past us, Father led me onward through the fog.

We were on the left side of the street. When we came to a major inter-secting street, Father said, "If I'm right, this should be Tottenham Court Road. There. See the sign on the wall. Yes, Tottenham Court Road. We'll go this way. In my youth, I would stand here and imagine walking all the way to where the buildings ended and the trees of the countryside began."

Unable to see anything around us, we continued along Tottenham Court Road and then took a side street and another. Father's earlier ref-

erence to the labyrinths of London seemed apt. He had said, "Don't worry." In truth, I never worry, except about Father.

We walked for what seemed to be a mile. Most women in their hooped skirts wouldn't have been able to go even a few yards. But my "bloomers," as the newspapers disparagingly call them, give me freedom.

We reached what Father said was Great Russell Street, and soon, on another street, he assured me, "We're almost there."

But two figures loomed in the fog.

Father inhaled sharply.

The figures — two men, I saw now — were tall.

As the fog swirled, they blocked our way.

"Are you the people I've been waiting for?" Father asked.

"What are you talking about?"

"Ann."

"Ann? Who's Ann?"

"If you don't know who Ann is, step aside," Father ordered.

When they didn't, Father shifted to move around them.

But the men changed their positions and again blocked our way. Their features were haggard, unshaven.

"Damn you, step aside!" Father demanded.

The first man's shapeless clothes resembled those of a street ruffian. The other man had a strange hat. I calculated which way Father and I might need to run.

"I have no money!" Father told them. "Do what you wish to me, but let my daughter go into the house!"

"I'm not leaving without you, Father!"

"Are you the Opium-Eater?" the ruffian demanded.

"What?"

"Thomas De Quincey?"

"What possible business could—"

"I'm Detective Inspector Ryan. This is Constable Becker."

As the fog parted slightly, I saw that the second man's strangely shaped hat was actually a policeman's helmet and that he wore a constable's uniform.

But the ruffian was in charge. "I need to ask you to come with us to Scotland Yard."

4

"Among Us Are Monsters"

CHOLERA CAUSES UNCONTROLLED, rice-colored diarrhea that rapidly leads to dehydration and probable death. Three months earlier, in September of 1854, London had suffered its worst epidemic in decades, losing seven hundred people in the frighteningly short time of two weeks. Dr. John Snow had ended the outbreak when he proved that cholera wasn't caused by breathing foul air but rather by drinking fecal-contaminated water. The center of the outbreak was the Broad Street area of Soho, and after extensive interviews, Snow determined that people who had access to the public water pump in that area were the ones who contracted the disease. Excavation revealed that the well had been dug next to a cesspit from which excrement was leaking. To the surprise of foul-air theorists, Snow ended the epidemic by the simple expedient of arranging for the pump's handle to be removed.

Detective Inspector Ryan had helped Dr. Snow conduct his cholera investigation. When Ryan aimed the lantern over the wall and saw Becker covered with blood, lying beside two dead pigs near an excrement-filled ditch, he had no doubt where Becker needed to be taken for immediate medical treatment.

Ryan ordered a police wagon to hurry Becker to Dr. Snow's residence at 54 Frith Street in Soho, near where the recent cholera epidemic had occurred.

The thin-faced, forty-one-year-old physician took a while to light an oil lamp and respond to the urgent pounding on his door.

"Who the devil?" Wearing a housecoat, he came to attention at the sight of two constables holding Becker.

"Detective Inspector Ryan says to give you this note, sir," a policeman said.

Snow read the note with growing alarm.

"Take his foul clothes off right there. Throw them in the street. Then bring him into this vestibule. No farther than that. I'll bring hot water and fresh rags. We need to clean him thoroughly before he comes into the office."

Once cleaned, Becker was placed on a sheet on a chair in Snow's office. Mid-Victorian physicians had desks in their offices rather than examination tables. After all, there wasn't any need for an examination table. Physicians were gentlemen and almost never laid hands on a patient, except to determine the speed and strength of a pulse. The disagreeable task of actually touching a patient was left to socially inferior surgeons.

But Snow had once been a surgeon and retained some of his habits even after having been elevated to the higher medical rank. Holding his lamp, he looked closely at the bite marks on Becker's arms and legs and exclaimed, "If the pigs were diseased, if excrement seeped into those cuts..."

Snow quickly disinfected the bites with a strong solution of ammonia, a shocking hands-on procedure for a physician to perform.

Becker grimaced from the sharp sting of the ammonia. The sounds of animals made him look around in confusion. On counters, he saw cages in which mice, birds, and frogs were agitated by the sudden commotion.

"Am I seeing things?"

"I use them for experiments to determine dosage," Snow explained.

"Dosage of what?"

"I need to apply stitches to the worst of these bites. The pain will be extreme. This will help make you comfortable."

The "this" Snow referred to was a metal container that had a mask attached to it.

Snow brought the mask toward Becker's face.

"What's *that?*"

"Chloroform."

"No." Becker pressed back in alarm. He knew about chloroform, a newly developed gas anesthetic. The previous year, London's newspapers had printed stories about how Queen Victoria had made the controversial choice to be given chloroform during the birth of her eighth child. Dr. Snow was the physician she had chosen to administer it.

"It's perfectly safe," Snow assured him. "If Her Majesty trusted me, surely you can. There's nothing to be afraid of."

"I'm not afraid of anything," Becker emphasized. "But I don't dare go to sleep."

"Given the fight I gather you've been through, you can use the rest." Snow again brought the mask toward Becker's face.

"No!" Becker raised a hand, keeping Snow at a distance. "I can't go to sleep! I want to be a detective! If you put me to sleep, the investigation will continue without me! I'll never have this chance again!"

MEANWHILE, more constables arrived at the murder scene.

"Keep knocking on doors. Keep questioning neighbors. Widen the search," Ryan ordered. "Ask for anything, no matter how slight, that wasn't normal."

Accompanied by two constables holding lanterns, he again climbed the wall behind the shop. Avoiding the two dead pigs, he eased down on the other side and crouched to study the footprints. They remained more perfectly preserved than he had dared to hope.

Good work, Becker.

The two constables handed down an empty pail, a pitcher of water, and a sack of plaster of Paris. Then they joined him. Recalling that he'd promised to show Becker how to do this, Ryan put water and the powder into the empty pail and stirred them, adjusting the proportion until the mixture had the consistency of pea soup. He poured the mixture into the footprints.

"Stay here," he told the constables with the lanterns. "Don't let anything touch the plaster as it hardens. I know this is harsh back here. I'll have someone relieve you in two hours."

Ryan made his way to the noisy street outside the shop, where he greeted privy excavators he had sent for. During the cholera epidemic, one of Dr. Snow's arguments against the theory that miasma caused cholera had been that privy excavators, who constantly breathed foul air, didn't contract the disease any more than other people did.

Since privies were normally excavated during the night — hence the term "night soil" — the four-member team, which consisted of two tub-men, a ropeman, and a holeman, hadn't thought it unusual to be summoned at this hour, although the urgency of the summons had made them curious about what sort of emergency a privy might cause.

Their interest increased as Ryan explained. "The killer might have dropped something down the hole and used a stick to poke it beneath the surface. Excavate the privy and spread the contents over the courtyard. Don't come through the shop. Use a ladder to climb over the wall in the alley next to here."

As the night-soil men followed orders, Ryan saw a police wagon arriving with a bearded man whom he recognized as a sketch artist for the *Illustrated London News*.

"Same arrangement as the last time," Ryan told him amid the nightmarish zigzag of police lanterns. "I keep the originals. You can make copies, but you can't use them until I give you permission. That might not happen for several weeks."

"What's all the commotion?"

"How's your stomach?"

"Am I going to wish you hadn't asked me to come?"

"Not when your editor sees the illustrations. I want you to draw everything you can until your hand becomes numb."

"It's going to take that long?"

"I hope your wife isn't expecting you to be home in time for church."

"She moved out a month ago."

"Sorry to hear it. But going to church might be something you'll want to do after you finish this."

When Ryan showed him what was in the shop, the illustrator turned pale.

"God in heaven."

Ryan left him in the shop and stepped outside, discovering that Police Commissioner Sir Richard Mayne had arrived. Fifty-eight, with an aristocratic bearing and thick gray side-whiskers almost to his chin, Mayne listened to Ryan's report, was shown the crime scene, managed to maintain an impassive, professional reaction, and looked as pale as the sketch artist when he emerged from the shop.

"It's the worst I've seen," Mayne concluded.

Ryan nodded. "And it wasn't a robbery."

"There'll be considerable pressure from the home secretary to find the madman responsible," the commissioner predicted. The home secretary controlled all aspects of domestic security, including London's police force. He was Commissioner Mayne's powerful superior. "Lord Palmerston will be eager for us to settle this in a hurry. Before there's a panic."

"I think we have both murder weapons. The mallet, and *this*." Ryan showed him the ivory-handled razor.

"Expensive."

"Yes. And the footprints don't have hobnails on the soles, again suggesting a man of means."

"Unthinkable," Mayne told him. "A man of means wouldn't be capable of this ferocity. The razor must have been stolen."

"Possibly. We'll check burglary reports to see if a razor like this is missing. Also we'll question shopkeepers who sell expensive razors and see if anyone can identify this one. As for the mallet, the owner might not be difficult to find. There are initials on it."

"Initials?"

"J. P."

"No." Mayne's face seemed to shrink with distress. "Are you certain?"

"Why? Is there a problem?" Ryan asked.

"J. P.? I'm very much afraid there is indeed a problem."

"We found him!" a voice shouted. "The murderer! We caught him!"

Ryan pivoted toward confusion in the fog. The noises grew stronger as lanterns revealed men yanking a figure into view. The figure's rumpled coat was covered with blood. He struggled.

"Hiding in an alley!"

"Wasn't hiding! I was asleep!"

"Fought us when we grabbed him!"

"What was I supposed to do? You attacked me!"

"Butchered Jonathan and his family is what you did, and that poor servant girl of his!"

"Jonathan? I never heard of—"

"That's his blood on your coat!"

"I had too much to drink! I fell!"

"You killed my brother!" A man punched the captive's face.

"Hey!" Ryan yelled.

The man struck again, the captive wailing and lurching back.

"That's enough!" Ryan ordered. "Let him explain!"

"It'll all be lies! The bugger slit my brother's throat!" The man struck yet again, blood flying.

Ryan rushed to intervene. Abruptly the captive fell, people falling with him.

"I can't see him! Where *is* he?" the brother demanded.

"Here! I have him!"

"No, that's *me!*"

Bodies tumbled in the fog.

"There! Over there!"

The turmoil shifted toward an alley, the crowd chasing a desperate shadow. Someone swung a club and barely missed the fugitive's head.

Ryan charged after them. Sensing someone next to him, he glanced that way and reacted with amazement.

"Becker?"

WEARING A CLEAN UNIFORM, Becker kept pace with Ryan despite the tightness of the stitches and bandages under his clothes. "I came back as soon as I could."

"You should be resting."

"And miss the chance for you to teach me?"

Ahead, the mob surged into the alley.

"He found a broken bottle!" someone screamed. "My eyes! He slashed my eyes! God help me, I can't see!"

More people squeezed into the alley.

"I can't breathe!" someone moaned.

Ryan strained to pull them away.

Becker did the same. Fifteen years younger than Ryan, taller, with broader shoulders, he yanked men out of the alley, throwing them onto the cobblestones.

The odor of alcohol was overwhelming.

"Move!" Ryan ordered.

But the mob was like a wall.

To the left, Ryan saw light through an open door, a heavy woman gaping out.

"There!" he told Becker.

They rushed past the woman and found themselves in one of the many taverns in the area. Charging past benches and a counter, they entered a corridor and reached a storage room on the right.

"The window!" Ryan yelled.

Becker ran around beer kegs and tugged up the window. Outside, the noise of shouts and curses was overwhelming. Ryan brought a lantern to the window, piercing the outside gloom enough to reveal the fugitive swinging a broken bottle at the mob. Faces were bleeding. In fright, the pursuers now strained desperately to retreat from the broken bottle, colliding with those behind them.

Becker's long arms stretched through the window and seized the fugitive's shoulders, pulling him inside. Out there, two men grabbed the fugitive's legs.

The fugitive screamed as if he were being torn apart.

Ryan set the lantern on a table and grabbed a broom from a corner. With the pointed end, he thrust out the window toward the men clutching the fugitive's legs. He aimed toward their chins, jabbing, striking so hard that a man cried out and grabbed his face. Ryan lunged the broom at the other face, and with a wail, the men out there released the fugitive's legs.

Suddenly freed from resistance, Becker lurched backward, pulling the fugitive into the room, the two men falling onto the floor.

"Get away!" the captive shouted, swinging the broken bottle.

Ryan grabbed his arm and twisted until, with a scream, the man dropped the bottle, its jagged points shattering. Becker pulled handcuffs from his equipment belt, their new spring-loaded design holding the clasps in place as he used a key to lock them.

"I didn't do anything!" the man screamed.

"We'll find the truth of that soon enough," Ryan said, trying to catch his breath. "How did blood get on your coat?"

"They damned near killed me. *That's* how it got on my coat." The man's lips were swollen and mangled.

"If you passed out from alcohol and you weren't hiding," Becker said, "they did you a favor."

"How the hell do you work that out?"

"The night's so cold you might have froze to death."

"Some favor. Freezing to death or getting beat to death."

"You can thank us for stopping that from happening."

"Where were you drinking?" Ryan asked, impressed by Becker's effort to make the prisoner trust him.

"A lot of places."

"What's the name of the last one? When did you leave?"

"I don't remember." The man reeked of gin.

"Keep him here until he's sober enough for us to question him," Ryan told the patrolmen who'd joined them.

Still breathing hard, he and Becker went to the front room, where Commissioner Mayne waited in the tavern, looking much older than his fifty-eight years. His skin seemed to recede behind the side-whiskers that hemmed his jaw.

Outside, the loud noises of a scuffle filled the street, constables shouting, striking with their truncheons to disperse the mob.

"This is only starting," Mayne said gravely.

"We can hope the gin will put them to sleep," Ryan offered.

"No, this will become worse. I know from experience. The mallet and the initials on it. I —"

The commissioner suddenly stopped as he looked at the heavyset woman who helped to manage the tavern. A red-faced man who seemed to be her husband came in and stood next to her.

"I need to speak to you," Mayne told Ryan, pointedly ignoring Becker's presence. "In private."

The tavernkeepers obviously thought it strange that the commissioner paid attention to a red-haired Irish ruffian instead of a uniformed constable.

"Constable Becker is my assistant," Ryan said. "He needs to know everything."

Although Becker couldn't have expected that, he hid his surprise.

"A constable as an assistant?" The commissioner still didn't look at Becker. "Isn't that a bit irregular?"

"Well, as you indicated, there'll be pressure from Lord Palmerston to solve this in a hurry and avoid a panic. We want to assure people I had access to every resource. If you can tolerate going back to the shop, no one will overhear us there."

"Except the dead," the commissioner murmured.

THE MAN FROM THE *Illustrated London News* was drinking from a flask when they came in. He showed no embarrassment at having been discovered.

"I don't believe this is a job for me. When I couldn't tolerate being in here any longer, I went outside and tried to sketch the riot, but —"

"For God's sake, don't put anything in the newspaper about a riot," the commissioner pleaded.

"Don't worry about *me*. I could hardly see anything in the fog, let alone draw it. But I counted at least two dozen reporters out there, so you can bet you'll be reading about a riot on top of what happened here tonight."

The commissioner groaned. "I'll be hearing from Lord Palmerston for certain."

"Things got so rough out there I came back to this damned place."

The odor of blood remained strong.

"Definitely not a job for me."

"Perhaps more to drink," Ryan suggested.

"A *lot* more to drink. If I didn't need the money…"

"We need some time in here alone," Ryan said. "The street's quiet now. Perhaps some fresh air will help. Or the tavern down the street."

"Some time in here alone? You're welcome to as much of it as you want." The illustrator quickly went outside and closed the door.

Commissioner Mayne stared toward the counter behind which the unseen but impossible-to-ignore presence of the shopkeeper's body made the room feel small.

"The initials on the mallet. Are you certain they're J. P.?"

"Absolutely," Ryan answered.

"I was only fifteen, but I remember how frightened I was. How frightened my mother was."

"Frightened?" Becker asked.

"My father never admitted to feeling threatened by anything, but I could sense that he was frightened also."

"I don't understand," Ryan said.

"You're both too young to have been alive then. Day after day, I read everything about them in every newspaper I could find."

"Them?"

"The Ratcliffe Highway murders."

As Ryan and Becker frowned in confusion, the commissioner explained.

Saturday, 7 December 1811

The events of that night caused a wave of terror throughout England that had never been equaled. Ratcliffe Highway derived its name not from rats but from a red sandstone cliff that dropped toward the Thames, but in 1811, there were plenty of rats nonetheless, and the desperation associated with squalor.

One of every eight buildings in the area was a tavern. Gambling was commonplace. Prostitutes populated every corner. Theft was so widespread that a fortresslike wall needed to be constructed between Ratcliffe Highway and the London docks.

Shortly before midnight, a linen merchant, Timothy Marr, asked his apprentice, James Gowen, to help him close the shop, which had remained open to accommodate sailors newly arrived in port with money they were eager to spend. Marr sent his servant, Margaret Jewell, to pay a bakery bill and bring back fresh oysters, a cheap, common food that didn't need to be cooked. But Margaret discovered that the bakery was closed, as was every place that sold oysters. Disappointed, she returned to the shop, only to find that the door was bolted. As she knocked repeatedly, she attracted the attention of a night watchman making his rounds as well as a neighbor whose late supper had been disturbed by the noise.

The neighbor crawled over a shared fence, entered through an unlocked back door, proceeded along a corridor, and discovered the body of the apprentice. The young man's head had been bashed in. Gore covered the walls. The neighbor stepped shakily farther into the shop and gaped at Mrs. Marr sprawled near the front door. Her head had been smashed repeatedly, portions of her brain leaking out. Terrified, the neighbor freed the bolt on the front door. A crowd rushed in, knocking him aside. Among them was Margaret Jewell, who looked behind the shop's counter, saw the battered corpse of Timothy Marr, and screamed.

But the horrific discoveries were only beginning. Close inspection revealed that Marr, his wife, and his apprentice all had their throats slit. In Marr's case, the cut was so deep that his neck bone could be seen. In a back room, the searchers found a shattered cradle and an infant whose head had been pounded, its throat cut the same as the others.

No money was stolen from Marr's cashbox," Commissioner Mayne said. "In a bedroom, a ship carpenter's mallet with the initials J. P. was discovered. Its striking surface was matted with blood and hair."

"But..." Becker hesitated, his thoughts in disorder. "That's what happened here, except that two children were killed, not one."

The commissioner seemed not to notice that Becker had violated protocol by speaking before Detective Inspector Ryan did.

Ryan now spoke. "Ratcliffe Highway is only a quarter of a mile away. Saturday, December seventh, eighteen hundred and eleven, you said."

"Forty-three years ago," the commissioner murmured.

"Today's December tenth, not the seventh, but these murders happened on Saturday night, too, so it's nearly the same."

Mayne nodded. "I was raised in Dublin. My father was a judge in Ireland."

Ryan hadn't realized that Mayne was Irish like himself and had removed nearly all traces of his accent, the same as Ryan.

"In those days, before the railway, London's newspapers and magazines were sent via mail coach. Thanks to improved roads, they traveled at an amazing ten miles an hour," Mayne explained. "As word about the savage murders spread relentlessly, so did the terrified reactions to them. When the mail coaches reached the port at Holyhead, their contents were transferred to packet boats that sailed to Dublin. Before steam, the boats were at the mercy of the wind and storms. Sometimes it took two days for the boats to cross the Irish Sea. My father had political aspirations. The London news was important to him. Reports about the Ratcliffe Highway murders reached him five days after the butchery occurred."

The building with its five corpses seemed to contract.

"Within my father's memory, within *anyone's* memory, so many people had never been murdered at once," the commissioner continued. "Yes, a highwayman might shoot a traveler at night. Someone passing an alley might be dragged in and stabbed for his purse. A drunken brawl in a tavern might end in someone being beaten to death. But no one could remember three adults killed together, and the child! An infant! All murdered so violently.

"The news spread from town to town, gathering strength as local newspapers reprinted the details. No one could imagine what sort of lunatic was responsible. Receiving the newspapers five days after the murders, my father told a business acquaintance who visited our house that by then the murderer could have traveled almost anywhere. Indeed, the killer might very well have been on the packet boat that brought the news to Ireland. The killer might even be in Dublin itself. Then my father realized that I was listening at the door and closed it."

The house of death felt colder. The commissioner looked at Ryan and Becker with terrible distress.

"People were afraid to leave their homes. They suspected every stranger. I heard of a wealthy woman who had locks installed on doors within doors in her house. Everyone was certain that every sound in the night was made by the murderer coming for them. Only gradually did the panic subside. But it quickly returned with greater force when twelve days after the first mass killing, there was another."

"What?" Ryan asked in amazement. "Another? Twelve days later?"

"Only a half mile from Marr's shop. Again in the Ratcliffe Highway area."

THIS TIME, it happened on a Thursday," the commissioner said. "A week before Christmas. A man named John Williamson owned a tavern. A customer hurried toward it just after closing time, hoping to get a pail of beer, when he heard someone shout, 'Murder!' The cry came from a half-naked man who hung from an upper window, suspended by bedsheets tied together.

"The half-naked man was a lodger in the tavern. He fell toward the street, where a night watchman caught him. As the lodger kept shouting, the watchman pounded on the locked front door while a crowd quickly gathered. They pried up a hatch in the pavement where beer kegs were delivered. When they charged into the basement, they found Williamson's body. His head had been bashed in by a blood-covered ripping chisel that lay next to him. His throat was slit. His right thumb had been slashed almost completely off, apparently when he tried to defend himself.

"When the crowd ran upstairs into the kitchen, they found Williamson's wife in a pool of blood, her head pounded in, her throat slit also. A servant girl lay near her, similarly mutilated. The lodger who'd escaped reported that he'd heard a loud noise and crept downstairs from his room to investigate. Close to the bottom, he'd peered into the kitchen and seen a man near Mrs. Williamson's body. Dreading any sound he might make, the lodger had crept back up the stairs and tied sheets together to climb from the window.

"News of the slaughter spread everywhere. Fire bells clanged. Men grabbed pistols and swords, swarming through the streets, hunting anyone who seemed even remotely suspicious. One volunteer chased a man he believed was the killer but who was innocent and who pulled out a pistol, blowing off the volunteer's face. Anyone who was foreign, particularly Irish, was assumed to be guilty."

The commissioner paused after the Irish reference, seeming to take for granted that Ryan would understand the terror.

"Strangers hid and were blamed for hiding. Every window was shuttered. Watchmen were hired to guard houses and then were suspected of being the killer. As the mail coaches transported the newspapers to every community throughout the land, the panic multiplied. Isolated villages armed themselves, convinced that the killer would flee London and pass through their area, leaving more bodies in his wake. I remember being frightened when I overheard one of my father's friends tell him, 'We are no longer safe in our beds.' I read that in London people hurried to churches to beg God for their lives, only to find notices nailed to doors that warned, *among us are monsters.*"

"Monsters," Ryan said.

"Imagine everyone's relief when an anonymous source directed investigators to a young merchant seaman, John Williams, who had recently returned from a long voyage and whose tendency to get into fights had attracted attention."

"John Williams?" Becker asked, puzzled.

"That's right. He rented a room at a boardinghouse a short walk from both murder scenes. A ship's carpenter had previously stayed there and left a box of tools. Those tools included a mallet with the carpenter's initials J. P. stamped by a nail into its top."

"J. P. The initials on the mallet we found tonight," Ryan said.

"You can understand why I'm troubled. The mallet was familiar to the boardinghouse's owner. He identified it as the same mallet that was found at the scene of the first murders. The night of the second murders, Williams was reported to have acted strangely when he returned to the boardinghouse after news about the killings spread. Someone remembered blood on his clothing, which he claimed was due to a fight in a tavern.

"Williams was detained and spent Christmas Eve, Christmas Day, and Boxing Day in Coldbath Fields Prison, where he waited to be questioned after the holiday. But when the magistrates reconvened and spectators squeezed into the court, expecting to see the presumed killer being brought in for questioning, word arrived that prison guards had discovered Williams dead in his cell."

"Dead?" Becker asked in surprise.

"A suicide. A pole extended across the top of his cell. The jailers used it to air out bedding. Williams had been allowed to keep his clothes and had tied a handkerchief around the pole, hanging himself. But more horrors were yet to come."

"That's difficult to imagine," Ryan said.

"The authorities concluded that Williams's suicide was the same as a confession. A public hanging normally demonstrated what happened to monsters. But that wasn't possible in this case, so instead, on New Year's Eve day, his body was placed on a horse-drawn cart. A slanted platform allowed his corpse to be fully in view. The mallet was put into a slot to the left of his head. The ripping chisel lay behind his head. Opposite the mallet, to the right of his head, another object was placed into a slot, soon to have a major role in the ceremony.

"Spectators gathered as the cart was led along Ratcliffe Highway. Numerous politicians walked before and after it, wanting to be seen by the crowd. The procession came to a halt at Marr's shop, where the first four murders had occurred. The cart was positioned so that Williams's corpse appeared to view the scene of his inhuman acts. After ten minutes, the cart was led to the tavern where the second set of murders had occurred. Twenty thousand people lined the streets, watching the procession. They were strangely silent as if stunned by the sanity-threatening crimes that Williams had committed. The only outburst came from a coachman who leapt down and lashed the corpse several times across the face."

Ryan's cheek twitched.

"The cart halted a final time at the crossroads of Cannon and Cable streets. Paving stones were torn up. A hole was dug. Williams's body was dumped into it. The object that had been put in a slot opposite the mallet was pulled out. It was a stake."

"What?" Ryan asked.

"A man acting as the equivalent of an executioner jumped into the hole and pounded the stake through Williams's heart. Unslaked lime was thrown onto the corpse. Dirt followed. The paving stones were hammered back into place. When I heard about this, I asked my father why they used a stake. He told me it was an old superstition, that the stake was the only way to prevent an evil spirit from returning to commit more unspeakable crimes."

"And the crossroads?" Becker wondered.

"Another superstition. If, despite the stake, the ghost of the monster somehow returned, it would be trapped forever, unable to choose which of the four roads to take. At first, the replaced paving stones were uneven enough that travelers could tell where the monster was buried and avoid the contamination of driving over his grave. But gradually the stones became level with the others. Over the years, people forgot where Williams was buried or that he was buried there at all."

"I go through that crossroads often," Ryan said. "I never realized."

"Knowing that the terror had ended allowed me to sleep at last without worrying that Williams was outside in the dark," the commissioner told them.

"And *had* it ended? Were there any further murders?"

"No, there were not."

Something in the house made a creaking sound, as if a corpse had moved, but, of course, the noise could only be due to the cold night causing window joints to shrink. Nonetheless, Ryan, Becker, and Commissioner Mayne stared toward the closed door that led to the bodies in the passageway, the kitchen, and the bedroom.

"The murders here...do you think that someone found an old mallet and hammered the initials J. P. into it to draw attention to the parallel?" Becker asked. A troubling thought made him shake his head from side to side. "Or else...no, that's hardly possible."

"Say what's on your mind," Ryan told him. "If you're going to work with me, I don't want you holding back."

"Could this be the same mallet that was used in the original murders?"

The door opened, startling them.

The bearded artist for the *Illustrated London News* stepped in.

"Is this yours?" he asked Ryan. He held a newspaperboy's cap in his hands. "One of the patrolmen found this. He thought it looked like one you lost."

"Yes. Thanks." Ryan pushed the cap down over his head, at last able to hide his red hair. "How long do newspapers keep old issues?"

"The *Illustrated* has copies from eighteen forty-two, when it began."

"We're interested in eighteen eleven. And any illustrations that might have been made of a weapon used in a crime that year."

"Weren't any drawings in newspapers back then. We were the first to use 'em. Crime? What crime?"

"The Ratcliffe Highway murders."

"Oh, right, them," the artist said matter-of-factly.

"You *know* about them?" the commissioner asked in surprise. "How? You're too young to have been alive in eighteen eleven."

"Sure. I read about them last week."

Becker's voice demonstrated as much surprise as the commissioner's. "You *read* about them?"

"'On Murder Considered as One of the Fine Arts.'"

"What in blazes are you talking about?" Ryan asked.

"The Opium-Eater. Thomas De Quincey."

"Everyone knows who the Opium-Eater is. What does Thomas De Quincey have to do with—"

"I sketched him on Friday for our newspaper. His collected works are being published. He's been talking to reporters so they'll write about him and get people to buy his books. Undignified, if you ask me. But when was the Opium-Eater dignified?"

"I still don't—"

"'On Murder Considered as One of the Fine Arts.' That's something else De Quincey wrote besides the opium-eating book. Since I'd drawn a sketch of him, I decided I'd read what all the fuss is about."

As if to make a point, the bearded man pulled out his flask and tilted it above his lips, finishing its contents. "De Quincey didn't just write about being addicted to opium. This 'Fine Art' thing describes the Ratcliffe Highway murders."

"What?"

"The Opium-Eater went on and on about them. The bloodiest thing I ever read. Gave me nightmares. He piled on so many gruesome details, it's like he was there."

5

The Sublimity of Murder

During the 1300s, Paternoster Row acquired its name because monks could be heard chanting the Pater Noster, or Our Father, in nearby St. Paul's Cathedral. In that century, stores there sold religious texts and rosaries. But by 1854, the street was the center of London's publishing world. At 6 a.m. (according to the bells at the cathedral, telling the faithful to waken and prepare for church services), Ryan and Becker descended from a police wagon.

In early light, a breeze chased the fog and allowed them to study the multitude of bookshops on each side of the street. Many were owned by publishers who, during business hours, placed stalls on the street to promote their various offerings. But 6 a.m. on a Sunday morning was hardly the start of business hours, so Ryan and Becker pounded on various doors in the hope that someone lived on the premises.

An elderly man raised an upper window and leaned out sleepily. "What's all the noise?"

"Do you work here?" Ryan yelled up.

"Yes. Go away." The old man started to close the window.

"Police. We need to talk to you."

"Police?" Although the old man seemed impressed, it took a while before he managed to come downstairs and open the door. He wore nightclothes, including a cap. His white beard curved into his sunken cheeks.

"Those bells are loud enough without you hammering," he complained. Fumbling to put on his spectacles, he clearly wondered what a uniformed policeman was doing with a ruffian whose red hair wasn't quite concealed by a newspaperboy's cap.

"The Opium-Eater," Ryan said.

"Thomas De Quincey?" Ignoring Ryan and his shabby clothes, the clerk spoke to Constable Becker. "Yes, what about him? You won't find him here. Saturday was the time to talk to him."

"We're looking for *books* that he wrote," Ryan said.

The clerk kept directing his attention toward Becker and his uniform. "They've been selling briskly. I have only a few left."

"We need to read them," Ryan said.

The clerk continued to ignore him, telling Becker, "We're not open on Sunday. But come back after church. I'll make an exception for a constable."

"We need to read them *now*."

Ryan passed him, entering the shop.

THE LEATHER-BOUND VOLUME had pages that needed to be cut. Becker hid his surprise when Ryan raised a trouser cuff, pulled a knife from a scabbard strapped to his leg, and slit the book's pages.

"Be careful how you do that," the clerk objected. "Customers are particular about how their book pages are cut. Constable, since when do you let prisoners carry knives?"

"He's not a prisoner. He's Detective Inspector Ryan."

"Irish." The old man nodded as if his suspicions were confirmed.

"Tell us about 'On Murder Considered as One of the Fine Arts,'" Ryan said.

"Seems like you'd know more about that subject than *I* would."

Ryan stared at him so directly that the old man raised his hands in surrender.

"If you mean De Quincey's essays..."

"Plural? De Quincey wrote more than one essay about murder?" Ryan asked.

"Three. All in that book you're trying to destroy. De Quincey does enjoy his murders."

"Murders?"

"After he wrote *Confessions of an English Opium-Eater,* he promised his next book would be called *Confessions of a Murderer.*"

The two police officers gaped.

"But instead of a book about killing, he wrote three essays about it," the clerk said, opening the book to show them.

Astonished, Ryan and Becker read about a men's club where lectures were delivered about the great murders of history. The lectures were called the Williams Lectures, after John Williams, the man accused of the Ratcliffe Highway multiple killings.

"My God, look at how De Quincey praises the murders," Ryan said. "'The sublimest that ever were committed. The blaze of his genius absolutely dazzled.'"

"And *here.*" Becker quoted in amazement: "'The most superb of the century. Neither ever was, or will be surpassed. Genius. All other murders look pale by the deep crimson of his.'"

"De Quincey sounds insane."

Ryan and Becker discovered that De Quincey's latest essay about murder had been published only a month previously. In it, the Opium-Eater described Williams's two killing sprees for fifty astoundingly blood-filled pages—murders that by 1854 had occurred forty-three years earlier and yet were presented with a vividness that gave the impression the killings had happened the previous night.

Williams forced his way through the crowded streets, bound on business. To say was to do. And this night he had said to himself that he would execute a design which he had already sketched and which, when finished, was destined on the following day to strike consternation into the mighty heart of London. He quitted his lodgings on this dark errand about eleven o'clock P.M., not that he meant to begin so soon, but he needed to reconnoiter. He carried his tools closely buttoned up under his loose roomy coat.

Ryan pointed at the next page. "Marr kept his shop open until midnight. Williams hid in the shadows across the street. The female servant left on an errand. The watchman came by and helped Marr put up the window shutters. Then…."

Williams waited for the sound of the watchman's retreating steps; waited perhaps for thirty seconds; but when that danger was past, the next danger was that Marr would lock the door. One turn of the key, and he would have been locked out. In therefore, he bolted, and by a dexterous movement of his left hand turned the key, without letting Marr perceive this fatal stratagem.

"His left hand. How does De Quincey know Williams used his left hand?" Becker wondered.

Having reached the counter, he asked Marr for a pair of unbleached cotton socks.

"Unbleached socks? How does he know *that?* Only the victim and the killer were in the room."

The arrangement had become familiar to the murderer. In order to reach down the particular parcel, Marr would find it requisite to face round to the rear and at the same moment to raise his eyes and his hands to a level eighteen inches above his head.

"Eighteen inches? How can De Quincey be that precise?" Ryan exclaimed.

This movement placed him in the most disadvantageous possible position with regard to the murderer who now, at the instant that the back of Marr's head was exposed, suddenly from below his large coat, unslung the heavy ship-carpenter's mallet and with one solitary blow so thoroughly stunned his victim as to leave him incapable of resistance.

"It's the same as what happened last night, complete with the unbleached socks we found on the floor. The shopkeeper must have been reaching for them," Becker said. "Look at this about the baby."

He found himself doubly frustrated—first, by the arched hood at the head of the cradle, which he beat into a ruin with his mallet; and secondly, by the gathering of the blankets and the pillows about the baby's head. The free play of his blows had thus been baffled, and he therefore finished the scene by applying his razor to the throat of the little innocent, after which, as though he had become confused by the spectacle of his own atrocities, he busied himself by piling the clothes elaborately over the child's corpse.

"It's the same as what we found."

"Two," Ryan suddenly said.

"What?"

"Williams committed *two* sets of killings." Ryan turned a page to find more horrors: the slaughter of the tavernkeeper, his wife, and the servant twelve days later.

"The tavernkeeper's name," Becker said.

"What about it?"

Becker pointed at a line in the book. "John Williamson."

"So?" Ryan asked.

"The killer's name was John Williams. In the second set of murders, the victim's name was John Williamson."

Ryan looked at him in confusion.

"John Williams. John Williamson. As if they were in the same family," Becker said, "like a father killing his son."

"That has to be a coincidence," Ryan told him. "The commissioner would have mentioned if the killer was related to the victim. Besides, the parallel doesn't work. Williams was young enough to be the tavernkeeper's son, not his father. Thinking that way doesn't make sense. The point is, look at the detail with which the Opium-Eater describes the murders."

The housemaid was caught on her knees before the fire-grate, which she had been polishing. That part of her task was finished, and she passed on to filling the grate with wood and coals at the very moment when the murderer entered. Mrs. Williamson had not seen him, from the accident of standing with her back to the door. Before he was observed, he had stunned and prostrated her with a shattering blow on the back of her head. This blow, inflicted by a crow-bar, smashed in the hinder part of her skull. She fell, and by the noise of her fall, roused the attention of the servant, who uttered a cry, but before she could repeat it, the murderer descended on her with his uplifted instrument upon *her* head, crushing the skull inwards upon the brain. Both women were irrecoverably destroyed, so that further outrages were needless, and yet the murderer proceeded instantly to cut the throats of each. The servant, from her kneeling posture, had presented her head passively to blows, after which the miscreant had but to bend her head backward so as to expose her throat.

"It's as if I'm in the room," Becker murmured. "Forty-three years after the murders, and the Opium-Eater writes about them as if they happened yesterday."

"He describes the blood with glee." Ryan grabbed the book and quickly stood. "We need to talk with him."

A voice asked, "Who? De Quincey?" Footsteps rumbled down the stairs, preceding the elderly clerk, who held a hymnbook and was dressed to go to church.

"He was here on Saturday, you told us?" Becker asked.

"In that chair over there. Wasn't comfortable. His forehead gleamed with sweat. Even sitting, he kept moving his feet up and down. Probably needed laudanum. But his daughter brought him cups of tea, and he answered questions from customers, and I must say I sold plenty of books. Are you planning to buy the one you mutilated, by the way?"

"A discount for police business."

"Who said anything about a discount?"

Ryan put half the price on the desk. "Do you know where he went?"

"Well, I know he lives in Edinburgh."

"All the way to Scotland? No!"

"But I got the impression that for the next week he and his daughter were remaining here in London."

"Where?" Ryan demanded.

"I have no idea. Unlike the police"—the old man gave Ryan's shabby appearance a disparaging look—"I don't ask people their personal business. Perhaps his publisher would know."

"Where do we find his publisher?"

"The address is in the book for which you demanded a discount. But if you need to talk to the Opium-Eater anytime soon, I don't think the address will help you."

"Why?"

"The publisher's in Edinburgh, also."

RYAN AND BECKER hurried from the bookshop and climbed onto the police wagon.

"Waterloo Bridge train station," Ryan told the driver.

As they sped away, people walking toward St. Paul's Cathedral looked with disapproval toward Ryan's rough clothes, seeming convinced that he'd been arrested.

"De Quincey wrote about *two* sets of murders," Becker said.

Ryan reacted as if Becker had stated the obvious. "Yes, there were two sets of Ratcliffe Highway killings. What's your point?"

"Do you suppose there'll be *another* set of murders?"

As the wagon came to Waterloo Bridge, buildings gave way to the open expanse of the river with its steamboats, barges, and skiffs adding wakes to the surging waves.

Becker noticed that Ryan looked down at the wagon's floor rather than at the wide, powerful water. The detective's grip was tight on the side of the wagon. Only when the wagon arrived on the other side and the river was behind them did Ryan relax his grip and look up from the floor of the wagon.

"Are you all right?" Becker asked.

"What makes you think I'm not?"

"Crossing the river seemed to bother you."

"Murders are what bother me."

They reached the arches that supported the Waterloo Bridge train station and ran into its massive structure.

Ryan could remember when railways hadn't existed. The first one—from Liverpool to Manchester—had been built in 1830, when he was sixteen. Before then, most transportation had been via horse-driven coach, which—as Commissioner Mayne had noted—could proceed as fast as ten miles per hour, although only the mail coaches, with their system of horse relays, could maintain that pace. Now, with railways crisscrossing the nation, it was possible to travel at a once-inconceivable *sixty* miles per hour.

For the system to function, however, arriving and departing trains needed to maintain a strict schedule. The result was a profound change in the way communities thought of time and distance. Prior to the railway, a village in northwestern England might have had its clocks set at ten minutes after seven while a village a hundred miles away might have had *its* clocks set for twenty minutes later. The discrepancy couldn't be noticed when someone traveling via a horse-driven coach required more than ten hours to go from one village to the other.

But now, with trains speeding across that hundred miles in one hour and forty minutes, the difference between the clocks in those two villages was significant. If similar differences existed in every community, a coordinated schedule would have been impossible. Using the measurement of time as determined by the Royal Greenwich Observatory in London, every railway clock (and soon every other timepiece throughout England) was set for the same hour and minute, in what became known as Railway Time.

Amazingly, information could travel even faster than passengers on a train, crossing hundreds of miles not only in a few hours but in an astounding few seconds, because as the railways spread, telegraph lines were erected next to them. The click-click-click of operators' keys relayed messages with what had once been impossible speed.

In the train station's telegraph office, Ryan told the operator to send a message to James Hogg Publisher at 4 Nicolson Street, Edinburgh, Scotland, the address inside the book.

People at risk. Send London address for Thomas De Quincey at once.

"You make it sound as if De Quincey's in danger," Becker said.

"It might get us a quicker response."

As they spoke, the message would arrive at the Edinburgh telegraph station. In minutes, a messenger would set out to deliver a sealed envelope to Hogg's business address, where if the publisher wasn't available (as he wasn't likely to be on a Sunday morning), the messenger would ask every neighbor he could find until Hogg's home address was located.

Ryan sent a separate telegram to the Edinburgh police force.

Murder investigation. Urgent you find James Hogg at this address. Need London location of Thomas De Quincey.

"Now you make it seem as if De Quincey's a suspect," Becker noted.

"Well, isn't he? Edinburgh's small compared to London. One of these messages ought to get results this afternoon. Twenty years ago, when I was a constable like you, there wasn't even a train to Edinburgh, let alone a telegraph line. This could have taken weeks."

"What if Hogg traveled somewhere?" Becker asked. "He might even be in London."

"Then I'll order patrolmen to ask at all the hotels in London. One way or another, I intend to find out where the blazes De Quincey is."

THE MURDER SCENE remained a welter of activity.

As Ryan and Becker jumped down from the police wagon, a constable reported, "The neighbors I spoke to didn't notice anything, Inspector."

"Same here," another said. "The fog and the cold kept everybody inside."

"I found a dollymop who claims she saw a stranger," a third added.

"Working the streets last night, she must have been desperate," Ryan told the policeman.

"That's one reason she noticed him. Nobody else was in sight."

"*One* reason?" Ryan asked.

"She says when she started to approach the stranger, he gave her a look that warned it would go nasty for her if she came any closer. Hardest eyes she ever saw, she tells me."

"Did she describe him?"

"Tall. Big shoulders. A sailor's coat and cap. A yellow beard."

"Yellow? There aren't many men with that color of beard. We'll go through the catalogue system and look for a match." If the man had been arrested in the past ten years, Ryan knew, his aliases, age, height, weight, tattoos, birthmarks, scars, and other identifying characteristics would have been recorded as part of the arrest procedure. "Did she notice where he went?"

"She says she was smart enough to go one way when he went the other."

"Keep questioning the neighbors. Extend your search even wider."

Ryan and Becker entered the tavern and went to the back room, where two patrolmen watched the handcuffed prisoner.

Still claiming to have been drunk, the prisoner didn't remember where he'd been the previous night or who could vouch for his presence at the time of the murders.

"His boots have hobnails," Becker pointed out to Ryan. "The prints we found didn't."

" 'Course my boots've hobnails. Can't afford to keep resoling 'em," the prisoner muttered.

"There's always a chance he changed his boots," Ryan said. "But he can't change their size."

"Let's find out." Becker tugged a boot from the complaining prisoner and went outside to compare it to the prints, the casts of which were now dry.

"Too small," he reported when he came back.

Ryan rubbed the back of his neck. "Almost out of possibilities."

"Detective Inspector Ryan?"

Ryan turned toward a constable in the doorway.

"There's a boy here looking for you. He has a telegram."

When Ryan opened it, he smiled. "De Quincey's London address."

Continuing the Journal of Emily De Quincey

In all my adventures with Father, I can now add one more: being arrested. Constable Becker and the ruffian who said his name was Detective Inspector Ryan insisted that was not the case, but the somberness of their expressions and the haste with which they wanted to place us in a police wagon belied their assurances.

"Go with you to Scotland Yard? Why?" Father demanded as the fog swirled around us.

"We have questions," the ruffian said.

"About what?"

"The Ratcliffe Highway murders."

"Everything I have to say about them is in my latest book. Why do you care about something that happened forty-three years ago?"

"Not forty-three years ago," the ruffian said. I have difficulty referring to him as a detective inspector.

"Of course it was forty-three years ago," Father replied. "Do detectives not have schooling? Subtract eighteen hundred and eleven from—"

"Last night," Ryan said.

"I beg your pardon?"

"The murders happened last night."

The statement made the air feel colder. Even in the fog, I could see Father straighten.

"Murders last night?" he whispered.

"Can anyone account for your activities between ten and midnight?" Becker asked. From Ryan, the question would have been challenging, but the constable made it sound respectful.

"No."

"Please tell us where you were." Again, the constable's tone was assuring.

"I don't know."

"*You don't know?*" Ryan interrupted rudely. "*Does your laudanum habit weaken your memory?*"

"*My memory is excellent.*"

"*Then perhaps you were too affected by the drug to know what you were doing last night.*"

"*I know what I was doing. I just don't know where.*"

Ryan shook his head. "*What opium does to people.*"

Constable Becker stepped forward, kindly asking me, "*May I have your name, miss?*"

"*Emily De Quincey. I'm his daughter.*"

"*Can you help us understand what your father is trying to say?*"

"*I meant what I said. It's perfectly clear,*" Father told them. "*If you'd asked me what I was doing instead of where I was, I could have told you I was walking.*"

"*Walking? That late?*" Ryan interrupted again as the fog continued to engulf us.

I began to sense a stratagem that they had calculated before we arrived, the ruffian trying to make us feel threatened while the constable was solicitous, in the hopes that the contrast between them would confuse us into making careless statements.

"*My father walks a great deal,*" I explained. "*Especially if he is making an effort to reduce his laudanum intake, he spends much of his time walking.*"

"*One summer in the Lake District,*" Father said proudly, "*I walked two thousand miles.*"

"*Two thousand miles?*" Ryan looked puzzled.

"*It's cold out here,*" Father said. "*Instead of pursuing this conversation for the neighbors to hear, may we go inside?*"

"*Where we need to go is Scotland Yard,*" Ryan insisted.

"*And is there a necessary on your wagon, or will you stop on the way so that we can use one?*" Father added with a turn to me, "*Excuse the reference, my dear.*"

Now Father *was* the one employing a stratagem. He has never used a genteel synonym for a privy.

"*I forgive you, Father.*"

"*The necessary in the house is remarkable,*" Father told Ryan and Constable Becker. "*Our housekeeper tells me it is modeled after a water device introduced at the Great Exhibition in Hyde Park three years ago. 'A flush with every push,' I believe the motto is. She says that the inventor charged a penny a flush. Almost six million visitors to the Great Exhibition. Imagine, a penny from each of them.*"

Ryan sighed. "Very well. Let's go into the house."

Mrs. Warden hovered as the four of us entered the parlor. Her look suggested that she expected nothing less than that the Opium-Eater would be questioned by the police.

"*I'll light a fire,*" she said, obviously wanting to overhear.

"*Don't bother,*" Ryan told her. "*We won't stay long enough for the room to get warm.*"

"*Father hasn't eaten anything since breakfast. Please, bring tea and biscuits,*" I told Mrs. Warden.

But she didn't move.

"Please," *I emphasized.*

Mrs. Warden reluctantly went to do her duty, her hooped dress brushing against the doorway. I assumed she would do her best to eavesdrop from the kitchen.

There was a lot of activity after that, with everyone — thanks to the cold outside — using what Father kept calling the necessary. It is on the main floor. Although this well-to-do section of London is serviced by a company that pumps water into homes, the pressure of the water is not dependable. A necessary on the upper floor would not receive enough water to function.

During the confusion of the coming and going, I noticed that Father went upstairs, however. Soon afterward, he returned to the parlor. Despite the cold temperature of the room, his brow had a film of moisture. This morning the moisture — caused by exertion — had been shiny, but now it was dull, and from experience, I knew that could mean only one thing.

"*Oh, Father,*" I said with disappointment.

He shrugged. The left side of his overcoat had a bulge, no doubt caused by a flask of laudanum. I might have expected it, given the pain he feels when relating to strangers.

"What do you mean, 'Oh, Father'? Is something the matter?" Constable Becker asked, glancing from my face to my father's. The lamp in the parlor showed that the constable has a scar on his chin. Despite it, he is not difficult to look at.

"My daughter is merely indicating that she is fatigued."

"Quite the contrary, Father."

"Last night," Ryan said. "You went walking?"

"I have been restless lately," Father said. "I do not feel shame by admitting that my debts are considerable. At one time, I had obligations to pay rent on six lodgings."

"If not for all your books, Father, you wouldn't have needed most of them." I turned to tell Constable Becker, "He fills one house with books and then rents another and another."

"That is family business, Emily. No need to share the details. Some landlords were so pitiless that they pursued me into court and even into jail."

"Jail?" Ryan asked, straightening.

"In jail, how was I to work and pay my debts and support my dear now-departed wife and what were then eight children? Thanks to friends who paid my bond, I was released, but then of course I owed my friends as well as the landlords, the butcher, and the baker, and you can see how everything mounted. Sometimes, to avoid the bailiff, I was forced to sleep in haystacks, but that was nothing compared to when I lived on the cold streets of London when I was seventeen."

Becker frowned. "Miss De Quincey, does your father always talk this way?"

"What way?" Father wanted to know, puzzled.

"So many words so quickly."

"Not quickly," Father rejoined. "It's everyone else who talks slowly. I hang on to their words, wishing they would proceed with their thoughts. Constable Becker, I don't wish to be forward, but blood is seeping through the left knee of your uniform."

"Blood?" Becker looked down. "Oh. I must have torn one of my stitches."

"Stitches?"

"Last night, I was attacked by two pigs."

Now it was Father's turn to look baffled.

Mrs. Warden squeezed her hooped dress through the doorway, carrying a tray of tea and biscuits that she set on a table. She poured the tea but then stood in the background.

"Thank you," Ryan said with a tone of finality.

Disappointed, Mrs. Warden returned to the kitchen, where she no doubt continued to eavesdrop.

"The murders," Father said.

"Yes," Ryan said. "Last night near Ratcliffe Highway."

Father's blue eyes contracted. "How many victims?"

"Five. Three adults and two children."

"Oh, my," Father said. With a look of defeat, he reached into the left side of his coat, pulled out a flask, and poured a ruby liquid into his teacup.

"What are you doing?" Ryan asked.

"Taking my medicine."

"Medicine? What kind of medicine comes in a flask? Is that alcohol?"

"No. Well, yes, in a manner of speaking. But no."

"Don't tell me that's laudanum.*"*

"As I said, I'm taking my medicine. I'm subject to severe facial pains. Laudanum is the only way to relieve them."

"Facial pains?"

"And a stomach disorder." Father took a deep swallow from his teacup. "It dates back to when I was a young man."

Constable Becker pointed. "But you poured at least an ounce."

Father took another swallow.

"Stop." The constable reached for the teacup. "Good heavens, man, are you trying to kill yourself?"

Father pulled the teacup close to him, preventing Constable Becker from grabbing it. "Kill myself?" The film of sweat on Father's brow became more noticeable and yet duller. "What a strange idea." He pointed toward an object that Ryan held. "I see you have my latest book."

" 'On Murder Considered as One of the Fine Arts,' " Ryan said.

Father swallowed more liquid from his cup. "Yes, that is an essay in the book."

Becker looked at me and said, "Miss De Quincey, perhaps you'd like to join your housekeeper in the kitchen or else go to your room."

"Why on earth would I wish to do that?"

"I'm afraid our conversation might disturb you."

"I've read Father's work. I know what it contains."

"Even so, what we need to talk about might shock you."

"In that event, if I find it shocking, I shall leave," I pronounced.

No one said anything for a moment. Ryan and Constable Becker glanced at one another, as if determining how to continue.

"Very well, if you insist on remaining," Ryan said. "In eighteen eleven, on Ratcliffe Highway, John Williams entered a linen shop that was about to close. He used a mallet with the initials J. P. to shatter the heads of the shopkeeper, his assistant, his wife, and his infant. Then he slit the baby's throat."

It was my impression that Ryan was needlessly graphic in an effort to persuade me to leave the room, but I steeled myself and showed no reaction.

"That is correct," Father said.

"The same thing happened last night in the Ratcliffe Highway area," Ryan told him. "Except that two children were killed, not one."

"Two children?" Father slowly set down his cup. "Oh."

"We have numerous questions," Ryan continued. "Why do you know so many precise details about murders that occurred forty-three years ago? Why, in all that time, did you persist in praising those murders? Why did you feel compelled to write about them in extremely graphic detail as recently as last month? Finally, I'll ask you again, where were you at ten o'clock last night?"

"And I'll answer again, I was walking the streets."

"Which streets?"

"I have no idea. I was lost in my thoughts."

"You expect us to believe that you paid no attention to your surroundings?"

"In the fog? Even if I hadn't been preoccupied, there weren't any surroundings to notice."

"Preoccupied about what?"

"A personal matter."

"When it comes to murder, no topic is too personal for us to ask about."

I couldn't keep silent any longer. *"This is outrageous. Surely, you are not suggesting that my father had something to do with the murders?"*

"He's an expert in them. He's obsessed about them."

"Murders forty-three years ago!" Embarrassed that I'd raised my voice, I moderated it, but my tone was nonetheless stern. *"My father is a professional magazine writer. On occasion, he writes about sensational topics so that he can help publishers sell their magazines. Murder is a popular topic."*

"Last night it certainly was," Ryan said. He looked at Constable Becker, as if giving him a cue to take over.

"Miss De Quincey," Becker said, obviously trying to win me over, *"do you have any idea when your father might have returned from walking the streets?"*

"No."

"Do you know when he went out?"

"I heard his footsteps on the stairs about nine o'clock."

"An hour to reach the shop at ten," Ryan said to himself. *"It's possible for a man accustomed to walking a great deal."*

"Did you hear him return?" Constable Becker asked me.

"No."

"Three o'clock!" Mrs. Warden called from the kitchen.

"That is true," Father said. *"I returned at three o'clock."*

"Plenty of time for you to have walked back from the shop," Ryan murmured to himself.

I no longer cared that I raised my voice. *"Look at this man! He's sixty-nine! He's short! He's frail!"*

"Thin," Father said. *"But please, Emily, not frail. This month alone, and it's only the eleventh, I walked one hundred and fifty miles."*

"Do you honestly believe my father has the strength to bludgeon three adults with a ... what did you say was used?"

"A ship carpenter's mallet," Becker answered.

"It sounds heavy."

"A sturdy tool."

"Look at my father's arms."

They turned in Father's direction, and perhaps it was the effect of the laudanum, but he seemed smaller in the chair, his shoes barely touching the floor.

"What you describe would have been impossible for him," I emphasized.

"Alone," Ryan said. *"But two people could have done it, one with the knowledge and one with the strength."*

"You are making me impatient," I said. *"The next thing, you'll suggest that I'm the one who helped Father kill all those people. Would you like to know where I was at ten o'clock last night?"*

"Honestly, Miss De Quincey, I don't think —"

"In bed. But I'm afraid I don't have a witness."

Color rose to both men's beard-stubbled cheeks.

"A ship carpenter's mallet?" Father asked.

"Yes," Ryan answered. *"You understand the significance?"*

"The parallel was that exact?"

"More than can be imagined. The mallet had initials stamped into it by a nail. Would you care to guess what the initials are?"

"J. P.? It's not possible."

"But it is. The initials are indeed J. P., the same initials that were on the mallet used in the murders forty-three years ago, the same initials that you wrote about in your essay on how murder is such a wonderful art. Now I must insist" — Ryan stood — *"that you come with us to Scotland Yard, where you can answer our questions in a more appropriate setting."*

"No," Father said. *"I won't come with you to Scotland Yard."*

Ryan stepped closer. *"You're mistaken. Believe me, sir, you will come with us to Scotland Yard. Whether under your own power or under duress, that is your choice."*

"No," Father repeated. He drank the last of the laudanum in his cup. *"Not Scotland Yard. I'm afraid there is only one place to discuss this."*

"Oh? And where might that be?"

"Where the murders occurred."

6

The Patron of Gravediggers

DARKNESS MERGED WITH THE THICKENING FOG. On the street outside the shop, the lights of police lanterns no longer zigzagged urgently. The investigation had reached its limits — no more neighbors to question, no more places to search.

Nonetheless the street was chaotic. As Ryan and Becker climbed down from the police wagon, they assessed the troubling circumstance that confronted them. Although most of the daytime crowd was gone, having retreated from whatever terrors the new night concealed, those who remained were drunk and made enough noise for a crowd ten times larger. They carried clubs, swords, and rifles. There was nothing Ryan could do about their weapons. In the absence of gun laws, even children could own firearms.

"How long will you stay and keep us safe?" a neighbor demanded from a constable outside the shop.

"As long as we're investigating."

"But how long? Tomorrow night?"

"Possibly," the policeman replied.

"*Possibly?* What about next week? Will you be here *then?*"

"I'm not certain. A lot of streets aren't being patrolled while we're here. Soon we'll need to get back to our districts."

"My God, we'll all be murdered unless we find the killer ourselves!"

Amid the clamor, Ryan noticed that the Opium-Eater and his daughter had climbed down from the police wagon without assistance. Despite his considerable efforts to dissuade her, De Quincey's daughter had refused to be left behind while De Quincey had refused to go without her.

"I need to make certain that Father takes care of himself," she had said, and to prove it she'd insisted that De Quincey eat several biscuits as the wagon transported them. "The state of his stomach is such that he eats as little as possible. This is his first food since breakfast."

Ryan had never encountered a pair quite like them. At five feet ten inches, Ryan was taller than most people in 1854, a requirement for being a policeman. In contrast, De Quincey was shorter than the average height of five feet four inches, his thin frame making him seem even shorter, perhaps only five feet. Yet the Opium-Eater had a way of talking that was out of proportion to his size, making him fill the space he occupied.

As for the daughter, she was the most strong-minded female Ryan had ever met. Her "bloomer" style of dress indicated her independent attitude. While he reluctantly admitted that she was attractive, with pleasing features, blue eyes that matched her father's, and smooth, brown hair pulled back behind her head, he barely controlled his exasperation when he told her, "You see how inconvenient it was for you to have insisted on coming with us. Now you'll be forced to stand here in the cold with a constable to protect you from this rabble while we go inside."

"And why, please tell, would I wish to remain out here in the cold?"

"You surely can't come inside."

"Why not? I've seen death before, especially my mother's long, wasting illness."

Ryan gave Becker a look that suggested, *Maybe* you *can deal with her.*

But before Becker could say anything, the Opium-Eater opened the door and stepped into the shop. Trying to stay in control, Ryan entered, moving ahead of him. The next thing, Emily was inside, followed by Becker.

Although the bodies had been removed, the room continued to have a foul odor. Ryan glanced back at Emily, concerned that she might faint. But although she looked pale and held a handkerchief to her nose, she surprised him by seeming more curious than horrified.

Becker closed the door and stopped the cold fog from drifting in.

"Apart from the absence of the bodies, is everything as the murderer left it?" De Quincey asked.

Or as you *and an accomplice possibly left it?* Ryan wondered. "No."

"How is it different?" De Quincey continued.

"My purpose in agreeing to bring you here is to ask *you* questions, not the other way around," Ryan informed him.

"But how is it different?" De Quincey indicated an open door to the left of the counter. "I see considerable dried blood on the passage floor. There are contours as if the blood pooled around bodies. Where were they taken?"

"After an artist made detailed sketches, the remains were removed to the basement."

De Quincey nodded. In 1854 London, there weren't any funeral parlors. Corpses were kept at home until burial. Family members placed the body of a loved one on a bed, cleaned and dressed it, and made the corpse look as if it were sleeping. Sometimes a death mask was made, and with the advent of the daguerreotype process, photographs sometimes were taken. After that, friends were allowed to enter the bedroom and view the remains. The visitations might last five days until it became obvious that a coffin was required.

After a religious ceremony at the deceased's home, the coffin was transported via a horse-drawn hearse to a cemetery, but London's rapid growth put a strain on burial capacity. Cemeteries designed for three thousand burials were forced to accommodate as many as eighty thousand, eventually piling ten, twelve, and even fifteen caskets on top of one another. As the bottom caskets disintegrated, cemetery workers helped the process by digging down and jumping on the remains to compact them so that additional caskets could be placed on top.

New cemeteries were located miles from the center of London, with the result that a horse-drawn funeral procession would take most of the day for the body to arrive at its resting place. But only a month earlier, in November, an innovation had occurred with the construction of the London Necropolis Railway Station. A funeral procession could now board a special train that transported mourners and the coffin to the recently created Brookwood cemetery, twenty-five miles away. After the interment, the train would then bring the mourners back to London, all in a previously impossible single day's round trip.

An abrupt noise interrupted De Quincey's questions. It came from the rear of the building, not the creak of beams shrinking in the cold but of footsteps climbing stairs.

Becker stepped in front of Emily, his hand over the truncheon on his belt.

A shadow lengthened in the corridor, reaching the top of the basement stairs.

Becker heard Emily inhale with apprehension.

At once a figure approached them, stepping around the dried blood on the passage floor.

Becker recognized the man he'd discovered pounding on the door the previous night in an effort to deliver a blanket to his sick niece. This was also the man who'd led the mob's assault on the stranger who the mob had believed was the killer.

The burly man frowned toward the group before him. His hair was unkempt. Dried tears streaked the grime on his beard-stubbled cheeks.

Seeing strangers, he tensed until he focused on Becker's uniform. "I'm Jonathan's brother."

"This is Detective Inspector Ryan," Becker said.

The brother nodded. "I saw you earlier."

"In the fracas. Yes."

"The constable outside said it was all right for me to come in."

"It is," Ryan agreed.

"Did the best I could for 'em. Poor Jonathan. Never should've come here from Manchester. None of us should've. I set up trestles and planks in the basement. Put 'em on the planks. Tried to make 'em look natural, I did, but God help 'em..." The man's voice wavered. "After what the bugger did to 'em...excuse me, miss...how can I possibly make 'em look natural? The undertaker wants sixteen pounds for 'em for the funeral. Says I need white coffins for the two children. The baby..." Fresh tears welled from his eyes. "Even the baby costs for a funeral. And where will I find sixteen pounds? Ruined I am. The bugger destroyed Jonathan and his family, and now I'm ruined too."

Snot mixed with his tears. He shook his head in despair.

Emily surprised Becker by saying, "I'm sorry."

She further surprised Becker — and Ryan and especially the grieving man — by crossing the room and touching the man's arm. The only person who didn't look surprised was De Quincey.

"My heart goes out to you," she said.

The man blinked, unaccustomed to kind words. "Thank you, miss."

"Mr....?"

"Hayworth."

"Mr. Hayworth, when did you sleep last?"

"A few hours here and there. Hasn't been time. Truth is, my mind won't allow me."

"And when did you eat last? I can smell that you've been drinking alcohol."

"Apologies, miss. With the shock of everything, I..."

"No need to apologize. But when did you eat last?"

"Maybe this morning."

"Do you live around here?"

"Five minutes."

"Do you have a family?"

The man wiped at his face. "My missus and a little boy."

"Detective Inspector Ryan will arrange for someone to escort you home."

Ryan blinked.

"Mr. Hayworth, I'm giving you strict orders to let your family know that you're all right," Emily continued.

"Strict orders?"

"Yes. Your wife and son must be worried sick. What's more, given what's happened, they must be afraid. They depend on your safety."

"You're right, miss," the man told her sheepishly.

"I want you to go home immediately and eat something. Then I want you to rest your head. Even if you can't sleep, lying down will do you good. The man who escorts you to your home will tell me where it is. I'll go there when I have the opportunity. If I discover that you haven't followed my orders, I shall be displeased, and you do not wish that."

"No, miss. I promise, miss."

Ryan gave Becker a subtle nod.

"I'll take care of it," Becker said. "One of the constables will escort Mr. Hayworth home."

"Thank you," Emily said to Becker and Ryan.

"Thank *you,* miss." Hayworth sniffled, wiping his sleeve across his face.

"And we'll give some thought to how your funeral expenses might be alleviated," Emily added. "But right now, your priorities are your family, food, and rest."

Hayworth nodded. Hope mixing with exhaustion, he sniffled again and allowed Becker to lead him from the shop.

WE'LL GIVE SOME THOUGHT to alleviating his funeral expenses?" Ryan asked Emily as Becker returned and closed the door against the cold fog.

"Yes. I'm confident that a solution will come to us," Emily replied.

"*Us?*" Ryan asked. "The Metropolitan Police can't assume that obligation."

"Manchester," De Quincey interrupted. "The victim was from Manchester. The family's name is Hayworth."

"That's what he told us. Why?" Ryan asked. "You look as if you think those details are important."

"Perhaps. May I see the sketches of the bodies?"

"You're still asking questions instead of answering them. How do you know so much about the original Ratcliffe Highway murders? What age were you in eighteen eleven?"

"Twenty-six. Old enough to have the strength to commit the murders, if not the size. Your next question should be, Where was I during that December night forty-three years ago?"

"Precisely."

"I was in Grasmere in the Lake District, residing in William Words-worth's former home, Dove Cottage. At that time, it was a several-days' journey to London via coach, although I suppose I could have managed it if I were desperate to slaughter a family on Ratcliffe Highway. However, I would have been missed because at the time I was engaged in a much-protracted disagreement with William and his family over shrubbery that I chose to have ripped from their former garden. William's wife, Mary, and his sister, Dorothy, were much displeased. Believe me, they would have noted my absence. William and Dorothy have joined the majority, God bless them. But Mary is still alive and assembling new editions of her husband's poetry. I am not certain where she resides, but perhaps she still remembers the rancor of that December."

"Since you're both asking and answering the questions, what should my *next* question be?"

Becker noted that Ryan didn't sound frustrated any longer. The detective had found a way to make De Quincey cooperate.

"The one with which you started. How do I know the details of the original murders? Because I researched them, Inspector Ryan. I was so impressed by the paralyzing effect the murders had on the nation that I accumulated copies of every newspaper with even the slightest informa-tion about them. The panic of those days was exceptional and widely reported. You'll find the newspapers in one of the many lodgings for which I do my best to pay rent in order to store things. Unfortunately I can't recall which of those lodgings they're in."

"Lothian Street in Edinburgh, Father," Emily said.

"Are you sure, Emily?"

"You asked me to fetch them from there when you were writing your third murder essay."

"Thank you, Emily." De Quincey turned toward Ryan. "May I see the sketches of the bodies now?"

"They're at the end of the counter."

De Quincey drank from his laudanum flask, making Ryan raise his eyes in disgust.

De Quincey then proceeded to the counter and examined one sketch after another.

Becker expected a reaction of horror, but instead the short man displayed only intense concentration.

When he finished, his voice was filled with sadness. "From lightning and tempest; from plague, pestilence, and famine; from battle and murder, and from sudden death, Good Lord, deliver us."

"Pardon me?" Ryan asked.

"It's a prayer from the general petition of the Anglican Church," De Quincey explained. "Odd how the Church considers sudden death to be worse than pestilence and famine. Julius Caesar viewed it in a different light. The night before his assassination, he happened to be asked what he considered to be the best mode of death. He replied, 'That which is most sudden.' He meant a death that would cause neither pain nor terror. Interesting that the Anglican Church prefers a lingering death in which pain tortures the victim, giving him time to settle not only with God but with the grocer."

Becker had never heard anyone speak this way. The Opium-Eater's strange thoughts made his mind spin. "Well, the shopkeeper didn't feel terror. From the looks of things, he didn't know what hit him."

"Yes." De Quincey pointed at one of the sketches. "It appears that he was struck twice from behind before his throat was slit." Significantly, De Quincey didn't apologize to his daughter, seeming to take for granted that she had heard conversations of this sort before. "He wouldn't have known what was done to him. Nor the infant. But the wife, the servant, and the young girl were struck from in front. They saw what was coming. *They* definitely felt terror."

"And your point is...?" Ryan asked.

"Was any money taken?"

"No."

"If the motive wasn't profit, what else could it have been?" De Quincey wondered. "Revenge? On whom? The shopkeeper? It's a poor revenge when the victim doesn't know he's being punished. Revenge on the wife because she rejected the advances of the killer in an earlier encounter?

Perhaps. But then why kill the servant, the young girl, and the infant? The wife wouldn't have seen her children being killed. She wouldn't have experienced the maximum torment. Could the servant have been the true victim? If so, why did the killer then brutalize the infant?"

"These questions already occurred to us," Ryan said impatiently.

"Sometimes our minds trick us into seeing things in a way that they aren't."

"I haven't the faintest idea what you're talking about."

"Father, explain about the Indian emperor and the coach," Emily suggested.

"Thank you, Emily. An excellent example."

"The Indian emperor and the coach?" Ryan raised his hands in frustration. "Can we please confine the conversation to the murders?"

"That's precisely what I'm doing. A British diplomat once gave a coach to an Indian emperor. The coach had a high roof with four seats inside and an outside forward seat for the driver. It was ornate to the point of magnificence, but at that time, coaches didn't exist in India, and after the official departed, the emperor didn't know what to make of the gift. What he did know was that his exalted stature required him to be above everyone, so he and his advisers climbed to the top of the coach, where the emperor sat in the precarious throne of the driver's seat. Meanwhile the driver, whose status was so low that he didn't deserve to be seen, climbed into the coach and threaded the reins through a hole he created beneath the driver's seat. In that position, unable to view where he was going, the driver urged the horses forward. At first, the emperor enjoyed the excitement of the violent ride, but after he was tossed this way and that for a sufficient length of time, he ordered the driver to stop. Not wishing to appear undignified, he smiled as he was helped to the ground, after which the coach was put away and never seen again."

"And what is the point of that story?" Ryan demanded.

"We see things from a perspective that we take for granted, such as the emperor thinking that the driver's seat was preferable because it was high. But what if our perspective is incorrect? Looking at the scene of these murders, what we think is one thing might be something else entirely. The bodies have been removed. What else has been changed?"

"All the doors were closed," Becker responded, the first he'd spoken in a while.

"Who discovered the bodies?"

"I did," Becker added. "I came upon the brother pounding on the front door. It was locked, so I climbed a wall and came in through the back."

"Where you saw ... ?"

"The mother and the young girl on the floor in the passage."

"Then you ... ?"

"Opened that door"—Becker indicated the doorway next to the counter—"entered the shop, and found the body behind the counter."

"And after that?"

"I opened the doors to the kitchen and the bedroom and discovered the other bodies."

"The killer didn't achieve his full design."

"I don't understand," Ryan said, exhaustion straining his voice.

"In my essay about the fine art of murder, I refer to pity and terror as the ultimate goals. We feel pity for the victims. But who feels the terror? The shopkeeper didn't. The infant didn't. Yes, the wife, the servant, and the young girl felt terror, but only for the briefest of moments as they gaped at the mallet coming toward them. Constable Becker, what time did you reach the shop as you made your rounds?"

"Ten fifteen, the same as every other night."

"The reliability of every constable's schedule. I assume that the killer would have known your schedule and intended to wait until ten twenty before he unlocked the front door and stepped outside into the darkness. He couldn't have known that the brother would arrive and interfere with the plan. In the normal order of things, the next day someone would have wondered where the shopkeeper and his family were. That person would have knocked on the door, found it unlocked, and entered. The odor and the blood spatters would have led to the discovery of what lay behind the counter. Horrified, the person would have run for help. More people would now have entered the shop, and with each door they opened, further horrors would have greeted them, until the spectacle achieved its maximum effect with the opening of the final door and the discovery of the slaughtered infant."

De Quincey walked toward the doorway that led to the rear of the building.

Surprised by his sudden movement, Becker and Ryan followed as he entered the passage, took a wide step around the dried blood, and peered into the kitchen.

"Teeth on the floor," De Quincey commented. "Sublime."

"You're insane," Ryan said.

"The coach and the Indian emperor," De Quincey told him. "To understand what happened here, you need to pretend you're the killer. If you're disgusted, you won't truly see. You need to admire the butchery as a masterpiece."

"The laudanum has twisted you."

"To the contrary, it allows me to see perfectly straight."

Becker looked back to make sure that Emily wasn't following. She remained in the shop, seeming to feel sorry for them.

De Quincey entered the kitchen and studied the mallet on the table. "May I pick it up?"

"By all means. I'd like to see how you manage it," Ryan agreed.

The Opium-Eater assessed the matt of hair and dried blood on the striking surface. "Note how ungainly it is in my hand. Only someone large would feel comfortable with this."

He inspected the top of the mallet, where the wooden handle was secured to a hole in the metal head. "And here are the initials punched with a nail into the metal. J. P. The same as on the original mallet. That mallet also had an imperfection on its striking surface, a zigzag pattern in the metal. May I scrape away some of the hair and dried blood?"

Ryan stared at him for several seconds.

"*I'll* do it," the detective said.

De Quincey showed no reaction when Ryan produced his knife from a scabbard under his right trouser leg.

Ryan gently picked at the hair and blood, taking care not to scratch the metal.

He frowned at what he uncovered. "A pattern like *this*?"

De Quincey's blue eyes narrowed intensely.

"Yes. An imperfection that resembles a lightning bolt. Exactly the same. In all probability, this is the mallet that was used in the original killings."

The kitchen became silent.

De Quincey pointed toward a white cloth on a chair. "What's this?"

"A smock that the killer used to keep blood from spattering his clothes," Ryan answered. "I made inquiries. It's ordinary. No shop clerk would remember who purchased it."

De Quincey held it at arm's length, studying the blood pattern on it. "Ordinary? No. You might not be able to find a clerk who remembers selling it, but the smock itself has a special purpose. It's an *artist's* smock."

Now the kitchen seemed colder.

"Murder as a fine art," Becker murmured.

"These killings were committed less for the pleasure of slaughtering the victims and more for the dramatic way they would be discovered. Forty-three years ago, the Ratcliffe Highway deaths spread a wave of terror throughout the country. But they were amateurish compared to these. Five corpses instead of four. Two children instead of one. An artistic arrangement of bodies. The same murder weapon. What an improvement!"

"Improvement?" Ryan asked in dismay.

"Tomorrow when the newspapers report what happened and the telegraph instantly spreads the news, the killer will receive the artistic satisfaction he craves. Pity and terror. Terror throughout England, even more than forty-three years ago. And as for pity, we'll receive none from the killer when the next set of murders happens. We need to pity each other and hope that God pities us all."

"The next set of murders?"

In the front room, Emily screamed.

As the scream persisted, Becker charged from the kitchen. Desperate to reach Emily, he raced down the passage and into the shop, where he froze at what he encountered.

The rapid footsteps of Ryan and De Quincey joined him, those men also halting in astonishment at what they faced.

The door was open. Fog drifted in, hovering around a man whose features had the color and grain of mahogany. He was extremely tall — taller even than Becker. He wore an oddly shaped head cover, gray, that Becker took a moment to remember from a drawing he'd seen in a newspaper. A turban, he thought it was called. Despite the cold night, the newcomer's only garments were a long, billowy shirt hanging over equally billowy trousers. Of Oriental design, they too were gray. Other than in the *Illustrated London News,* Becker had never seen anything like them. Apart from diplomats and military personnel stationed in India or other parts of the subcontinent, almost no one in England had ever encountered them.

Emily stood to the side of the shop, lowering her hands from her face. "I'm sorry. The door suddenly opened. When he appeared, I didn't know what was happening. I've never seen..."

"A Malay," De Quincey said.

"You know this man?" Ryan asked in amazement.

Outside, constables hurried through the fog to form a wall behind the exotic figure.

"It can't be." De Quincey kept staring. "After so many years."

"Then you *do* recognize him?"

"No."

Baffled, Ryan turned to the newcomer. "What do you want? How did you get past the constables outside?"

"We heard a shout down the street, like someone being attacked, Inspector," a policeman said.

"But while they ran to investigate, I stayed," another policeman said. "I wasn't twenty feet away. He couldn't have passed me."

"Of course he could," De Quincey said. "He's a Malay."

"What do you want?" Ryan repeated to the newcomer.

The only response was a puzzled narrowing of the intruder's dark eyes.

"What are you doing here?" Ryan insisted.

The man shook his head in confusion.

"I don't think he understands English," Becker said.

"The Malay I met many years ago didn't understand English, either," De Quincey said.

"Many years ago?" Ryan asked.

"A man who looked like this man once came to my home in the Lake District," De Quincey explained. "His sudden appearance was astonishing. It was as if he'd arrived from the moon. I tried Latin and Greek, with no effect. When communication failed, he lay down on my kitchen floor and slept. After an hour, he rose abruptly and walked down the road, vanishing into the countryside. The experience was so unreal I had many dreams about him. But that was so long ago, he can't possibly be the same man."

"...omas," the man said.

"What's he trying to say?" Becker wondered.

"...omas...incey." The Malay seemed to have memorized words without understanding them.

"Thomas?" the Opium-Eater asked. "De Quincey? Is that what you mean to say?" He pointed toward himself. "Thomas De Quincey?"

The Malay nodded. "...incey." He reached under his shirt.

Becker quickly stepped forward and grabbed the Malay's hand, making certain that he wasn't withdrawing a weapon. Instead what the Malay produced was an envelope.

De Quincey grabbed it and tore it open. As he read the message, his face became pale.

"What is it, Father?" Emily asked.

His hand trembling, De Quincey gave her the piece of paper.

Emily read the message aloud, her voice becoming as unsteady as her father's hand.

To learn what happened to Ann, to find her, come to Vauxhall Gardens at eleven tomorrow morning.

"*Ann?*" Ryan asked. "You mentioned that name when we met you returning to your house. Who's *she?*"

"My lost youth."

"What?"

"There is no such thing as forgetting." Although De Quincey stared at the note in Emily's hand, his blue eyes seemed to focus on something far away. "When I was seventeen and starving on the streets of London, I fell in love with a streetwalker."

Ryan and Becker looked amazed by De Quincey's frankness. They weren't shocked only by his reference to a prostitute—and in front of his daughter. Almost equally surprising was that he expressed an emotion as personal as love. Candor of this sort, especially in public, was unimaginable.

"I promised to meet Ann at a certain hour on a certain street, but unavoidable circumstances prevented me from being there."

Haunted, De Quincey pulled out his laudanum flask, taking a long swallow from it.

"When I finally managed to arrive on a later day, Ann wasn't waiting, and I never saw her again, no matter how many years I spent searching for her. I never would have come to London now if I hadn't been promised that I'd be told what happened to her."

"Who promised you this?" Ryan demanded.

"I have no idea, but he also arranged for the rent of the townhouse where Emily and I are staying. I was lured here to be connected with the killings. Am I the murderer's audience? For certain, he's been following me."

"Following you?"

"How else could he have known I was here tonight so that he could send the Malay to deliver the message? And then there's the matter that he chose a victim who came from Manchester and whose last name was Hayworth."

"You thought that was important earlier, but you didn't tell us why," Becker said.

"I was raised near Manchester. My family home was called Greenhay."

"Greenhay. Hayworth. It's a coincidence," Ryan told him.

"No."

"You're seriously suggesting that the killer chose the shop owner as his victim because you both came from Manchester and his name is similar to that of your family home?"

"It's not a coincidence that these killings occurred a month after my latest publication. Detail by detail, they match what I wrote in the postscript to 'Murder as a Fine Art.' To make the association with me more perfect, the killer selected a victim with echoes to me. He connects me with his crimes. God help me, how else does he plan to involve me in his butchery?"

7

A Garden of Pleasures

In 1854, THE BRITISH EMPIRE was the largest the world had ever known, far greater than Alexander's conquests or that of the Romans. Its territories encircled the globe, including Canada, the Bahamas, Bermuda, Gibraltar, Malta, Cyprus, a third of Africa, and a significant portion of the Middle East as well as India, Burma, Malaya, Singapore, Hong Kong, Borneo, New Guinea, the Solomon Islands, Fiji, Samoa, Australia, New Zealand, and portions of Antarctica.

The man at the center of it, arguably the most powerful man on earth, was Henry John Temple, known officially as Lord Palmerston. For almost half a century, beginning in 1807, Palmerston had developed an expanding, profound influence in the British government, first as a member of Parliament, then as secretary at war (nineteen years), secretary of state for foreign affairs (fifteen years), and currently the home secretary, a position that put him in charge of almost everything that happened on domestic soil, particularly with regard to national security and the police. Most observers were confident that Palmerston would soon become prime minister, but prime ministers came and went, whereas a man who had a lifetime of influence in the War Office, the Foreign Office, and the Home Office in effect controlled the government. Prime ministers and even

Queen Victoria herself frequently summoned Palmerston, demanding to know why he enacted policies that neither Parliament nor the prime minister had authorized.

At nine o'clock Monday morning, Ryan sat in front of this great man in his Westminster office. Palmerston was seventy years old, with long, thick, brown-dyed side-whiskers that extended all the way to his strong chin and framed his dominating gaze. His age had affected neither his energy nor his ambition. His office was decorated with a large map of England and another of the world, with every British territory colored in red and stuck with a pin of the British flag.

Palmerston's wealth was manifest in his garments, their cut and their stitching of such obvious quality that Ryan felt poorly dressed, even though he had put on his only fine clothes: the expected gray trousers, matching waistcoat, and black coat that came down to his knees. In keeping with fashion, straps attached to the bottom of Ryan's trousers were looped under his boots, applying tension to prevent the trouser legs from wrinkling. The tightness of the legs, especially when sitting, made Ryan wish for his loose, comfortable street clothes.

Seated next to Ryan was Police Commissioner Mayne. In a corner, taking notes, sat Palmerston's male secretary. Next to the office's closed entrance stood Palmerston's protective escort, retired colonel Robert Brookline. Years earlier, Palmerston had been shot by a would-be assassin. He had resolved that it wouldn't happen again. Brookline, a twenty-year military veteran with battle experience in India and China, was more than qualified to protect him.

"I was in the cabinet when the first Ratcliffe Highway murders occurred," Palmerston told them. "I remember the fright that spread through the nation and how the Home Office bungled controlling it. Now that I'm home secretary, I won't allow that fright to happen again." He pointed toward a stack of newspapers on his desk, the five dozen that were published in London. "The hysteria of these reports is bound to lead to more incidents like the riots after the murders on Saturday night. Inspector Ryan, I understand that you were involved in both those riots."

"Yes, Your Lordship. At one point, the crowd decided I was a suspect and turned on me."

"Indeed." Palmerston glanced at Ryan's red hair.

"Then it turned against someone else. We stopped him from being seriously injured and possibly killed."

"I haven't heard you mention him, so I gather that the mob was mistaken."

"Yes, Your Lordship. He isn't the killer."

"You're certain?"

"Definitely."

"How refreshing to hear someone say he is definite about something. What about the Malay?"

"He appears not to be able to speak English, Your Lordship, and despite the best efforts of the Foreign Office, we haven't found anyone who speaks Malay."

The reference to the Foreign Office, which Palmerston had once controlled and which, it was rumored, he continued to control, made His Lordship's eyes even more alert.

"We have the Malay in custody," Ryan added, "but his foot size doesn't match the prints at the murder scene. I'm inclined to think that he wasn't involved, except as a paid messenger."

Palmerston shook his head impatiently and turned his withering attention toward Commissioner Mayne. "What's being done to assure the population that the streets are safe?"

"Your Lordship, all detectives and constables are working extra hours. All rest days have been canceled. Patrols have been doubled. A witness says she was suspicious about a tall man with a yellow beard. The man wore a merchant sailor's cap and coat."

"What sort of witness?"

"A prostitute."

"A prostitute," Palmerston said, unimpressed.

"We searched our card catalogue at Scotland Yard to determine if any criminals have that color of beard."

"And?"

"The only criminal who matches that description died three years ago," the commissioner replied.

"A sailor with experience in the Orient might know how to speak the

Malay's language," Palmerston granted. "He would also know which ships arriving in London might have a Malay working on them. But if the killer is indeed a sailor, he might be at sea again by now."

"Yes, Your Lordship," Mayne responded. "Our constables are making inquiries at the docks. If anyone remembers a sailor who matches that description, we'll send a message via the next ship to warn the authorities at the suspect's destination."

"Which could take weeks or even months, by which time the suspect could be on another ship," Palmerston responded with greater impatience.

"Yes, Your Lordship. Without a transocean telegraph, our options are limited."

"At the moment, I wish the telegraph hadn't been invented. Colonel Brookline, what's your opinion of it?"

The strong-featured man who stood at military ease replied, "It's been of immense help in the Crimea, Your Lordship. Commanders are able to communicate orders with remarkable speed."

"It didn't stop those idiots Raglan and Cardigan from perpetrating that disaster with the Light Brigade. If I still controlled the War Office, I'd have relieved them of their command. Raglan sends an imprecise order. Cardigan gallops off with his cavalry, not certain where his objective is but determined to be a hero. After nearly destroying the Light Brigade, he has a champagne dinner aboard his yacht in a nearby harbor. Thanks to the telegraph, everyone instantly knows what happened thousands of miles away, and the government might fall because of the bungling of the war. Forty-three years ago, it took three days for mail coaches to spread throughout the country. But yesterday the telegraph sent reports of Saturday's murders to every town in the land even before the newspapers could be put on trains. People are huddled in the streets. Many have pistols. My informants tell me the sole topic of conversation is how everyone plans to leave their places of employment early so they can hurry home before the fog returns. It's not only in London that this is happening. The whole country's terrified, and I'm the one responsible for reassuring everybody."

"Your Lordship," Ryan said. "There's another possibility that we're investigating."

"You have my attention, Inspector."

"The footprints we found did not have hobnails in the soles, suggesting that the killer is not a laborer. The razor I found is almost certainly the second murder weapon. Its handle is well-crafted ivory. Its steel is high quality. Very expensive. That too suggests the killer is not a laborer."

"Stop using negatives, Inspector."

Ryan felt heat rise to his cheeks. "Your Lordship, we need to consider the possibility that the killer might be someone of means and education."

"Consider...? Good heavens, man, that's inconceivable. The razor must have been stolen. Someone with means and education couldn't possibly be responsible for these hideous crimes. Their extreme violence makes that obvious. Only a common person could have committed them. Or else a drug abuser."

"A drug abuser, Your Lordship?"

"The Opium-Eater is everywhere in these newspapers. A month ago, he wrote in lengthy, bloody detail about the original killings. It's as if the murderer used the Opium-Eater's essay as an instruction manual. Or could the Opium-Eater himself be responsible for the murders?"

"Your Lordship, he's barely five feet tall. He's sixty-nine years old. It would have been physically impossible for him to have killed all those people."

"Whether he's innocent isn't the point. Someone whose faculties have been corrupted by a lifelong opium habit is an obvious suspect. Arrest him. Make certain that the newspapers know about it."

"But..."

"If we put him in prison, the public will breathe easier, convinced that we're doing something. I do not wish to be argued with, Inspector. Arrest him."

"Your Lordship, I merely want to point out that, if the pattern holds true, there'll be another multiple killing. If De Quincey's in prison when the murders occur, it'll be obvious we arrested the wrong man."

"In twelve days, Inspector. That's when the next murders occurred forty-three years ago. Twelve days ought to be enough time for you to find the madman responsible. It had better be, or else you won't be a detective any longer, and that'll be the least of your worries. Meanwhile, De Quincey's arrest will prove we're doing something. Putting him in prison will make the population feel safe."

"Perhaps earlier than twelve days, Your Lordship."

"Pardon me?"

"De Quincey believes that the killer is exaggerating the Ratcliffe Highway murders. If he's right, the next killings will happen much sooner than the last time and be more savage."

To avoid attracting attention, Becker used a cab instead of the police wagon to transport De Quincey and Emily from their townhouse near Russell Square. He chose a roundabout route and looked back to see if any vehicle stayed behind them, a task made less difficult because fewer than usual carriages were on the streets.

Their first destination was the office of the undertaker in charge of burying the Hayworth family. True to her word, Emily had visited the victim's brother the previous evening and made good on her vow of determining that he was with his wife and son.

Now she told the undertaker, "The deceased had one pound, eight shillings, and two pennies in a cash box. That will serve as a down payment for the funerals."

Standing in the background, Becker was amazed by Emily's forthrightness, while De Quincey seemed not to find it unusual.

"One pound, eight shillings, and...!" the undertaker exclaimed. "But all five funerals amount to sixteen pounds! Someone stole my hearse last night! If I'm not paid beforehand, I don't see how I can arrange for the disposition of the remains in a timely way!"

"I'm sorry about your hearse, but the deceased's brother is capable of paying only one pound a month until the debt is retired," Emily responded calmly.

"At *that* rate..."

"Yes, sixteen months. Delayed but assured. The alternative is that you lose the opportunity to gain a desirable reputation."

"Lose *what* opportunity? What are you talking about?"

"These murders have attracted the attention of the newspapers."

"They certainly have. The murders are all everyone is talking about. Everywhere I go—"

"If you accept one pound a month, my friends in the police force will tell reporters that you're the undertaker in charge of helping the deceased's brother in his time of anguish. Your firm's name will become highly regarded. Your business will prosper."

"Well, that's excellent, but I still don't see…"

"If you refuse, my friends in the police force will tell every reporter how heartless you are at a time when you're supposed to provide comfort. Everyone in London will read about your cold manner."

"But…"

"A moment's reflection will persuade you that one alternative is better than the other." Emily stood. "In the meantime, here are one pound, eight shillings, and two pennies. Your firm has a stellar reputation. I am confident that you will give the deceased and his family a funeral that people will praise for a long time."

BECKER HAD NEVER HEARD any woman speak that way. Concealing his amazement, he escorted her and De Quincey outside to the cab, where he scanned the street and observed that no vehicle had stopped in wait for them to emerge from the undertaker's.

"I don't think we're being followed," he remarked as they continued toward their ultimate destination.

"The killer doesn't need to follow," De Quincey said pensively. "After all, he knows where I'll be at eleven o'clock."

"But I need to plan for other possibilities. He might intend to surprise you en route."

"Yes," De Quincey conceded, "he does not lack surprises."

FIVE MINUTES AFTER paying the toll and crossing the stone piers of Vauxhall Bridge, Becker told the cabdriver to go beyond the railway tracks and stop at Upper Kennington Lane. He helped Emily down, then turned toward De Quincey, but discovered that the man, surprisingly limber for his age, was already beside him on the ground.

Amid the odor from a nearby distillery, Becker scanned the working-class neighborhood, mostly shops with rooms above them.

The news of the murders had visibly affected the mood even here on the south side of the Thames, a distance from Ratcliffe Highway. Pedestrians no longer had a leisurely pace. Their expressions were pensive and guarded. A man selling roasted potatoes from a cart appeared suspicious of any customers who approached him, for fear one of them might attack him.

To avoid notice, Becker had been given permission to exchange his uniform for plain clothes. It was a further step in his goal to becoming a police detective, but he wished it had happened under other circumstances.

A few people looked with disapproval at Emily's unorthodox unhooped dress, in which the movement of her legs was visible. Otherwise no one paid attention as they walked along a wooden wall on their right and came to a wide, tall building. Above a large entryway, a faded sign announced VAUXHALL GARDENS.

De Quincey took his laudanum flask from his coat pocket.

"That's the third time you drank from it since we left the house," Becker said.

"Thank you for keeping count."

"The volume of laudanum you consumed so far today would kill most people."

"It's medicine prescribed by a physician. When I try to stop, *that* is more likely to kill me." De Quincey's brow was filmed with sweat as he looked at his daughter and changed the subject. "Pleasure gardens were once the rage, Emily. I came here when I was in my thirties to watch a reenactment of the Battle of Waterloo."

"A reenactment of Waterloo? That seems impossible."

The morning sky was again clear, a breeze having chased the fog.

"One thousand soldiers took part in it," De Quincey said, talking to distract himself from what he needed to do. "The audience, perhaps ten thousand, was transported by the din of the muskets and the smoke from the gunpowder."

"This place is big enough for that?"

"More so."

"It's almost eleven," Becker pointed out.

De Quincey took a nervous breath and nodded.

"Remember," Becker said. "A dozen constables wearing street clothes gradually came here one at a time, pretending to be customers. If there's an incident, they'll rush to help. I still think you should allow me to walk with you so I can defend you in case of an attack." He looked down at the bulge of the truncheon and handcuffs under his civilian overcoat.

"Whatever the killer has planned, it won't happen if you're at my side," De Quincey responded. "If I'm wrong and this becomes violent, at least I know that Emily has your protection. As for me, I need to take the risk on the chance that I'll learn about Ann."

"After all these years, she still means that much to you?" Becker asked.

"When I begged on the streets of London, I owed her my life."

De Quincey stepped through the entryway.

After counting to twenty, Becker and Emily followed.

The gate was in dire need of fresh paint. Its wood was splintered and in some places broken.

The ticket seller barely looked up from a newspaper he was reading. The item on the front page was about the murders.

"Two shillings," he said distractedly.

Becker paid from coins he'd been given at Scotland Yard.

Beyond the entrance, they surveyed the almost deserted facility and watched De Quincey proceed along a white gravel path between leafless trees. He seemed to expect that someone would approach him as he passed a concert stage. When that didn't happen, De Quincey looked ahead toward a long line of open compartments in which dining tables provided a view of the concert area. Again, no one approached from the stillness.

Pretending to admire their surroundings, Becker and Emily passed a building that had the spires, arches, and domes of an East Indian palace. They turned toward a man in circus clothes who walked across a tight-rope stretched between trees across a lawn. The performer held a pole to maintain his balance. His once-red costume was faded and frayed.

Becker wondered where the other constables were positioned. Perhaps some had joined a handful of people who looked with indifference at the tightrope walker and seemed to wish for the return of their money. They were far more fixated on the somber topic of their discussion, and Becker had no doubt that the topic was the murders.

Leafless trees stretched into the distance. Bare bushes surrounded a statue of a man on horseback. The horse's tail had fallen off.

"Perhaps in spring when the leaves return, this place will be more appealing," Emily conjectured, looking ahead toward her father.

The smell of smoke and the crackle of a fire brought them to a large canvas balloon where customers could pay to be taken aloft. Like the tightrope walker's costume, the colors on the balloon were faded. The fire had a screen that prevented sparks from igniting a canvas tube attached to a chimney. The tube captured hot air from the chimney and used it to swell the balloon, beneath which was a wicker basket for passengers. Smoke leaked from the balloon.

A sign proclaimed, SEE VAUXHALL BRIDGE FROM THE HEIGHTS! WESTMINSTER BRIDGE! ST. JAMES'S PARK!

"And maybe a close view of the Thames if the balloon crashes," Emily suggested.

De Quincey kept walking ahead of them, moving deeper into the gardens.

"There used to be acrobats, jugglers, and musicians," Becker said. "Fireworks. At one time, I was told, fifteen thousand lamps illuminated the grounds at night, so many that the glow could be seen across the Thames. But now..." He pointed toward shattered globes on poles along the path. "The owners had financial difficulties. The evening festivities used to glitter like a royal ball. But the things that happen here at night became unsuitable."

"You're referring to prostitution?" Emily asked.

Becker felt himself blush.

"I don't mean to embarrass you," she said.

"The truth is, I was worried about embarrassing *you*," Becker said.

"Father always speaks directly with me. Even when I was a child, he didn't treat me like one. In Father's household, among my six surviving brothers and sisters, I grew up fast."

"Yes, with the bailiff searching for him, I imagine you learned about life quickly."

"Father called me his spy."

"Oh?" The word attracted Becker's attention.

"In Edinburgh, many times he couldn't live with us for fear of being arrested, so he found secret lodgings, where I brought him food and other necessities such as pen and ink. With the bailiff watching our home, I squirmed from back windows, over walls, and through holes in fences. When I finally reached Father in whatever room he'd managed to find refuge, he gave me manuscript to take to his publishers. But his publishers were being watched also. Again I needed to go over walls and through back windows to deliver the pages, receive payment, and return to Father. Of the money I gave him, he subtracted the minimum he needed and told me to take the bulk of it to Mother."

"Sounds like you had a difficult childhood."

"To the contrary, it was fascinating."

Becker heard rapid footsteps behind him.

"Stay close," Becker told her.

Ready for trouble, he turned, surprised to see Ryan hurrying along the path.

Ryan didn't look his usual self. In place of his scruffy street clothes, he wore a dress overcoat that hung open, revealing formal gray trousers, a matching waistcoat, and a black coat that came down to his knees. If not for the newspaperboy's cap concealing his red hair, he could have passed as a commissioner rather than a detective.

"Everything's quiet," Becker reported.

But Ryan's features were troubled. The sky matched his gloom, dark clouds now drifting in.

"What's wrong, Inspector?" Emily asked.

"When I met your father yesterday, I'd have been pleased to do it. But now..."

"To do what? I don't understand."

"I've been ordered to arrest him."

"Arrest him?" Emily exclaimed. "You can't be serious."

"I wish I weren't. Where *is* he?" Ryan asked.

"Ahead of us," Becker told him.

"But *where?*"

"On the path. He's…" Becker turned to indicate De Quincey's location. "My God, he isn't there. What happened to him?"

THE OPIUM-EATER PROCEEDED along the path. Decades of drinking large quantities of laudanum had created many realities for him. The unnatural combination of elements at Vauxhall Gardens — the spires and domes of an East Indian pavilion, the outdoor concert stage, the tightrope walker, the hot-air balloon, smoke leaking from it, and even a statue of Milton — so resembled his opium dreams that he didn't know if this was a wide-awake nightmare or if he was still in bed, asleep.

Disoriented, he wondered if perhaps he had never left Edinburgh. Perhaps he had never received the message that promised to reveal what had happened to Ann if he came to London. More than anything, he hoped that he was dreaming because that would mean the murders had not occurred on Saturday night and that even worse would not soon happen.

The front area of the gardens was devoted to public events such as dances, plays, concerts, and banquets. But the rear section provided an amazing forest in the middle of the city. At one time, the forest had been scrupulously maintained, inviting people to walk among the trees, but over the years, negligence and lack of funds had caused it to revert to a wild state of which his friend Wordsworth would have approved but which in fact was so densely overgrown, filled with so many hiding places, that De Quincey felt threatened.

Adding to the sense of chaos were *faux* ruins among the trees, reproductions of ancient Greek and Roman landmarks that appeared to have collapsed in a weird concatenation of centuries, pillars of the Parthenon lying next to a segment of the Colosseum, dead weeds and vines obscuring them.

Again the Opium-Eater had a dizzying sensation that what he saw was the result of laudanum. But no matter how much he attempted to assure himself that he was enduring an opium nightmare in Edinburgh, he kept remembering the smell of the murder scene and the grief on the face of the victim's brother.

An intersection gave him a choice of three directions: left, right, or straight ahead. Arbitrarily he chose the white gravel path on the left. Thicker forest flanked him: a skeletal tangle of leafless shrubs and trees. His chest felt swollen. His breathing was rapid.

Ann.

He had never forgotten the long-ago evening of his youth when he had told her how much he loved her. He had vowed to return to London in eight days, to share his future with her just as she had shared her meager resources with *him*.

But Ann had understood the future far better than *he* had. Tears had trickled down her cheeks. She had returned his embrace, but she hadn't said a word, and indeed he had never heard her speak again.

How he longed to walk hand in hand with her once more, to listen to the music of the street organ with her, to kiss her. Countless times he had dreamed about her. Again and again in various essays and books he had written about her — accounts that the killer had obviously studied. There was always the chance that the summons here wasn't merely a taunt. Perhaps the killer had become similarly obsessed with Ann and had discovered crucial information about her.

De Quincey resisted the urge to take out his flask and swallow more laudanum. But more than by fear, he was motivated by hope — and the need to punish himself for leaving Ann. If there was even the slightest possibility that he could learn something about the woman he had searched for throughout his life, he couldn't turn away.

On each side, the trees and bushes seemed to reach for him. A cold wind seeped beneath his overcoat. His boots crunched unnervingly on the gravel. Branches scraped. The wind made a faint keening sound.

Then he realized that the keening sound wasn't the wind but instead a voice. A *woman's* voice.

"Thomas."

It came from his right — a high-pitched, mournful plea.

"Thomas."

"Is it you, Ann?"

"Thomas."

Unsure if he was imagining the voice, he stepped from the path. His boots crushed dead leaves as he shifted between bushes and tree trunks, straining to see in the accumulating shadows.

"Ann?"

"Here I am, Thomas."

"Where?"

A woman stepped from behind a tree.

He stared. Then he gasped and stumbled backward, certain that he was indeed experiencing a nightmare.

The woman was wizened, almost bald. Her face was gaunt, her eyes sunken. Sores festered on her cheeks.

"Here, Thomas. Take me. Your Ann."

"No."

"You didn't return when you promised. You abandoned me."

"No!"

"But now we're together." Dressed in rags, the festering woman held out her arms. "Love me, Thomas. We'll always be together now."

"You *can't* be Ann!"

"This is what you want." The woman raised her ragged coat and skirt, exposing her wrinkled nakedness. "Love me, Thomas."

As a scream formed in his throat, another plaintive voice startled him.

From another tree, another wizened, festering woman emerged, raising her coat and dress, exposing herself. "Here I am, Thomas. Your sister Jane. Do you remember me? Do you remember playing with me in the nursery? Do you want me? You can have me."

Now he did scream as another woman stepped from a tree, raising her coat and dress.

"Here, Thomas. I'm your sister Elizabeth. Remember how you sneaked into the room where I lay dead? You stared at my body all afternoon. Then you kissed me. You can kiss me again now, Thomas. You can have me."

"I'm Catherine, Thomas." Yet another woman emerged, exposing herself. "Remember me? The little girl who lived near you at Dove Cottage? Wordsworth's daughter? Remember how you lay on my grave for days, sobbing, thinking of Jane and Elizabeth and Ann. The terrible loss. But not any longer. We're here, Thomas. You can have us all."

Weeping uncontrollably, De Quincey watched even more women step from the trees, their features destroyed by pustules.

"*I'm* Ann!"

"No, *I'm* Ann!"

"I'm Jane!"

"Elizabeth!"

"Catherine!"

"Love us, Thomas!"

He shrieked, the wail coming from the depth of his soul, from the pit of his despair. His tears burned his eyes. He sank to his knees, screaming, "No! No! No!"

WE NEED TO SEPARATE!" Ryan said. "You take that path! I'll—"

"Wait. I hear something," Becker said.

"Voices. Women's voices," Emily said. "They're calling names."

"That way!" Ryan pointed to the left and started to run.

Becker hung back, needing to stay with Emily and protect her. But she surprised him by rushing ahead, her bloomer dress and her frantic need to reach her father giving her a speed that Becker had difficulty matching.

They rounded a corner.

"No!" De Quincey's voice shrieked from the trees.

"Ann! Jane!" the women's voices shouted.

"Here!" Ryan charged into the undergrowth.

"Elizabeth! Catherine!" the women chanted.

"Emily, stay back!" Becker warned.

But she was too determined. Branches snapped as they forced their way through the trees.

De Quincey kept wailing.

"Ann! Jane! Elizabeth! Catherine!" the women chanted.

Becker pulled his truncheon from beneath his coat, charging past bushes.

Emily hurried to follow.

Ahead, Ryan abruptly stopped at the sight of De Quincey on his knees, sobbing. Becker joined him, gaping at ragged women—streetwalkers, old and infected—who shouted the mystifying names.

"Emily, you shouldn't see this!"

"But what's *happening?*"

Becker had no idea. He braced himself, scanning the trees for a threat. All he saw was the women.

De Quincey's shoulders heaved, his convulsions rising from the deepest part of his soul.

"Father!" Emily ran to him. "Are you hurt?"

De Quincey sobbed too forcefully to answer.

The women focused on the truncheon in Becker's hands. With panicked sounds, they backed into the trees.

"Stop!" Becker ordered.

But the women hurried away.

De Quincey sank all the way to the ground.

"He doesn't seem injured!" Emily said, straining to hold him up. "I don't understand!"

Becker removed another piece of equipment from beneath his coat — the clacker that he used to sound emergencies. He gripped the handle and spun the blade. Its ratcheting alarm was ear-torturing, easily heard throughout the gardens.

The last of the wizened women vanished into the trees.

"Inspector!" a man yelled. The newcomer hurried toward them through bushes, one of the plainclothes constables who'd arrived earlier and positioned themselves throughout the grounds.

"Run to the entrance!" Ryan shouted. "Lock the gates! Don't let anybody out!"

As the newcomer raced away, other constables charged through the undergrowth.

"There are women in the forest!" Becker told them. "Prostitutes! Catch them! Be careful — they might not be alone!"

Continuing the Journal of Emily De Quincey

In all my years with Father, I have seen him weep only twice before: at the deaths of my brother Horace and that of my beloved mother, his dutiful wife, Margaret. But now the severity of his grief far exceeded his deep reaction to those losses, and when I came to realize the significance of the names the women had shouted, I understood why.

Constable Becker lifted Father and carried him through the trees. The constable is so tall and Father so short that Father seemed like a child in the constable's arms. Inspector Ryan walked with me, warily looking around at the forest as if he expected that at any moment we might be attacked. That Becker now wore street clothes instead of his uniform and Ryan now wore go-to-church clothes instead of his ruffian's costume only made the world seem even more upside down.

We reached the performance area of the gardens, passing the hot-air balloon and the tightrope walker, who now stood on the lawn and looked fearfully at the commotion.

The spires, arches, and towers of the East Indian pavilion beckoned us. Inside, a spreading flower was painted on the vaulted ceiling. The walls depicted Oriental scenes: a tiger in a jungle, a turbaned man on an elephant, a magician playing a flute to an upright hooded snake, a crowd marveling at wonders in a colorful bazaar.

Constable Becker set Father on a bench against a wall. No matter how fervently I tried to calm Father, he didn't seem to hear me. His sobs came from a part of him that I couldn't reach.

Becker and Inspector Ryan were manifestly disturbed by this dramatic show of emotion. I suspect that they had never seen a man weep before, ever, so strenuously have most people been taught to keep their feelings to themselves.

The constables who brought in the pathetic women I'd seen in the forest were disturbed by Father's weeping also, as were the captives who almost certainly had never seen a man weep and who had probably allowed themselves to weep only if alone or with a few trusted friends. Everyone in the strange pavilion had been trained to believe that a show of emotion is a weakness, and Father's helpless display of absolute sorrow was something they couldn't comprehend, almost as foreign as the Oriental scenes on the walls.

More constables came in, bringing more women. Many of the prisoners were weak from visible illness, but all of them struggled as best they could and cursed with such crudity that heat singed my ears.

"Perhaps you should go," Ryan told me.

"I won't leave Father," I responded.

The women were handcuffed in a line, right wrist to a neighbor's left wrist, then led around a pillar where the final two wrists were secured and the group formed a circle.

Although I had witnessed streetwalkers in Edinburgh, I had never seen any in a worse condition. Disease had ravaged them. Their faces were riddled with sores. Some had almost no hair. Their shriveled mouths showed gaps where teeth had been. Their complaints reverberated off the arched ceiling.

"Quiet!" Becker yelled.

"You won't get my money!" one shouted.

"We don't want your money!" Ryan yelled back. "Not that I believe you have any for me to steal."

"Got plenty of money."

"Sure."

"Earned it, I did!"

"I'm definitely sure of that."

A constable brought in another woman and handcuffed her to the others.

"How many so far?" Ryan asked.

"Twenty-three," Becker answered. "And here comes another one."

"Found these on her," the arriving constable said, holding up two gold coins.

"Them's mine! Give 'em back!"

"Two sovereigns. That's more than most clerks earn in a week. Where'd you steal them?"

"Earned 'em."

"Tell me another one," the newly arrived constable said. "Nobody paid two sovereigns to play Bob-in-the-Betty-box with you."

"Constable," Ryan warned and nodded in my direction, making the newcomer aware of my presence. "A lady's here."

"Oh. Sorry, Inspector. I apologize, miss." The man turned red. "Sometimes they don't understand unless I speak to them in their language."

"Didn't play Bob-in-the-Betty-box," the woman objected. "Earned 'em, I tell ya. Honest work."

Becker studied the women and said, "If one of them has gold coins, maybe others do." He approached a woman on his left. "What's your name?"

"Doris."

"Show me the inside of your pockets, Doris."

"No."

"I'll search you if you don't."

"Now I'm scared. He wants to search me, girls."

They laughed.

"I charges for men to search me," Doris said. "How much do you want to pay for me to search your pollywog?"

The women laughed harder.

I tried to make it seem that I heard this kind of talk every day.

"Gibson, give me some help," Becker told the newly arrived constable. With distaste, the two men searched Doris's pockets.

"The bugger's thievin' from me!" Doris objected. "Yer my witnesses!"

"I'm not trying to steal from you," Becker insisted. "Stop fighting. What have you got here?"

Becker held up two gold coins. "Who else has these?"

A noisy, frenzied struggle resulted in the discovery that each of the women, all twenty-four of them, had two gold coins.

Becker frowned. "Where'd you get your coins, Doris?"

"Worked for 'em, and not the way you think."

"Then how?"

"A gentleman paid me."

"To do what?"

"To sneak in this morning before the gardens opened."

"And then what?" Ryan interrupted.

"To hide in the forest."

"And then?" Ryan persisted.

"When he came along"—the woman pointed toward Father—"I was to call to him." Doris mimicked the tone that I had heard earlier among the trees. "Thomas. Thomas."

She sounded as if she were pleading for help.

At the sound of his name, I felt Father become tense.

"Thomas! Thomas!" the other women joined in. The sound boomed violently off the Oriental walls.

It hurt my ears.

Father stopped weeping.

"All right!" Ryan shouted, raising his hands. "Stop! If you want your sovereigns returned, shut up!"

Gradually, they quieted.

"The gentleman told me to say I was Ann," one of the women volunteered.

"And I was to say I was Jane," another said.

"Elizabeth," a third joined in.

"Catherine," a fourth added.

"No, I'm Ann."

"I'm Jane."

"I'm Elizabeth."

"I'm Catherine."

I felt Father's head rise from where he slumped next to me. Holding him, I looked down and was struck by how red his eyes were from sobbing and how hard the blue of them was.

The litany of names resounded off the walls.

Again Ryan shouted, "Damn it, stop!"

His stern look had its effect, although the harsh echo of their voices took long seconds before the room became still.

"A gentleman told you to say these names?" Ryan demanded. "What gentleman?"

They pouted and didn't answer.

"I asked, what gentleman? Describe him!"

Doris looked at Becker. "I don't like the way he speaks to me. You're much nicer."

"Thank you, Doris," Becker responded. "Tell me about the gentleman, and I'll bring you hot tea."

"Hot tea?"

"I promise." Becker turned toward a constable by the door. "Webster, would you mind taking care of that?"

The constable looked at Ryan, who nodded his permission.

"The gardens have a shop just down the path," Webster said.

"And you'll give us our sovereigns back?" Doris asked Becker fretfully.

"I promise to give you your sovereigns back."

Doris smiled, showing toothless gaps.

As when Ryan and Becker had first met Father and me, I suspected the two had a stratagem in which Ryan made the women feel threatened while Becker was solicitous, winning their cooperation.

"Doris, what did the gentleman look like?" Becker asked.

"Tall, he was. Strong-looking."

"How old?"

"Wasn't young, wasn't old." Doris pointed toward Ryan. "Like him."

"Did he have a beard?"

Doris nodded emphatically. "Yellowlike."

I felt Father sit up beside me.

"How was he dressed?" Becker asked.

"Like a sailor," Doris answered. "But he didn't fool me. No sailor ever gave me two sovereigns. A shilling if I was lucky. Never two sovereigns."

"Forty-eight pounds all told," Ryan noted. "A man of means."

"Doris, how did he talk?" Becker asked.

"Not like any sailor I ever met. This one was educated, he was. A gentleman."

"Weren't you afraid? After all, he was lying about himself."

"'Course I was. Since Saturday night, everybody I know is afraid. But he gave me two sovereigns." Doris spoke as if that was all the fortune in the world. "Ain't never seen two sovereigns before. Sometimes he used fancy words I didn't understand."

"Like what?"

Doris searched her memory. "Like 'rehearse.' Didn't have the faintest. Turns out it means he needed to get us together in an alley and tell us what to say and be satisfied we remembered it."

"Tonight we go back and get another sovereign," a woman near Doris said proudly.

"Another one?" Ryan asked in surprise.

"Hush, Melinda," Doris warned.

"No, tell me." Ryan stepped forward.

"To make sure we did what we was supposed to, he said if we was good he'd give us another sovereign tonight," Melinda said.

"Where?"

"In the same alley where we ..." Melinda looked at Doris.

"Rehearsed," Doris said, pleased that she remembered the word.

"Tell me where," Ryan persisted.

"Oxford Street."

The name made Father stiffen as I held him.

"Can we have our tea now?" Doris asked. "I was cold in them woods."

"It's on its way," Becker promised.

"Melinda, will you take me to where the alley is?" Ryan asked.

"No!" Doris objected. "Then the gentleman'll see you and he won't show up to give us the other sovereign." She scowled at Melinda. "I told you to hush."

"He won't see us, I guarantee," Ryan assured her. "And for cooperating we'll bring you biscuits with your tea."

"Biscuits? Lordy, you treat me just like a lady."

"Just like a lady," Ryan agreed.

"Yellowlike," Father said, startling me. It had been a long time since he'd spoken.

Everyone looked in his direction.

"Pardon me?" Ryan asked him.

"She said 'yellowlike.' The beard was 'yellowlike.'"

Father surprised me even more by standing. His sobbing had made his face seem narrower than usual. His blue eyes were even more stark.

"Yellowlike. That's what I said," Doris agreed, uneasy about Father's intensity.

"Which means not yellow but somewhat like it," Father said. "Could the color have been closer to orange? Perhaps a cross between the two?"

Doris cocked her head one way and then the other, thinking. "A little orange, a little yellow. Ain't seen many beards like it."

"That's the color I describe in 'Murder as a Fine Art,'" Father told Ryan. "In the essay, I suggest that the color might have been a disguise."

"Disguise?"

"John Williams worked on ships that sailed to India. Some criminal sects there change the color of stolen horses with dyes, one of which is the color Doris describes and which I mentioned in my essay. I raised the question of whether Williams dyed his hair to disguise his appearance when he committed his crimes."

"You're suggesting that our man dyed his beard for the same purpose as well as to imitate what was in your essay?" Ryan asked.

"I'm suggesting far more. I have trouble imagining that the killer grew a beard, a several-months' process, and kept dyeing it. Meanwhile, he would also be forced to dye his hair to match it, lest the discrepancy between his hair and his beard attract more attention than the unusual color of the disguise. It's all too complicated."

"The beard itself is a disguise?"

"Without question. Just as he disguises himself in sailor's clothes. Perhaps he has a theatrical background."

"An actor?"

"Someone who is an expert in changing his appearance. Make inquiries at shops that sell wigs and makeup to performers."

Ryan turned to one of the constables. *"You know what to do, Gibson."*

"On my way, Inspector." The constable hurried from the pavilion.

Becker asked Father, *"What about the names the women called to you? We know about Ann. But who are Jane, Elizabeth, and Catherine?"*

"I don't want to talk about it."

"But..."

"I wrote about them in my work. The killer read about them and used them to hurt me. That's all you need to know."

"He kissed his dead sister is what he did," Doris said.

"Be quiet!" Father shouted.

"Lay on his neighbor's dead girl's grave, he did. Clawed at the ground for nights on end. The gentleman told us what you was. Told us not to feel sorry if we made you upset and worse by calling those names at you. Said you deserved it."

"Shut up!" Father raised his hands and made a pushing motion, as if shoving away apparitions. I have never seen him so agitated. "Damn you, not another word!"

Abruptly the door opened, and the constable who'd gone for tea came back with four waiters carrying trays.

"The biscuits! I don't see the biscuits!" Doris complained.

I turned toward Father, but he wasn't there. He had left the pavilion, closing the door behind him.

"Father." I hurried out to him.

He stared down at the gravel path. His hat was in his hands. The cold wind ruffled his short brown hair. Dark clouds covered the sky.

"There is no such thing as forgetting," he murmured.

The door opened, Ryan and Becker stepping out.

"De Quincey," Ryan said.

Father didn't reply to them, either.

The two men stood in front of him.

"I'm sorry," Ryan said. "I need you to explain why the names disturbed you."

"It isn't your business."

"The killer made it my business," Ryan persisted. "Whatever twisted connection he feels with you, I need to understand it."

"Leave him alone," I said. In the woods, when I had recognized the names the women called out to Father, their horrid significance had become apparent to me—and why Father was so devastated. "You can see how this affects him."

"Miss De Quincey, surely you can understand," Ryan insisted. "I can't depend on your father for help if the killer is able to manipulate him. It jeopardizes the investigation."

"Once," Father said.

His voice was so faint that it took me a moment to realize what he said.

"Once?" Ryan asked. "I don't understand."

"This time only," Father said more audibly.

He looked up at Ryan and Becker. His gaze was anguished and determined.

"The killer manipulated me this time only. I won't permit it to happen again. He's twice the monster I imagined him to be. But now I'm prepared. Never again."

"And the names?"

"To keep secrets," Father said, "to push them down, to try to hide them is to be controlled by them. I have written about them, but I have never been able to speak about them. Why is that, do you suppose? I find an empty page friendlier than speaking to another person. I allow strangers to read my deepest troubles, but I cannot allow myself to disclose my troubles face-to-face."

Father removed his laudanum flask and drank from it.

"You'll kill yourself with that," Becker said, repeating what he'd warned Father earlier.

"There is more than one reality," Father said.

"I don't understand."

"And some realities are more intense than others. You wish to know about Jane, Elizabeth, and Catherine?"

"Not wish to. I need to," Ryan insisted.

"Jane was my younger sister. She died when I was four and a half." *Father took a deep breath.* *"She was as bright as the sun, too young to be anything except innocent. How I loved to play with her. She contracted a mysterious fever and was hidden away in a sickroom. I never saw her alive again. My grief became more extreme when word traveled through our house that Jane's vomiting had so annoyed a servant that the servant had slapped Jane to make her stop. Slapped a dying child. It is no exaggeration that I was overwhelmed by a revelation that the world of my nursery was not as it seemed, that evil existed, that the universe is filled with horror. Please tell them your middle name, Emily."*

"It is Jane," I said proudly. "In honor of Father's dead sister."

"There is no such thing as forgetting," Father emphasized. "By paying those pathetic women to call out Jane's name, the killer wants me to remember the servant who slapped my dying sister. He wants me to know that he is slapping me."

Father's words came faster, his torment pushing him.

"And now for my sister Elizabeth. She was nine. I was six. She had a large head, which physicians believed was caused by hydrocephalus."

Ryan and Becker looked confused.

"Water on the brain," Father rushed on. "Perhaps her large head explained her amazing intelligence and sensitivity. Although I had two remaining sisters with whom I played, Elizabeth was my second self. Where she was, there was Paradise. We enjoyed endless games together. She read to me wonderful stories from The Arabian Nights. *Sometimes the stories were so beautiful they made Elizabeth weep. In those cases, she read the stories to me a second time. I slept in the same room with her. I was secluded in a silent garden from which all knowledge of oppression and outrage was banished."*

Father stared up at the darkening sky.

"One Sunday afternoon, Elizabeth visited a friend at the nearby house of a servant. She drank some tea. As evening came, the servant escorted her home through a meadow. The next morning, Elizabeth had a fever. The illness grew rapidly worse. In a week, she succumbed. Was the water in the tea she drank contaminated? Was there something about the meadow through which she walked that made her sick? I can never know. The physicians thought that perhaps her large head had been the cause."

Father trembled.

"You don't need to do this," I said.

"Inspector Ryan says he requires an explanation," Father answered bitterly. "When a nurse told me about Elizabeth's death, I could not take it in. Six years old, I literally felt as if I had been knocked unconscious. During her rapid illness, I had not been allowed to see her, but when I learned that her corpse had been laid to rest in an upstairs bedroom, I could not stay away. At one in the afternoon, when the servants were eating and everyone else was resting, I crept up the back stairs and stared at the door to the room. It was locked, but the key had mistakenly been left in place, so I used it to open the door. Hearing the voices of the servants downstairs in the kitchen, I entered and closed the door behind me so softly that no echo ran along the passage.

"*The front of the bed obscured my view. I stepped forward, slowly bringing Elizabeth's body into sight. Dear sweet Elizabeth. The frozen eyelids, the marble lips, the rigid hands crossed on her chest — they could not possibly have been confused with those of anyone alive. Only her large noble forehead was the same. The window was open. Gorgeous sunlight streamed in, and yet a wind seemed to blow, mournful, a wind that swept the fields of mortality for a hundred centuries.*"

Father braced himself and continued.

"*A vault seemed to open in the blue sky beyond the window. I was taken away as if flying. Frost surrounded me, making me shiver. At once, I was back in the room, realizing that a long time had passed, that I was standing next to Elizabeth's corpse. I suddenly heard a footstep outside the door. In a rush, I kissed Elizabeth on the lips, then waited for the footsteps to pass, and crept from the room without being discovered.*

"*The next day, the physicians arrived with a surgeon, who cut Elizabeth's magnificent head open, believing that a defect in her brain had caused her death. I know this because I was able to sneak into the room again and saw the bandages that concealed what the surgeon had done to her skull. I dreamed many times about the opening that lay under those bandages, the gateway to what used to be her mind. I later heard that the surgeon described Elizabeth's brain as being the most beautiful he had ever seen.*"

"Dear God," Ryan murmured.

"And now Catherine," Father said, more determined. "She was William Wordsworth's daughter. William was my idol. As a youth, I wrote him letters of admiration. To say that his poems transported me is an understatement. His belief in the freedom of emotion, of opening ourselves to new perspectives, seemed to me the only way to conduct my life. He answered my letters and even suggested that I visit him in the Lake District. Twice I made the journey there, but each time, my insecurity prevented me from knocking on his door. Only much later, accompanied by Coleridge, whom I also befriended, was I able to muster my resolve to meet him. I soon established a residence in the area and frequently visited Wordsworth at Dove Cottage, the home he rented. How quickly circumstances changed. When William decided that he needed a larger *home, I rented Dove Cottage. I wanted to sleep in the room where* he *had slept, to eat in the room where* he *had eaten.*

"But unfortunately idols turn out to be imperfect. William could be petty and was maddeningly indecisive about the details of a project that I agreed to help him self-publish. We sometimes argued, and our disagreements affected my relationship with his wife, Mary, and his sister, Dorothy. What kept the friendship going was the affection I felt for his three-year-old daughter. Her name was Catherine. I spent as much time with her as I possibly could. We played for entire afternoons, just the two of us at Dove Cottage. The killer wants to make something evil of that, but my affection for Catherine was simply a version of the love that I felt for my dead sister Jane and my dead sister Elizabeth. With Catherine, I was a child again. I was in the nursery garden of my boyhood from which all oppression was banished.

"I received a note from William's sister, Dorothy, which I remember to this day. 'My dear friend, I am grieved to the heart when I write to you, but you must bear the sad tidings. Our sweet little Catherine was seized with convulsions on Wednesday night. The fits continued till a quarter after five in the morning, when she breathed her last.' "

Father paused.

"Breathed her last. Like Jane and Elizabeth. After Catherine's burial in a churchyard near Dove Cottage, I went there every night and lay on her grave and did indeed claw at the earth as the diseased woman in the pavilion told you I did. I would have died to bring Catherine back. And Jane and Elizabeth. Truly I would have given my life to bring them back—and Ann, I grieved for Ann. I grieved for all the losses of my life.

"Again and again, I wrote about each of them. I revealed my anguish on the page in a way that I never until now allowed anyone to hear from my lips. Until Catherine's death, I drank opium only sparingly to alleviate my stomach and facial pains. But afterward, it became the extreme that I wrote about in my Confessions.*"*

Ryan and Becker didn't express any reaction for several seconds. But the looks on their faces made clear how stunned they were.

Father stared at the dark sky and then at the bare tree branches, which now were motionless.

"The wind stopped," he said. "I thought perhaps a storm was coming, but now it appears"—he pointed to the north—"that the fog is forming early over the Thames."

He turned toward Ryan and Becker. "The killer wants me to identify him with the servant who slapped my dying sister for her uncontrolled vomiting. My work is not *vomit. It is my attempt to understand the pain that made me who I am, just as I hope my readers will understand who they are. The killer perverts my work to suit his foul intentions, and by God, I will make him pay for that as much as I will make him pay for brutally stealing the lives of those five poor souls on Saturday night."*

"And probably even more lives to come," Ryan found the voice to say.

8

The Year of Revolution

DURING THE 1600s, a mallet-and-ball game known as pall mall was so popular in the Westminster district that a street where it was played acquired that name. By 1854, Pall Mall—located to the north of St. James's Park—acquired a reputation for something quite different, a series of luxurious gentlemen's clubs where men of similar views could share a meal, have a drink and a cigar, enjoy quiet time in the library, and even find lodgings. While some used their club to avoid their families in the evenings, the bigger appeal was gambling.

Clubs existed for political parties, religious groups, actors, writers, artists, just about any common interest for which approved-only members were willing to pay a 20-guinea initiation fee and a 10-guinea yearly assessment. The denomination of payment indicated the exclusivity of the membership, for while guineas had once been actual coins, they no longer existed except as a concept used for professional fees and luxurious items. If someone requested a guinea, he would receive two coins—one pound and one shilling—the implication being that a guinea (which didn't exist) was a cut above the common currency of the pound.

On Pall Mall, as many as four hundred gentlemen's clubs catered to various interests. As a consequence, it wasn't difficult for some clubs to become anonymous, avoiding attention among their neighbors. In addition, members who preferred not to be seen arriving and departing could take advantage of curtained tunnels that some clubs erected between the street and the entrance. A coach could pull up, its occupants could step into the tunnel, the coach could pull away, and no one on the street would know who had arrived.

This happened at 2 P.M. on Monday, when a coach that looked no different from any other (but the interior of which was well appointed, complete with cigars and brandy) pulled away from the Reform Club and disappeared into Pall Mall traffic. A sign in front of the club announced, CLOSED FOR RENOVATIONS.

Three men stood within the curtained tunnel: Lord Palmerston; his security chief, Colonel Brookline; and a member of Brookline's team. The last remained in the tunnel and watched the street while Brookline approached a man whose uniform indicated that he was the club's doorman but who in fact was another member of the security team.

"Nothing out of the ordinary, Colonel," the man reported.

Brookline entered the club, surveyed its polished marble lobby, and noted the strategic positions of two other security operatives, both of whom nodded that everything was under control. Apart from them, the lobby had no occupants.

"Ready, Your Lordship," Brookline said.

Palmerston stepped inside and proceeded past an abandoned counter, the clerk for which had been instructed to remain at home.

The stained-glass door of a bar beckoned on the left while a restaurant invited straight ahead. But Palmerston and Brookline turned to the right and climbed a marble staircase. Despite his seventy years and heavy frame, Palmerston moved with the confidence of immense political power.

He walked purposefully along a passage and stopped at the second door on the right, where he waited for Brookline to knock three times, then once.

When the door was opened, an attractive young woman in a beguiling dress stood before them.

"Thank you, Colonel," Palmerston said. "Return in ninety minutes."

"Very good, Your Lordship."

Palmerston smiled to the young woman, stepped inside, and closed the door.

PALMERSTON'S PASSION FOR female companionship was so well known that gossip about it had spread from the upper class until it became the topic of ribald jokes in the poor sections of London. The *Times* gave him the nickname Lord Cupid.

It was a reputation that Palmerston encouraged, using it as a way to disguise his other activities. On this particular afternoon, the woman in the room — an actress recruited by Colonel Brookline — had allowed herself to be seen entering the club's curtained tunnel. Brookline took for granted that the club was under surveillance. The arrival of the actress in a men's club closed for renovation would be a sufficient explanation for Palmerston's own arrival five minutes later. Even the security guards had been deceived about the reason for Palmerston's arrival. If an unfriendly observer managed to identify the actress, so much the better. It would reinforce Palmerston's reputation for preferring exotic liaisons.

The moment Palmerston locked the door, he gave the actress a slight bow. "You are well?"

"Thank you, Your Lordship, yes."

"You have something to amuse you?"

"A script for a new play I need to study."

"Is there plenty of blood in it?"

"Yes, Your Lordship. A stabbing in a pool onstage. And two explosions."

"I look forward to attending."

Palmerston left her in the sitting room and proceeded to the bedroom. He locked the door and slid a wardrobe away from a wall, exposing stairs that led to the next floor.

At the top, he entered a room that had a long table. Six men sat at it, three on each side. Each had taken care that he wasn't followed to the building. They were all dressed in laborer's dusty clothes and had arrived separately at the servants' entrance at 7 A.M., carrying bags of tools, presumably the workmen accomplishing the renovations that the sign announced outside the club.

"André, you're thinner than when I last saw you," Palmerston commented. The man was in fact English, but Palmerston preferred his French alias.

"Not from illness, Your Lordship."

"Indeed not. You have a new female friend."

André looked surprised.

"Her name is Angelique," Palmerston reported. "She is twenty years old and comes from Reims. She likes to dance. Her father is a cabinetmaker."

"Your Lordship, I am careful about what I tell her. She is part of my cover. She does not know my secrets."

"No need to be alarmed, André. I determined that she isn't a threat. I mention these details merely to emphasize that even though we meet only twice a year, I think about each of you every day."

"Your Lordship," the Englishman who called himself Giovanni said quickly, "if you heard that I was drinking, it is not to the excess that I pretend. It is all for appearances, so that the Italian authorities won't suspect that I am serious."

"I am aware of that," Palmerston responded. "I'm not disappointed in any of you."

They looked relieved.

"I trust that you *won't* disappoint me. You are truly always on my mind."

Palmerston focused his gaze on each of them, one at a time, displaying the powerful presence that had made him variously war secretary, foreign secretary, and home secretary.

"Face-to-face every six months, we reestablish our bond. We reaffirm from the solid looks we give one another that I can depend on you and that you can depend on me. Can I? Can I depend on you?"

"You know you can, Your Lordship," Niels assured him.

"Anselmo, Wolfgang, Mikhail?" Again Palmerston used aliases that identified the countries to which the English operatives were assigned.

"You have my complete loyalty, Your Lordship," Mikhail asserted. "The mission is all that matters."

The others nodded resolutely.

"Make your reports."

One by one, they described their progress.

"I am encouraged."

"Thank you, Your Lordship."

"Do you need more resources?"

"Additional weapons, ammunition, explosives, and printing presses," Wolfgang responded. "Not to mention the alcohol to prime mobs into using them."

"And all of that will require?"

"Twenty thousand pounds."

The others identified the amounts they needed in France, Spain, Italy, Denmark, and Russia.

"The funds will be provided through the usual means," Palmerston told them, taking the huge sums of money for granted.

"I hear rumors that the queen is with child again," André said.

"No," Palmerston replied, "although I'm assured that she plans to keep trying. Eight children aren't sufficient for her. Her Majesty wants more offspring and intends to marry all her children to the royal houses of Europe in the hopes of guaranteeing that Europe won't threaten the British Empire. She wishes to be known as the grandmother of the Continent. But that will take many years, and Her Majesty is foolish to imagine that blood relations won't quarrel. Our way is more assured. Eighteen forty-eight proved the wisdom of our method. Destabilizing Europe is the only way to protect the empire."

EIGHTEEN FORTY-EIGHT. The widening division between rich and poor became so extreme that revolutions spread throughout almost every nation on the Continent.

The upheavals began in France, where the original blood-filled revolution of 1789 was still being felt and where a near civil war in 1848 brought an end to the recently returned monarchy. The furor spread to the Italian and German states, to the Habsburg Empire, to Belgium, Switzerland, Denmark, and Poland. In many cases, the effects of the uprisings were short-lived, with aristocrats soon returning to power. But a mere six years after the Year of Revolution, fear still preoccupied the upper class throughout Europe.

Great Britain was one of the few countries not to experience a revolution, with the result that it rose to the height of world power, becoming the master of the globe. What only a handful of the inner circle knew was that Lord Palmerston's methodical progression from war secretary to foreign secretary to home secretary had allowed him to establish a network of provocateurs, who incited the workers of the Continent to rebel against their rich masters. By keeping Europe in turmoil, he assured Great Britain's dominance.

As he told his espionage operatives, "Destabilizing Europe is the only way to protect the empire."

But for all his apparent confidence, Palmerston knew that he had gone almost too far. The spirit of revolution that he had created on the Continent had inadvertently infected England. In 1848, a total of 150,000 members of a labor group called the Chartists had assembled in London, south of the Thames on Kennington Common near Vauxhall Gardens. They intended to march on Parliament and demand yearly elections, universal voting privileges for every man in England, and the right for non–property owners to be elected.

Fear of the consequences caused Palmerston to commission 150,000 special constables to preserve order, one for every Chartist. Military units blocked all the bridges across the Thames. In the end, the Chartists agreed that only a few representatives would cross the river and present their petition to the government, which pretended to consider it but ultimately did nothing. The Chartists returned to their homes throughout the country. The crisis was averted.

But Palmerston knew that things might have turned out quite differently because of the demon that he had created.

HE DESCENDED THE HIDDEN STAIRWAY, slid the wardrobe back into place, crossed the bedroom, unlocked the door, and greeted the beguiling young actress in the sitting room.

She peered up from the script of the new melodrama that would include a stabbing in an onstage pool as well as two explosions. With a smile she asked, "Are you finished with me, Your Lordship?"

Palmerston studied his pocket watch and sighed. "Unfortunately."

"Always at your service, Your Lordship."

"You're very charming."

Someone knocked on the door—three times, then once. Palmerston peered through a peephole and opened the door, where Brookline waited for him.

"Ninety minutes. Punctual as always, Colonel."

They proceeded along the club's corridor, passed the security officer at the top of the marble stairs, and descended to the club's ornate lobby. Meanwhile, on the topmost floor, the agents disguised as workers left the meeting room and continued pretending to renovate the club. At sunset, they would exit through the servants' door. A different set of workers, these legitimate, would arrive the next morning.

"Colonel, you were in India in 'forty-eight," Palmerston said at the bottom of the stairs. "Did word reach there about the near-revolt in London?"

"The Chartist rebellion, Your Lordship? Yes. Most alarming. We were always alert against a similar attempted mutiny by the natives in India."

Outside the club, they passed the security agent dressed as a doorman. At the end of the curtained tunnel, a different-colored coach awaited them.

"You're using another vehicle?" Palmerston asked.

"It's one of my new security precautions, Your Lordship. Anyone who followed you here might have continued following the earlier vehicle in the expectation that it would return here for you. That would be easier for them than waiting for you to leave and taking the risk that they'd be noticed on the street."

"You suspect I'm being followed?"

"That's always my assumption, Your Lordship."

Brookline and the operative guarding the tunnel flanked Palmerston so that no one could see him step into the coach. As a final precaution, just before Brookline climbed inside, he scanned the area.

He looked for the telltale indicator of surveillance—someone who wasn't moving amid the constant commotion of the street. Today, it was easier to look for surveillance because the street was less populated than usual, nervous people hurrying home before dark and the further set of murders that were predicted to occur.

Brookline sat opposite Palmerston in the well-appointed interior as the coach drove into Pall Mall traffic, a security operative at the reins, a second operative next to him.

"Your Lordship, is there a reason you mentioned the Chartist rebellion?"

"It happened only six years ago and remains fresh in people's minds. The only time I saw comparable fear in the streets was after the Ratcliffe Highway murders decades earlier. After Saturday night's murders, that fear is on the streets again. We need to do everything to stop it."

BROOKLINE CALLED TO THE DRIVER, "Turn left onto Marlborough Road."

"That isn't the way to my home," Palmerston objected. "I need to return for a reception Lady Palmerston has arranged for the prime minister. We should be going to the right up St. James's Street."

"That would be the expected way, Your Lordship. For another security precaution, we're taking an unanticipated route."

"*Another* security precaution. Do you expect trouble?"

"To repeat what you said, Your Lordship, fear is on the streets again. As home secretary, you might attract the displeasure of someone who believes you haven't done enough to keep the streets safe." While he spoke, Brookline didn't look at Palmerston but instead directed his attention toward the windows on either side of him, studying the street. "I can't change where you live and work, but I *can* change the route you use to go to them."

The coach passed Buckingham Palace on the left and proceeded to the right, up Constitution Hill.

"I'm not reassured that Her Majesty suffered six assassination attempts on this very street," Palmerston said.

"Because she lives here, Your Lordship. But no one can anticipate that you're taking this route home."

"Four years ago, someone tried to kill Her Majesty by striking her head with a cane—outside my home when her cousin Lord Cambridge owned it."

"As I mentioned, Your Lordship, I can change the route, but not where you live."

The coach turned to the right at Wellington Arch and entered Piccadilly, the street on which Palmerston had his mansion. The area had once been countryside. A tailor who earned a fortune from selling then-fashionable stiff collars with perforated lace borders, known as piccadills, built a mansion there, Piccadilly Hall, and the name became synonymous with the area. Other mansions soon were built. The prestigious location was directly across from Green Park, famous for its fireworks on special occasions.

As the vehicle approached the walled gates to the semicircular driveway in front of Palmerston's mansion, Brookline kept scanning the street and noticed a man emerge from the park.

The man was distinctive because he walked with determination across the street, so focused on the coach that he paid no attention to the carriages that were forced to stop abruptly, horses rearing in protest.

The man had a revolver in his right hand.

"Get down on the floor, Your Lordship."

"What?"

"Down on the floor, Your Lordship! Now!"

Brookline recognized the revolver as an 1851 Colt navy model. Its specifics came automatically to him: a repeater whose cylinders were front-loaded with 280 grains of powder and a .380 ball.

The man kept coming.

One of the gates opened slowly.

"Forster!" Brookline shouted to the driver. "You and Whitman get His Lordship through the gate! I'll distract the man!"

The coach came nearer to the slowly opening gate.

Brookline jumped from the coach.

"Stop!" he told the man with the gun. He held up his hands in a placating gesture. At the same time, he moved forward.

The man came relentlessly.

"You're too late! Lord Palmerston's going into the house!" Brookline warned him.

"Not yet he isn't!"

The man had a German accent. He dodged to the side, gaining a view of the coach where it was only beginning to enter the open gate.

He raised the pistol.

A woman screamed.

"I know what the bastard's doing in Germany!" The man aimed. "But he won't do it anymore!"

Brookline lunged.

The man pulled the trigger.

The revolver exploded.

Amid a burst of gray smoke, Brookline swung his fist down like a club, knocking the revolver from the man's grasp. The next instant, he collided with the assassin, slamming hard against him.

But the man was strong and solid. Absorbing the blow, he lurched back but didn't fall.

Brookline swung his fist toward the man's throat.

The man blocked the blow and swung toward *Brookline's* throat, a maneuver that indicated that he too was a trained fighter.

Brookline jumped backward, avoiding the lethal punch.

A horse reared.

Someone shouted from the closing gate, "His Lordship's inside!"

The attacker darted around the front of the horse, slapped its haunches, and startled it into charging at Brookline.

As Brookline dove toward the pavement, feeling a rush of air from the stampeding cab, the attacker used the vehicle to shield him while he raced across the street and into the park.

Brookline surged to his feet and charged around the back of the cab, only to see another panicked horse speeding toward him. He hurried in front of it just in time and chased the attacker into the park.

Paving stones gave way to grass. Lampposts became trees. As the attacker sped along a path, a servant with a baby's pram cried out and shoved the pram toward bushes, choosing one collision over another.

Brookline ran past her and the now-wailing baby. Stretching his long legs, he came closer to his target, but at once the man veered from the path, crashed through bushes, and disappeared down a slope.

Brookline reduced his speed and studied the bushes.

Abruptly he dove to the ground as a fireball sped at him. Sparks flying, it shrieked over his head and struck a tree, the skyrocket exploding. Despite the cold weather, Brookline felt heat pass over him.

A second skyrocket sped horizontally through the park, exploding against a bench.

A third struck another tree.

Now every other manner of fireworks erupted. The slope burst into flames: red, green, yellow, blue. Sparks gushed as if from a fountain or spun on the ground as if on a wheel. Others shrieked or crackled like gunfire. Debris flew everywhere, smoke making it impossible to see down the slope.

Brookline pressed hard against the grass, compacting his body as much as possible. He squeezed his hands over his ears, as if he were under bombardment. His heart pounded against the frozen earth. He could almost hear the screams of battle.

Gradually, the explosions stopped. Glancing up, he saw the smoke dwindle. He rose carefully to a crouch, scanning the devastated bushes and slope. Branches smoldered. Dry grass was blackened.

THE REVOLVER HAD TOO MUCH gunpowder in it?" Palmerston asked, still in shock.

"Yes, Your Lordship. Overcharging it can cause that model to explode."

They were in Palmerston's mansion, in the ballroom on the second level, where tables glittered with champagne glasses ready to be filled at the soon-to-occur reception. The destroyed weapon sat on a polished tray.

"And you couldn't find him?"

"Not after the fireworks diversion he prepared. By the time the explosions ended, he was nowhere in sight."

"But why would the madman have wanted to kill me?"

"To quote him, Your Lordship... forgive my language."

"Just tell me."

"As he prepared to try to shoot you, his exact words were, 'I know what the bastard's doing in Germany! But he won't do it anymore!'"

"Germany?"

"Yes, Your Lordship. Do you have any idea what he was babbling about? It didn't make sense to me. Our current quarrel is with Russia in the Crimea. We don't have any hostile involvement with the German states. Besides, you're the home secretary now, not the foreign secretary or the war secretary. Anything that happens in Europe doesn't concern you any longer, only what happens here at home."

"Exactly. How could I have anything to do with Germany? The man was delusional."

Lady Palmerston, his former mistress, appeared in the doorway, her look indicating that the guests would soon arrive.

"Do you think you should cancel the event?" Brookline asked.

"And disappoint the prime minister?" Lord Palmerston asked in dismay. "Admit that the current instability is having an effect? Emphatically not. But Colonel Brookline..."

"Yes, Your Lordship?"

"Increase my protection."

9

The Separate System

A TRAIN CHUGGED PAST VAUXHALL GARDENS. Beyond the tracks, numerous boats navigated the Thames. Ryan watched the train's black smoke merge with the fog forming above the river. His summoned-to-meet-Lord Palmerston clothes felt stiff and uncomfortable, especially his high collar and the straps that looped under his boots, keeping his trousers taut.

Those weren't all that made him uncomfortable. He turned toward the many constables who led the twenty-four prostitutes from the gardens and put them into police wagons. The women were complaining again. But dealing with them was simple compared to the problem with De Quincey.

"I wish I could believe that laudanum hasn't unhinged his mind," Ryan told Becker as the Opium-Eater and his daughter emerged from the gardens. "Did any of what he said make sense to you about his two dead sisters and the Wordsworth child? My older sister died when I was ten. She fell into a river and drowned. I grieved for her, but I adjusted. I hardly think about her now."

"Yesterday, when we crossed Waterloo Bridge to go to the telegraph office, I noticed that you looked uncomfortable," Becker said.

"What does that have to do with De Quincey? Right now, I'm uncomfortable about a lot of things."

"Perhaps crossing a river is one of them."

"Surely you don't mean because of what happened to my sister. Have you been drinking laudanum also? Last night you seemed to agree with De Quincey that we do things without understanding why. Heaven help me, while he talks, it all makes crazy sense, but a half hour later, it's like the fog that's coming in. Oh, my, here comes his daughter. I confess I find her attractive, but she's as difficult as..."

"Inspector, what will happen to these women?" Emily asked.

"We'll transport them back to Oxford Street."

"And nothing else?"

"The gold coins they were paid might last as long as a month if they don't spend the money on gin instead of food and lodging."

"But isn't there some way you can help them?"

"It's a life they chose. The Metropolitan Police Service isn't responsible for them."

"A life that was forced upon them by poverty. You can't possibly believe any woman would willingly be in their state. Are there surgeons to whom you can send them for their sores and bad teeth? Can you transport them to farms, where they can work in respectable conditions and regain their health?"

"Miss De Quincey, the police force isn't a charitable association. We're not equipped to do what you're suggesting."

"But if these women were given an alternative to the streets, there would be less crime and men would be less tempted to fall from virtue. Constable Becker, isn't there any way *you* can help? Surely we can all come to a solution."

We? Ryan thought, fascinated by how she always managed to involve others.

Becker answered, "Tonight, perhaps they'll receive another gold coin from the man who paid them the first two. We'll have plainclothes constables watch the alley where they'll wait for the killer to return."

De Quincey overheard and came over. "The one place in London the killer won't be is that alley. He wants you to put men there so that other areas of the city won't be protected. Did you question every customer who was in the gardens? Almost certainly he was here today, enjoying his game."

"All the people here could account for themselves."

"A skilled actor *would* be able to account for himself," De Quincey pointed out.

"We're continuing to investigate the possibility that the killer has a theatrical background," Ryan said. "We might also have a name."

"A name?" De Quincey raised his head.

"Before I arrived, I received new information that I didn't have a chance to mention until now. The house where you're staying is owned by a businessman who travels frequently on the Continent. He uses a rental agent who tries to keep the house occupied while he's away."

"My own inquiries determined that," De Quincey said. "The owner's name is Westfall. He sells fabric to clothing manufacturers across the Channel. But the rental agent wouldn't tell me who paid for us to stay in his house."

"Because the rental agent was given an additional fee not to disclose the name," Ryan explained. "But as soon as he understood the gravity of the situation, he cooperated and revealed that the man who signed the rental papers is Edward Symons."

De Quincey's expression darkened. "No."

"Do you recognize the name?"

"Is it spelled S-y-m-o-n-s?"

"Yes. Not the common spelling," Ryan answered. "How did you know?"

"That's *not* the name of the man who rented the house for us."

"But—"

"Edward Symons is dead."

Ryan and Becker looked at each other in surprise.

"Thirty years ago, Symons committed several murders in Hoddesdon in Middlesex," De Quincey told them. "He was hanged."

"Thirty years ago? But how do you—"

"Symons was a farm servant who developed a fondness for his employer's wife. When he revealed his affections, she responded that the differences

in their stations—his lack of education, means, and physical attractiveness—
made his suggestion laughably unsuitable. The woman had two sisters
living with her, and they joined in his humiliation. His employment was
terminated, but although he departed from Middlesex, he did not forget
their insults. He brooded night and day until he could no longer resist the
impulse to return to the farm. The women had long since forgotten about
him when he surprised them in the farmhouse. In a perfect epilepsy of
fury, he swung his knife right and left until all three women lay dead and
the kitchen floated in blood."

Ryan noticed that Emily looked away.

"Are you all right, Miss De Quincey?"

"Yes. It seems that I too can be affected by Father's manner of speaking. Please continue, Father."

"Just before Symons was hanged, he told the prison chaplain about an
odd sensation he experienced in the midst of his frenzy. He claimed there
was someone else in the room, a dark figure on his right who kept pace
with him during the murders."

"Someone else?" Ryan asked.

"The chaplain believed that the dark figure was Satan, who urged
Symons on. But Symons was so steeped in rage that he didn't need any
devil to encourage him."

"Then who was the dark figure?"

"His shadow."

"His shadow?" Ryan frowned. "I don't understand. From sunlight
coming through a window? From a lamp in the kitchen?"

"From Symons himself. In his frenzy, Symons imagined that the dark
part of his personality emerged from him and mirrored all his actions."

Ryan looked at Becker. "This is what I meant. He speaks like the fog
coming in."

"I wrote about Symons in one of my essays. The killer is taunting me
again, comparing himself to Symons, threatening to do to me what
Symons did to those women."

"Mr. De Quincey, you provided new ways to look at these murders,
and I thank you. But I'm afraid that I now have an unpleasant duty to
perform."

"Unpleasant?"

"Father, I didn't have a chance to warn you," Emily said quickly.

De Quincey looked more baffled. "Warn me about what?"

"When Inspector Ryan arrived here, his preposterous intention was to arrest you."

WHILE RYAN DEBATED whether Lord Palmerston's orders obligated him to put handcuffs on De Quincey (he decided not to), across the river a seemingly insignificant, elderly woman was on the verge of a dismaying discovery. Her name was Margaret. She slept in a corner of a bakehouse where she worked not far from the notorious rookery of Seven Dials, so called because seven streets intersected in that slum. The bakehouse was filled with ovens to which the poor, who didn't have access to a stove, took their main meal to be cooked after the day's bread was removed. They gave Margaret pots filled with bits of raw meat and potatoes. They came back later to retrieve the baked food and carry it to whatever meager shelter they called home.

Margaret cooked her own modest meals in the ovens, and although the bakehouse could be stifling in summer, its heat was welcome in winter and even soothed her aching bones. Her main requirements were so sufficiently met that, except to use the privy in back, she seldom left the building. Thus she wouldn't have known about Saturday night's murders if they hadn't been the main topic of conversation for everyone who visited the bakehouse on Monday. They brought their pots of food earlier than usual, indicating their need to make certain they returned to their hovels before the yellow fog again engulfed the city and the murderer perhaps repeated his terrible crimes.

"There was two sets of murders back then, you know," a ragged woman said.

"What murders?" Margaret asked. Her left cheek showed a scar from a long-ago fire. To hide it, she had a habit of turning away from people to whom she spoke.

"Why, the Ratcliffe Highway murders, of course. Ain't you heard? It's all over the street."

The mention of the Ratcliffe Highway murders so startled Margaret that she almost lost her grip on the pot the woman handed across the counter.

"No, I haven't been out," Margaret said quickly. "The Ratcliffe Highway murders happened ages ago. Why are people talking about *them?*"

"Because of the murders Saturday night," another ragged woman said, handing Margaret a pot.

"What murders?"

"You really haven't heard? Happened again near Ratcliffe Highway. A shop that sells to sailors. Socks and underdrawers, linen and such. The same as the last time, except there was more of 'em. Just after the shop closed, five people had their heads bashed and their throats slit."

"No," Margaret said.

"My grandpa remembers back then," a third woman said. "He told me there was *two* sets of murders all those years ago. Twelve days later, more people had their heads bashed and their throats slit, this time in a tavern. My grandpa says everybody was so terrified nobody went onto the streets."

The first woman complained, "The constable on the corner promises he'll keep things safe, but what do peelers care for the likes of us? I'm not taking any chances. I'll be back in an hour to get my pot and hurry home. Constable or not, anything can happen in the dark."

"Margaret, your hands are shaking," another woman said with concern.

"All this talk of murders. Whose hands *wouldn't* be shaking?"

Margaret had an unusual number of customers for most of the day. But by late afternoon, the bakeshop was nearly empty, a few nervous people hurrying in with blankets to carry their steaming pots away. Except for her trembling hands, she managed to conceal how startled she was by news of the murders.

Her worst fear was coming true. *It was happening again.* Back then, there had been four murders in a linen shop, whereas this time there had been five. That there would be another set of murders, Margaret had no doubt, just as she was certain that the next set of murders would take place in a tavern, the same as the last time.

She was certain of something else. They would come sooner.

And be worse.

She slumped against a back corner of the bakeshop.

"Margaret, are you ill?" one of the other workers asked.

"I need to leave on an errand."

"But you *never* leave. The fog will soon be here. Aren't you afraid to go out?"

"This can't wait."

Margaret hurriedly put on her thin coat and emerged from the warm building onto the grim, cold street. Its usual bustle was absent.

"How do I get to Scotland Yard?" she asked the constable on the corner. Again, she turned her head so that the scar on the left side of her face didn't show.

"The Yard's a distance, ma'am."

"I need to talk to whoever's in charge of investigating Saturday night's murders."

"That would be Inspector Ryan. What do you know about those murders?"

"Not them. The others."

"The others, ma'am?"

"The ones that happened forty-three years ago."

"The recent ones are what concern us."

"But I know the truth about the ones that happened back then, and Lord help me, I'm afraid I know who killed those people on Saturday night."

You're MAKING A MISTAKE," De Quincey insisted as the police wagon transported the four of them up Farringdon Road. Having returned to the north side of the Thames, they were only a mile east of the Russell Square neighborhood where the killer had arranged lodgings for De Quincey and his daughter. But the contrast in the areas was extreme. Farringdon Road was dismal, on the verge of poverty. Normally it would have been crowded with dustmen, street sweepers, and costermongers desperate to earn a living by selling fruit, vegetables, and fish from their carts, but with the fog spreading, everyone was hurrying home before an early dark threatened to bring new violence. The nervousness on the faces the wagon passed was obvious.

"I ask you not to do this," De Quincey protested.

The wagon wheels clattered. High, stone walls loomed as the vehicle turned left onto Mount Pleasant Street. The gray of the approaching fog made the stone walls even more somber.

"Coldbath Fields Prison," De Quincey said. "No."

"I don't have a choice," Ryan told him. "I take Lord Palmerston more seriously than I do the prime minister. If I don't arrest you, I'll be dismissed from the force, and right now, the city needs every detective and constable it can muster to stop the killer from slaughtering more people."

They reached an ugly, arched, barred entrance flanked by stern-looking guards. A group of men in civilian coats stood impatiently nearby. When the wagon stopped, the men rushed forward, ready with pencils and notepads.

"Is he the Opium-Eater?" one of them shouted.

"Why did you kill all those people?" another demanded.

"Newspaper reporters?" Emily exclaimed. "How did they know we were coming?"

Becker jumped down and spread his arms. "Stay back!"

"Did the opium make you do it?" a third reporter shouted.

The guards near the gate hurried to help Becker.

"Keep away!"

"Lord Palmerston must have spread the word," Ryan told De Quincey in disgust. "He thinks that by arresting you, people won't be afraid while we continue hunting for the killer."

"But it's *good* for people to be afraid," De Quincey said. "If they're suspicious, it might save their lives."

"The only thing Palmerston cares about is his political reputation. If you don't walk in there on your own..."

"No need to resort to the alternative."

De Quincey stepped down from the wagon, shielding himself behind Becker.

"Did you kill the Marr family and the Williamsons forty-three years ago?" a reporter shouted.

Ryan looked at Emily and then at the commotion. "I hoped you could wait here while we went inside. But now..."

"Even if the reporters were absent, I wouldn't have agreed to remain outside."

Emily stepped down before Ryan could help, amazing him with her agility. No woman in a hooped dress could have ridden in the wagon, let alone climbed down easily, so difficult was it to keep a hooped dress from popping up and revealing undergarments.

"After you bashed in their heads, why did you slit their throats?" a reporter yelled.

"Why did you slaughter the baby?"

As Becker struggled to make a path through the reporters, more guards ran from the barred entrance.

"Don't force us to get nasty!" Becker told the reporters. "Clear the way!"

Doing his best to shield De Quincey and Emily, Ryan guided them past the guards and through the entrance.

Instantly the air became darker and colder.

COLDBATH FIELDS PRISON derived its name from a field in which a spring had once provided the opportunity for bathing on the outskirts of London. But then the metropolis had spread to the north and overtaken the field. The wet ground upon which the prison had been built made the walls feel permanently, achingly damp.

As soon as Becker joined Ryan, De Quincey, and Emily, the barred entrance clanged shut. They stood in a courtyard, the cobblestones of which were dirty and worn. A puzzling rumble vibrated from the center of the complex. On the left was a bleak structure with the sign GOVERNOR'S QUARTERS. On the right, an equally bleak structure had the sign GATEKEEPER'S QUARTERS.

From the former, an overweight man in a tight suit emerged, wiping his mouth with a food-stained cloth napkin. His cheeks were florid.

"Inspector Ryan," he said in hurried greeting, "Lord Palmerston sent word that you'd be arriving, but I had no idea when. I was just catching a bite. Sorry to keep you waiting. This is the prisoner, I take it."

"His name is Thomas De Quincey."

Prison administrators were known as governors. This one was not only taller than De Quincey but three times his girth, making De Quincey seem even smaller. The governor spoke as if De Quincey weren't present. "The Opium-Eater. Well, when he sees what I have in store for him, he'll wish he'd kept his mallet and his razor in his pocket."

"Perhaps there's been a misunderstanding," Ryan said. "Mr. De Quincey is here for protective custody."

"Mister? We don't call prisoners 'mister.' The note Lord Palmerston sent implied that this man is a principal suspect."

"The newspaper reporters are supposed to think so, yes, but in reality Mr. De Quincey is a consultant whose safety we want to guarantee."

"This is very irregular." The governor pivoted toward Emily. "And the presence of this young lady makes the situation even more so. Miss, I'm afraid you'll need to be escorted outside. This is no place for—"

Becker interrupted. "May I present Miss Emily De Quincey, our consultant's daughter?"

"You may, but she still needs to be escorted outside."

"Not with those reporters making trouble out there," Becker said.

"And who might *you* be?"

"Constable Becker."

"Why aren't you in uniform?"

Before Becker could reply, Emily extended her hand, saying, "Governor, I'm delighted to meet you."

"Really?" Suspicious, the governor nonetheless appeared captivated by Emily's bright, brown hair and lively blue eyes as he took the hand she offered.

"You'd do me a great service if you'd explain your responsibilities," Emily continued. "They must be immense. What are your theories about prison reform? I imagine they're extremely interesting."

"Prison reform? Theories?"

"I've read Jeremy Bentham. The greatest good for the greatest number and so forth, but I'm sure that your own theories must be equally enlightening."

"Jeremy Bentham?"

The group stood on a pathway that led to stark buildings from which the low rumble continued to vibrate. As fog gathered overhead, particles of soot drifted down.

"Jeremy Bentham?" the governor repeated, baffled. He wiped the falling soot from his sleeve. "Perhaps we should step inside."

They entered a clammy structure from which corridors radiated like spokes in a wheel. There were five corridors, for each of which a barred, metal door provided a barrier to the rows of cells. The design allowed an observer to stand in the hub and see any activity in any of the corridors merely by turning to the right or left. Although aboveground, the place felt like a cellar.

In addition to the persistent rumbling vibration, there was now a low clank-clank sound from the cells along the five corridors.

A sharp-nosed guard stepped from a room on the right in which truncheons and manacles hung from pegs. Rare among prison guards, he had a mustache, perhaps a sign that he felt entitled to his own rules.

"Which one's the lodger? I met Ryan before. It's obviously not the lady. So it's either of these two gents, but I'm guessing it's you," he said to Becker.

"Actually I'm a constable."

"But not in uniform?"

"A detective in training."

"Cushy. So it's the little man here."

"The Opium-Eater," the governor said.

"I love locking up the famous. Brings 'em down to our level. I'll take your braces and neckerchief for starters, gent. Wouldn't want you to hang yourself. Wouldn't want you bringing in knives or other unfriendly objects either."

"The only knife I use is for cutting book pages," De Quincey said as the jailer felt along his clothes.

"And here it is," the jailer said, removing the folded knife from De Quincey's coat. "Ridiculous little thing. Here, what's *this*?"

"My medicine." De Quincey removed his flask from his coat, finished the last few swallows, and gave it to Emily.

"Medicine." The jailer chuckled. "That's a good one."

"Please refill it, Emily."

"But don't be in a hurry to bring it back," the jailer advised. "He won't be drinking it here."

The clank-clank sounds continued from the radiating corridors of cells.

"Jeremy Bentham," Emily said to the governor.

"Yes, you mentioned Mr. Bentham." The governor wrinkled his brow in concentration. "I can't seem to..."

"The greatest good for the greatest number. Prisoners who are well nourished, made healthy, and taught a trade can become assets to society when they're released."

"We don't see many assets here," the jailer said before the governor could respond.

"The theory is that correction is more productive than punishment," Emily told them.

"As for that," the jailer replied, again speaking for the governor, "punishment makes them correct their ways, I guarantee it."

"There are cockroaches on the floor."

"Indeed. If they weren't already in residence, we would need to import them to make things even more disagreeable for the prisoners."

"I saw a rat scurry down a passage."

"If you stay here long enough, you'll see many more," the governor interrupted, trying to regain control of the conversation, "which isn't likely to happen because it's time for you to be escorted to—"

"Through the bars to the corridor straight ahead, I saw a man with a hood," Emily said. "In fact, *several* men with hoods. Guards were pulling them on a rope."

"Your Jeremy Bentham might call it guiding them rather than pulling them," the governor said, appearing pleased for attempting a joke. "We practice the separate system here."

"Good. You promised to explain your theories. I'm eager to hear them."

"The purpose of a prison is to isolate the offender and force him to meditate on his transgressions."

"Isolate?" Emily asked.

"Each cell has a size that is adequate for only one prisoner. He eats alone. When he is taken out for exercise or work, he wears a hood that allows him to see only toward his feet."

"What sort of exercise?"

"He and other prisoners walk outside each day for a half hour in a walled yard."

"I'm such a dunce that I'm sure I'm missing something," Emily said. "If the prisoners can see only their feet while they wear the hood, how do they stop from bumping into one another?"

"They clutch a rope that has knots tied twenty-four inches apart. A guard supervises them while the line of prisoners walks in a circle."

"And while they walk, they never see the other prisoners nor, I assume, can speak with them."

"That's correct," the governor said. "The same applies when they are removed from or returned to their cells. The hoods allow us to use fewer guards than we might otherwise be forced to."

"May the prisoners speak with the guards at least?"

"Good heavens, no."

"But if the prisoner can never speak to another person, wouldn't this lead to severe mental stress?"

"Some prisoners do go insane or commit suicide," the governor admitted. "The point is that we wish them to occupy their minds with thoughts about the crimes that brought them here. As for their souls, each prisoner is provided with a Bible."

"You say they are removed from their cells in order to work." Emily made the statement sound like a question.

"In the treadwheel house," the governor acknowledged.

"That sounds fascinating." Emily's tone invited him to explain.

"The prison has a laundry, a carpenter shop, a flour mill, a kitchen, and various other units that make us nearly self-sufficient. All the machines are linked to and turned by a large treadwheel, fifty feet wide, with grooves in it onto which prisoners step, as if they are walking up stairs. But of course, the wheel keeps turning, so the prisoners never actually rise."

"Is that the source of the vibration I've been hearing?"

"Indeed."

"The noise is wearing on the nerves."

"The prisoners learn to dislike it, yes. The guards in the treadwheel room put cotton balls in their ears. If the prisoners are unruly, the guards tighten the screws on the wheel, making it more difficult to turn. That is why the guards are sometimes referred to as 'screws.'"

"I have heard the expression. Thank you for explaining it. How many prisoners are on the wheel?"

"As many as necessary to keep the wheel turning so that the various smaller machines linked to it in the bakery, the laundry, and so forth keep turning as well."

"And how long is each prisoner required to keep stepping on the treadwheel?"

"Eight thousand steps," the jailer said before the governor could.

Until that moment, Emily's questions had been rapid, but now she seemed unable to say anything further.

"They climb eight thousand feet each day?" she finally managed to ask.

"Yes."

"Day after day?"

"It's like Sisyphus rolling his rock," De Quincey said, the first time in a while. His tone suggested emotion held rigidly under control as he peered along the corridor.

"I don't know anything about Mr. Sisyphus any more than I do about Mr. Bentham," the governor said. "But I do know how to make prisoners regret their crimes."

"It's time to show Mr. Opium-Eater his quarters." The jailer pulled a ring of large keys from his belt.

"May I remind you that Mr. De Quincey is not here as a convicted criminal or even as a suspect," Ryan said. "He is a police consultant about whose safety we have reason to be concerned. Please treat him accordingly."

"All I know is, Lord Palmerston wants him locked away, and the home secretary gets what he wants. If there's anything in the country he doesn't control, I'd like to know what it is." The governor motioned for the jailer to open the barred door in the middle corridor. "Stay here, miss."

"I intend to see where my father will spend the night."

"And probably a lot more nights after that," the governor said. "If you're determined to view what a lady's eyes were never meant to, very well, come along. We're understaffed, and I don't have anyone to watch you."

Their footsteps echoed as they proceeded along a dank corridor. The cell doors were made of rusted metal, with a peephole and a slot through which objects could be passed. The clank-clank sound kept emanating from each of them.

"What causes that dreadful noise?" Emily asked.

The corridor was filled with it.

"It's easier to show you than to explain it," the jailer said.

When he pulled a door open, a clammy smell drifted out.

Emily and De Quincey entered warily, finding there was space barely for the two of them.

The cell was seven feet wide, nine feet high, and thirteen feet long. A tall man, such as Becker, could have raised his arms to touch the ceiling and spread them to touch the walls. For him, pacing the cell would have been impossible. For a short man, such as De Quincey, the room was only slightly less confining.

The cell had shadows, its light provided by a small, barred, grimy window high in a wall. With the fog thickening, afternoon seemed like evening.

The window was at one of the narrow ends, the cell's other narrow end occupied by the door. Beneath the window, a hammock was folded and attached to a ring on the wall. A blanket and a thin mattress hung inside it.

De Quincey stared at the ceiling. "No pipes."

"Of course there aren't any pipes," the jailer said from the corridor. "Why would there be pipes?"

"In eighteen eleven, there was a pipe across the ceiling. Perhaps in this very cell."

"What are you talking about?" the jailer demanded. "Were you a guest here in eighteen eleven?"

"Only in my nightmares."

"Well, you'll have many more nightmares here."

The only other objects in the small room were a pail for body wastes, an old chair, a table upon which sat a Bible, and ...

"Why is there a wooden box attached to the wall?" Emily asked. "Why does it have a handle?"

In the corridor, the clank-clank sounds echoed from the other cells.

"This is more of the prisoners' work," the governor answered from outside.

"Work?" The cell was so narrow that Emily required only a short step to reach the box. "What sort of work is this?"

"Work for the privilege of eating," the governor replied from the corridor, his voice echoing. "The box is half filled with sand. When the prisoner turns the handle, a cup inside scoops up some of the sand. When the cup reaches the top of the box, it releases the sand. When the cup reaches the bottom, it scoops up more sand."

"And releases it and scoops up more sand as the handle is turned," Emily said.

"Exactly."

"Is there effort involved?"

"The crank is stiff. The sand is heavy."

"But…"

"Continue, miss. I am happy to answer your questions."

"I confess to being confused. What does the box accomplish?"

"The work occupies the prisoner's time."

"You call it work? But nothing is produced," Emily said. "At least the treadwheel produces energy for the machines in the laundry and the kitchen."

"The box produces an incentive to avoid crime when the prisoner is released."

"Surely, if the prisoners were taught to make their own clothes, that would be more productive and equally time-consuming. In addition, they would be equipped with a trade by which to earn a living when they are released from their bondage."

"Are these the sort of ideas that your Jeremy Bentham proposes? Teaching prisoners to make clothes? How strange." The governor looked truly perplexed. "I wonder if these wretches can even be taught."

"Are boxes like this the cause of the sounds in the corridor?" Emily asked.

"Indeed. In every cell."

"You say they do this for the privilege of eating. How many times must each prisoner turn the handle each day?"

"Ten thousand times."

Emily inhaled sharply, overwhelmed by the immensity of the number that the governor had told her.

"Do you have any other questions?"

Emily couldn't voice them.

"In that case, I'll bring Mr. Opium-Eater his prison clothes," the jailer said from the doorway.

"No need," Ryan told him. "Mr. De Quincey is here for protection. He is not a prisoner and can keep his clothes."

"Perhaps Lord Palmerston has other ideas," the governor decided. "I'll make inquiries."

"Also Mr. De Quincey will not be required to turn the handle on the box in order to receive food."

"Again, Lord Palmerston might have other ideas. In any case, the Opium-Eater will find his menu limiting." The governor still referred to De Quincey as if he weren't present. "Tonight he'll receive a boiled potato with some of the water in which it was boiled."

"My father's stomach problems prevent him from eating anything more complicated, unless it's boiled rice or bread soaked in warm milk," Emily said.

"And if beef is served, it must be thinly sliced diagonally rather than longitudinally," De Quincey added.

"Longitudinally? What in blazes is he talking about?" the jailer demanded.

"You'll become accustomed to his method of speaking," Becker assured him.

"No, you won't," Ryan said.

"This is wrong." De Quincey turned toward Ryan. "Were you able to determine how the killer obtained the mallet that was used in the original murders?"

"It was in what we call our evidence room as an object of historical interest."

"And yet the killer was able to get his hands on it. If he can do that, what other places does he have access to? We know the killer follows me. I'm not safe here."

"Tonight, with you in custody, this is the safest place in London," the governor vowed.

"No," De Quincey objected. "John Williams, the man accused of the original Ratcliffe Highway murders, died in this prison. Perhaps in this very cell. Supposedly he committed suicide, hanging himself from a bar in the ceiling. But there are theories that he had an accomplice who arranged for him to be murdered, lest Williams attempt to bargain for his life by identifying the accomplice."

"You're suggesting that the killer might try to do the same to you here tonight?" the jailer asked, as if he considered the idea preposterous.

"The killer is obsessed with the murders forty-three years ago. And obsessed with *me*. Inspector Ryan, don't leave me here."

"Lord Palmerston himself gave the order," Ryan pointed out. "There's no alternative."

"I beg you. Prisons are designed to keep people inside, not the other way around. It might be a lot easier to break *into* this place than to break out of it."

"Well, for certain, *you're* not breaking out," the jailer said.

Emily took charge. "Father, I'll do my best to make this place comfortable for you."

She needed only two steps to reach the narrow back wall, where she removed the blanket and thin mattress from the folded hammock. Then she reached up to unhook the hammock and stretched it across the back wall, anchoring it on another hook. Finally, she put the mattress and the blanket on the hammock.

"Good night, Father." She embraced him, holding him for a long time. She whispered something in his ear. Then she pulled back, her voice unsteady. "Rest as well as you can. I shall see you in the morning."

"Maybe not," the governor cautioned. "We'll find out what Lord Palmerston has in mind. Maybe the Opium-Eater won't be allowed visitors."

"Miss De Quincey, I'll escort you back to your lodgings," Becker told her.

"I do not think so," Emily responded.

"I'm sorry. If I did anything to offend…"

"The last place in the world I plan to go is the house where we're staying. Has it slipped your mind that the killer rented it for Father and me?"

The implications had a solemn effect.

"If Father is in danger, so am I. The killer might decide to torment me as a way of tormenting Father. Inspector Ryan, are you prepared to post guards at the house? How many would be required? Is there any guarantee that the guards would be effective?"

Ryan didn't have an answer.

"Very well," Emily concluded, "since we know that the killer has been following Father and me and since the governor assures me that this prison is the safest place in London, I shall remain here."

BEYOND COLDBATH FIELDS PRISON, the smoke from London's half-million chimneys mingled with the yellow fog spreading from the Thames, obscuring the city. Ash drifted down. But even without the concealing presence of the fog, the artist of death would not have attracted suspicion. The few people he encountered — unavoidable business forcing them to muster their bravery and hurry along the otherwise deserted streets — gave him a look of gratitude. He nodded reassuringly in return.

He carried a ripping chisel concealed up the sleeve of his coat. Eighteen inches long, it had a sharp edge on one end and a hook on the other, it too possessing a sharp edge. The tool was favored by demolition workers, who swung the hook into walls and then yanked down, tearing out chunks of wood or plaster.

A ripping chisel had been employed in the second Ratcliffe Highway murders forty-three years earlier. Those murders had occurred in a tavern near the shop where the first murders had been committed twelve days previously. Three people had died in the second attack while there'd been four victims in the first, one of them an infant. Already the artist had improved on those events by slaughtering five people, two of them children. But while he intended to demonstrate his talents in a tavern tonight, just as the killer had done forty-three years earlier, this tavern would not be near the shop in which he had performed his skills on Saturday night.

No, a great artist needed to expand his horizons, just as he needed to compress the time in which he showed his creations to his public. Twelve days between masterpieces was too long. A space of a mere two days would achieve a greater effect.

A man scurrying through the fog looked frightened when he almost bumped into the artist, but then the man's tense expression relaxed. Nodding with relief, the man hurried on while the artist walked with a confident, easy, assuring manner. Gas lamps provided only slight halos. Except for the clatter of a few distant carriages, the night was silent.

The artist passed a constable — he'd lost count of the number of policemen guarding the streets tonight — and made a gesture that all was well. As he reached his destination, he nodded to a frantic man hurrying by. The man carried a basket of something that must have been important, perhaps his family's evening meal. Did the fool believe that the evening meal was worth his life?

The artist saw yet another constable, this one standing beneath a nearby gas lamp. Again, an all-is-well signal was exchanged.

When the artist stepped into the tavern, the occupants jerked their heads up, startled. At the sight of him, however, all except one man relaxed and returned to their conversations or their beer mugs or their pipes.

There were eight occupants in the smoke-filled room. The tavernkeeper, wearing a white apron looped around his neck, stood behind a counter on the right. Two men sat on stools at the counter. In back, a barmaid — also wearing a white apron — brought a plate of bread and cheese to three men sitting at a table near the fireplace. At a table in front, a weary-looking constable jumped to his feet, the only man who wasn't assured by the artist's arrival.

"Sorry, Sergeant," he blurted. "I've been outside so long and it's so cold out there, I couldn't—"

"Not to worry, Constable. I understand. The truth is my feet are frozen, and I came in here for the same reason *you* did. What are you having? Tea? Perhaps I'll join you."

The tavernkeeper grinned. "Better yet, Sergeant, I'll pour you a pint. No charge."

"No, thanks," the artist replied. "Breaking one rule is bad enough. But drinking alcohol on duty — I don't think so."

"You're on duty sure enough. Keeping us safe. We thank you for it. Hot tea on the house."

"You're very kind."

The constable's helmet was on the table. It contained a metal liner that strengthened it sufficiently for the constable to be able to stand on it and peer over fences. It was also strong enough to withstand a heavy blow to the head from someone sneaking up behind him. But not when it was on the table.

As the artist walked past the constable, he dropped the ripping chisel from inside his sleeve and swung it, using the blunt part of the hook to crush the constable's skull. Without stopping, he pivoted and swung three more times, right, left, right, shattering the heads of the three men about to eat their sandwiches. The barmaid gaped. The curve of the hook whacked across the side of her head and drove her unconscious onto the floor.

"Hey!" the tavernkeeper managed to say.

By then, the two men at the counter had blood erupting from their skulls as the iron bar found its targets. The tavernkeeper never had a chance to say another word before the artist swung powerfully.

In a rush, the artist turned the iron bar so that the sharp end of the hook was now available. He toppled the constable off the bench, placed a foot on the constable's chest, and brought the hook to his throat.

The artist did the same to the men who'd been about to eat their sandwiches. To the barmaid. To the men lying near the counter. To the tavernkeeper.

But the masterwork was not yet complete. After leaving the ripping chisel on the counter, the artist propped the victims over tables or the counter so that, except for the blood, they gave the appearance of having drunk too much and fallen asleep.

His uniform was spattered with blood, but he needed more. He scooped two handfuls from a pool on the floor and smeared it over his face and his neck, obscuring his features.

He opened the back door.

Then he hurried to the front door, took several deep breaths to make it appear he was winded after a struggle, and staggered outside, moaning to the constable under the gas lamp, "Murder!"

"Sergeant!" The constable rushed toward him.

"Help!"

The artist fell to the cobblestones.

Overwhelmed, the constable pulled his clacker from his equipment belt and frantically swung its handle. Its racket couldn't fail to be heard for a considerable distance, attracting every constable in the area.

"Inside," the artist moaned. "They're all dead."

The narrow, fogbound street erupted into chaos, neighbors racing toward the tavern and the clacker's din, their voices rising in fear.

"What's happened?"

"My God, look through the door!"

"Butchered!"

"It can't be! I saw Peter only an hour ago!"

"Martha's dead also? No!"

Constables charged along the street, their murky forms like ghosts in the fog.

"What's happened?"

"Murdered? *Who?*"

"Everybody, keep away from the door! You can't go in there!"

"Do what he says! Keep away!"

"Sergeant." The constable who'd sounded the alarm knelt beside the artist, who lay on the cobblestones, moaning, his face and uniform covered with blood. "I sent for a wagon. We'll get you to a surgeon."

"Too late."

"We'll do everything we can. The man who did this—did you see him?"

"Dressed like a sailor."

"Did he have a yellowish beard?"

"No beard. He looked like any other sailor."

"Did you see where he went?"

"Out the back door. Your face is a blur."

"Here's the wagon. We'll get you to a surgeon. You two! Help me put the sergeant into the wagon! The rest of you, the killer escaped out the back! Look for a sailor!"

With his eyes closed, the artist felt arms lift him and settle him into the wagon. Amid the shouting in the street, the wagon bumped forward.

"Easy!" the constable warned.

"You can get him to the surgeon quick, or you can take your time and get him there dead!" the driver shouted back.

The constable made sounds as if climbing aboard. "Well, we don't want him dead from the damned ride either!"

Two other constables climbed aboard.

"Look out for sailors!" someone in the crowd yelled. "A blasted sailor did this!"

Sailors won't be difficult to find, the artist thought. *The docks are only a quarter mile away.*

The wagon bumped over more cobblestones.

"He stopped moaning," the constable said. "I think we're losing him! Hurry!"

The clatter of hooves increased, as did the violent motion of the wagon. The angry roar of the crowd receded into the fog.

"The surgeon's house should be just up ahead," the driver insisted. "In the fog, I can't quite... There!"

Someone pounded on the surgeon's door while hands lifted the artist from the wagon and carried him toward lamplight that he saw through squinted eyes.

"Inside!" a man ordered.

Hands carried him through a doorway, then another doorway, setting him on a table.

"There's so much blood," the surgeon exclaimed, "I don't know where he's been wounded."

Through squinted eyes, the artist saw that the surgeon wore nightclothes.

"Is he dead?"

"No, I feel him breathing. I need room to work. You two go outside. *You,* help my wife bring hot water."

Footsteps hurried in various directions.

Hands unbuttoned the artist's coat.

"Can you hear me, Sergeant?"

The artist moaned.

"I'll do everything possible to save you."

The artist allowed his eyelids to flicker open. A spectacled, gray-haired man in his fifties leaned over him.

The artist glanced around the room. It was empty.

Resolve and skill meant everything. The artist slipped a dagger between the surgeon's ribs, piercing the man's heart. He slid from under the collapsing surgeon and positioned the corpse on the table. At once he heard footsteps in the passage and stepped to the side of the door.

A constable rushed past him, carrying a bowl of steaming water. A gray-haired, middle-aged woman hurried after him. Since her hands were free and a possible, though unlikely threat, she died first, with a dagger to her right kidney.

Hearing her moan and fall, the constable turned, holding the steaming bowl of water. The artist slashed his throat, incapacitating his voice box so that he couldn't cry out. As the constable slumped, the artist grabbed the bowl so that it wouldn't fall and shatter, attracting the two policemen who'd been sent outside.

Unfortunately, blood had gushed into the water, making it useless. But presumably there would be more in the kitchen. After setting the bowl on the floor, the artist hurried toward the back of the house. No one was in the kitchen. More water was in a pot that dangled over the hearth.

He washed blood from his hands and face. He took off the crimson-streaked sergeant's uniform. Under it, he wore the ragged clothes of a beggar. The double layers had not been conspicuous because the cold forced many people to wear extra garments. From filthy trousers, he removed a filthy hat and tugged it over his head, concealing his features.

At the front of the house, a door opened, one of the policemen calling in, "How *is* he? Will he live?"

The artist opened the back door and stepped outside, disappearing into the fog. From nearby streets, the shouts of hunters and the screams of quarry reverberated through the night. The artist's masterpiece was already in progress, sounding as if it would be even more splendid than he hoped.

THE GERMAN SAILOR had a workable knowledge of English. That morning, he'd arrived after a six-month voyage from the Orient, the British

East India Company's vessel laden with tea, spices, and opium. After he'd found a boardinghouse, he paid for a servant to carry a tub and pails of hot water to his room. Sitting with his knees drawn to his chest in the small container, he'd luxuriated in the cleansing heat of the water. Decent food came next, anything that didn't have fish in it. Tomorrow, he would use his voyage money to buy fresh clothes, but for now, he had greater needs. A woman serviced him at the end of an alley, no language necessary—all he needed to do was extend two shillings.

Then a tavern. By all means, a tavern. The German sailor hated English beer, but he hated gin even worse, and English beer was better than nothing. His pent-up need for alcohol couldn't be satisfied, no matter how many mugs he drank and how many times he visited the privy behind the tavern. A woman at the bar gave him a look that suggested she also might be in the market for two shillings, but then a man perhaps offered her *three* shillings because she went upstairs with him. Finally the sailor felt bloated and tired enough to return to the boardinghouse, provided he could remember which direction to take.

The cold, yellow fog surrounded him as he stumbled along narrow streets. In the tavern, his limited English had made him understand parts of conversations, most of them about killings that had occurred two nights earlier, but he didn't understand the details, and he was too tired to care, although it did strike him as odd that the mood in the tavern had not been as energetic as he had expected.

Putting a hand to a soot-covered wall to steady himself, he heard a terrible noise in the distance and was slow to identify it as a London policeman's clacker. Immediately he heard other clackers as well as shouting, a panicked commotion at the end of the street. The din was enormous.

"Murder!" someone yelled.

Someone else shouted something about "Sailors!"

The shouts merged with boots rushing along the street, some of them coming in the sailor's direction. Dim streetlamps showed the fog swirling as figures charged through it.

The sailor ducked into an alley. The crowd roared into view. Hiding in shadows, he watched the murky shapes run past. They continued to shout something about sailors.

Trembling, he again felt pressure in his swelling bladder. He held it, waiting for the mob to pass. Some had knives. Others had swords. One carried a rifle.

The pain in his bladder intensified. Shifting deeper into the alley, he waited until he couldn't see the lamp or the street. Urgently he unbuttoned his trousers and released a trickle against a wall. Despite the night's chill, sweat beaded his face as his bladder insisted on being emptied more swiftly.

"What do I hear?" someone asked from the street.

The German sailor's English was good enough for him to understand. Instantly he stopped.

"I don't hear anything," someone said from the darkness at the end of the alley.

"Down there. Sounded like somebody taking a piss."

"I still don't hear anything. Without a light and a lot more people, I ain't going in there anyhow. Even if you're right, it could be anybody. Could be one of us."

"I probably imagined it. We'd better catch up to the others. You're right — it ain't safe being out here alone."

Footsteps hurried down the street toward the sound of the mob.

In the darkness, the German sailor trembled and listened and waited and finally the pressure in his bladder was again too great to be denied. Once more, he released a stream against the wall.

At last, he buttoned his trousers. Fear purged the effects of alcohol from his mind. He now remembered the location of his boardinghouse, but he needed to reach it without being seen. Perhaps if he removed his sailor's coat, that would stop him from attracting attention. The night was bone-chilling, but since the boardinghouse was only a quarter mile away, he could probably reach there in just his shirtsleeves without becoming numb.

He eased toward the alley's exit. As the fog-haloed lamp came into view, he dropped his sailor's coat and stepped into the street.

"See, I told you somebody was in there," a man said.

Threatening figures emerged from the fog. The sailor gasped.

"What's that he dropped?"

"A sailor's coat!"

"He wouldn't have thrown it away if he was innocent!"

The sailor blurted to them in German that they were making a mistake.

"A foreigner!"

"He's the murderer!"

The German ran.

The pain that entered his back felt like a punch. He looked down stupidly at a sword protruding from his stomach. As blood streamed down his trousers, he tried to stagger forward and instead toppled.

"That's what you get for killing Peter and Martha, you bastard!"

10

In the Realm of Shadows

IN 1854 LONDON, a journalist who spent several years compiling a four-volume study, *London Labour and the London Poor,* estimated that "there are upwards of fifty thousand individuals, or about a fortieth part of the population of the metropolis getting their living on the streets." Some pulled bones from rotting animal carcasses they came across and sold them to fertilizer makers. Others picked up dog shit, known as "pure," and sold it to tanners, who used it in the chemical process of removing hair from leather. Crossing sweepers swept horseshit from street intersections so that well-to-do pedestrians could move from pavement to pavement without soiling their shoes. Street musicians, ragmen, umbrella menders, match sellers, organ grinders, patterers who delivered the dying speeches of famous men, these and hundreds of other vagrants and wanderers ("a separate race," the journalist called them) filled the two thousand miles of London's streets.

Another term for them would be beggars, and under the calmest of conditions, beggars attracted little attention. After all, to notice them might lead to a compulsion to give them money, but one couldn't alleviate the condition of fifty thousand of them, not without becoming a beggar oneself, so it was wiser to pretend that they didn't exist. Especially on this hellish night, when mobs roamed the streets searching for strangers and foreigners to punish for the terror that threatened the city, beggars received little attention. How could nonpersons be seen as a threat when they weren't truly seen at all?

One such ragged nonperson limped unchallenged through London's squalid East End. With the fog so thick, his shabby figure was even more invisible than usual as he navigated a labyrinth of dismal lanes. Hearing the gratifying roar of mobs in the distance, he reached a sagging building with a faded sign above its double doors: LIVERY STABLE. Barns for horses and vehicles were commonplace in London, where fifty thousand horses (their number matched that of beggars) were necessary for the carriages, cabs, coaches, carts, and omnibuses that crammed the city. Those vehicles would definitely cram the panicked streets tomorrow as even more people used any means they could find to escape from London.

The beggar knocked twice, once, and three times on a rickety side door, then stood close to a dusty window, allowing himself to be seen. Inside, a curtain was pulled away. A lantern was raised, illuminating the beggar's features. The curtain was repositioned.

Someone freed a bolt and opened the door, providing only enough room for the beggar to slip through without revealing anything that was in the stable. Even if someone had managed to glimpse the interior, only the side of a stall would have been visible, certainly not the two vehicles that stood in a row before the locked double doors of the main entrance. A dark cloth concealed each vehicle.

After securing the door, the beggar (no longer limping) followed the man holding the lantern and joined two other men, who were seated on barrels.

"No need for me to ask if your mission was successful," the man with the lantern told the beggar. "The frenzy out there is proof. After what'll happen at the prison tonight, the panic will worsen."

"Yes, the prison. Anthony always enjoys a challenge," the beggar agreed. "But I wish I were there to do it in his place."

"You had your own mission tonight," the second man emphasized. "A more important one."

"That depends on your viewpoint about what's important." The beggar walked toward the cloaked vehicles. "You made arrangements for the horses?"

"Yes. They'll be ready whenever we need them."

Raising a cloak, the beggar peered at one of the vehicles.

It was a hearse. The gloom emphasized its black exterior. Through a window along the hearse's side, an open coffin was visible.

"Very nice."

"The other hearse is in even better condition," the third man said. "No one questioned us when we drove them here after we stole them."

"Yes," the beggar agreed. "Hearses can go almost anywhere and not be challenged."

WITH A SCRAPE OF METAL, the jailer locked De Quincey's cell. Becker studied the intense way Emily looked for a final time through the door's peephole toward her father. Then he and Ryan accompanied her along the corridor, escorted by the jailer and the governor, whose girth nearly filled the corridor and whose slow movements required him to come last.

They entered the hub from which the five corridors radiated. With another scrape of metal, the jailer locked that door also. Through the bars in that door, Becker saw a rat scurry along the corridor.

"Miss De Quincey, we need to get you settled for the night," Ryan said. "There's a boardinghouse across the street. Relatives stay there when they visit prisoners. The rooms aren't to the standard of the house where you've been living, but they are adequate."

"The killer has been following Father and me. For all I know, he is watching the entrance to the prison from a room in that very house. I do not feel safe with that arrangement. I feel perfectly safe *here,* however."

"A woman has never stayed here as a visitor," the governor objected. "We aren't equipped to accommodate—"

Emily scanned the rooms that were situated between the radiating corridors. "I see a cot in this office."

"Yes, the guards take naps there when they have a rest period," the jailer explained. "However—"

"If it's good enough for a guard, it is good enough for me."

"But we have no appropriate sanitary facilities for a lady," the governor protested.

"Are you referring to a privy?"

Becker was amused that the governor's face turned red with embarrassment, just as he himself had blushed when first hearing Emily speak so frankly.

"Well, miss, I, uh —"

"The alternative is that I might have my throat slit in the boardinghouse across the street. With that as an option, I believe that the privy here is suitable."

"But a guard would need to be assigned to you," the jailer objected, "and the prison is understaffed."

"You won't need to use a guard," Becker offered. "I'll stay with Miss De Quincey."

"Highly, highly irregular."

"But preferable to what the newspapers will say, and what *Lord Palmerston* will say, if I'm murdered because of negligence," Emily noted.

"This gives me a headache," Ryan said. "Deal with it, Becker. I need to get back to the investigation."

He opened a door and stepped onto the fog-obscured path that led to the prison's exit.

In that distraction, before the governor and the jailer had the chance to say another word, Emily entered the office and sat on the cot. She gave the sense that she had taken possession of it.

"Very well. I have important matters to attend to," the governor said. "We shall see how you enjoy a night in a prison."

"And I must supervise the distribution of the evening meal," the jailer said. "We shall see how you enjoy being alone here."

"She won't be alone," Becker reminded them.

As the governor and the jailer departed through the door that Ryan had used, closing it more loudly than they needed to, Becker followed Emily into the office.

The room was small and cold, illuminated by a solitary gas lamp hanging from the ceiling. Other than the cot, the only furniture was a battered desk and chair. Truncheons and restraints hung on the walls.

On the cot, Emily's back was rigid. She pulled her coat tighter around her shoulders.

"The governor was right," Becker said.

Emily didn't look at him.

"This isn't a proper place for you," Becker continued.

"Wherever Father is, I belong."

"Loyalty to a parent is admirable."

"And?"

"And?"

Now Emily did look at him. "I get the impression that you intend to add a qualification, such as 'But loyalty can be taken too far.' "

"No. Not at all. Loyalty to a parent is admirable." Becker sat behind the desk.

"That's it?"

"That's it."

Emily considered him. "You have nothing further to say on the subject?"

"Not a word."

"You surprise me, Constable Becker."

The outside door suddenly opened. The jailer entered from the cold, bringing three other guards who pushed carts upon which metal bowls were arranged.

"Still here, I see," the jailer said. "Here's your evening meal. I trust you'll find it to your liking."

He set two bowls on the table. Seeming amused by something, the jailer left the room and unlocked a door in one of the corridors so that the guards could distribute the food.

The bowls had several dents from having been roughly handled for a long time. When Becker looked into them, he understood why the jailer had seemed amused.

Each bowl contained a meager potato. An inch of soapy-looking broth surrounded it. Flecks of what might have been meat floated in the broth.

"I need to determine if Father can tolerate the food," Emily said.

She stood and came over to the table, where she assessed the contents of the bowls.

"This is what the prisoners normally receive," Becker apologized.

"But this is perfect!"

"It is?"

"Father's stomach can't tolerate much more than this. Even so, I need to taste it to be certain it's bland enough." Emily looked on either side of the bowl. "The jailer forgot to leave utensils."

"Actually," Becker said, "he didn't forget. For security reasons, the prisoners aren't given spoons or forks and certainly not knives."

"They eat with their hands?"

"They raise the bowl to their lips and pour the food into their mouths." Emily nodded and picked up one of the bowls.

"What are you doing?"

"There's no other way."

"Wait. I have something that might help. Please turn your head away."

"But—"

"Please," Becker repeated. "I need to do something that might offend you."

Emily started to say something more but relented and looked to the side.

Becker lifted his right trouser leg. Exposing his bare skin, he removed a knife from a scabbard strapped above his ankle, a strategy learned from Ryan.

"You can look now. It's clean," he assured her, setting the knife on the table.

Emily maintained her composure, as if she expected every man to have a knife hidden under a trouser leg.

After cutting the potato, she hesitantly chewed a slice, pronouncing, "The most perfectly tasteless potato I ever ate. Ideal for Father's stomach."

"In that case, I'll tell the jailer to send your compliments to the cook."

Emily delighted him by smiling. "This ordeal could have been worse for you. At least I don't wear any of those hooped-dress horrors that would have impeded you and Inspector Ryan."

"What you wear is called a bloomer, is that correct?"

"Named after a woman who championed this mode of dress. Unfortunately she's in a minority. Constable Becker, do you believe it's immodest for a woman to show the motion of her legs?"

"Immodest?" Becker felt heat in his face, which surprised him because he believed that he had become immune to being embarrassed by her. "I…"

"If so," Emily continued, "why is it not immodest for men to show the movement of *their* legs?"

"I, uh, never thought about it."

"How much do your clothes weigh?"

"My clothes." Becker felt more heat in his face. "Uh…this time of year, perhaps eight pounds."

"And how much do you estimate the clothes of a fashionable lady weigh, a woman with a hooped dress?"

"She would wear more garments than I do, certainly. Perhaps *ten* pounds?"

"No."

"Fifteen?"

"No."

"Twenty? Surely not more than twenty-five."

"Thirty-seven pounds."

Becker was too surprised to respond.

"The hoops that swell the underside of the dress are made from heavy whale teeth," Emily explained. "New models will be made from metal, which is even heavier. Several layers of cloth cover the hoops, the outside of which is flounced with twenty yards of satin. Imagine what it would feel like to carry twenty yards of satin all day. But of course, since a hooped dress sways, it's in danger of exposing a woman's legs, so several layers of undergarments are required. Meanwhile, similar layers of cloth are necessary above the waist so that the upper part of the dress won't seem flimsy compared to the bulk of the lower part of the dress. If you carried a thirty-seven-pound weight while going about your duties, I expect that you would become tired."

"Just thinking about it makes me tired."

"What is your waist size, Constable Becker?"

By now, she couldn't say anything that fazed him. "Thirty-six."

"Some idiot decided that the ideal waist size for a woman is eighteen inches. To accomplish that, a rigid corset is required, with tightly secured stays. I refuse to submit to that torture. Add the strangulation at the waist to the thirty-seven pounds of clothing, and it isn't at all surprising that many women faint. And yet they look askance at me, even though I'm the one who has freedom to move and breathe. Why are you smiling, Constable Becker?"

"If I may be forward..."

"Since *I* am, I don't know why *you* shouldn't be."

"I enjoy hearing you speak."

"Eat your potato, Constable Becker."

WHAT BECKER DIDN'T KNOW, or the governor or the jailer or Ryan, was that Emily and her father had a secret.

After having arranged De Quincey's hammock in his cell, Emily had told him, "Good night, Father." She had embraced him, holding him for a long time. Simultaneously she had whispered something in his ear. Then she had pulled back, her voice unsteady. "Rest as well as you can. I shall see you in the morning."

What she had whispered, her voice so low that De Quincey had barely heard it next to his ear, was "I brought this from the pleasure gardens, Father. It's the best I could do."

Simultaneously, using a hand that couldn't be seen by the four men waiting at the door, Emily had inserted an object into De Quincey's coat pocket.

He had concealed his surprise as she was led away.

Hearing his door being locked and the harsh echo of footsteps receding along the corridor, De Quincey waited, not daring to remove whatever the object was, lest the jailer be lurking outside the locked door, watching through the peephole.

He had once spent a day in a pauper's prison. That experience had been almost more than he could bear, even though the cell had been larger than this one and books had been allowed to him. Here, he faced only despair.

The cell's table and chair occupied a significant part of the compact area, along with the hammock and the wooden box on the wall. Two paces in either direction would take him to the walls. The solitary tiny window had bars and was the only source of light. As the fog thickened beyond the soot-covered pane, the cell appeared to become even smaller.

Forty-three years earlier, John Williams had been found dead in a cell much like this, De Quincey remembered. He was certain that the killer's determination to replicate the slaughters of forty-three years earlier would lead him to replicate other elements from that period. In particular, De Quincey was convinced that the killer would make sure that the suspected perpetrator of the current murders would die in a cell in this prison just as Williams had died here. The killer's obsession with De Quincey's writings reinforced that certainty.

He'll come for me, De Quincey thought. *What I told the governor is true—it's much easier to break into a prison than to break out of it. Sometime tonight, he'll attempt to kill me in a manner similar to the way John Williams died. But how can I protect myself in one of the smallest rooms I've ever been in?*

With only a few steps, he reached the door. In the continuing silence of the corridor, he listened for any sound that would indicate the presence of someone watching through the peephole. After a long time, he tested the door and found that it was indeed locked.

Only then did he remove the mysterious object that Emily had stealthily inserted into his coat pocket.

The object was an iron spoon. It was one of those used to stir the tea that the police had provided for the prostitutes who taunted him at Vauxhall Gardens. Tea had been provided for Emily also. She had known that Ryan intended to arrest him. How desperate her thoughts must have been, how carefully she must have looked around, making certain that no one saw her steal the spoon.

What she hoped that he might accomplish with the spoon was another matter. As she said, "It's the best I could do." But it at least was something.

De Quincey tensed as he heard a door being unlocked at the end of the corridor. Footsteps were accompanied by the sound of objects banging together, bowls, he soon learned, one of which was shoved through a slot in his door.

Through that slot and the peephole, he could see the yellow flame of gas fixtures positioned along the corridor. That meager light through the two apertures was barely sufficient for him to see that the metal bowl contained broth and a boiled potato with its skin on.

His distress made his stomach cramp with greater pain, but he knew that he couldn't expect to survive the night if he didn't attempt to build his strength, so he carried the bowl to the shadowy table and sat on the chair, listening to guards deliver food to the rest of the prisoners.

He waited until the noises stopped and the door at the end of the corridor was again locked.

Not surprisingly, no eating utensils were provided. But thanks to Emily, he had a spoon, although he suspected that this was not the reason she thought he might need it. Mindful of his uncertain digestion, he scraped off the potato's skin. Hesitant, he raised a chunk of the potato to his mouth. He tried to insert it and chew it. He really did. But his stomach protested too much, its pain insistent from the need for laudanum. At last, he returned the piece of potato to the bowl.

He looked at the hammock that Emily had prepared for him, a thin mattress and blanket on it. What alternative did he have except to crawl onto it and cover himself with the blanket to keep from shivering as cold gathered in the stone walls of the cell?

After all, where could he possibly hide to elude the killer? Under the table? His short, thin body would fit under there. He would even have space to pull in the chair some of the way. Scrunched throughout the night, his muscles would protest, but that was better than being strangled. If he hid his bowl of potato and broth in the slop pail, it would appear that the room had never been occupied.

Nonetheless, would the killer be deceived? One of laudanum's gifts was the ability to see outside himself, and the perspective that now came to the Opium-Eater was that of the killer standing in the open doorway. The yellow light from the gas fixtures in the corridor would stream weakly into the room, dispelling the shadows sufficiently to reveal the empty hammock. A glance to the right and left would disclose that the corners were empty. That would leave only one place for someone to hide. The killer would lunge under the table and...

Helpless and afraid, De Quincey sought to use the strange focus that laudanum provided.

There are many realities, he thought desperately. *View the cell from the killer's perspective. There must be a better place for me to hide.*

OUTSIDE COLDBATH FIELDS PRISON, a messenger emerged from the fog and walked along misnamed Mount Pleasant Street toward the barred entrance. To the southeast, from the direction of the docks, a commotion filled the night. For the sound to travel a distance in the fog, its cause must have been extreme, and the messenger knew that it indeed was. Mobs roamed the streets, hunting for sailors. Three had already been killed, two others beaten badly. Still others had been captured and were being interrogated by thugs. Those who rented beds in boardinghouses had locked themselves inside, securing shutters over windows shattered by rocks. A group of twenty had taken shelter in a warehouse at the docks, arming themselves to withstand an assault. Constables who formerly were assigned to guard the streets were now straining to control the mobs.

The messenger banged the knocker on the prison's entrance.

A peephole opened, a guard demanding, "State your business."

"I have a message from the home secretary. It demands immediate attention from your governor." The messenger held up an envelope, a gas lamp over the entrance revealing the envelope's official wax seal.

"The governor's asleep."

"The document concerns the Opium-Eater. I was instructed to deliver it now. Lord Palmerston is waiting for the answer."

Uncertain, the guard kept staring through the peephole.

"I strongly suggest that you wake the governor," the messenger said, "or else tomorrow you might find yourself employed as a dustman rather than a prison guard."

Another moment's hesitation. Then...

"Wait here."

The peephole closed.

Well, of course I'm going to wait here, the messenger thought. *Since he didn't let me in, where the hell else am I going to wait?*

In the distance, the outcry of the mob persisted. Several screams rose above the babble.

After counting to thirty, the messenger raised his hand to bang on the entrance a second time. Before he could do that, however, the heavy lock scraped, and the entrance swung open.

"The governor is waiting for you."

"Good."

"I'll show you the way."

"I already know it. Right through here."

The messenger nodded in curt greeting to two other guards on duty near the entrance. He turned toward the bleak structure on the left and opened the door.

Wearing a robe over his nightclothes, the governor sat behind his desk. The office was cold, the fire having been allowed to dwindle. Closed curtains did little to keep out the chill. The governor leaned close to the only heat source, a lamp on the desk, which revealed that his normally puffy face was even more so because he'd been suddenly wakened.

"From Lord Palmerston?" the governor asked nervously.

"Yes. About the Opium-Eater."

The messenger closed the door, crossed the office, and handed the sealed envelope across the desk.

The governor used a letter opener to break the seal. As he removed the folded document, he absently told the messenger, "You may sit."

"Thank you, but I've been instructed to return promptly to assure Lord Palmerston that his orders are being followed."

"At this institution, Lord Palmerston's orders are *always* followed."

"He appreciates obedience."

As the governor read the document, the messenger plunged the letter opener into his throat, destroying the governor's larynx, making it impossible for him to cry out. While the governor struggled for air, choking on his blood, the messenger went to what resembled an accountant's ledger on a side table.

The ledger contained a diagram of the prison, with notes indicating which prisoner was in which cell.

By the time the messenger gained the information he wanted, the governor had toppled forward onto the desk, his weight pushing the letter opener farther through his throat, its tip projecting from the back of his neck.

The messenger opened the door only wide enough for him to step outside, preventing the guard from viewing the office.

The yellow fog drifted around them.

"The governor has gone back to bed. He wants me to speak to the Opium-Eater," the messenger said.

"I'll take you to the jailer."

"Thanks. Sorry if I sounded officious at the entrance. Lord Palmerston is a difficult man to please, not that you heard it from me. Sometimes when he doesn't like the messages I bring back, he blames me instead of the sender."

"The governor isn't much better."

Their footsteps sounded along the cobblestone path. A lamp above the hub's entrance gradually became visible.

The guard unlocked the door. "What's all the noise from the river?"

"Several riots."

"What?"

"The killer slaughtered eleven more people tonight, including a surgeon and a constable."

"A surgeon? A constable? Then *nobody* is safe."

"The mobs think a sailor did it."

"But isn't the Opium-Eater the killer?"

"Seems not. The mobs are grabbing every sailor they can find."

"Lord save us."

And Lord save you, the messenger thought, *if you don't follow the suggestion I'm about to make.*

"I know what to do from here. The jailer's just behind this door. Better get back to the gate in case the mobs come in this direction."

"You're sure you can find your way back to the entrance?"

"Returning, all I need to do is follow this path."

The guard hesitated.

The messenger prepared to kill him. "Better hurry to the gate in case there's trouble. It sounds as if one of the mobs is almost here."

The young man rushed through the fog.

When the messenger could no longer hear the guard's urgently retreating footsteps, he opened the door to the hub.

* * *

INSIDE, THE YELLOW flames from gas fixtures showed the barred doors to the radiating corridors. The flames also showed the open doors to four rooms situated between the corridors.

The doors were open. In the first room, the jailer was slumped over his desk. In the second, a guard was similarly slumped. In the third, a big man in street clothes lay unconscious across a desk while the Opium-Eater's daughter slept on a cot.

The fourth room was empty, the prison's efficient, secure design requiring no other personnel to be on night duty here.

Each man had a bowl in front of him. While the guards' food was of better quality than that of the prisoners, all of it was prepared in the prison's kitchen, and all the food brought to the hub and the radiating corridors, whether to prisoners or guards, had been drugged by someone who worked in the kitchen and owed the messenger a great favor.

The sight of the Opium-Eater's daughter and her escort was unexpected but convenient.

The messenger removed a ring of keys from the drugged jailer's waist. He unlocked the door to the middle corridor and proceeded past the quiet cells. He found a door on the right whose number matched the entry in the governor's ledger that indicated where the Opium-Eater was being held.

He unlocked that door. It could be opened only outward. The gaslight in the corridor cast his shadow into the cramped cell.

The light was sufficient to reveal that the cell appeared unoccupied.

The messenger frowned. Had he made a mistake when he'd examined the governor's ledger? Perhaps he'd misread the number next to the Opium-Eater's name. No. The messenger didn't make mistakes. It was far more likely that the governor had made a mistake when he wrote the entry.

Remaining just outside the doorway, the messenger peered in toward the corner on the right. No one. He peered in toward the corner on the left. No one was there either.

He slowly entered the shadowy room. At the opposite end, the hammock hung against a wall, its thin mattress and its blanket upright within it, awaiting a new prisoner. The messenger directed his attention toward the table. Its chair was slightly askew, as if making room for someone under there. Ready to complete his mission, he yanked back the chair and lunged under the table.

His hands grabbed air.

There wasn't an empty bowl on the table. Only a Bible.

The governor wrote the wrong number! the messenger inwardly bellowed. *Now I need to go from cell to bloody cell!*

He returned to the corridor and closed the door so that his view of the corridor would not be impeded. Arbitrarily, he chose the cell on the right. He unlocked the door and stepped into the fetid confinement, which smelled of night soil in the pail that served as a chamber pot. An empty bowl on the table showed that the cell's occupant had eaten the drugged food. A large man—*too* large to be the Opium-Eater—snored on a hammock.

Blast it.

The messenger proceeded to the next cell and the cell after that. In each case, the Opium-Eater was not the occupant.

How much time do I have before the guard who escorted me here comes looking for me? I can't search every cell in all five corridors! That'll take hours!

THE OPIUM-EATER SLOWLY released his breath after the intruder abandoned the cell and closed the door. He was hidden in the only place available.

In desperation, he'd concealed the bowl of potato and broth in the pail that served as a privy. He'd pulled the chair partway from under the table, making it look as if he might be under there.

Detecting a sound at the far end of the corridor, he'd removed the blanket and mattress from the hammock. Fear shooting through him, he'd unhooked one end of the hammock and pulled it across to hook it to the other end, folding the hammock so that it hung against the wall the way it had been positioned when he had arrived. In a rush, he'd set the mattress upright inside the folded hammock and placed the rolled blanket on top of it—again as they'd been positioned when he'd entered.

Hearing footsteps in the corridor, he'd squirmed fearfully behind the upright mattress. Squeezed into the corner behind it and the hammock, his short, thin body blended with the shadows.

To all appearances, the cell had not been assigned a prisoner.

Or so he prayed the intruder would conclude.

He strained not to breathe as the intruder surveyed the room, grabbed under the table, noted the absence of a food bowl, and decided that the cell was empty. Further sounds indicated the door being closed and an adjacent door being unlocked. Then another door. Then the door after that. The intruder made no attempt to muffle the sound of his impatient footsteps.

The Opium-Eater didn't understand. Why wasn't the intruder afraid of waking the prisoners whose cells he invaded? Were they so trained not to talk to anyone that they wouldn't dare cry out even if someone burst into their cells in the middle of the night? Was it possible for the prisoners to be cowed so severely?

Or could there be another explanation? Could the prisoners have been...

The dark suspicion strengthened.

Drugged?

The Opium-Eater thought of the potato in the bowl that he had hidden in the slop pail.

The intruder proceeded angrily from cell to cell, not caring how much noise he made.

Squeezed into the corner behind the folded hammock, the Opium-Eater allowed himself to breathe more freely as the sounds went farther and farther from him.

The corridor lapsed into silence.

The Opium-Eater strained to listen. The silence deepened.

The cell door banged open.

The intruder stepped furiously inside.

"It took me a while to wonder why this door was locked if the cell was empty. There's no need to lock a cell that doesn't contain a prisoner."

The intruder closed the door, blocking the exit.

"He warned me you're a clever little shit."

He?

The Opium-Eater flinched as the intruder charged toward the folded hammock, yanked away the upright mattress, and lunged into the corner. The Opium-Eater gasped as the attacker grabbed him, lifted him, and slammed him against the wall.

The impact took his breath away.

But people do not submit to die quietly. They run, they kick, and they bite. Panicked, he did much of that now. The intruder was tall. Suspended in the air against the wall, the Opium-Eater felt his boots against the intruder's knees.

He kicked those knees repeatedly. Right, left, right, left. Despite his age, his legs had the strength of walking thousands of miles a year. He kicked fiercely, frantically, striking the intruder's groin.

With a roar, the intruder slammed him harder against the wall. The impact of the Opium-Eater's head against stone sent a flare through his mind. Abruptly the flare dimmed, and he feared he was going to pass out.

He managed to turn his head and sink his teeth into the intruder's right hand, which held him off the ground, squeezing his throat. Biting, he felt the attacker's blood spurt into his mouth. He gnawed deeper, twisting his head from side to side. As his teeth tore flesh from the intruder's hand, blood dribbled from his lips.

The intruder threw him to the floor. The crack of his body against it stunned him and made him feel that the cell was spinning. But his desperation to live was greater than his pain. When the attacker reached down, he rolled. As small as the cell was for him, it was even smaller for a man as big as the intruder, with almost no room to maneuver. On the floor, the Opium-Eater squirmed this way and that, evading the intruder's arms. When he banged against the slop pail, he grasped its handle and swung it, bashing it against the intruder's face.

He swung the pail a second time, but the attacker grabbed it and hurled it away. On his back, the Opium-Eater pushed from the attacker's hands. He felt the chair behind him and tried to use it as a shield, but the attacker grabbed it and hurled it away also.

The Opium-Eater kicked at shins and knees in a frenzy, but the attacker only exhaled in rage and dragged him back toward the folded hammock.

"I can't hang you in here the way John Williams died. No overhead pipe. But I can do *this*."

Using one large hand to press the Opium-Eater against the floor, the attacker pulled the blanket toward them.

The Opium-Eater writhed and kicked and felt the attacker add the weight of his knee onto his chest. It became almost impossible to breathe. He opened his mouth to draw in more air.

And gagged as the attacker shoved a corner of the blanket between his lips.

Terrified, he flailed, desperate to get free, to push away the attacker's hands and spit out the portion of blanket. But the attacker pressed his knee harder onto his chest. Struggling for air, the Opium-Eater reflexively opened his mouth wider and gagged as the attacker shoved another section of the blanket into it.

Past his tongue. Into the top of his throat.

Dry and dusty, the blanket absorbed all the moisture in his mouth. His lungs convulsed. His stomach propelled bile toward his mouth, but the wedge of blanket deflected the bile into his lungs.

His heart pounded with such frantic force that he feared it would burst. In the greatest frenzy of his life, he felt the shadows of the cell become darker.

His arms weakened. His sight narrowed. The attacker shoved even more of the blanket into his mouth, cramming it down his throat.

At once he had a floating sensation, a dream state overtaking him, much like the effect of opium. As a child, he'd had a persistent nightmare about a lion threatening him. In the nightmare, he'd been so frightened that paralysis seized him. He'd been tempted to lie down before the lion in the hope that the lion would spare him if he acquiesced.

As his mind dimmed and his chest heaved with less force, he thought that it would be so easy to lie down in front of the lion now.

So peaceful to surrender.

No!

He groped in his coat pocket. Rage filling him, he clutched the spoon Emily had given him.

In fury, he gripped the round end of the spoon and thrust its handle up with all his remaining strength.

Something popped. Warm, thick liquid streamed onto his fist as the spoon's handle rammed into what he suddenly realized was the attacker's left eye.

The attacker stiffened.

Screamed.

Shoving with all his remaining might, the Opium-Eater thrust the spoon's handle deeper into the man's eye.

Wailing, the attacker raised his hands to his face.

The Opium-Eater shoved him, hearing an impact as the attacker's head struck the wooden box on the wall.

The Opium-Eater struggled to pull the blanket from his mouth. He tugged and tugged. Dear God, how was it possible for so much of the blanket to have been crammed into his mouth? Abruptly the thing was out of him. He drew a frantic breath, but his stomach kept heaving, and bile kept rising, burning in his throat.

He twisted his head and vomited.

The attacker crawled toward him. The Opium-Eater kicked, feeling his boot shove the spoon deeper into the man's eye socket.

Delirious, he rolled. He struck the wall and used it to grope to his feet. The attacker grabbed his ankle. The Opium-Eater kicked his hand away and staggered toward the door. Behind him, the attacker struggled upright.

The Opium-Eater shoved the door open and was almost blinded by what would normally have been faint gaslight. Dizzy, he heard the attacker charging toward him. He stumbled into the hall, slammed the door, and struck the attacker's face.

With one hand against the wall, he staggered along the corridor.

Behind him, the cell door crashed open.

He strained to move faster toward the hub at the end of the corridor.

Footsteps lurched after him.

He struggled to increase speed.

A hand grabbed his shoulder.

BECKER SLUMPED ACROSS THE DESK in the office in the hub. The last thing he remembered was that Emily complained of drowsiness and set down the knife he'd lent her to eat the potato.

"It's been a long, stressful day," he had told her. "I'll go into the next room so you can sleep."

But as Emily rose from the desk and lay on the cot, he felt drowsy also. He set down the potato he'd been eating and made an effort to stand from the desk, but his knees had no strength, and he felt his eyelids flickering shut.

Gradually he became aware that his head was on the table. He had a vague sense that a lot of time had passed. He strained to open his eyes and saw his right hand in front of him. Blurred, it held the potato he'd been forcing himself to eat.

Metal clattered, as if a pail had been thrown. A wooden object struck a wall—perhaps a chair. But the noises were distant, as if in a dream.

A scream brought Becker's eyes fully open, it too from a distance but definitely not in a dream.

Dizzy, he raised his head. Beyond the desk, Emily lay on the cot.

The sounds of a frantic struggle echoed beyond the room. A door banged. Footsteps stumbled along a corridor. The door banged again, other footsteps stumbling along the corridor.

Legs unsteady, Becker managed to stand. He didn't understand why the jailer wasn't responding to the sounds. Where was the other guard who watched the corridors at night?

A cry of pain made him grab his knife from the table. Light-headed, he stepped from the room and turned toward the middle corridor.

What he saw made him waver in confusion. De Quincey was out of his cell. A huge man, with blood on his face, pressed De Quincey against the wall and squeezed his throat.

"Hey!" Becker managed to shout.

The tall man kept choking De Quincey. The contrast between the tiny man and the large attacker was grotesque, like a giant choking a child.

"Stop!" Becker yelled.

The door to the corridor was ajar. With increasing strength in his legs, Becker stepped through. The shock of what was happening cleared the fog from his mind. He ran along the corridor and rammed the butt end of his knife against the attacker's skull.

The blow should have knocked the attacker unconscious. Instead, the man merely turned in fury and startled Becker with the discovery that something protruded from his left eye socket. God in heaven, it looked like a spoon. Gore dripped from the socket.

The man released his hands from De Quincey's throat, dropping him to the floor in a heap. With an intense glare in his remaining eye, he reached under his coat. The next instant, he thrust a hand toward Becker. The hand held something that glinted, and Becker ducked back in time to realize that the object was a knife. The blade slashed across Becker's chest, slicing his coat, nicking his skin. He lurched farther back as the attacker spun the knife so that its glint resembled a furiously pivoting wheel. The movement was too fast for Becker to follow. All he could do was keep stumbling away from the terrifying blur, moving just fast enough that pieces of his coat parted but not his skin.

At once the attacker lurched rather than lunged. He jerked forward, falling. Becker saw that De Quincey had grabbed the attacker's ankles, tripping him.

The attacker dropped, face forward, onto the floor. He cried out, trembled, and suddenly became still.

Becker shook, straining to adjust to what had happened. De Quincey gasped for air, his throat red from the finger marks of the attacker.

Cautiously, Becker turned the attacker onto his back. The spoon had been rammed all the way into the man's head, the round part barely visible. The man's expression was lifeless.

"Can't," De Quincey murmured, "breathe."

Becker hurried to him. De Quincey had blood spattered on his face and his clothes, but as much as Becker could determine, the blood wasn't his.

"Take shallow breaths," Becker told him. "Your throat's swollen, but nothing's broken, or else you wouldn't be able to talk."

De Quincey nodded.

"Take shallow breaths," Becker repeated, "and let your throat relax. You'll soon breathe normally."

"Was...?"

"Don't try to talk."

"...real?"

Becker didn't understand.

"Was it real?" De Quincey sounded as if he were more afraid for his sanity than he was for his life. "Did it happen? It wasn't the laudanum?"

"It definitely happened," Becker assured him.

"Father!"

Becker turned and saw Emily clinging to the bars at the end of the corridor.

He ran to her as the jailer staggered from his office, rubbing the back of his neck.

"I think we've been drugged," Becker told them.

Outside, footsteps charged toward the door. Accompanied by two guards, Ryan hurried in from the darkness.

He wore his shapeless street clothes again, his cap covering most of his red hair. Bewildered, he looked at Becker's slashed coat before he noticed the body in the corridor.

"That's the killer," Becker said.

DRUGGED," the jailer confirmed. "Every prisoner and every guard who works in this building."

"The food?" Ryan asked.

"Yes. What the outside guards ate wasn't tampered with. Only in here," the jailer elaborated. "We use civilians to prepare the food. One of them must have been bribed."

"The guard at the gate says the dead man claimed to have a message from Lord Palmerston," Ryan said. "A sure way to get into the prison. We found the note in the governor's office. All it says is 'Treat the Opium-Eater as harshly as possible.' The governor probably didn't have a chance to read it before he was stabbed."

"Then the killer came to this building, saw that we were all asleep, found the key, and went to Mr. De Quincey's cell," Becker concluded. He drank coffee to help clear his mind from the drug. "I searched him, but he doesn't have anything on his clothes to identify him."

"A message from Lord Palmerston?" Ryan sounded doubtful. "I know several people on Lord Palmerston's staff, but I never saw *this* man before. Maybe a newspaper sketch artist can produce a good likeness of him. Possibly someone can identify him."

The group was in the room where Becker and Emily had fallen asleep. Emily sat with her father on the cot. The attacker's blood remained on De Quincey's face.

"You haven't explained the spoon," the jailer noted with suspicion. "How did you get the spoon?"

De Quincey seemed not to hear the question. He trembled from the effects of the fierce battle for his life.

And from the cramps of laudanum withdrawal.

"Emily, did you refill my flask?"

"I never had the chance, Father. I never left the prison."

De Quincey shuddered.

"Tell me how you got the spoon," the jailer persisted.

"I gave it to him," Emily said.

The jailer's mouth hung open.

"Inspector Ryan"—De Quincey's voice was hoarse—"who knew I was being brought to this prison?"

"For starters, all the newspaper reporters you saw when you arrived. Lord Palmerston spread the word far and wide. By late this afternoon, it was common knowledge. He wanted to make certain that people thought you were the main suspect and that you were off the streets."

"To make people feel safe." After everything that had happened, De Quincey looked even smaller than usual, trembling on the cot.

"That's right."

"But now other murders have occurred."

"That's what I came to tell you. Two sets of them," Ryan said. "Eight people at a tavern, and three at a surgeon's house."

"Not to mention the governor. Murders I obviously couldn't have committed since I was imprisoned here. So there's no reason to keep me locked away any longer."

"Lord Palmerston hasn't given permission for that," the jailer objected.

"Yes, I expect at the moment he has numerous other things to occupy his attention," De Quincey noted. "The riots that Inspector Ryan described, for example. Nonetheless, there's no reason to keep me locked away any longer, and *every* reason to let me go."

"Such as?"

"I need to study the murder scenes."

Emily raised her head in surprise. "What are you talking about, Father?"

"Take me to the tavern, Inspector Ryan. I need to find what else the killer unwittingly told us about himself. Before something worse happens."

"But we don't need to worry now," Becker objected. "The killer's lying in the corridor out there. It's over."

"*A* killer is lying in that corridor. Yes. But *the* killer? No."

"What on earth makes you believe that?" Ryan demanded.

"When he burst into my cell, he said something that's too indelicate to repeat."

"For you to feel such, it must indeed be indelicate," Emily said. "But I don't intend to leave."

"Very well. He called me a clever little shit."

"Some might not disagree," the jailer said.

"Specifically, the sentence was 'He warned me you're a clever little shit.' "

" '*He* warned me'?" Ryan asked.

"Someone gave instructions to this man. Whoever that other person is, now that he has replicated the original murders, he'll feel free to create his own masterpieces."

I I

The Dark Interpreter

THE FOG WAS WORSE than the night before, the soot particles in greater quantity, sticking to skin and clothing. Ryan had managed to find a wagon with a cover, shielding De Quincey, Emily, Becker, and himself as a constable drove them toward the tavern. But apart from the shelter that the canvas walls and roof provided, Ryan would have preferred to see the smothering fog and try to guess the cause of possibly threatening shadows moving within it.

The faint lantern hanging under the canvas revealed that De Quincey continued to tremble. Now that he'd washed the attacker's blood from his face, it was clear that he was alarmingly pale.

"Are you all right?" Ryan asked.

"Thank you, yes. I have suffered through this before."

"You've been attacked before? You needed to fight for your life before?"

"The attack did in fact happen?" De Quincey asked Becker again.

"Most definitely."

"I can tolerate anything if I have my medicine." De Quincey hugged himself.

"Why do you insist on calling it medicine?" Becker asked.

"Without it, my facial pains and stomach disorders would be intolerable."

"Worse than you're feeling now?"

"Sometimes I can reduce the quantity until I finally discontinue it." De Quincey's voice wavered. "But the pains worsen, like rats tearing at my stomach, and eventually I can't resist the need."

"Could the pains be caused by the body's craving for the drug?" Ryan asked. "Perhaps if you became accustomed to not having the drug, the pains would go away."

"How I wish that were the case."

Becker felt pressure next to him and realized that Emily, still groggy, had fallen asleep with her head against his shoulder. Neither her father nor Ryan seemed to think that the situation was unsuitable, so he continued to provide support for her.

"My mind demands it more than my body," De Quincey continued, as if talking helped to distract him from his need. "Our minds have doors."

"Doors?" Ryan asked in confusion.

"Opening them, I discovered thoughts and emotions that controlled me but that I didn't know I possessed. Unfortunately, self-knowledge can turn out to be a nightmare. Too many nights, I dream about a coach driver who turns into a crocodile."

"Thoughts that control you but that you don't know you possess? A crocodile?" Ryan shook his head from side to side. "For a moment, I almost seemed to follow what you said."

"My friend Coleridge was a well-known opium-eater."

"I have heard such, although I confess I have not read his poems," Ryan said.

De Quincey lapsed into a singsong way of speaking that made Becker fear De Quincey had lost his mind. His words seemed to refer to hallucinations.

> *The shadow of the dome of pleasure*
> *Floated midway on the waves;*
> *Where was heard the mingled measure*
> *From the fountain and the caves.*
> *It was a miracle of rare device,*
> *A sunny pleasure dome with caves of ice!*

"That is Coleridge," De Quincey concluded. "From 'Kubla Khan.'"

"It rhymes insistently."

"Indeed it does." De Quincey hugged himself and trembled.

"It has a child's rhythm."

"That also. Coleridge uses childlike rhyme and rhythm to make you feel that you are under opium's spell. In fact, he *was* under its spell when he wrote his poetry. But as much as it helped him create beauty, it destroyed his health. He tried desperately to gain his freedom, but it isn't easy to leave the pleasure dome."

Shouts made the wagon stop. Bodies jostled the sides, shaking Emily awake.

"What's that noise?" she murmured.

"Inspector, you'd better get out here!" the driver yelled.

Becker and Ryan jumped hurriedly down, confronted by shadows storming from the fog.

A shrouded streetlamp revealed men holding swords, knives, rifles, and clubs.

"What's your business here?" one of the men demanded.

"I could ask you the same," Ryan answered.

"But we know who *we* are, and you're a stranger."

"We're police officers."

"Look like beggars to *me*." The smell of gin wafted from the man. "The bloke next to you has a coat that's almost in rags." The reference was to the knife slashes that De Quincey's attacker had inflicted on Becker's garment.

"And blood!" another man shouted, pointing.

One of the knife slashes had nicked Becker's chest, the blood now dried.

"Still has the victims' blood on 'im."

"It's my own blood," Becker told them. "I'm an off-duty constable. This is Inspector Ryan. If you want to see a uniform, look at the driver."

"Yes, the driver's wearin' a constable's uniform, but so was the killer when he slaughtered fifteen poor souls in a tavern. People first thought he was a sailor, but it turned out he was a constable. Dressed as a sergeant."

"Not fifteen victims in a tavern," Ryan insisted. "Eight."

"And six people in a surgeon's office!"

"Three," Becker corrected him.

"How would *you* be so certain unless you was there! Uniform, my arse. The killer was disguised as a policeman, so how can we believe a stranger wearin' a uniform?"

"Look, this other bloke has red hair peekin' under his cap!"

"Irish!"

"Wait! I'll show you my badge!" Ryan reached into his coat.

"He's goin' for a knife!"

"Get 'im!"

The mob charged, pinning Ryan and Becker against the wagon. The impact knocked Becker's teeth together. A club struck his shoulder.

Ryan groaned.

Abruptly a woman screamed.

A man attacking Ryan swung toward the fog. "Who's *that?*"

"Help!" the woman shrieked.

"Where?"

"There!"

"Help! He attacked me!"

Astonished, Becker saw a woman stumble from the fog. Her bonnet hung from her neck. Her coat was torn open, the top part of her dress ripped.

The woman was Emily.

"He grabbed me! He tried to—"

"Where?"

"Down that alley! A policeman! He ripped my dress! He tried to—"

"Let's go! The bastard's gettin' away!"

The mob raged past Ryan and Becker, disappearing into the fog toward where Emily pointed.

"Hurry," Becker told her, helping her into the wagon.

Under the canvas roof, Becker heard Ryan jump up next to the driver. "Get out of here fast."

As the wagon jostled rapidly over the cobblestones, Emily fumbled to secure the top of her dress and to close her coat.

"Well done," Becker told her.

"It was all I could think of." Working to catch her breath, Emily adjusted her bonnet.

"And if that didn't distract them," De Quincey indicated, "this was the other plan."

De Quincey had taken the lantern from its hook in the wagon and held it as if to throw it from the wagon.

"The crash when it landed and the explosion of flames might have confused them enough for you to escape into the fog."

"But what about the two of *you? The mob would have turned on *you.*"

"A short, elderly man and a young woman?" De Quincey shrugged. "We were prepared to claim to be your prisoners. Not even drunkards would have thought we were dangerous."

"But you are," Becker said, studying them with admiration. "You're two of the most dangerous people I ever met."

THE RUMBLE OF THE MOB in front of the tavern made Ryan tell the driver to stop. After Becker, De Quincey, and Emily dismounted from the wagon, he asked two constables to escort them through the crowd.

But the crowd had little respect for constables and made way with barely controlled hostility.

"Brilliant," De Quincey murmured.

"What are you talking about?" Ryan asked.

"First, the killer tricked them into attacking every sailor they could find. Then he made them believe that a policeman, *any* policeman, is the killer. They trust no one and suspect everyone. Brilliant."

"Forgive me if I don't share your enthusiasm."

The group reached the tavern, where two nervous constables stood guard.

"Glad you're here, Inspector."

"Yes, it appears you can use plenty of help."

"For certain, there aren't enough of us," the other policeman agreed.

Ryan turned to Emily. "There are eight corpses inside. I can't leave you out here with this mob. Tell me what to do with you."

"I'll shield my eyes. Constable Becker can lead me to a corner where I'll look away from the room."

"There's an odor."

"I can bear it if *you* can."

"The conversation will be disagreeable."

"More disagreeable than the conversations I've already heard? That is difficult to imagine."

"Becker..."

"I'll take care of her."

The group entered the tavern.

There was indeed an odor. Of bodily fluids and the beginning of decay.

As Becker escorted Emily to a table on the right, Ryan gestured for De Quincey to offer his opinions.

But De Quincey barely looked at the carnage. He walked deeper into the tavern, sidestepped blood, and reached the entrance that led behind the counter. He seemed oblivious to the tavernkeeper slumped forward as if asleep. His total attention was devoted to the shelves behind the counter.

"It's here. I *know* it is."

He scanned bottles of gin and wine. He searched behind rows of glasses. He stooped, inspecting the area around the beer kegs.

"It *must* be."

Desperation made De Quincey move faster, his short figure pacing back and forth behind the counter. Only his shoulders and head showed above it. He barely glanced down to make sure that he didn't step in blood.

"Where in God's name...? There!"

Like an animal that had found its prey, he pounced toward a shelf under the far end of the counter. He disappeared from Ryan's view. Then he rose, holding a decanter filled with ruby-colored liquid. He grabbed a wineglass and filled it with the liquid. Hand shaking, he raised the liquid to his lips, fearful that he might spill some of it, and took a deep swallow.

Another.

A third.

Ryan watched in shock. A stranger might have thought that De Quincey was drinking wine, but Ryan had no doubt that this was laudanum. One swallow would have made most people unconscious. Two swallows would have killed them. But De Quincey had just consumed three, and now he drank a *fourth*, finishing the glass!

De Quincey stood as if paralyzed behind the counter. His empty gaze was directed past corpses drooped over a table, centering on the fireplace in the back corner, where chunks of coal smoldered.

But De Quincey didn't appear to see that fireplace. Instead his blue eyes seemed to stare at something far away. They became blank.

The moment lengthened.

"Father?" Emily asked from the front corner, her back turned to the room, unable to see him. "You are very quiet. Are you all right?"

"I'm fine now, Emily."

"Father..."

"Really, I'm fine."

But despite his assurance, De Quincey continued staring intensely at something far away in the fireplace.

At once his eyes gained focus. Darkness in them lightened. His face became less pale. His forehead acquired a glistening sheen.

He stopped shaking.

He breathed.

"Inspector Ryan, I don't suppose you've read Immanuel Kant."

The statement was so surprising, seeming to come out of nowhere, that Ryan needed a moment before reacting. "That's correct." Pride made him refrain from adding, *I've never heard of him.*

De Quincey breathed again and slowly withdrew his gaze from the fireplace.

He set down the empty glass and surveyed the room as if seeing the corpses for the first time.

"Yes, that's understandable. Since Kant wrote in German, his works can be difficult to find in London. I translated several of his essays. I shall send you some. May I touch the corpses?"

As with so much of what De Quincey said, the request suddenly seemed to be the most normal in the world. "If you think it's necessary."

"I do."

De Quincey stepped toward the tavernkeeper slumped over the counter.

"If not for the blood, it would seem that he had worked too many hours or else had overindulged on gin and fallen asleep."

"That is the appearance," Ryan agreed.

"Until I attempt to rouse him."

De Quincey grasped the sides of the tavernkeeper's head and lifted, exposing a neck that had been so torn open by the ripping chisel on the counter that the larynx was exposed. Bone grated.

"Oh…"

"Yes," Ryan said. "Oh."

De Quincey pulled the body back a little farther, inspecting the tavernkeeper's apron, which covered his chest to his neck. Formerly white, it was splattered with blood.

"The pattern is impressive. If it's possible to create art by randomly throwing paint or in this case blood at a canvas, this is a fine example."

"You are deranged," Ryan decided.

De Quincey seemed not to have heard. "The ripping chisel on the counter has blood on its hook. A similar weapon was used in the second Ratcliffe Highway murders. The killer left it behind forty-three years ago just as he did now."

"Yes, you mention that in 'Murder as a Fine Art.' Again, the killer used your essay as his guide."

"Emily, does this conversation distress you?" De Quincey asked.

"I would prefer to be at home in Edinburgh," she answered with her back to him, her voice rebounding into the room.

"I, too, my dear. I can't wait to return home and resume avoiding debt collectors. They no longer seem a pack of Furies. Would a handkerchief soaked with wine help to conceal the odor if you breathed through it?"

"Anything would help, Father."

De Quincey pulled a handkerchief from a pocket, found an open bottle of wine, soaked the cloth, and offered it to Ryan.

"I'll get it," Becker said. He came over and took the handkerchief back to Emily.

Staring toward the corner wall, she raised the handkerchief to her face. Her voice was muffled. "Thank you."

"To return to Kant," De Quincey said.

"By all means." Ryan sighed. "It's not as if we have anything more important to consider."

"The philosopher raised the question of whether reality exists objectively or whether it is a subjective projection of our thoughts."

"I haven't the faintest idea of what you mean."

"You will."

De Quincey made his way along the counter and moved around it into the room. He examined the two dead customers who were propped across the counter.

He turned toward the table near the fireplace, where three more customers and a barmaid were slumped as if asleep. A plate of blood-specked bread and cheese was next to them. He pulled back the barmaid's head and assessed the blood on her previously white apron. He moved toward the final corpse, a constable, who lay across another table, a teacup in his hand.

"Magnificent. Weary customers in a tavern at the end of the day. Their elixir has made them so peaceful that they fell asleep. The blood is a discordant element, but art should have contrast. And of course there's the further discordant element of what I discovered when I lifted their heads. No longer the neat slits created by a razor. Now the damage amounts to mutilation. Extreme violence beneath apparent peace. A fine art."

Ryan muttered something indelicate, adding, "You haven't said anything that will help me catch the madman who did this."

"You think a madman did this, Inspector Ryan?"

"That's obvious. No money was taken. The violence was unthinkable."

"My brother William was so unmanageable that my parents sent him away to live at a private school."

"I don't see the relevance. The laudanum has made you incoherent."

"After my father's early death, my mother brought William home to Manchester in the hopes that he had improved. Her hopes were ill-founded. He was a restless bully, constantly inventing new preposterous schemes in which the rest of us were forced to participate. He gave nonsensical lectures to which we had to submit. He compelled us to perform in plays that featured violence he inflicted on us. He invented imaginary countries that he and I separately controlled, but he was always expanding his country until he overran mine and destroyed it. He tortured cats by tying sheets to them and throwing them off the roof to see if he could make a parachute. I lived in fear every day."

"What does this have to do with—"

"Eventually William's violent behavior became so extreme that my mother again sent him off. I have seldom felt more liberated than the day he was put in a carriage and taken away. I have often wondered what horrid crimes he might have committed if he hadn't died from typhus when he was sixteen."

De Quincey turned from the corpses and faced Ryan. "An odd thing occurred almost at the same moment that my brother was taken away to London. A dog ran to our closed front gate. Then it ran along the edge of the property. Curious about the animal's unusual appearance, I followed its progress. A brook formed the boundary of our property—a good thing because the water prevented the dog from attacking me. I looked searchingly into its eyes and observed that they were glazed as in a dream but at the same time suffused with a watery discharge, while its mouth was covered with masses of white foam."

"The dog was mad," Ryan concluded.

"Precisely. A rabid dog's hatred of water is all that prevented it from attacking me. Some men came running along the road in pursuit of the dog. It raced ahead of them, but eventually the men returned, saying that they had caught it and killed it. I learned later that the dog had bitten two horses in the village and that one of them succumbed to rabies. Inspector, do you believe that a madman killed these people, a rabid human, responding to irresistible, uncontrollable impulses?"

"How else can so much violence be explained?" Ryan demanded.

"If the killer's impulses were uncontrolled, how do you account for the careful arrangement of the bodies? On Saturday night, he hid the corpses behind a counter or behind doors so that whoever discovered them would receive a series of shocking revelations. In this case, he practiced concealment in another fashion, by making the corpses appear to be asleep, their slumping posture hiding the terrible disfigurement to their throats, providing a surprise for each viewer who looks closer. Even though a constable stood watch beneath a streetlamp outside, the murderer risked taking the time to arrange his artwork. These are not the acts of an uncontrolled man."

"For a change, I follow your logic."

"Immanuel Kant asked the question, Does reality exist objectively, or is it a subjective projection of our thoughts?"

"And again you've lost me."

"Inspector Ryan, when you look at the stars, where are they in relation to you?"

"Pardon me?"

"Are they above you, for example?"

"Of course."

"But the earth is a globe, is it not? London is not at the northern pole. It is located approximately one third down the sphere. We stand more or less sideways. The force of gravity keeps us from spinning off into space."

Ryan looked as if he had another headache. "Yes, the earth is a globe, so logically we do stand sideways on it. But it always *appears* that we're on the top."

"Inspector, I don't believe that Kant himself could have been so eloquent. It does in fact *appear* that we are on top of the earth, even though we are on its side. We act upon assumptions that control our view of reality, even though reality might be quite different. Tell me what it would feel like if you were at the bottom of the earth, gazing at the stars."

"In that event…" Ryan looked uncomfortable. "By your logic, I would be upside down, dangling by my feet, staring…" The inspector swallowed. "Down."

"With all of vast space below you, stretching toward infinity."

"The thought makes me dizzy."

"As does the true reality before us. We encounter violence of this magnitude and we are tempted to react automatically by stating that only a madman could have done this. Someone irrational, uncontrolled, obeying savage impulses. But what we see does not match that idea. Eight people in one room. The killer dispatches them before any of the victims, even the constable, has a chance to fight back."

De Quincey gestured toward the murder scene.

"The constable was nearest the door as the killer entered, so this man needed to be dealt with first, then the three men at the table near the fireplace, then the barmaid, then the two customers at the counter, and finally the tavernkeeper behind it."

De Quincey walked through the room and pretended to swing a murder weapon toward each victim.

"How many seconds did I require to do that, Inspector?"

"Perhaps ten."

"But it must have been done in far less time than that. Otherwise at least one of the victims would have been able to shout for help. These murders were committed rapidly and without hesitation. With artistry and precision. There is only one way to become this adept. With practice. This was not the killer's first experience with inflicting death."

"You're telling me he did this before, and not just on Saturday night?"

"To accomplish this task, he must have killed many people many times before."

"Impossible. Surely I would have heard. Even if the crimes were committed far from London, news about the atrocities would have spread."

"The news did spread. You read about these deaths every day in the newspapers, except that they aren't referred to as crimes."

"Becker, does any of this make sense to you?" Ryan demanded. "Multiple murders that aren't called crimes?"

"The killings aren't even called murders," De Quincey elaborated.

"Becker?" Ryan pleaded.

"I have a suspicion where he's going."

"And?"

"I don't want to follow his logic. It's unthinkable."

"That's my point," De Quincey continued. "By definition, what is unthinkable isn't part of our reality. Inspector, your assumptions about what is possible prevent you from accurately seeing the reality before you."

Becker interrupted, walking toward Ryan. "Remember the bootprints behind the shop? They didn't have hobnails, suggesting that the murderer was someone of education and means, not a laborer. The expensive razor suggested the same thing."

"I proposed that idea to Lord Palmerston," Ryan insisted. "He thoroughly rejected it. He told me that a man of education and means couldn't possibly be capable of savagery."

"Lord Palmerston is wrong, of course," De Quincey said. "It happens every day."

"Not that I'm aware of," Ryan objected. "Bankers, owners of corporations, and members of Parliament do not go about bashing heads and gashing throats."

"Perhaps metaphorically they do," De Quincey said.

"What?"

"Never mind. I agree. These murders weren't committed by a banker, an owner of a corporation, or a member of Parliament. But imagine a context in which killings are not called murders."

"Perhaps if I swallowed some of that laudanum, I would understand."

"The killer is practiced at his art. He has killed many times before. He is comfortable using disguises. He speaks a language that the Malay who delivered the message last night would understand. Those pieces of information narrow the range of suspects considerably."

"The Malay. You're suggesting that the killer has been to the Orient and speaks some of its languages?"

"Yes."

"Experience in disguises suggests a criminal," Ryan continued.

"Or someone who wishes to blend with criminals and defeat them. You, for example, dress in disguise" — De Quincey indicated Ryan's shapeless, common clothes — "in order to blend with lower elements."

"I should be looking for a detective who worked in the Orient?" Ryan asked in confusion.

"Not a detective. In the Orient, who else serves as a law enforcer? In India, for example, where cults are notorious for their disguises?"

Ryan looked baffled. But then as his thoughts seemed to click together, his eyes displayed sudden clarity.

"A soldier."

"Yes. A soldier. A man trained to kill without hesitation. A man who had many opportunities to practice his craft in the Orient, learning some of its languages. But when he killed, it wasn't called a crime. It was called heroism. And he wasn't just any soldier. The man we're looking for had duties that required disguises."

"A soldier." Ryan sounded breathless. "I do indeed feel like I'm dangling by my feet from the bottom of the earth."

12

The Education of an Artist

THE ARTIST OF DEATH locked his bedroom door and placed crumpled newspapers on the floor. Anyone who improbably gained access to the room would brush against those papers. The noise would prompt the artist to roll from his cot while drawing a knife from a sheath strapped to his arm.

The cot was identical to one he had used in India. After enduring his nightly penance, he lay on the cot and hoped that he would not suffer his usual nightmares. Although the bedroom had a fireplace, he never burned anything in it, wanting winter's chill to be another penance, just as he never opened windows during summer's sultry nights, refusing to allow a breeze to cool his sweat.

India's mountains had been bitterly, bone-achingly cold, while its lowlands had been oppressively, smotheringly hot.

Twenty years of cold and heat.

Of death.

Of the British East India Company.

"Two hundred years it's been here," a sergeant had told the artist's unit when they arrived in Calcutta in 1830. "The British East India Company claims its profit comes from shipping tea, silk, and spices back home. And the niter that's the main ingredient in saltpeter. Can't have an empire without saltpeter. You!" The sergeant challenged one of the new arrivals. "What's it used for?"

"My mother used it for pickling, Sergeant."

"You idiot, pickles don't make an empire great. Saltpeter along with sulfur and powdered charcoal gives you what?"

"Gunpowder, Sergeant," the artist of death volunteered, standing at attention under the furnace of the sun.

He was eighteen. He had been in the army from when, as a tall twelve-year-old, he had walked into a London enlistment center and claimed to be fourteen. That had made him eligible for what was called boy service, first as a courier and later as a hospital helper. He preferred the hospital because while he hurried bandages to male nurses or took away slop pails, he had the chance to study the pain of injured soldiers. At the age of seventeen, he had officially become part of the regiment, but the daily routine of marches and maintenance had bored him after the fascination of the agony he saw in the hospital. Because enlistment was for a minimum of twenty-one years, the only way the artist could leave the army was by deserting, but given that the police were already looking for him, he didn't see any point in having the army search for him also. When news spread that the regiment was sailing to India, the artist pretended to share the concern of others about yellow fever and murderous natives, but in truth the prospects made him feel overjoyed.

"Gunpowder. Yes. Very good, laddie." The sergeant looked at the artist of death as if he meant the compliment. His sun-browned and -creased face suggested that the sergeant had been in India forever. The cynical tone with which he delivered the briefing implied that he'd given it more times than he cared to recall.

"Gunpowder," the sergeant emphasized. "The empire can't very well carry on its wars unless it has saltpeter to make gunpowder, right? And India has the greatest reserves of saltpeter ingredients on the planet."

The sun was so fierce that as the artist of death stood at attention with the other arrivals, he stopped sweating. His vision paled. Spots wavered before his eyes.

"But saltpeter, tea, silk, and spices aren't why we're here to help the

British East India Company do business, laddies. The reason we're here is this little beauty."

The sergeant held up a pale bulb. "This is the head of a poppy plant."

He used a knife to cut the bulb. "And this white fluid seeping out is called opium. It dries to a brown color. When it's powdered, you can smoke it, eat it, drink it, or inhale it to make you think you're in the clouds. I don't doubt one day somebody'll figure out how to stick it directly into your veins. But if you value your life, do not—I repeat do not—*ever*—use this stuff. Not because it can kill you if you take too much, and too much is only a little. No, if I catch you using this devil, *I'll* be the one who kills you. I can't depend on someone whose mind drifts into the clouds. The natives hate us. If they get the chance, they'll turn against us. When the shooting starts, I want to know that the men I'm fighting with are focused on their business and not on swirling dervishes. Do I make myself clear? You! What did I just say?"

The sergeant spoke challengingly to the artist, who fought to clear the spots from in front of his eyes.

"Sergeant, you said don't use opium! Ever!" the artist responded.

"You'll go far, laddie. Not once, everybody! Oh, you'll be tempted to learn what the talk's all about! You'll want to ride the clouds! Resist that temptation, because I swear, before I kill you for using it, I'll break every bone in your body! Everybody, am I clear about that? Do not let this devil tempt you!"

"Yes, Sergeant."

"Louder!"

"Yes, Sergeant!"

"I CAN'T HEAR YOU!"

"YES, SERGEANT!"

"Good. To give you an idea of the disgusting depths into which opium can lead, I want each of you to read this piece of filth that I'm holding. This foul book is called *Confessions of an English Opium-Eater*. Its author is a degenerate named Thomas De Quincey. Those of you who can't read will listen to someone read it out loud. You," the sergeant challenged the artist. "Can you read?"

"Yes, Sergeant!"

"Then make certain these other men know what's in this perverted dung heap of a book!"

"Yes, Sergeant!"

The sergeant dropped the poppy bulb and crushed it with his boot, making a dramatic show of grinding its white fluid into the dirt.

"Now let me tell all of you how the British East India Company works and why you're risking your life for it. The company has plenty of opium from here in India, but it earns more profit from the tea in China. So which makes more sense? Does the company sell the lower-priced opium at home in England and then bring back the money to buy the higher-priced tea in China? Or does it save itself the trouble and keep much of the opium right here, trading it to the Chinese in exchange for tea? Tell me!" the sergeant demanded from the artist as more spots wavered in front of his eyes.

"Trade the opium for the Chinese tea, Sergeant!" the artist of death answered.

"You really show promise, laddie. Exactly. The British East India Company trades the opium for the Chinese tea. There's only one small problem in this scheme. Opium happens to be illegal in China. The Chinese emperor isn't eager for his millions of subjects to become opium degenerates. Imagine the emperor's nerve standing up to the British East India Company and by extension the British Empire. By the way, did I explain that it's very difficult to tell the difference between our government and the British East India Company?"

"You didn't, Sergeant!" the artist replied. "But we wish to know!"

"You'll be a corporal in a couple of weeks, laddie. Everybody, pay attention. All the empire's wars need financing, and we have the British East India Company to thank for making them possible. It lent the British government millions of pounds to finance the Seven Years' War alone. Generous, don't you think? But then, in exchange, the government gave the British East India Company the exclusive right to trade with India and China. It's no coincidence that the chairman of the company's board of directors is the British government's foreign secretary. The result of this cozy arrangement is that when you protect the British East India Company, you protect the British government. Keep that thought foremost in your minds and you'll never wonder why we're here."

A recruit toppled, a victim of the sun.

Two other arrivals stooped to help him.

"Did I say you could move?" the sergeant demanded. "Leave him alone! Both of you remain at attention for an hour after everyone else is dismissed!"

The sergeant walked up and down the line, glaring at all of them. In the background, two elephants used their trunks to carry logs to a construction site. The artist feared that he was going insane.

The sergeant confronted the artist.

"If opium is illegal in China but if the British East India Company wants to trade its opium for Chinese tea, how can that transaction be managed?"

The artist thought carefully, fighting his heat sickness. "By smuggling the opium into China, Sergeant!"

"I hereby officially promote you to corporal. See that you punish the two men who broke ranks just now. Yes, the opium is smuggled into China. That is accomplished via ships to Hong Kong or via caravan through India's northern mountains. When you men aren't making sure the natives don't rebel against us, you'll guard the opium as it's loaded onto ships and caravan wagons. It's a busy life here, laddies, provided you don't weaken the way *that* man did."

The sergeant pointed toward the man who'd collapsed.

"Is he dead?"

"I think so, Sergeant," a recruit answered.

"Well, what doesn't kill us makes us strong."

COUNTLESS OPIUM BRICKS, the color of coffee, awaited shipment to China or else home to England, there to be blended with alcohol and made into laudanum. All the warehouses had a faint biting odor of the slaked lime that was part of the water solution in which the opium paste was first boiled.

The artist became very familiar with that odor because his first assignment in India was to guard those warehouses. Each night, he and other sentries patrolled the walkways between the buildings. Ignoring the bites of insects, he focused on the shadows ahead, aware that the insects, even if they infected him, would be nothing compared to the anger of the sergeant if someone broke into the warehouses and stole any of the opium.

A slight scraping noise made him pause.

When a shadow scurried from a warehouse, he raised his rifle.

"Stop!"

The shadow ducked behind some crates.

The artist stepped closer, aiming. "Identify yourself!"

"I know that voice. Is it *you*, Corporal?" a man whispered.

"Step out!"

"Thank God. We thought you was the sergeant. Keep your voice down."

Figures emerged from behind the crates, three privates with whom the artist had sailed to India.

"We was just grabbin' a brick." One of them grinned. "Reckoned we'd have a smoke before goin' to sleep. This damned heat. These bloody insects. You want some?"

"Put it back in the warehouse."

"You want it all to yourself, eh? Fine. Here it is. We'll walk away. Pretend you never saw us."

"I said, 'Put it back in the warehouse.'"

"And then what?"

The artist didn't answer.

"You're not gonna turn us in, are you?"

The artist kept aiming.

"Damn it, the bastard's gonna turn us in!"

When they lunged, the artist shot the first man in the chest. Pivoting with the rifle, he drove his bayonet into the second man.

The third man crashed into him, knocking him against crates. The man thrust a knife at him. Twisting to avoid it, the artist grabbed the man's hand and bent it, forcing him to drop the knife. Ramming his elbow into the man's throat, he heard something crack.

The man sank, clutching his throat, gasping for air.

Voices and footsteps raced toward the artist. Soldiers surrounded him.

"My God," one of them said, holding a lantern over the bodies.

"Who fired that shot?" The sergeant pushed his way forward. "What happened?"

"That opium brick," the artist explained. "I caught them stealing it from the warehouse."

"So you killed them?" the sergeant asked in surprise.

"Those were your orders."

"Yes, those were indeed my orders."

"Plus, they tried to kill me."

"Three," a soldier said in the background. "He killed all three."

"Not only three, but three of your own." The sergeant studied him. "It's easy to kill natives. But three of your own? Did you ever kill anybody before?"

"No," the artist lied.

"Someone else might have hesitated."

"Sergeant, I didn't have time to think."

"Sometimes not thinking is good. There's someone I want you to talk to."

IGNORE MY RANK. No need to address me as 'sir,'" the major said. "Tell me about your father."

"Didn't know him. My mother wasn't married. When I was four, she met a former soldier and lived with him."

"Where did he serve?"

"With Wellington at Waterloo."

"You lived with a man who helped make history."

"He never talked about it. He had a big scar on his leg, but he never talked about that, either. Nightmares sometimes woke him."

"My father fought at Waterloo, also," the major confided. "Nightmares woke *him*. The reason I asked is, sometimes it's inherited."

"Inherited?"

"The ability to stare a threat in the face and not flinch. But since you never knew your father, we have no way of telling what you might have inherited from him. The fear of being killed or of killing can paralyze a man. Only twenty percent of our soldiers are able to overcome those fears. The rest provide cover for the actual warriors. It seems that *you* are one of those warriors."

"All I did was defend myself."

"Against three trained men, but you didn't flinch."

Beyond the major's tent, an instructor showed ten soldiers how to tie a knot in a rope to make an effective garrote. The instructor explained that the weapon, a favorite of the Thug cult, crushed the windpipe in addition to strangling.

The artist listened with interest.

"This is a special unit I'm assembling. You speak better than your fellows. Where did you learn?" the major asked.

"Every Sunday in London, I went to a church where a teacher gave me a biscuit if I learned to read Bible verses."

"The Bible says, 'Thou shalt not kill.'"

"There's a lot of killing in the Old Testament."

The major chuckled. "Why did you become a soldier?"

"When I was an infant, my mother carried me on her back while she gathered chunks of coal along the Thames. Until I was nine, I worked for a dustman, collecting ashes. After that, I shoveled horse droppings from the streets and put them in bins for the fertilizer makers to pick up. When I was eleven, I helped clean privies."

"There seems to be a common denominator."

"After a year of digging out privies, I decided that the army couldn't be much worse, so when I was twelve, I claimed to be fourteen and signed up."

The major's eyes crinkled with amusement. "Enterprising. Your mother and the man she lives with, did they approve?"

"They died in a fire long before I was shoveling horseshit."

"I'm sorry about your difficult life. Did you ever consider that you were *meant* to join the army?"

THE HARDSHIPS OF SURVIVING on London's streets had seemed the worst that anyone could endure, but the artist's new training took him far beyond his former ability to withstand fatigue, heat, hunger, thirst, and lack of sleep. The strange part was, he welcomed it. He proudly developed resources of strength and determination that he hadn't imagined were possible. He learned to ignore the threat of pain and death. Fear became an unfamiliar emotion, even as he vowed to make the enemy suffer fear in the extreme.

He was transformed into one of the warriors that the major had spoken about.

He received better food.

His lodgings were less cramped.

He was given respect.

He loved it.

"Your mission is to guard the opium caravans," the major told the artist's elite unit. "The land distance from India to China is less than the sea distance. In theory, the shorter distance should be quicker, but overland has these mountains"—the major tapped a pointer against a map on a wall—"where marauders attack our caravans and steal the opium. We send heavily armed cavalry to protect the caravans. It doesn't matter. The caravans continue to vanish. Tons of opium have been stolen."

The major directed his attention toward the artist. "We believe that the marauders are Thugs. Repeat what we taught you about the Thugs."

The artist responded without hesitation. "Major, they're a criminal cult that worships Kali, the Hindu goddess of death. She's sometimes called the Devourer. That's why she has so many arms in paintings of her. The Thugs specialize in stealing from travelers, usually killing them by strangulation."

"Correct as always," the major said.

The artist kept his face impassive but felt the pleasure of receiving approval.

"The British East India Company wants you to stop them," the major commanded the unit. "No, not merely stop them. Make them understand the unspeakable consequences of challenging the empire."

Forty natives accompanied the caravan. They managed the oxen that pulled the twenty wagons. They herded goats that were used for milk and meat. All were trusted employees of the British East India Company.

Each day, the artist and two members of his unit walked next to the wagons and assessed the behavior of the natives. Each night, they stepped into the dark and studied the camp, looking for secret conversations.

The cavalry escort amounted to forty, its captain sending riders ahead to look for ambushes. Villages became widely separated. As the land rose, trees gave way to grassland and boulders. The higher altitude made the animals and men breathe harder. Streams rushed from the distant mountains, their water so cold that it made the artist's teeth ache.

"Three days to the pass through the mountains," the native guide said.

"Any risk of snow?"

"Not this time of year, but anything is possible."

Indeed anything was possible. Two cavalry outriders galloped back in alarm. The caravan crested a plateau. Ravens and vultures erupted into the air, revealing the remnants of a caravan that had departed two weeks earlier. That caravan had included other members of the artist's unit.

Bones lay everywhere, scattered by predators. The bones of humans only. All the oxen, horses, and goats were missing, as were the wagons and their contents. The bodies had been stripped, no fragments of garments on any of the skeletons.

Portions of foul-smelling flesh remained, but not enough to indicate wounds. None of the bones showed signs of violence from firearms or blades, however. If those weapons had been used, at least some of the bones would surely have displayed damage. That forced the artist to conclude that all eighty-three people in the caravan — cavalry, natives, and three highly trained members of the artist's unit — had been strangled.

"I don't see how this is possible," he told the cavalry commander. "Granted, the natives didn't know how to defend themselves, but our horsemen did, and they had rifles as well as swords. The members of my special unit were even more capable. Nonetheless all of them were overpowered."

The odor of decay was strong enough that the artist and the soldiers worked quickly, handkerchiefs tied over their faces, to collect the bones into a huge pile and cover them with rocks. Normally the races wouldn't have been mingled, but because there wasn't any way to distinguish the bones of natives from those of the English cavalry, it seemed better to group all of them together and be certain that the English received a Christian burial. Prayers were said. The oxen, horses, and goats kept reacting to the smell of death, so to quiet them, the caravan moved a mile ahead, formed a circle, and camped near a stream.

The night sky was brilliant. With so much natural illumination, the wagons were already exposed, so there was no reason not to build cooking fires.

The cavalry commander assigned sentries. As the natives and the soldiers prepared food, the artist and the two members of his unit hoped that so much activity would conceal them from anyone watching. They crawled from camp and established their own sentry posts at three equal compass points, northeast, northwest, and south. They each took a packet of biscuits and a canteen filled with stream water.

Away from the fires, the night was bitterly cold. The artist lay among rocks and used force of will to keep from shivering. *I can withstand anything,* he told himself, remembering the sergeant's words. *What doesn't kill me makes me strong.*

The fires didn't last long, their fuel coming from grass, animal droppings, sparse bushes, and the branches of a solitary, long-dead tree.

The artist kept scanning his surroundings.

A shadow moved among the wagons, perhaps a guard coming back from his watch while another man took his place. A later shadow might have been a native relieving his bladder beyond a wagon.

The camp settled into sleep.

Another shadow appeared, detaching itself from the circle of wagons. Close to the ground, it came in the artist's direction.

As the artist drew his knife, the moon cast a shadow of someone behind him.

The artist rolled an instant before a figure leapt toward him. The moon's illumination was enough to reveal that the figure had a rope with a knot in it and that the figure looped it over where the artist's throat had been. The artist stabbed him, stifling his moans. He surged up to meet the second figure, surprising him, thrusting under his rib cage while pressing a hand against his mouth.

The artist didn't allow himself even a moment to exult in his victory.

What he felt now were the tightened nerves and compacted muscles of an animal confronted by an enemy. Something terrible was happening to the camp, and he had the even more terrible sense that he might not be able to stop it.

He crawled silently in that direction, then stopped as he realized that just as he had seen the shadow crawl toward him, so an enemy in the camp could see him approaching. That shadow had been a decoy, drawing his attention while the true assassin had come from behind him.

Are there others behind me? he thought.

He hugged the ground, trying to assess which direction posed the greater threat. Three clangs from an oxen bell puzzled him. Soon, he noticed silhouettes moving among the wagons. They bent and tugged at various objects. His stomach hardened when he realized what they were doing — stripping clothes from corpses. The silhouettes put the clothes in the wagons, along with various objects that had been unpacked to prepare the night's meal. They hitched the oxen to the wagons. They herded the goats together and tied the horses to the backs of the wagons.

The artist had no doubt that everyone in the camp was dead.

He had no doubt about something else as well. The silhouettes moving among the wagons would soon want to know why the two men sent to kill him hadn't returned.

He crawled away from the camp, scanning the horizon for threats. The two members of his unit who had established their own sentry posts — had they possibly survived? When he judged that he was far enough away, he moved in a circle, searching for where the other men had taken their positions.

Now he again saw moving shadows — two silhouettes tugging clothes from a body that could only belong to one of his comrades.

Loyalty fought against common sense. So far, he had counted at least twenty silhouettes. He knew that one man in his special unit was dead. What were the odds that the other man had survived? If so, what would that man decide to do? There was no way to save the caravan. The mission now became to determine how the caravan had been overwhelmed and to pass that information to the next caravan that would come through here in two weeks.

The artist knew that his comrade wouldn't be foolhardy. If the man was alive, he would back away and hide, as the artist now planned to do. They were trained to be self-reliant. They would survive to defeat this enemy another day.

Hide? Where? The landscape was barren, except for boulders and the stream. Using the cavalry horses, the marauders who overwhelmed the caravan would easily be able to search the area for miles in every direction.

The artist made a wide semicircle. Staying low, he retraced the route that the caravan had used to arrive here. He didn't know if the attackers had the skill to follow his tracks. To eliminate the risk, he walked backward where the animals and wagons had crushed grass and torn up the ground.

A glow over the eastern hills warned that the sun would soon rise. No matter how low he stayed as he ran, he would soon be visible. Horsemen could easily catch him. He needed to conceal himself.

He suddenly realized where he was—near the mound that contained the bones of the previous caravan. As the light increased, the artist sprinted toward the rocks, removed some, made a tunnel among the bones, crawled in, pulled the rocks back into place, and arranged the bones so that they concealed him.

The stench of the rotting flesh made him vomit the biscuits he'd eaten while watching the caravan. Willpower wasn't enough to keep him from throwing up. The odor was so disgusting and visceral that his body took charge. Buried by death, he fought not to shiver from the cold of the rib cages and skulls above and below him and all around him. Tense, he listened for the sound of approaching horses and voices.

They came soon. Although the artist didn't understand their language, their tone was urgent and angry. Evidently the marauders had found the bodies of the men who had tried to kill him. They knew that at least one member of the caravan remained alive, and they were determined to find him.

The majority of the horses galloped past. Some did not, however. The artist heard the animals shy from the stench, making it difficult for their riders to control them. Someone seemed to suggest that they pull the rocks off the mound and search through the bones. The others protested in disgust. The horses became more upset.

The horsemen finally galloped on, following the caravan's tracks down the slope. The artist assumed that other searchers pursued in other directions.

Feeling crushed by the bones, he took shallow breaths, working to control his nausea. His muscles ached from tension and cramps because of not being able to move.

He thought about the knotted rope with which an attacker had tried to strangle him. The weapon was favored by the Thug cult. But that didn't explain how they'd been able to overwhelm forty cavalry soldiers, forty natives, and one, if not two, members of his highly trained unit. Surely one of the soldiers could have fired a shot before being strangled, or else one of the natives would have cried in alarm. But all of them had died silently.

How was that possible?

The artist lay among the bones, shivering and brooding, trying to understand how the attack had occurred. Presumably the Thugs had watched from a distance and approached the wagons after dark.

But how had they soundlessly overwhelmed so many so quickly? Had some of the natives rebelled? But those natives had worked for the British East India Company many years. Why would they suddenly have become traitors?

The artist's mind retraced the route of the caravan. At one point, they had allowed a one-legged old man to join them so that he could travel to reach his son's family in a mountain village. Later, a wizened grandmother with a little girl had also joined the caravan. The little girl had needed a doctor's attention, and now they were returning home.

The artist had objected, but the natives had told him that it was customary to allow the helpless to join a caravan, and after all, how could a one-legged old man, a wizened grandmother, and a little girl be threats?

Rethinking the decision to let them come along, the artist couldn't disagree with that logic. There was no way that those weak people could have overcome so many natives and soldiers.

That took him back to his initial thought, that some of the natives had betrayed the caravan.

The vibration of hooves brought his mind to attention. He heard the rumble coming closer. Returning, the attackers sounded even more angry and frustrated. How he wished that he could understand what they were saying. Had they decided to stop hunting him? What were their plans? If he survived, he swore, he would learn as many local languages as he could.

They galloped back in the direction of the wagons. Soon, the artist heard the distant clatter of the caravan departing. Wary, he didn't move. Even after he could no longer hear the animals and wagons, he didn't move. Someone might have been left behind to study the landscape and see if he crept from cover.

The morning became silent. His arms and legs demanded to be allowed to move, but he remained immobile beneath the cold bones and the heavy rocks. The small amount of sunlight that reached him changed direction as morning turned to afternoon.

But he didn't move. He occupied his mind by trying to understand how the caravan had been overwhelmed.

The specks of light dimmed as the sun changed direction, afternoon turning to twilight.

Then everything was dark.

The artist had long since urinated on himself. His mouth was so dry that his tongue stuck to the roof of his mouth.

He remained in place.

When he realized that despite his discipline and determination, he had fallen asleep, he bit his lower lip, drawing blood to rouse himself, and decided that if he didn't take the chance of leaving his burrow he might lapse into unconsciousness there.

Slowly, silently, he pushed rocks away from the bones. His arms didn't want to work. With small, careful movements, he emerged from the massive grave, but no matter how deeply he breathed, he couldn't clear the odor of decay.

The night sky was again brilliant. Crawling so slowly that he hoped his movements would be imperceptible, the artist moved toward the stream. He plunged his head into it, the icy water shocking him into alertness. Like an animal, he looked cautiously around to make certain that he wasn't being stalked. He took a deep swallow. Another. And another. The cold water pained his tongue and throat, and made him more alert.

Scanning the area for moving shadows, he reached into his pockets and nibbled the remainder of the biscuits that he had taken with him the night before. His stomach protested, but he forced down the food, needing strength.

The departing wagons had gone to the west. His own direction needed to be southeast, toward the caravan that would reach this area in two weeks. Staying low, he followed the stream down the slope.

And stopped.

The bodies of the soldiers and natives he had traveled with beckoned him. As much as he wanted to leave, the dead men insisted. He hadn't been able to protect the caravan. That left him with the obligation of learning how so many men had been overwhelmed.

Mustering grim resolve, he turned and approached where the wagons had stopped the previous night. He was ready with his knife, expecting that at any moment a shadow would attack him. In the moonlight, he saw long objects on the ground. Some were pale.

They were bodies stripped of their clothing. Vultures had torn off parts of them. A wolf raised its head from eating, sensed how dangerous the artist was, and skulked away.

Perhaps one of the attackers had remained and pretended to be a corpse. The artist doubted it. The night was so cold that he couldn't imagine anyone being able to lie naked on the ground for hour after hour.

He would know soon enough. Ready to defend himself, he examined each body, eighty of them, plus his two comrades whose bodies he discovered at their sentry positions.

Eighty-two.

He assumed that the raiders would have taken the bodies of the two men who'd attacked him. But even so, there should have been eighty-five corpses, including the one-legged old man, the wizened grandmother, and the little girl. The latter three were nowhere to be found.

They'd been Thugs.

But it didn't make sense. How could a crippled old man, a bent-forward grandmother, and a little girl have silently overpowered so many people, including soldiers with combat experience?

The beginning odor of death hung over the moonlit field as the artist inspected the corpses to determine what had killed them. But in only two cases was the cause of death obvious—his two compatriots all had marks on their throats that indicated they'd been strangled. As for the others, except for what the wolves and the vultures had started to do, there weren't any injuries.

How is this possible? It's almost as if eighty people fell asleep and never woke up.

Fell asleep? At once, the artist understood what had happened. The crippled old man, the wizened grandmother, and the little girl had poisoned the food that was being prepared, probably adding powder to the pots of water that were boiled for tea. They must have been trained to do it so they wouldn't be noticed. After the poison had its effect, they had rung the oxen bell three times, signaling for the rest of their band to enter the camp and collect their spoils. The only reason that the artist and his two comrades hadn't been poisoned was that they'd put biscuits in their pockets and left while the meal was being prepared, wanting to use the activity in camp to conceal their stealthy movements as they chose their sentry positions.

Poison.

Yes.

The artist crept from the field of death. He ran southeast in a crouch for several miles, then felt safe enough to straighten. By then, the sun was up, adding its warmth to the heat generated by his urgency. Eventually he was forced to moderate his pace, eating a few biscuits from his pockets as he moved. Soon he ran again. When he slept, it was only briefly. At all costs, he needed to reach the next caravan. He couldn't take for granted that the Thugs would wait until the caravan reached this area. They might change their tactics and attack earlier.

He pushed himself to his limit. On the second day, he reached a farm, where he paid for food and a robe. All the while, he kept his wary attention on the farmer and his family, suspecting they might be Thugs.

He hurried on, watching for anyone who might follow him from the farm. He reached a village, but instead of entering, he veered around it during the night, suspicious that Thugs might live there. He descended relentlessly.

On the seventh day, he staggered across a field and found the next caravan. By then, he looked so haggard, windburned, and wild that a cavalry patrol challenged him, believing him to be a native.

"English," he managed to say past his swollen tongue as they aimed rifles at him.

"That's right. We're English. Put your hands in the air."

"No, *I'm* English." His raw throat made his speech indistinct.

"The beggar can barely talk. Search him for weapons."

"Wait. I think I recognize him. Robert? Is that you, Robert?"

The artist strained to get the words out. "You're Jack Gordon."

"It *is* Robert! I trained with him! He's part of my unit!"

"You're . . . attacked."

"I can't understand what you're saying, Robert. Drink this water."

"You're going to be attacked."

Gulping from a canteen, the artist staggered along the caravan. He suddenly pointed at the same one-legged old man, wizened grandmother, and little girl who had joined his own caravan. After soldiers grabbed them, a search revealed that the man was neither old nor one-legged. Makeup made him look elderly. The seemingly absent leg was bent back and up from the knee, strapped in place beneath his robe.

The stooped, wizened grandmother turned out to be a middle-aged woman of excellent strength. As with the old man, makeup had aged her. The little girl was indeed a little girl, but she was so well trained that she might as well have been an adult. A bag of poison was under her robe.

The artist rested only briefly, then tortured the captives, wishing that he didn't need to rely on a native translator. Again, he vowed to learn the area's languages. He confirmed the signal the Thugs used to tell the rest of the band that everyone in camp was dead from the poison: three clangs from an oxen bell.

Where would the next attack occur?

They resisted telling him.

He inflicted more pain. The little girl finally couldn't bear it any longer and revealed everything.

He shot them.

The caravan reached the area where the attack was supposed to occur. They formed the wagons in a circle for the night, took care of the animals, made an evening meal, and pretended to go to sleep, presumably to die from the poison. The artist rang the oxen bell.

When twenty Thugs snuck through the darkness, the artist killed five of them himself while the rest of the command took care of the others. He made sure that one Thug was kept alive, and promised to set him free if the Thug would teach him the cult's methods of disguise. The captive endured unimaginable pain before he finally revealed secret after secret: about makeup, about blackening teeth to make it seem that some were missing, about applying wigs and fake beards and thickening eyebrows, about putting a pebble in a shoe to create a convincing limp. The Thug also revealed various places where his band of marauders camped.

When the Thug no longer had things to teach, the artist shot him.

The artist led cavalry to the various Thug campgrounds, destroying everyone there: men, women, and children.

He was promoted to second lieutenant. Most officers were gentlemen of means who paid to be given authority in the military, sometimes with disastrous results. But the artist received his commission based on merit and reputation.

Soon he was a full lieutenant.

The Opium War with China provided even more reasons for him to be promoted. The English government was determined to earn millions of pounds by flooding China with opium. The Chinese emperor was determined to prevent his millions of subjects from becoming mindless. Thus, there needed to be a war that lasted four brutal years, from 1839 to 1842, and the artist needed to kill increasing numbers of people.

Opium. The lime odor of the countless bricks of it stacked in warehouses made him nauseous. Even the coffee-colored look of the drug affected his stomach. He could no longer drink coffee because of that color. Or tea — after all, tea was what the opium bricks were traded for. He drank increasing quantities of alcohol, however.

Nightmares woke him, images of bones and corpses swirling as if he were under opium's influence. The faces of his victims resembled poppy bulbs that exploded with white fluid gushing from them instead of blood.

A loud noise shocked the artist out of his night terror. He pulled the knife from the scabbard on his wrist, tumbled from his cot, and braced himself for an attack.

The loud noise was repeated.

Someone was outside on the street, pounding on the door.

With visions of the hell of India still turning in his mind, the artist crept around the cot, stepped over the crumpled newspapers, and approached the small window to his bedroom, so small that not even a child could squeeze through it. The window had bars as a further protection.

The artist pulled a curtain aside and saw darkness beyond the glass. As the pounding on the door continued, he unbolted the window, swung it out, and peered down toward a fog-shrouded man standing under a gas lamp.

"What do you want?" the artist shouted.

"You've been summoned!"

13

The Inquisition

FOG SWIRLED ON THE STREET known as Great Scotland Yard. Eager to escape the cold, a constable opened a door marked METROPOLITAN POLICE and entered a corridor lit by gas lamps mounted along the wall. He took off his gloves and rubbed his hands together.

On his left, an elderly woman slumped on a bench, with her head tilted back against the wall. Her eyes were shut, her mouth open. The constable peered close, thinking she might be dead. Then he noticed a slight movement of her chest.

She had a faded burn scar on her left cheek.

He turned to his right, addressing a constable behind a counter. "Who's the old woman on the bench?"

"Came in four hours ago. Says she wants to talk to Inspector Ryan. Says she has information about the murders."

"Which ones? Saturday or tonight?"

"Neither. The killings forty-three years ago."

"Forty-three years ago? Ha. A little late to offer information about *them*."

"Claims she knows something about *those* that'll help us solve *these*."

"Poor soul. Look at her. Too old to think clearly, confusing then with now."

"I asked her what she wanted to tell us. The answer was always the same—she's so ashamed, she won't say it more than once, and even then she says she's not sure she can say it to a man instead of a woman."

"Seeing as how we don't have a woman constable, she'll be waiting a long time. What do you suppose an old woman could be ashamed of?"

Continuing the Journal of Emily De Quincey

With the mob outside the tavern and with no other place to spend the night, Inspector Ryan and Constable Becker sequestered Father and me in an upstairs room. The bed's rumpled blankets made it obvious that the room had a previous occupant, probably the tavernkeeper, but I remained groggy from having been drugged, and my exhaustion was greater than my revulsion at sleeping on a dead man's bed. Cushions provided a place for Father on the floor. Ryan and Becker slept outside the room. Despite the corpses downstairs, I managed to sleep.

A loud noise jolted me awake.

The pounding of a fist.

Pounding on the tavern's door.

One of Father's essays is titled "On the Knocking at the Gate in Macbeth." It describes the moment when Macbeth and his wife realize the enormity of the murder they conspired to commit. Lady Macbeth says she feels unsexed while Macbeth claims not to be of woman born. Time seems to stop, along with the beating of their hearts. Abruptly a knocking at the gate startles them. The pulse of the universe begins again, rushing them toward their destiny.

I felt that way as I wakened to the pounding on the tavern's door. Briefly, while I slept, I had managed to forget the horrors of the past three days, of the prison, of the dead in their slumber below me. But suddenly the pounding on the door caused the world to rush at me again, and I had the terrible premonition that the outcome of this wide-awake nightmare would overtake us horribly soon.

"Who is it?" I heard Inspector Ryan demand, hurrying down the stairs.

The pounding continued as I heard him unlock the door.

Indistinct voices drifted up.

Ryan closed the door and climbed the stairs, his sounds less quick, giving the impression of reluctance to deliver whatever message he had received.

I opened the door before he could knock. He and Becker, unshaven and weary-looking, faced me.

"What's wrong?" Father asked behind me.

"Lord Palmerston wants to see all of us immediately."

As our vehicle proceeded through the increasing fog, creating the greater impression of unreality, I saw the vague shapes of guards on every corner. Two of them stopped the coach that Lord Palmerston had sent for us. After leaning inside and recognizing Inspector Ryan, they told the driver to continue.

The gloom was dispelled by a growing radiance that troubled me. Every other building on the street was dark, but the wall outside Lord Palmerston's mansion was illuminated by numerous lamps, as were all the windows of the wide structure's three levels.

Father had retrieved his flask from me and refilled it with laudanum at the tavern. Now he drank from it as a gate admitted our coach to a curved driveway flanked by more guards.

We stepped down and walked past guards into an enormous foyer, the marble floor of which reflected flames in a chandelier. At the top of a wide staircase, we entered a ballroom in which numerous glasses on tables and the strong smell of champagne provided evidence that an event had occurred the previous evening.

The event must have been joyless, given the stern look we received from a heavyset man of perhaps seventy, with long, thick, brown-dyed side-whiskers and the narrow eyes of someone accustomed to giving commands. He wore evening clothes, evidently not having retired after the conclusion of the event.

Next to him was a tall, straight-backed man in his early forties. His strong, harsh features reinforced the impression of discipline that his military posture communicated.

When Inspector Ryan respectfully removed his cap, exposing his red hair, both men gave him a disapproving look.

"I'll take care of this business quickly." Lord Palmerston pointed toward a tall stack of newspapers. *"These will soon be on the streets. I don't know how reporters obtained information about the attempt on my life this afternoon, but—"*

"Someone tried to kill you, Your Lordship?" Ryan asked in surprise.

Lord Palmerston's sharp gaze left no doubt of its meaning—Don't interrupt me.

"The city is already in a panic. Reports of my near assassination will only make things worse. Eight people slaughtered in a tavern. A surgeon, his wife, and a constable killed at the surgeon's home. Mobs attacking sailors and constables. The governor of Coldbath Fields Prison killed during a rescue of the Opium-Eater."

"Rescue? No," Becker objected. *"That was an attempted murder."*

"What's your name?" Lord Palmerston demanded.

"Constable Becker, Your Lordship."

"Not any longer. You're relieved of authority. Your coat is in rags. Why is there blood on it?"

"At Coldbath Fields Prison, I attempted to stop the intruder from killing Mr. De Quincey, Your Lordship."

"From rescuing him, you mean." Lord Palmerston turned away. *"Ryan, you're relieved of authority also. Not twenty-four hours ago, I warned you what would happen if you failed to control this crisis. Instead you chose to put yourself under the sway of the Opium-Eater."*

With each reference to that disparaging term, I sensed Father become more rigid beside me.

"When I ordered you to arrest the Opium-Eater, my motive was to assure the population that events were under control," Lord Palmerston continued, as if Father were not in the room. *"Putting a logical suspect in prison gave us time to discover the actual murderer while calming the citizenry. But now I believe that the Opium-Eater is in fact responsible."*

"This is wrong!" I exclaimed.

"Colonel Brookline, tell them what you discovered."

The tall man with a military bearing stepped toward several documents on a table. *"The Opium-Eater can't account for his activities at the time of the murders on Saturday night. He argues that his age and lack of strength make him incapable of overpowering so many people. That his daughter helped him isn't credible."*

The colonel's dismissive tone in my direction made me feel insulted.

"But that doesn't mean he didn't have help. The accomplice who tried to rescue him from prison proves that he isn't working alone."

"No," Becker insisted. "The man was trying to kill Mr. De Quincey, not rescue him."

"If you become more argumentative, I shall order you removed and perhaps arrested," Lord Palmerston warned. "Colonel Brookline, continue."

"After the Opium-Eater's arrest, I conducted a thorough inquiry. The evidence here proves his intention to instigate a rebellion comparable to what happened during the Year of Revolution six years ago. From his earliest days, he demonstrated contempt for authority. He ran away from a school in Manchester and settled among the worst elements of London, living on the streets with prostitutes. When he became a student at Oxford, he participated in almost no educational activities. In fact, he left the university during his final examinations, apparently realizing that the requirements to demonstrate facility in Greek were too demanding for him to bluff his way through."

"No, the examination was too easy—in English rather than in Greek!" Father protested. "I left because I felt insulted!"

Colonel Brookline continued to act is if Father were not in the room. "While the Opium-Eater pretended to be a student at Oxford, most of the time he appears to have actually been in London in the company of radicals. He had a fascination with atheism."

"Atheism?" Father repeated indignantly.

Colonel Brookline turned on Father, for the first time acknowledging his presence. "Do you deny your familiarity with Rachel Lee, the notorious atheist?"

"She was a guest at my mother's house."

"Which tells us about the dubious nature of your home environment," Brookline noted.

"Leave my mother out of this."

"While you posed as a student at Oxford, you made contact with Rachel Lee during the infamous trial in which she accused two Oxford *students of abducting and attempting to rape her. Their own testimony indicated that she had gone willingly with them in an effort to leave her husband and engage in a ménage à trois. The trial came to a startling conclusion when she was asked to give testimony on a Bible but she refused on the grounds that she did not believe in God. The proceedings were immediately halted, the students exonerated. These are the sorts of dangerous people with whom you enjoy collaborating.*

"Your association with the poets Wordsworth and Coleridge is even more suspect. You followed them to the Lake District, a well-known radical enclave. There, Coleridge created a socially disruptive newspaper to which you pledged both money and enflaming articles. You assisted Wordsworth in publishing a pamphlet that was libelous in its attack of Parliament. Wordsworth's disruptive praise of the common man — farmers and milkmaids and so forth — impressed you to the point that you showed your contempt for the structure of society by descending beneath your station and actually marrying a milkmaid."

"My dear departed wife was not a milkmaid." Father's expression became rigid.

"Call her what you will, her father was the most extreme radical in the Lake District, constantly urging the overthrow of the gentry." Brookline's accusations rushed on. "You have frequently been sought by law-enforcement officials. You often assumed aliases and concealed your numerous addresses, sometimes having as many as six lodgings at one time."

"Because of debts, I changed my name and moved frequently to avoid bill collectors."

"Or were you avoiding Home Office agents assigned to keep track of your rebellious activities?" Brookline demanded. "You wrote aggravating essays for both conservative and liberal magazines, urging both sides to extremes."

"To pay my bills, I worked for whoever wanted my services. The editors encouraged me to be reactionary."

"In one case, your invectives contributed to a lethal argument between the editors of two magazines. In a duel, one of the editors was mortally shot. No doubt you hoped that both of them would be killed and that the resultant outrage would lead to more violence."

"You twist things."

"It is your mind that twists things. You advocated the immoderate use of laudanum."

"I described my own experience as a caution to others."

"You also indulged in a drug called 'bang.' "

"Bang?" Lord Palmerston sounded baffled.

"Otherwise known as hashish, Your Lordship, from which the word 'assassin' is derived."

"Good heavens."

"During the Crusades, fanatical Muslims smoked it before their murderous attacks on English officers, Your Lordship."

"No! Hashish encourages an appetite, not violence," Father insisted.

"Violence. Yes, you praised extreme violence in several of your essays, revealing your obsession with John Williams and the original Ratcliffe Highway murders. You called Williams a genius."

"An attempt to be humorous."

"The many people who were murdered recently are not amused. Through drugs, violence, and radical views, you persistently advocated the overthrow of the aristocracy. Now your obsession with violence has impelled you to encourage accomplices to re-create the original Ratcliffe Highway murders in an effort to destabilize London. I have proof, Your Lordship."

Brookline raised an item from the documents on the table. "In one of former inspector Ryan's few helpful acts, he arranged for a newspaper artist to sketch the face of the dead man at Coldbath Fields Prison. The man gained access to the prison by claiming to be a messenger from you, Your Lordship."

"From me? But I sent no one to that prison," Palmerston replied in confusion.

"He had a message in an envelope with your seal on it."

"Impossible."

"No doubt a forgery. The message inside turned out to be of no importance, merely a trick to gain entrance. Here is the sketch, Your Lordship. Certain grotesque aspects of his death have been eliminated in an attempt to achieve an ordinary likeness. Do you recognize this man?"

Palmerston held the sketch near a candelabrum on the table. "He didn't work for me. I've never seen this man in my life."

"Although he didn't work for you, you have in fact seen him, Your Lordship."

"I don't—"

"Granted, you saw him only fleetingly as I pushed you to the floor of your coach. This is the man who tried to assassinate you this afternoon."

"What?"

"The man who tried to kill you is the same man who attempted to rescue the Opium-Eater from prison. I strongly suspect that this isn't the Opium-Eater's only accomplice. With Your Lordship's permission, I think it would be appropriate to question the Opium-Eater in a persuasive manner after he is readmitted to prison."

Anger so controlled me that I raised my voice in defense of Father. "Persuasive manner. You can't be serious. Torture an old man?"

"No one used the word 'torture.' The British government does not torture prisoners," Brookline said.

"Then perhaps it's the British military who does the torturing, Colonel."

Brookline gave me the harshest glare I ever received. "I don't understand why this woman is allowed to be here. She doesn't serve our purpose, except to show by her scandalous clothing the contempt that she and her father have for the standards of society. Not only is the bloomer dress immodest by revealing the outline of her legs, but it is also synonymous with a notorious female activist who campaigns for the disruption of society by advocating the right of women to vote."

"Immodest?" Father said angrily. "First, you insult my mother."

"I merely state facts."

"Next you insult my dead wife."

"The daughter of an agitator."

"Now you insult my daughter."

"Don't try to distract us from our purpose."

"Which is to torture an old man!" I protested.

"Old?" Brookline scoffed. "Your Lordship, the Opium-Eater uses his age to deceive those who might otherwise suspect him. In the past few *days, he demonstrated more nimbleness than most men twenty years younger than he is."*

"I am thirsty," Father announced.

"What?"

Father went to a table in the corner and chose one of the half-full champagne glasses.

He swallowed its contents in one gulp.

My companions Ryan and Becker were accustomed to seeing this behavior, but Lord Palmerston and Colonel Brookline opened their mouths in astonishment.

Father selected a second half-full champagne glass and swallowed its contents as well. He looked around for a third.

"We'll see how insolent you are in Coldbath Fields Prison when you reveal the names of your accomplices," Brookline said.

Father turned toward Palmerston. "Your Lordship, the man you should be searching for is a British soldier who spent considerable time in the Orient. He learned the languages of that region sufficiently to be able to give instructions to a Malay. He became an expert in disguises there. He has extensive experience with killing."

"This is a laudanum fantasy, Your Lordship. British soldiers do not kill English civilians," Brookline objected.

"Are you suggesting that they kill only Oriental civilians?" Father asked him.

"Don't be impertinent."

"Only someone with extensive combat experience could have accomplished the recent skillful slaughters," Father elaborated. "Someone who was trained, someone who has done it many times."

"Outrageous! British soldiers are not madmen!" Lord Palmerston protested. "If we suspect British soldiers, there'll be no end of it. Your description could apply even to Colonel Brookline."

"Indeed it could." Father stared at Brookline. "Did you serve in India, Colonel?"

"This is another of the Opium-Eater's attempts to undermine society, Your Lordship. Through his accomplices, first he persuades the populace to believe that the killer is a sailor, with the consequence that many sail-

ors were attacked and work at the docks has halted. Then he convinces the mob that the killer is a constable, with the consequence that several policemen have been assaulted and faith in law enforcement has been eroded. Now he attempts to draw suspicion toward the military. By the time he's finished making accusations, no one will be above suspicion. Next, he'll claim that you're the killer, Your Lordship." Brookline turned toward our group. "Former constable Becker." He put the emphasis on "former."

"Yes?" Becker frowned.

"Even though you choose not to appear in uniform, I hope you are professional enough to possess handcuffs."

"They are in my coat pocket."

"Put them on the Opium-Eater."

"Pardon me?"

"When you address me, call me 'Colonel.' Put the damned handcuffs on the Opium-Eater."

Becker hesitated.

"Perhaps you too would enjoy a night's lodging at Coldbath Fields Prison," Brookline suggested. "You could pass the time with men you arrested."

"Do what he wants," Father said. "At the moment, there's no alternative."

"For a change, the Opium-Eater makes sense," Brookline noted.

I had difficulty catching my breath as Father held his wrists in front of him and Becker pressed the shackles onto them.

"The key." Brookline extended his hand.

"Any constable's key will fit any set of handcuffs," Becker said, "but if you're determined to have mine, here it is."

Becker gave him the key.

When Brookline reached for Father, his impatience prompted him to push Ryan out of the way.

Ryan bumped into me. "I'm extremely sorry, Miss De Quincey." In the confusion, he pressed something into my palm.

It was the key to the handcuffs that Ryan himself carried, I realized. The key would fit any set of handcuffs, including Becker's.

Brookline tugged Father toward the door.

I forced myself to burst out weeping. "No!" After pushing my way past Brookline, I grabbed Father, doing my best to sob hysterically.

"Everything will resolve for the best, Emily."

"We're wasting time." Brookline pulled Father toward the door.

"I'll pray for you, Father."

While I clung to Father, I put the handcuff key into his coat pocket.

"Your Lordship," Brookline told Palmerston as he pulled Father from the room, "it's dangerous for you to go to your office tomorrow. For the time being, I recommend that you conduct your business here.*"*

The next moments were a blur as Lord Palmerston's guards urged Becker, Ryan, and me down the marble stairs. We followed Father and Brookline across the foyer and out the front door, into the lamp-lit fog, where we watched them climb into the coach that had brought us to the mansion.

Father leaned out, shouting, "You know where I'll be, Emily!"

"Yes, in prison," Brookline mocked.

"Where I listened to the music."

"Completely insane."

"Remember, Emily! Where I listened to the music!"

Brookline pulled Father all the way inside the coach. A guard stepped in with them, slamming the door. Another guard joined the driver on top.

The gate opened. The horses clomped forward. Almost immediately, the coach disappeared into the fog.

"Please bring another coach," Ryan told a footman.

"Not for you."

"I don't understand."

"Colonel Brookline's instructions were emphatic. He said the three of you can walk."

Beyond the illumination of Lord Palmerston's mansion, the coach entered dense shadows, bumping over paving stones on the unseen expanse of Piccadilly. A lamp next to the driver cast a faint glow through an opening and permitted the occupants an indistinct view of one another's faces.

Colonel Brookline sat across from De Quincey. A security agent sat beside him.

The handcuffs pained De Quincey's wrists.

"I met your son, Paul, in India," Brookline said.

"Indeed?"

"In February of eighteen forty-six. After the Battle of Sobraon in the first Anglo-Sikh War."

"India's a massive country. How surprising that you happened to meet him."

"Yes, a remarkable coincidence. Your son told me he enlisted in the military when he was eighteen."

"That is correct."

"I received the impression that he wanted to get away from home. To put considerable distance between you and him."

De Quincey refused to show that his emotions had been jabbed. "My children who survived to adulthood turned out to be wanderers."

"Now that I think of it, another of your sons joined the military and went as far as China."

"That is true also."

"He died from fever there."

"I do not wish to be reminded of that."

"Perhaps if your son hadn't been so eager to get away from you, he would still be alive."

"You keep bringing my family into this."

The coach thumped over a hole in the road. The impact jostled them.

It also aggravated the grip of the handcuffs on De Quincey's wrists.

"When I pulled you into the coach," Brookline said, "I felt something in your coat pocket."

"I have nothing." De Quincey was very conscious of the key that Emily had put into his coat. His heart cramped.

"But you do. I felt it." Brookline reached toward his coat. "Surely you don't believe you can sneak something into prison."

De Quincey held his breath, trying not to betray his apprehension.

"And look at this," Brookline announced victoriously.

He yanked the flask from De Quincey's pocket and shook it, listening to the liquid inside. "Could this be cough medicine, or perhaps some brandy to ward off the night's chill? Let us investigate."

Brookline unscrewed the cap, sniffed the contents, and grimaced. "Why am I not surprised that it's laudanum?"

He unlatched the window and threw the flask into the street. "Even mixed with alcohol, its odor is disgusting."

In the dark, the flask clattered across paving stones.

"That's where filth belongs. In the gutter."

"You're familiar with the odor of opium, Colonel?"

"The lime used to process it reminds me of the quicklime that is dumped into mass graves. In both warehouses and battlefields, I encountered the deathly odor of lime almost every day of my many years in India. When I arrived there, I was eighteen, the same age as your son who fled to India to avoid you."

"Perhaps you were fleeing your own father."

"If you are trying to bait me, you won't succeed," Brookline said. "My father has no relevance. I never knew him. My mother lived with a former soldier. He never complained about the military, so after he died in an accident, I decided to give his former profession a try. In India, I was trained by a sergeant who explained about the British East India Company and the opium trade. The sergeant said that if he caught any of us using opium, he would break our bones before he killed us. He called it the devil."

"He was right."

"That is not the impression you give in your *Confessions of an English Opium-Eater.* You praise the drug for increasing your awareness. You claim that music becomes more intense, for example, almost as if you can see what you're hearing."

"Yes. But as I make clear in my book, the effect lessens with each taking. An increasing amount must be ingested in order to achieve the same effect. Soon, massive amounts are necessary merely to feel normal. Attempting to reduce the quantity produces unbearable pain, as if rats tear at the interior of my stomach."

"You should have emphasized that in your *Confessions,*" Brookline directed.

"I believe that I did."

"The sergeant who warned me about opium owned a copy of your book. He made all his trainees read it so that we would understand the devil. In fact, he ordered me to read your foul confessions to those soldiers who could not read. I read it so often that I memorized your offensive text. But he was mistaken to order us to read it. Your book is an encouragement to use opium rather than a caution."

"That was not my intention."

"How many people became its slave because of you, do you suppose? How many people did you trap in hell?"

"I can easily ask the reverse. How many people took my advice to stay away from the drug once they understood its false attraction? There is no way to know either answer."

"In India and China, every battle I fought, every person I killed, was because of opium. Over the centuries, hundreds of thousands died in conflicts because of it. Millions of people in China were corrupted by it. In England itself, how many slaves to opium are there?"

"Again, there is no way to determine that number."

"But with laudanum available on every street corner and in every home, with almost every child being given it for coughs or even for crying, there must be hundreds of thousands, perhaps millions, who require it without realizing the hold it has on them, do you agree?"

"Logic would say so."

"Fainthearted women who seldom leave their homes and keep the curtains closed and surround themselves with a swirl of patterns in their shadowy sitting rooms—do they not seem to be under the influence of the drug? Laborers, merchants, bankers, members of Parliament, members of every stratum of society—they too must be under the influence?"

"An argument can be made that you are correct."

"An influence that you encourage."

"No."

"My disgust for your opium-eating *Confessions* led me to investigate the rest of your vile work."

"I'm impressed. Some editors complained that I myself should have read my essays before submitting them."

"Everything is a joke to you. Not content with advocating opium abuse, you praised the Ratcliffe Highway killer, John Williams. 'All other murders look pale by the deep crimson of his,' you said. You described Williams as an artist."

"Yes."

"The Ratcliffe Highway murders were 'the sublimest that were ever committed,' you said."

"Those are indeed my words."

" 'The most superb of the century,' you described them."

"Your research is thorough."

"Extremely so."

" 'Obsessive' is the word that comes to mind."

"Opium abuse, killing, and death are not things to be mocked. In Coldbath Fields Prison, I shall demonstrate that truth to you."

Brookline lurched as the coach struck another hole in the road.

De Quincey had been praying that it would happen again. He had primed his reflexes, knowing that this might be his only opportunity. He had thought it through carefully, anticipating precisely what needed to be done.

As the impact jolted Brookline and the other man, De Quincey lunged toward the door.

The force of the wheel coming out of the hole knocked Brookline against the back of his seat. He grabbed for De Quincey too late. The Opium-Eater was already out the door, jumping into the darkness.

The force of coming off the moving vehicle threw him off-balance. He nearly toppled forward and smashed his face on the paving stones. But he managed to keep his balance, straightened, and ran panicked into the swirling fog. His direction was to the right.

Brookline shouted.

Boots landed hard on the street. Three sets: Brookline, the interior guard, and the man riding with the driver. As long as they made noise, the sounds that he himself made would be undetectable.

Brookline seemed to read his thoughts and yelled, "Quiet!"

Behind the Opium-Eater, the night became silent. Meanwhile his hurried bootsteps echoed.

"That way!"

De Quincey ran harder. The long strides of the tall men would soon close the distance he had managed to gain. Despite his age, fear gave him strength, as did his habit of walking thousands of miles a year. His only hope was to race back along Piccadilly in the direction of Lord Palmerston's mansion.

Green Park lay across from it. If he could reach that park, its grass would muffle the sound of his boots.

A lamppost suddenly loomed. Heart thundering, De Quincey shifted to the side. His shoulder jolted past it, sending a shudder through him, making him groan. Again he was in darkness.

"I hear him! He's not far ahead!" Brookline shouted.

De Quincey ran faster. His lungs burned. His shoulder throbbed. His legs felt the strain of greater exertion.

Another lamppost loomed, but this time he avoided it. Abruptly an uneven paving stone tripped him. He landed and groaned, but his terror was greater than his pain, and he struggled upright, lurching onward into the fog.

"He's close!" Brookline yelled.

At once the sounds on the street changed. Until now, echoes had come from both right and left, indicating that there were buildings on each side. But now the echo came only from the right.

The expanse of the park must be on his left.

Or perhaps his panic had distorted his hearing. If he was wrong, he would crash into a building.

"I see a shadow moving!" Brookline shouted.

In one of the greatest acts of faith in his life, De Quincey darted to the left. Reaching out, he touched the spike-topped palings that enclosed the park. As he raced along them, he heard one of his pursuers slam into the palings and curse.

Running, De Quincey drew his hand painfully along the palings, searching for the gate. Where was it? Had he passed it?

Bootsteps rushed closer.

De Quincey felt the gate. Frantically lifting the metal latch, he pushed and ran into the murky park. At the same moment, he heard the rush of a hand grab for him and miss.

The noises he made changed to silence as he veered to the right, leaving the stones of a path for the softness of grass.

The bootfalls behind him became silent also as Brookline and his two men entered the park. Or almost silent. The grass didn't entirely muffle sounds. Occasional dead leaves crunched under De Quincey's soles.

"Over there!" Brookline shouted.

De Quincey was forced to run slower, to lessen the impact he made. Despite the night's cold, his lungs felt on fire, but he couldn't inhale fully to cool them, lest the noise of his harsh breathing indicate where he was.

He heard one of the men strike something.

"Watch out for the trees!" Brookline's voice warned.

De Quincey reduced his pace even more. After the illumination of Lord Palmerston's house, the street had seemed in total darkness, but in fact, the lampposts had provided a periodic hazy glow. Now in the park the darkness was absolute. The fog was a veil through which he groped, the range of his cramped arms limited by the painful handcuffs.

The throbbing in his shoulder intensified. His chin swelled from where he had fallen and injured it.

Surprising him, his hands touched tree bark. He moved around the trunk. His waist struck a bench.

"There!" Brookline's voice yelled.

What had been an urgent race was reduced to a tense walk. Behind him, someone scraped against leafless bushes.

To his left.

He veered to the right, all the while moving deeper into the park.

"Reach under the benches! He's small enough to hide there!" Brookline ordered. "And under bushes!"

Again, De Quincey's shackled hands scratched against a tree. He shifted around it, bumped his head on a limb, and moved warily onward.

Abruptly he changed his mind. He couldn't allow himself to move so far from the street that he would be disoriented and walk in circles. It was essential that he go back to the street. His plan depended on that.

He returned to the tree, felt the limb that he had bumped against, and stretched up to determine if he could reach a higher one.

Indeed he could.

"Spread out!" Brookline commanded.

De Quincey's urgent pulse swelled his veins as he made another act of faith and climbed onto the first limb. His shackled wrists had sufficient space between them to allow him to grip the next limb and pull himself farther up.

His clothes brushed against the tree.

"There!" a man yelled.

Boots hurried quickly, crushing leaves. Using their sound to cover his own, De Quincey pulled himself higher.

"I heard him!" Brookline's harsh voice came from below him. "Somewhere around here!"

Braced between a branch and the tree trunk, De Quincey held his breath.

Trouser legs brushed against each other.

"Stop and listen," Brookline said.

The park became quiet.

The silence stretched on for several moments.

"While we search under benches and bushes, he can keep moving," one of the men noted.

"Yes, he could be anywhere in the park by now," Brookline agreed.

They lapsed into silence again and listened.

De Quincey's chest ached from not breathing.

"He can't keep running forever," one of the men said. "We'll catch him eventually."

"I want him *now*."

They waited longer. De Quincey became dizzy from not breathing.

"Colonel!" the coach's driver shouted from the unseen street. "Shall I summon more help?"

Brookline debated, cursed, then shouted, "No!"

He led his men back toward the street.

De Quincey parted his lips, trying to be as silent as possible when he released air from his lungs and slowly inhaled.

But he didn't dare move. For all he knew, Brookline had merely pretended to leave in the hope that De Quincey would feel confident and betray where he was hiding.

The faint sounds of Brookline and his men diminished.

At last, except for a distant barking dog, the night drifted into silence.

Wedged between the branch and the tree trunk, De Quincey's legs were cramped, but he couldn't allow himself to shift position, and no matter how much his lungs demanded air, he forced himself to inhale slowly and quietly.

The final hours of the night stretched on.

His shoulder ached. His chin throbbed.

The fog became less dense as dawn commenced. Still not feeling safe, De Quincey nonetheless needed to move. It was imperative that he reach the street while there was a chance of his not being seen.

Straining not to make a sound, he descended painfully. When he reached the bottom of the tree, his legs buckled. He needed to rub them, easing the cramps.

The heavy handcuffs irritated his wrists and made them swell. He desperately wanted to remove them. Thanks to Emily, the key was in his coat pocket. But the lock was on the outside of each cuff. There was no way he could reach his fingers around to insert the key into the locks.

As the air became gray, he snuck through the lessening fog, pausing to interpret any sounds he heard. Near the street, he crouched behind bushes and assessed the risk of moving forward.

No one seemed to be in the area. Creeping past benches at the edge of the park, he reached the gate. Would an enemy be waiting? De Quincey hoped that this would seem the last place to which he would go rather than a distant refuge. With no other choice, shoved by the terrible responsibility of the task he needed to perform, he stepped through the gate.

No one seized him. Hurrying despite his cramped legs, he moved to the right, away from Lord Palmerston's house. His destination was farther along the street, past the park, where buildings occupied both sides of the street.

Bent forward in the gloom, he scanned the edge of the pavement and felt his heart expand when he saw what he searched for.

The flask lay in the gutter where Brookline had tossed it. Brookline had said that it belonged there, and De Quincey agreed. It did indeed belong in the gutter.

Nonetheless he needed the flask. He snatched it up and raced back to the park.

But for once the laudanum wasn't for him. Although his body urgently craved it, he had a far more important use for it.

With its help, he might be able to prevent more people — a lot more, he feared — from dying.

14

The Woman of Sorrows

AT VAUXHALL GARDENS, if De Quincey had chosen to pay for an ascent in the hot-air balloon, he would have seen a perspective of London that made sense of the sprawling city in a way that a map could not provide. Rising, he could have viewed the majestic Thames and its numerous bridges. He could have admired Westminster Abbey and the Houses of Parliament.

But more than anything, what would have captured his attention was a stretch of royal parks that extended through the city. As a sign next to the hot-air balloon had advertised, one of the parks to be seen from above was St. James's, located directly to the west of the Whitehall government offices. That park blended into the next one — Green Park — which in turn blended into much larger Hyde Park, making it possible for someone to walk several miles through the heart of London and have the illusion of being in the countryside.

The Opium-Eater didn't walk, however. In the twilight of dawn, with the fog dissipating and the light growing, he ran as swiftly as he could manage, hoping that the trees and bushes gave him cover. The strain on his body compelled him to take a sip of laudanum from his flask. The drug subdued his agony and allowed him to push his body to its maximum. But he couldn't permit himself to drink much of it. He had a far more important use for the precious liquid.

His worst fright came when he needed to cross the street that separated Green Park from Hyde Park, but after that, he pressed on, stumbling now more than running as he used the dwindling fog for cover, finally arriving at Marble Arch, at the northeast corner of Hyde Park.

He had come here with Emily on Sunday morning, barely two days earlier, when the only complication in his life—apart from his opium habit and his poverty—was the necessity of explaining to Emily that when he was seventeen, starving on Oxford Street, he had fallen in love with a prostitute named Ann.

Oxford Street.

Beyond Marble Arch, it stretched before him. The gradually clearing fog made the street seem as gloomy as it had been fifty-two years earlier, when he had almost died there from hunger and the elements.

He moved past the dark shops on the street's left side, limping now, glancing nervously behind him to see if he was being followed. The noise of horseshoes on paving stones made him flinch. A vehicle was approaching. Was it a police wagon? Would Brookline, who had investigated his life so obsessively, guess that he would come to the one place in London with which he was more familiar than any other? But even Brookline couldn't know precisely where he would hide on Oxford Street.

The clomp of the horse's hooves was louder, closer.

De Quincey came to an alley, moved painfully along it, descended grimy steps, crawled through a hole in a fence, and descended again, this time into a tunnel, which led to another tunnel. There, in the shadows, bodies lay on granite, to all appearances dead but actually in an exhausted sleep made deeper by alcohol.

At the limit of his resources, De Quincey concealed his flask beneath a broken crate. Then he stepped to the middle of the bodies and lay among them.

No matter how cold the stones felt, the enclosure of the tunnel trapped a portion of the heat from the sleeping bodies.

Hiding among the beggars of Oxford Street, the Opium-Eater tried to doze as an angry chamber of his mind brooded.

* * *

With no other destination that they could think of at that early hour, Ryan, Becker, and Emily made their way to Scotland Yard. With luck, word would not have reached there yet that Ryan and Becker had been dismissed. They needed a place to rest while they decided on a strategy.

What would normally have been a twenty-minute walk took them an hour in the fog, but Emily didn't care about that or the numbing cold. What mattered was her father.

The sun was rising as they reached a building marked METROPOLITAN POLICE.

The warmth inside was welcome. Numerous doorways flanked a corridor. A stairway led to an upper level. Everything was quiet.

Ryan glanced at an elderly woman asleep on a bench, then stepped into an office on the right, where the constable on duty looked up from a desk.

Had the man been told that they'd been dismissed?

"Hello there, Inspector Ryan. Haven't seen you in a couple of days."

Ryan relaxed somewhat. "I've been busy."

"And likely to get busier."

"I'm afraid you're right. This is Constable Becker."

"Indeed, we've met. What happened to your coat, Becker?"

"Tangled with somebody."

"That's been happening a lot lately."

"And this is a witness we need to question," Ryan said, indicating Emily. "Can we use a room down the hall?"

"And get some hot tea?" Becker looked at Emily's frost-reddened cheeks.

"It's next to the stove."

They passed the old woman on the bench and entered a room that had three unoccupied desks near a stove. Emily took off her gloves and rubbed her hands together over the heat.

Ryan picked up a teapot and poured steaming liquid into three cups. "Enjoy it while you can. There's no telling when we'll be booted out of here."

A voice interrupted them.

"Ryan."

They turned.

The constable was in the doorway.

Has he learned that we're no longer policemen?

"A woman's been waiting for you," the man said.

"The one asleep on the bench?"

"Not anymore. When she heard you come in, she woke up. I told her you're the man she's wanting to see. Can you talk to her? She's been here since yesterday evening."

The woman stood behind him. Awake, she looked older than when they'd first seen her. She turned her face, as if hiding something. The portion of her face that showed was lined with wrinkles, tight like a net. She clutched her ragged coat as if she would never be able to get warm.

"It's something about the first Ratcliffe Highway murders," the constable explained. "I told her nobody cares about ancient history. It's the murders Saturday and last night that we want to solve. But she insists the first ones have something to do with the recent ones. She says she's ashamed about something. It wouldn't hurt to listen to her. Even if it's nothing, at least then she'll go home."

"Fine," Ryan said. "Let her in."

The constable motioned for the woman to enter the office.

She looked so tired and pathetic that Emily helped her to a chair at a desk. "Would you like some tea?"

"I don't have any money."

"This won't cost you anything," Emily assured her.

"Thank you. I'm thirsty."

"You have information about the murders?" Becker asked.

The woman nodded. "Forty-three years ago."

"What about the recent ones?"

The woman stared mournfully at steam rising from the cup Emily gave her. Although she had said that she was thirsty, she didn't drink. Emily was able to see that the woman's left cheek had a burn scar.

"What's your name?" Ryan asked.

"Margaret."

"Your last name?"

"Jewell."

Emily repeated the name so forcefully—"*Margaret Jewell?*"—that Becker and Ryan looked at her in surprise.

"What is it?" Ryan asked.

"From the Marr killings?" Emily asked the woman.

"Yes." Margaret's voice was edged with sorrow.

"What's going on?" Becker asked.

"Father wrote about this woman. She's the servant Timothy Marr sent to buy oysters just before the killings."

Ryan walked closer. "Margaret?"

The woman looked up at him.

"Tell us why you came here."

"Saturday midnight. Forty-three years ago."

"Yes, forty-three years ago." Ryan knelt before her, putting his face level with hers.

"Mr. Marr always kept his shop open until eleven on Saturday." Margaret looked at the teacup in her hands but didn't raise it to her lips. "That night...when Mr. Marr was ready to close, he told James—"

"James?" Becker asked.

"The shop boy. He told James to help him put up the shutters. He told *me* to go out and pay a bill at the baker's and then buy oysters for a late supper."

Margaret hesitated painfully.

"I always felt nervous being on the street that late, but Mr. Marr got angry over the slightest things, and I didn't dare refuse his orders without being dismissed. So in the dark I hurried to the oyster shop, but it was closed. Then I hurried to the baker's shop, and *it* was closed. I kept thinking how angry Mr. Marr was going to be. When I finally returned, I found the door locked. That proved to me how angry Mr. Marr was for me taking so long. But as much as I was afraid of *him,* I was more afraid of being robbed or worse on the dark street, so I knocked on the door. When that didn't bring him, I pounded. Soon I kicked it, shouting, 'Mr. Marr, let me in!'

"I put my ear against the door and heard footsteps. They stopped on the other side. Someone breathed.

"'Mr. Marr, I'm scared out here!' I shouted. But the door didn't open.

Instead the footsteps went away, and suddenly I had a feeling like a black cat had walked in front of me. It made me more afraid of what might be in the house than anybody on the street robbing me. I can't tell you how relieved I felt to see the lantern of a night watchman. He asked me what the trouble was, and then *he* pounded on the door, shouting Mr. Marr's name. The noise disturbed a neighbor, who crawled over the fence at the back, saw the door was open, and went in to find..."

The pause lengthened.

"Drink your tea," Emily encouraged her.

"The neighbor unlocked the front door. I never saw a man look more pale. By then a crowd was behind me. Everybody rushed in, taking me with them. I saw Mrs. Marr on the floor. Farther away, I saw James, the shop boy. Something wet dropped on me. I looked up and saw blood on the ceiling." Margaret shuddered. "Then the crowd pushed me past the entrance to the back of the counter, and that's where I saw Mr. Marr on the floor. Blood was on the shelves. *The baby,* I kept thinking. The Marrs had a three-month-old son. I prayed that he was all right, but then someone found the baby in a back room. The cradle was broken into pieces. The child's throat was..."

Margaret's hands shook, spilling tea.

Emily took the cup from her.

"That's something nobody's been able to understand," Becker said, "why the murderer killed the baby. Three adults would have been a threat to someone who tried to rob the shop. But a baby...from what I was told, the killer didn't steal anything."

"That wasn't why he did it."

"You confuse me."

"He wasn't there to steal."

"You sound as if you know."

Margaret nodded.

"What did he want? Why did he kill everyone? You told the constable at the desk that this had something to do with the recent killings," Ryan said.

Margaret nodded again, her face revealing her torment.

"Tell us, Margaret."

"Not to a man." Margaret turned toward Emily, her left cheek revealing her scar. "Maybe I can tell a woman."

"I believe I would understand," Emily assured her.

"So ashamed."

"If you finally talk about it, maybe you'll feel..."

"Better?" Margaret exhaled deeply, painfully. "I'll never feel better."

"We'll leave the two of you alone," Becker said.

He and Ryan stepped from the room, closing the door.

Emily pulled a chair next to Margaret. She put her hands on each side of Margaret's wrinkled face. She kissed Margaret's troubled forehead.

"My father says there is no such thing as forgetting," Emily said.

Margaret wiped at her eyes. "Your father is right."

"And yet my father writes compulsively about his memories, as if by putting them into words, he can dull them, no matter how sharply painful they are. Margaret, free yourself."

Even tears couldn't hold back Margaret's words.

A HALF HOUR LATER, Emily kissed Margaret's brow again. Shaken by what she had heard, she walked to the door and opened it.

Ryan and Becker waited on the bench in the corridor. The building was now full of sounds as constables arrived, the terrors of the previous night showing on their faces.

Emily recalled something her father had written. *The horrors that madden the grief that gnaws at the heart.*

Ryan and Becker stood.

"Emily, your father escaped," Ryan said.

"Escaped?"

"The news reached Scotland Yard while you were talking to Margaret. Your father jumped from Brookline's coach. Everyone's been ordered to search for him."

After what Emily had learned from Margaret, this further revelation made her reach for the wall to steady herself.

"We need to find him," Becker said. "Do you have any idea where your father might have gone?"

Emily continued to feel off-balance.

"Last night, when he was being taken away, your father shouted, 'You know where I'll be. Where I listened to the music.' Do you know what he meant?" Ryan asked.

"No."

"A concert hall perhaps."

"Father never mentioned one." Emily drew a breath, trying to clear her thoughts. "Thank heaven he escaped."

Where he listened to the music? Something stirred in a chamber of her memory, but although she did her best to bring it forward, it wouldn't come.

"Did Margaret tell you anything?"

"A great deal. Is there a church in the area?"

"She needs a church?"

"Very much so."

"Ten minutes away," Ryan said. "But it's a lot bigger than a church."

AN EARLY-MORNING SERVICE WAS IN PROGRESS. Under other circumstances, Emily would have marveled at the soaring vastness of Westminster Abbey, its columns and stained-glass windows, but all she could think about was that her father had escaped and what she'd learned from Margaret.

She placed Margaret in a pew. Tears continued to trickle down the old woman's face, wetting the scar on her left cheek as she knelt and prayed.

A surprising number of people were at the service, fear having brought them to beseech God for their safety amid the violence that gripped the city. Their slightest movement echoed in the cathedral's immensity.

A reverend began a sermon, the theme of which Emily imagined was the same as many sermons forty-three years earlier.

"The Lord is our shepherd." The reverend's voice reverberated. "The devil, like a wolf attacking us, is the Lord's enemy. If we have faith, the Lord will protect us."

Emily whispered to Margaret, "You did the right thing by telling me. Listen to what the reverend says. The Lord will not abandon you."

The sermon boomed in the massive structure as Emily led Ryan and Becker outside. Beyond the huge front doors, she barely noticed the abbey's dramatic forecourt.

"Until now, I have never spoken this way in front of men who are not members of my family," Emily said.

"That probably applies the other way around," Ryan told her. "It may be that we've never heard a woman speak the way I have the feeling that *you* are about to."

"Reasonable enough." Nonetheless, Emily hesitated, as Margaret had hesitated. "If I rush on, perhaps I can force myself to say it. Margaret was with child and without a husband."

The men weren't able to speak for a moment.

"Now I understand why she didn't want to talk about it," Becker said.

"You *don't* understand. Not yet. The father was John Williams."

"John Williams?"

"Margaret's parents died from typhoid fever when she was twelve. She worked in a number of factories and finally decided to look for a servant's position. Marr already had a shop boy, but now he needed a woman to help his wife while she was in a family condition and later after the baby was born. The pay was ten pounds a year, meals and a cot included. Margaret was allowed to leave the shop one night a week, a half day on Sunday, and a full day every month. She was seventeen.

"Marr was a bitter, angry man, always finding fault and shouting. Worse, he always complained when Margaret wanted her weekly night off or when she took her half day on Sunday. As far as her full day once a month was concerned, Marr threatened to put her on the street if she was absent for the entire day.

"Margaret met John Williams at a street festival on one of the rare occasions she was off duty. A merchant sailor, Williams was ten years older than Margaret, good-looking, with yellowish curly hair and an entertaining manner. He took a liking to her."

Emily paused, the shadow of Westminster Abbey weighing upon her.

"Then he took advantage of her," Becker suggested, trying to ease Emily's discomfort by saying it for her.

Emily nodded. "It appears that Williams wasn't merely trifling with her affections, although the consequence was the same. They spent company with each other whenever she could get away. Sometimes Williams was gone on a merchant ship for months. Early in October of eighteen eleven, he returned from a voyage to India. They were desperate to see each other."

Emily's face was red with embarrassment. She rushed on. "That's when the event occurred. Two and a half months later, Margaret finally had to admit that she was with child. She was sick every morning, and Marr recognized the symptom from when his wife had experienced similar sickness early in her condition. Marr challenged her with his suspicions. When Margaret admitted their truth, he was furious, saying that she'd signed a contract with him and he had relied on her to help his wife with the baby and now Margaret was unable to fulfill her obligations.

" 'I can work for many more months,' Margaret tried to assure him, but Marr shouted that he wouldn't tolerate a sinner in his home. He intended to look for another servant immediately, and as soon as he could find one, he would put her on the street with the rest of her kind."

Emily hesitated, trying to find the words to continue.

"John Williams was known for his temper. When Margaret told him about Marr's reaction, he became more furious than Marr was. She and Williams had planned to live together. Williams was scheduled to go on one more voyage to try to earn enough money for their lodging. The longer Marr kept her as a servant, the more time Williams and Margaret had to prepare. Now their prospects were ruined."

"Williams went to see Marr?" Ryan asked.

"Yes. The intent was to persuade Marr to keep Margaret working until Williams returned from his voyage. But you can imagine how two angry men handled the conversation. After they nearly came to blows, Marr swore that the next day, Sunday, could definitely be Margaret's half day off. The entire day, in fact. And every day thereafter because Marr didn't want her to return.

"This happened on Saturday afternoon. In a back room, Margaret heard the argument, but she was too afraid to intervene. She heard Williams storm from the shop. Then Marr made her do heavy work for the rest of the day. The reason he sent Margaret out near midnight supposedly to pay the baker's bill and buy oysters was to punish her because he knew how afraid Margaret was of the dark. She lied at the inquest."

"What?"

"The reason she failed to pay the baker and buy the oysters was that she had a premonition and was trying to find John Williams."

Numerous worshippers entered the church, the tension on their faces indicating that they were here to pray for their safety. The street in front of the abbey had little traffic. At eight in the morning, it should have been crammed as black-coated government clerks came to their offices, but many had apparently decided to remain home because of the crisis.

"The bloody government's not doing enough," a severe-looking man murmured to a companion as he entered the abbey.

Another man approached, telling a woman, "The peerage abandoned the city and fled to their country houses. They're so rich they can hire protection. But they don't dare rely on constables. A constable killed all those people last night."

"And sailors," the woman said. "Can't trust anybody. A man broke into Coldbath Fields Prison last night, killed the governor, and released a thousand prisoners. Heaven help us, they'll murder us in our sleep."

"For sure, the *government* won't help us."

"Lord Palmerston has reason to be worried," Becker observed as the man and woman took refuge in the abbey.

"Even more than he realizes," Emily replied.

"What do you mean?"

"You'll understand in a moment. Margaret couldn't find Williams because he'd been watching the shop. When he saw Margaret leave, he went in to confront Marr again. He'd been drinking. He had a ship carpenter's mallet that a sailor had left at his boardinghouse. Margaret believes that he only meant to frighten Marr."

"But the argument got out of control," Ryan concluded. "After Williams killed Marr, he needed to eliminate anybody who'd heard the argument and could identify him. But why the baby? The baby wasn't a threat to him. Why did he kill the baby?"

"In his drunken rage," Emily replied, "Williams decided that if Marr was determined to punish Margaret because of the baby she was going to have, then Williams was going to punish *Marr's* baby."

The abbey's bells rang, making the air tremble.

"Three days ago, that thought would have been impossible for me to consider," Ryan said.

"Margaret suspected that Williams was responsible," Emily continued. "The next morning, after the authorities questioned her, she found Williams at his boardinghouse. She asked him, but he denied it. She asked him again, this time strongly, and again he denied it. But she could see it in his eyes. What was she going to do? She couldn't tell everyone that she was with child and without a husband and that the man who fathered the child was the man who slaughtered the Marr family. Her future as anything except a woman of the streets would be ruined if she told the truth."

"So she didn't reveal her suspicions," Ryan murmured.

"She says, if only she hadn't met Williams, if only the event between them hadn't occurred, if only she hadn't been weak . . ."

"Yes, all those people would not have died."

"All these years, guilt tortured her," Emily told them.

"What about the Williamson killings twelve days later?" Becker asked. "I told Inspector Ryan how strange it was that a man named John Williams would kill a man named John Williamson."

"According to Margaret, Williams became distracted and moody. He drank so much that she couldn't bear to be with him. He sought her out, saying how much he loved her, but she sent him away. One of the taverns that he went to belonged to Williamson. People joked that the two might be related, that John Williams was young enough to be John Williamson's son, and yet Williamson was old enough to be Williams's father."

"Makes me dizzy," Ryan complained. "Now I'm thinking like your father. William*son.*"

"You understand?" Emily asked.

"Williamson. Son of Williams. The name kept torturing him. He'd killed Marr's son. Margaret had left him. He might never see his own child, possibly a son. Guilt tore him apart until he lost his senses. I think your father would say that when Williams killed Williamson, it was like he was killing himself.

"A few days later, he did in fact do that, hanging himself in Coldbath Fields Prison," Ryan concluded.

The abbey's doors banged open, startling them. Organ music boomed outward as nervous worshippers emerged, not seeming to feel any safer.

Organ music. Emily suddenly realized where her father had gone. But there wasn't time to explain.

"Margaret's baby," she said.

"What about it?"

"She delivered a son. She worked as a mudlark, scavenging coal along the river, but she managed to keep the child with her. When the boy was four, she met a former soldier. They lived together."

"And?"

"The boy took the soldier's name. Brookline."

"What?"

"Margaret Jewell's son... John Williams's son... is Colonel Brookline."

DE QUINCEY FELT HANDS TOUCHING HIM.

"Hey!"

Waking with a fright, he kicked with his sore legs.

Someone jumped back.

In the pale morning light, De Quincey's eyes jerked open. A dozen specters formed a semicircle before him. Their clothes were ragged, their faces gaunt, their skin marked with sores.

"Just feelin' for a razor," the man who'd jumped back said.

"You think I'm the killer?" Ignoring the pain in his injured shoulder, De Quincey used both shackled hands to grip the grimy wall behind him and stood. "A slight man of my age, what chance would I have against men as tall as you? Why would I want to harm you?"

"For our valuables," another man said with sarcasm.

"Maybe you were trying to rob me of *my* valuables," De Quincey told them.

"Your chin scabbed, the blood on your coat, you don't look like you have any more valuables than us. Why are you wearin' handcuffs?"

"I had a disagreement with Lord Palmerston."

"With Lord Cupid? Ha."

"Truly, Lord Palmerston took a dislike to me and ordered me arrested."

"If you don't want to tell us the truth, that's your business." A man stepped forward threateningly. "But what are you doin' here?"

"The same as you. I needed a place to rest."

"I meant *here*. How'd you know to find *here*?"

"If Lord Cupid's really after 'im, he'll bring the police," another man complained. "They'll search until they find this place. Let's throw the bugger out on the street."

"Down this tunnel, can you still smell the bread from the bakeshop?" De Quincey asked.

"Bakeshop?"

"The aroma used to make my stomach rumble. But after a while, when my stomach was so small that I knew I couldn't eat even if the bread were in my hands, I used to go down there and inhale the fragrance of the bread, imagining that it gave me nourishment."

"How'd you know about that?"

"And there used to be a turn in the tunnel, with steps that led up to a courtyard. A water pump was there. I never trusted it, but it was the only water I could find, so I drank from it anyway."

"How'd you know about *that*?"

"More than fifty years ago, this was my home for several weeks until I found shelter in an empty house close to here on Greek Street."

De Quincey looked around, feeling the weight of a half century. "Sometimes I think the pain I experienced here was nothing compared to what I later encountered. I need some favors from you good gentlemen."

"Gentlemen? Ha."

"We don't do favors for outsiders for nothin'," someone else grumbled. "We need to eat, you know."

"Believe me, I do know. Unfortunately, I find myself embarrassed by a lack of funds. I do have a means to pay you, though."

"How?"

"With these handcuffs. In my right coat pocket, you'll find a key to them."

A ragged man reached into De Quincey's pocket and pulled out the key, jumping away. "Now we have you. Without us, you can't get the cuffs off."

"I couldn't get them off anyway. The keyhole is on the outside of the cuffs, where I am unable to reach. Please unencumber me."

"The little guy talks funny," one man said.

"Let's keep him a prisoner," somebody suggested. "He can make us laugh by talkin'."

"Yeah. Like a toy we pull out of a box."

"Remove the handcuffs and keep them," De Quincey advised. "They are yours to sell. Police shackles and a key that opens them ought to be worth a couple of pounds to parties at odds with the police."

"I never thought about that."

"But do it quickly. I need to be on my way."

The men hesitated.

"A couple of pounds," one of them murmured. "Do it."

Soon De Quincey's wrists were free of the weight of the shackles. He rubbed the irritated, swollen skin, encouraging blood to flow.

"I have another means of paying you," he told the men.

"*Now* what's he talkin' about?"

"My clothes."

"Huh?"

"I need someone my size with whom to change garments."

"You want to trade your clothes with what *we* wear?"

"Someone my size," De Quincey emphasized. "The clothes I receive need to appear as if they are indeed mine."

"The only one of us your size is Joey over here. How old are you, Joey? Fifteen?"

A thin boy emerged from the group. His clothes were as ragged as the others, his face scarred by smallpox. "Think so."

"Would you like my better clothes?" De Quincey offered.

"They're too nice. How can I beg in 'em? I'll look like I don't need the pence."

"But you'll be warmer. And I have no doubt that the clothes I give you will become ragged soon enough."

In truth, De Quincey's trouser cuffs were slightly frayed. The elbows on his coat looked thin. But in his constant condition of debt, they were the best he could afford.

"And your hat, please, Joey. You have a full head of hair to keep you warm."

Five minutes later, Joey was pulling his new coat over his new trousers and looking proud. "I could go to a royal ball."

"The beggar's ball is more like it," someone chortled.

Meanwhile, De Quincey pulled on the rags that the boy had given him. He tugged the shapeless hat down over his forehead.

"Where do you expect to go like *that*?" a man wondered in amazement. "We're tryin' to get out of rags, and *you* want to get *in* 'em."

"Going somewhere is exactly why I need my next favor, good gentlemen."

"What? *Another* favor?"

"Which one of you pretends not to have legs?"

They glanced at each other, self-conscious.

"How'd you know about..."

"I am aware of all the dodges. One of you juggles. One of you does acrobatic tricks, presumably Joey, because he's the youngest and most nimble."

Joey couldn't resist showing off. He performed several somersaults and a flip before walking on his hands.

The other beggars clapped.

"Bravo," De Quincey said. "As for the rest of you, one of you sings. One of you pretends to be blind. One of you sweeps dirt from the street when a gentleman crosses with a lady. One of you pleads that you need the price of a train ticket to go home to see your dying mother. And *one* of you pretends not to have legs. I have an excellent offer for the man who engages in that trade."

"What are you offerin'?"

A man limped forward. Years of pinning his legs under him had damaged his knees.

"May I see your platform?" De Quincey asked.

The man looked puzzled for a moment. "Is that what you call it?"

"Please bring it forward."

The man limped beyond his companions and returned with a square wooden board that had old carpet attached to the top and rollers on the bottom. The carpet was thick, hollowed in the middle, so that the man could hide his legs under him, creating the appearance that his legs had been cut off at the knees.

"Never seen better," De Quincey said. "Dear man, please step down the tunnel with me a short distance. I need to speak confidentially to you."

While the others watched with suspicion, De Quincey led the man away. The beggar winced with each step he took.

"Good fellow, I need to borrow your platform."

"How am I goin' to beg without it?"

"Would I be wrong," De Quincey asked, "in assuming that on occasion you enjoy a touch of alcohol?"

"It is one of my few pleasures."

"And would I be wrong in assuming that you also enjoy opium in your alcohol?"

"You're talkin' about laudanum?"

"Exactly, my good man. To soothe one's bones from the chill air. Are you familiar with it?"

"My knees ache all the time without it. The pain keeps me from sleepin' without it."

"Would you be willing to exchange your excellent platform for a supply of it?"

"How's *that* goin' to happen?"

"I need to be assured that you are familiar with laudanum's potency. I want you to be warm in the cold and able to sleep without not waking up."

"You're talkin' about dyin' from it?"

"That has been known to happen to inexperienced partakers."

"I've been swallowin' laudanum since I was first on the streets. So have *they*." The man indicated the group farther along the tunnel.

"Perhaps you'd like to share with them. That way, no one consumes too much."

"Share? How's *this* supposed to happen?"

"Do we have an agreement?"

"Yes, yes, yes. Now where's the laudanum?"

De Quincey led the limping man back to the broken crate. He reached under it and produced the flask.

"What's *that*?" one of the beggars yelled.

"Another payment for your favors." As much as De Quincey craved a swallow, he handed the flask to the man with the limp. It was one of the most difficult things he had ever been forced to do: giving away laudanum. "When the flask is empty, you can sell it."

The man with the limp took the first sip. Each of them shared.

"I wonder if it would be too bold to request yet one more favor," De Quincey ventured.

"For a little bloke, you certainly have nerve."

"Fifty years ago, during my time on these streets, it was the custom that our group had territory within which we worked. I could beg from the Hyde Park end of Oxford Street to the corner of Bond Street. South to Grosvenor and north to Wigmore. But if I crossed from that area, I transgressed on another group's territory, and the consequences could be severe."

"It's the same now," a beggar agreed. "We have our spots. We don't compete. Live and let live."

"You would do me an important service. In fact, you would do London and England itself a service if you communicated with the neighboring groups and requested that they in turn communicate with *their* neighboring groups."

"What for?"

"I'm looking for a man. He's a retired military officer. He served twenty years in India and was celebrated for his combat achievements. He is in his early forties, unusually tall, with attractive features that are nonetheless unsettling because they do not reveal his thoughts or emotions. He is clean-shaven. He has light brown, curly hair. He walks with an extreme military bearing. He dresses with the elegance suitable to the man who controls security for the home secretary."

"Lord Palmerston? You *do* know Lord Cupid?"

"I met Lord Palmerston only once. That was last night, and the experience was disagreeable. The man I wish to know about is named Colonel Brookline."

"What do you want to know?"

"The location of Brookline's lodging, his whereabouts, his habits, anything that anyone can learn."

"To help England, you said? England ain't helped *us* much lately. What do we get for doing this?"

"The relief of knowing that he won't murder you in your sleep."

"Well and good, but I'm just as afraid of dyin' from starvation."

"I guarantee that everyone who helps me find Colonel Brookline will receive a plentiful supply of food."

"Without a penny in your pocket, I don't see how you can guarantee a blasted thing," a man complained.

"Lord Palmerston will arrange for the food."

"The man who wants you in jail? You expect us to believe that?"

"I promise that Lord Palmerston will overflow with generosity when shown the evil that hides next to him. Joey, since you now wear presentable clothes, you're the best person to sit on a bench in Green Park and watch Lord Palmerston's mansion on Piccadilly. Colonel Brookline will arrive there today. Probably several times. The description I gave you and the stern look in Brookline's eyes are unmistakable. Remember he is tall, with an extreme military bearing. He does not have facial hair, unlike the mutton-chopped politicians and bureaucrats who visit Lord Palmerston. His hair is curly."

"And what am I supposed to do if I see him?"

"Follow him. Then instruct a fellow knight of the street to come here and report to this gentleman who offered me the use of his platform."

"My word, you're makin' us into detectives," a beggar said with a toothless grin.

"Heroes," De Quincey corrected him.

On a usual Tuesday morning, Oxford Street would have been crammed with vehicles and pedestrians as well as various mongers with their coffee, pastry, and oyster carts. But on this particular Tuesday, traffic was half of what it normally would have been as the terror of years earlier was repeated.

The city's five dozen newspapers had printed extra copies of special editions but couldn't keep up with the demand. Rumors spread rapidly that more murders had been committed than were reported in the newspapers, some of them in neighborhoods of distinction. It was widely assumed that, after the governor of Coldbath Fields Prison had been killed, all the criminals had escaped with the purpose of violating London. The roads from the city were packed with coaches as the wealthy departed to their country estates. The railway stations were crammed with anyone who could afford a ticket.

Thus any observers studying Oxford Street in the hope of seeing a short, thin man of sixty-nine years had reason to believe that the absence of the street's normal chaos would make him more noticeable.

That there would be observers, De Quincey had no doubt. The previous night, he had told Emily, in Brookline's presence, that she would find him where he listened to the music. Brookline couldn't know what that meant. But perhaps Emily wouldn't know, either. De Quincey could only pray that she would remember when he had taken her to Oxford Street on Sunday and shown her the corner where he and Ann had listened to the barrel organ. But meanwhile Colonel Brookline would send men to every place in London where he and Emily were likely to reunite. Oxford Street — so important in De Quincey's past — would be at the top of the list.

What Brookline couldn't be aware of — what no one who hadn't nearly starved to death there could be aware of — was its underside, the secret world that only beggars inhabited.

Anyone watching now saw those beggars emerge from their crannies. They looked at the day's dismal prospects and proceeded with more than usual discouragement toward their corners. One of them was legless. The poor ragged devil transported himself on a small platform that had rollers under it. His head bowed, he used sticks to push at the paving stones of the pavement and move the platform along rather than abrade his hands on the stones.

EACH SEAM IN THE STONES sent a jolt through De Quincey's knees. The pressure of his legs pinned under him made him wish that he had sipped from the laudanum flask before giving it to his new companions in the tunnel. Soon his craving for opium would intensify his pain. Already his head throbbed while sweat slicked his forehead, sweat caused by withdrawal, not by the exertion of moving the platform.

Logic suggested that anyone watching the street would need to remain stationary, pretending to wait for someone or read a newspaper or look in a shopwindow. De Quincey noticed several possibilities, but as he wheeled past one of them, he attracted only the slightest, dismissive attention. The lowest members of society were beneath anyone's interest.

At another alley, De Quincey rolled the platform into shadows. Only when he was confident of not being observed did he dismount and carry the platform down steps. Making his way through deeper shadows, he reached another sequence of tunnels. Past a gap in a rusted barrier, he navigated what became a maze until he climbed steps and faced a cluster of shacks in a dismal courtyard.

A haggard woman peered out. "A customer this early, and he don't look like he has two pence to rub together."

Another haggard woman peered out. "Tell 'im we don't do charities for beggars."

"Good morning, dear ladies," De Quincey announced. He tipped his shapeless cap. His smile brought pain to the scab on his chin. "How is the linen-lifting tribe this morning?"

"Save your foolishness. A shilling, or no Bob-in-the-Betty-box for you."

"You misjudge my intentions, dear ladies." De Quincey put his cap back on. "I'm here to pay a social visit. Would Doris and Melinda reside here?"

"Doris and Melinda? How do you know...?"

"Some gracious paladins of the streets suggested that I'd find them here."

"The way you talk. I heard your voice before."

"Indeed you did, my dear lady. At Vauxhall Gardens, yesterday morning." De Quincey concealed his distress at the memory. "You all identified yourselves as Ann. My clothes were more presentable then."

"Gorblimey, it's the little man! What *happened* to you?"

"My fortunes have fallen since I encountered the same man who hired you to go to Vauxhall Gardens. Doris, I believe that is you."

"The bugger promised each of us another sovereign. Swore he'd give 'em to us last night. Didn't show up. We passed up customers while we waited."

"I can arrange for you to receive the sovereigns he didn't pay you."

"And how would *that* happen?"

"Melinda, is that you? I recognize your charming voice."

Melinda batted her eyelashes.

The other women laughed.

"Lord Palmerston himself will pay you the sovereigns," De Quincey said.

"And you'd be pals with Lord Cupid, would you?"

"We are definitely acquainted. If you kind ladies can spare me a few moments, I hope I can persuade you to become my spies."

15

An Effigy in Wax

MADAME TUSSAUD PREFERRED CORPSES. Living models, especially famous ones like Voltaire, Rousseau, and Benjamin Franklin, enjoyed the idea that their likenesses would achieve immortality, but when it came to practicalities, they complained about staying immobile for a considerable time while Tussaud made the casts from which she created her eerie wax impressions.

Corpses, on the other hand, displayed no impatience. During the French Revolution, Tussaud frequented morgues and looked for the separated heads of well-known victims of the Terror, making death masks of them. So skilled was she that revolutionaries compelled her to keep making wax models of prominent guillotine victims. Seeking a less dangerous environment, she toured Europe with her macabre collection and eventually settled in London, where she established her wax museum.

Although customers claimed that they went to Madame Tussaud's to see the dignified portrayals of notable personages such as Sir Walter Scott, the probability was that what they really wanted to see was the museum's Chamber of Horrors. For an extra sixpence, they could gaze at what appeared to be the bloodied heads of Robespierre, King Louis XVI, and Marie Antoinette. Visitors could decide if she was as beautiful as rumor suggested. They could also view wax effigies of notorious criminals depicted in the midst of their gruesome crimes.

The location of the wax museum was only a half mile north of Oxford Street, on the west side of Baker Street. There, a hansom cab stopped, and a clean-shaven man with curly hair, a stern look, and an extreme military bearing walked into the museum. Earlier, he had sent an operative to pay for the museum to be closed. When he showed a special ticket that his operative had purchased for him, an employee allowed him to enter.

Brookline did not linger to appreciate the eerily lifelike wax models of various admirable personages, such as Lord Nelson. Instead he verified that no one else was in the building and then made his way toward the rear of the museum, where the Chamber of Horrors was located. Rumors had reached him about a new exhibit that had opened after the murders on Saturday night — or rather had *re*opened, for this exhibit had been one of Madame Tussaud's most popular attractions when she toured through England many years earlier.

Brookline had seen it when he was young, before he joined the military. In fact, he had gone back to see it many times, although he had never been able to adjust to it any more than he had been able to restrain himself from returning to it again and again.

A plaque said:

JOHN WILLIAMS IN THE MIDST OF HIS FIRST
RATCLIFFE HIGHWAY MURDERS
(SATURDAY, 7 DECEMBER 1811)

"THE SUBLIMEST IN THEIR EXCELLENCE THAT
EVER WERE COMMITTED."
OPIUM-EATER THOMAS DE QUINCEY,
"ON MURDER CONSIDERED AS ONE OF THE
FINE ARTS"

Brookline stared at the scene, which was so vividly three-dimensional that, if not for a rope barrier, he could have walked within it. Before him was an inferior shop. Lanterns cast shadows, creating an ominous atmosphere.

A woman lay on the floor, her head bashed in. A young man sprawled farther away, *his* head bashed in as well. Blood was everywhere. A savage man was suspended in the motion of swinging a ship carpenter's mallet at someone slumped over a counter, behind which blood-spattered linen and socks were stacked on shelves.

Brookline knew that the scene wasn't portrayed correctly. Forty-three years earlier, the victim, Timothy Marr, had collapsed behind the counter. Similarly, a shattered cradle was visible beyond the dead shop assistant, a hint of a baby's bloodied head protruding from beneath a blanket. But in reality, the cradle and the baby could not have been visible from the shop. That particular murder had occurred in a back room.

Those inaccuracies weren't important, however. What mattered was the face of the murderer, who was viewed in profile as though he had turned for a satisfied look at his victims on the floor before he resumed his raging assault on Timothy Marr.

Madame Tussaud had not been able to see John Williams's corpse after he used a handkerchief to hang himself in Coldbath Fields Prison. Instead she had relied on a sketch that an artist had made of Williams's left profile shortly after he was taken down.

The sketch was not part of Tussaud's exhibit, but Brookline didn't need to have it there in order to know that the profile of the wax model before him was faithful to the artist's rendering.

Brookline knew this because he had found a copy of the sketch when he was young. He had kept it in a pocket, eventually wearing it out and needing to acquire another. He had studied it relentlessly, determined to learn its secrets. What kind of man had John Williams been?

What kind of man had his *father* been?

His mother, a coal scavenger along the river, had carried him on her back while she worked. They had lived in a shack near the docks, along with three other desperate women. As he grew older, he couldn't help noticing that she often wept in the middle of the night, concealing an anguish that she refused to explain, no matter how often he asked her what was the matter.

He never learned how her path crossed that of a retired army sergeant,

Samuel Brookline, or how the three of them came to live in a somewhat better shack near the docks. The former soldier, a veteran of the Battle of Waterloo, worked for a dustman, collecting coal ashes in a donkey cart, taking them to a warehouse near the docks. After the ashes were sifted in case they contained saleable objects that had mistakenly been discarded, they were sold to factories that made fertilizer or bricks.

Eventually the former soldier found a job for him with the dustman, and soon everyone thought of him as Brookline's son, just as his mother referred to herself as Mrs. Brookline even though they weren't married. But she always seemed sorrowful, and she continued weeping in the middle of the night.

One day he learned why. He and his mother were walking near the docks when a woman asked, "Margaret, good heavens, is that you?"

His mother kept walking, urging him along.

"Margaret? It *is* you. Margaret Jewell."

While his mother's first name was Margaret, she had always told him that her last name was Brody before she met the former soldier and took his name.

The woman caught up to his mother and asked, "What's wrong? Margaret, don't you recognize me? I'm Nancy. I used to work in the shop three doors down from Marr."

"Maybe I look like someone else," his mother said brusquely. "I don't know who Marr was. I'm sure I never saw you before."

"The Ratcliffe Highway murders. I would've sworn. You're really not Margaret? Sorry. I must've made a mistake. Really, I would've sworn."

The woman left them. The boy and his mother continued along the street.

"The Ratcliffe Highway murders?" the boy asked.

"Nothing to concern you," his mother told him.

But there was something in her eyes, a haunted look that made him resolve to learn what the Ratcliffe Highway murders were and who Margaret Jewell was.

One evening, he took a detour when he returned from the dustman's warehouse. He went to Ratcliffe Highway, asked about the murders, and was shocked to learn the details. Although they were eleven years in the past, their terror remained vivid to those who had lived in the neighborhood.

"Mother," he asked one evening when he found her alone in the shack, weeping, "did that woman the other day truly recognize you? Are you Margaret Jewell?"

His mother looked frightened then, as if he had accused her instead of asked her.

"Did you work for the Marr family that was murdered?"

Her look of fright changed to one of horror.

"Did you know John Williams? People say that they knew him in the neighborhood and that he sometimes came into the shop."

His mother screamed.

The former soldier rushed into the shack but couldn't calm her.

"What happened?"

"I just asked her about the Ratcliffe Highway murders," the boy said.

"Why would you ask about *them?*"

"Someone mentioned them. I was curious."

"I worked on the docks back then," the former soldier told him. "You can't imagine how terrified everybody felt. Twelve days later, they happened *again.*"

His mother put her hands to her face.

"What's troubling you, Margaret?" the former soldier asked. "Did you know someone who was killed in those murders?"

A few days later, the boy made another detour after working at the dustman's warehouse. He returned to Ratcliffe Highway, asked more questions, and was directed to the King's Arms tavern, where the second murders had occurred.

A printed copy of a sketch was displayed inside one of the tavern's windows for people going past to read. The sketch showed a man in left profile, with curly hair, a high forehead, a sharp nose, and a strong chin. A name was under the sketch, but the boy had not learned to read.

An announcement was next to the sketch, but the boy couldn't read that, either.

"Sir," he asked a man walking past, "would you please tell me what this says?"

The man had ordinary clothes and was not of sufficient standing to be called "sir," but the boy had learned that pretending to be polite could produce rewards, such as a piece of bread, when he visited households to gather coal ashes. The boy also paid the man a compliment by assuming he could read.

"Of course, boy. The words under this sketch give the name John Williams. A vicious sort he was, as the words on this other piece of paper tell us."

The man drew a finger along the window and the poster beyond it. "'On this site, 19 December 1811, the infamous murderer John Williams slaughtered tavernkeeper John Williamson, his wife, and a servant girl.' Poor form, using the murders to attract customers to the tavern."

The boy stared at the sketch of John Williams. A lamppost was behind him. People moving along the street caused the shadows to change and made him aware of reflections on the window. In particular, he became aware of *his* reflection, of his face next to that of John Williams: high forehead, sharp nose, and strong chin.

"Better not stare at him too long," the man advised. "With that curly hair of yours, you look a little like him. You don't want to give yourself nightmares."

"No, sir."

"Can't read, huh? Would you like to learn?"

The boy thought a moment and realized that, if he didn't know how to read, he wouldn't be able to learn more about John Williams and the Ratcliffe Highway murders.

"No, sir, I can't read. Yes, sir, I'd like to learn."

"Good lad. Do you know where St. Nicholas church is? It's down by the docks. St. Nicholas is the patron saint of sailors and merchants."

"The church is near the warehouse where I work for dustman Kendrick."

"A dustman, are you? Want to make something better of yourself?"

"Yes, sir."

"On Sunday morning, come to the nine o'clock service. I help the minister. After the service, I teach people how to read the Bible. I know that's your day of rest from being a dustman, but I always give a biscuit to any children who come to learn to read the holy word."

The boy's stomach rumbled at the thought of the biscuit. "Thank you, sir."

"With those good manners, you'll go far, boy. Now do what I say and stop looking at that sketch before it gives you nightmares."

To the puzzlement of his mother and the former soldier, the boy went to church every Sunday, sat through the service, attended his reading lesson, and received a biscuit. He became the best student the church had ever seen. Within a year, he could read any Bible passage his teacher presented to him.

He went to every newspaper and learned that they had archives in which reports about John Williams and the Ratcliffe Highway murders were stored. He read all of them until he knew them by memory.

He found a copy of a sketch of Williams and carried it in a pocket, studying it when no one saw him.

"Mother, who was my father?" the boy asked.

"He died a long time ago."

"But who *was* he? Tell me about him."

"It hurts me to think about him."

"How did he die? Is that why you sob at night?"

"I don't want to talk about it."

"What was his name?"

His mother turned away.

After work, the boy kept returning to Ratcliffe Highway. He frequently entered the building where Marr had been killed. It was still a linen shop, its layout exactly as described in the newspaper accounts. The boy imagined where the bodies had lain, where the blood had sprayed.

He returned to the King's Arms tavern, this time going inside, again imagining where the bodies and the gore had been.

He pretended that he walked next to the cart that had transported his father's body past twenty thousand people to the crossroads of Cannon and Cable streets, where his father had been buried with a stake through his heart. The boy positioned himself in the middle of the crossroads. As traffic rattled past and drivers shouted for him to get out of the way, he wondered if he stood on top of his father's bones.

He was under a dock when the former soldier discovered him.

"Stop!"

The boy spun. He had muzzled a cat so that it couldn't wail. Its legs were tied.

"Why would you do that?" the former soldier demanded.

The man grabbed the knife from the boy's hand, freed the cat's muzzle, and released the cords around the cat's legs. Despite its injuries, the cat managed to run away.

One night, the boy showed the sketch of John Williams to his mother.

"Is this my father?"

She recoiled from the image.

"John Williams. He's my father, isn't he?"

She stared at him in horror.

"Why did my father kill all those people?"

She wailed.

The former soldier hurried in, shouting at the boy, "What in blazes did you do *now*?"

"I asked her if John Williams was my father."

Weeping, his mother sank to her knees.

The former soldier shoved the boy toward the door. "Leave her alone! Get out! I don't want to see you here anymore!"

"*You're* not my father! You can't give me orders!"

With a gasp, the man staggered back. His breath driven from him, he peered down at the knife the boy had plunged into his stomach.

"Tell me, Mother. Am I John Williams's son?"

"You're a monster the same as your father was."

The boy plunged the knife into her also, hurled the shack's lantern onto the floor, and stepped outside.

Behind him, amid screams, flames crackled.

As BROOKLINE STUDIED THE WAX display of his father swinging the mallet, footsteps brought his attention back to the present.

He turned toward three men who appeared at the doorway. Two of them came into the room while the other remained at the entrance, making sure that no one eavesdropped from the corridor.

Brookline stepped toward them, positioning himself in front of another exhibit, one that showed the body snatchers, Burke and Hare, frozen in the midst of removing a corpse from a coffin they had excavated. A plaque explained that Burke and Hare sold corpses to surgeons who had few legal ways to obtain bodies for medical research. To provide even better specimens, Burke and Hare took to murdering people.

By conducting the conversation before this exhibit, Brookline distracted his associates from noticing the resemblance between him and John Williams in the later tableau.

"Anthony was killed at the prison last night," Brookline told them.

The three men adjusted to this information.

"The newspapers reported that *someone* was killed there in addition to the governor," the man at the door finally said. "Not the Opium-Eater. Someone else. I hoped it wasn't Anthony."

"He was very convincing as a would-be assassin outside Lord Palmerston's mansion," Brookline told them. "The fireworks he set off during his escape through Green Park were memorable."

"Godspeed to him," the two men said.

"Godspeed," Brookline echoed solemnly. "He was a man worthy to share combat with. Tonight we pay tribute to him."

Here," Margaret said.

"Stop," Ryan told their driver.

The coach halted outside a bakeshop on a gloomy street near the Seven Dials rookery. While most of the area near the slum was unusually empty, the shop bustled with activity.

"What's going on?" Becker asked with a frown.

He and Emily helped Margaret down and escorted her inside. Frantic people jostled past them, hurrying out, carrying bread.

"Reckoned you quit," the owner grumbled behind the counter.

"I had personal business," Margaret told him.

"Well, put on your apron and get back here with me. I can't keep up with all the customers. They want to make sure they have food at home so they don't need to go out tonight."

"Margaret," Emily whispered, "no one realizes this is where you work. You'll be safe here. We're going to need you. Don't leave."

* * *

Wʜᴇʀᴇ ʏᴏᴜʀ ꜰᴀᴛʜᴇʀ listened to the music," Ryan said as the coach took them along Oxford Street.

"It's the only place I can think of," Emily told him. "I kept imagining the violins and horns of a concert. But Father never mentioned any place where he listened to a concert. Then I heard the organ at Westminster Abbey, and I realized there were many kinds of music. *Organ* music. Father told me, when he was young, starving on this street, he and Ann used to come to a particular corner and listen to a man play a barrel organ."

"Do you remember the corner your father showed you?" Becker asked.

"Up ahead on the right."

"The street isn't busy. If he's here, we shouldn't have trouble seeing him."

"Nor would Brookline's men." Ryan pointed. "See there and over there? Those men appear to be reading a newspaper or looking into a shopwindow, but what they're really doing is watching the street. Brilliant. They work for Lord Palmerston, but Brookline can order them to do whatever he wants."

"This is the corner," Emily said. "I don't see Father anywhere."

"Maybe he's nearby." Ryan called up to the driver, "Stop."

He stepped from the coach and walked up the neighboring street, entering a shop as if on an errand.

"May I help you, sir?" a clerk asked, eager for business.

"Sorry. I made a mistake."

Ryan left the shop, didn't see De Quincey anywhere, and walked back toward the coach.

On the corner, a legless beggar banged a cup on a paving stone, pleading beneath his hat, "Kind sir, can you spare a pence?"

Ryan continued toward the coach.

"Inspector Ryan," the beggar continued pleading, "don't act surprised."

At the mention of his name, Ryan felt his skin prickle.

De Quincey?

Ryan had met informants under unusual conditions often enough that he controlled his reaction and dropped a sixpence into the beggar's cup.

"Meet me on the street behind this one," De Quincey told him, pulling the silver coin from the cup. "At Cavendish Square."

Ryan stepped into the coach and told the driver, "Go past two intersections, then turn toward the next parallel street."

"But what about Father?" Emily protested.

"Promise to look straight ahead."

"Why?"

"Whatever you do, don't look back."

"Inspector, please explain yourself."

"That was your father on the corner."

"The beggar without legs?"

DE QUINCEY BANGED HIS CUP on the paving stones a few more times. Occasional pedestrians went past and ignored him. When he saw the coach turn a corner, he pushed his wheeled platform in the other direction, passing one of the men who watched the street. A short distance beyond the man, he veered into an alley, dismounted from the platform, and descended into the tunnels.

A few minutes later, he reached the shadowy area where he had made his bargain with the beggars.

A man limped in one direction and then another, working his legs.

"I been on that...what'd you call it?...platform for twenty years. Walkin' feels strange. Hurts my legs more than scrunchin' 'em under me."

"I have no further use for it," De Quincey said. "Here's sixpence someone gave me. Many thanks, my good man. Did you receive any reports?"

"Someone thinks he noticed Brookline going in and out of Tussaud's wax museum on Baker Street. Someone else thinks he knows where this bloke might live."

"What's the address?"

When De Quincey heard the street name, he gasped.

I DON'T SEE HIM," Emily fretted. "We've been around Cavendish Square twice, but even when I pay attention to the beggars, I don't see him. Oh," she exclaimed.

From bushes in the square, a tiny ragged figure darted through an open metal gate, rushing toward the coach. Becker quickly opened the door, letting the beggar in.

"Hey!" the driver yelled.

"It's all right," Ryan assured him.

As Becker closed the door, De Quincey remained sprawled on the coach's floor, keeping his head below the windows.

"Did anyone notice?"

"Not that I can see," Becker answered.

"Father, you're shaking," Emily said.

"I need my medicine."

"We can't afford to buy laudanum for you," Ryan objected.

"I didn't ask you to do so." De Quincey's face glistened with sweat. "The man we're hunting—I know who he is."

"Yes. It's Colonel Brookline," Emily told him.

"What? You reached the same conclusion?" De Quincey asked, his amazement distracting him from his pain.

"Father, we met Margaret Jewell."

For once in his life, De Quincey was speechless.

Emily quickly explained what they had learned. "Margaret was too ashamed to tell the truth back then. She met a former soldier and took his last name: Brookline."

"Brookline is the son of John Williams?" De Quincey asked in greater astonishment.

"The boy became obsessed with his father. He haunted the Ratcliffe Highway murder scenes. During an argument about Williams, he stabbed the former soldier and Margaret, then set fire to the shack. The former soldier died, but Margaret managed to crawl away. She never saw the boy again."

"All we have are suspicions, though," De Quincey objected. "When I told Lord Palmerston that Brookline matched my description of the killer, the home secretary was outraged. Palmerston can't possibly imagine that a war hero, an officer, and the most trusted man on his staff, the man he depends on for his life, is capable of these murders."

"I know one man who might believe us," Ryan said.

"Who?"

"Commissioner Mayne. The man who told Becker and me about the original murders."

"Persuade him."

"God help me, I can't bear to see you shaking any longer," Ryan said. "Driver, stop."

Ryan hurried from the coach, entered a chemist's shop, and returned with a bottle of ruby-colored liquid. "That cost me one of my last shillings. Use it wisely."

De Quincey grabbed the bottle and seemed about to swallow its entire contents but suddenly stopped his trembling hand and took only a sip.

He closed his eyes and held his breath. Then he exhaled. When he looked at Ryan, his eyes were less anguished.

"Thank you."

"For heaven's sake, don't tell anyone I did that."

"You may count on my gratitude. Go to Commissioner Mayne. Meanwhile, Constable Becker, Emily, and I shall try to find Brookline."

"We're not police officers any longer. If Commissioner Mayne refuses to listen, we're on our own. We can't just wander through London, hoping to find Brookline."

"We're not on our own, and we won't be wandering. My informants gave me crucial information. I have no doubt where Brookline lives."

THE DESTINATION WAS so close that it surprised Emily and Becker. De Quincey instructed the driver to return to Oxford Street and proceed east, then south toward Soho Square.

"When I survived on the streets of London in my youth," De Quincey explained, "Soho Square was one of my haunts. I don't know what the Soho Bazaar over there is. That factory for Crosse and Blackwell pickles didn't exist. But the entrance ahead looks exactly the same as when I collapsed next to Ann fifty-two years ago. I see it as if it were yesterday. If Ann hadn't acted quickly to revive me..." De Quincey repressed the memory. "And here, just below the square..."

"Greek Street," Emily said, reading a sign on the side of a building. "You wrote about this area, Father."

"In my *Confessions.* I've come far, and yet I haven't come far at all. Please stop, my good man," De Quincey instructed the driver.

"Never had any fare treat me so polite," the driver responded, bringing the coach to a halt.

"Number thirty-eight," De Quincey told his companions. "In part, I survived the winter because a mysterious man took pity on me and allowed me to sleep in a house that he occupied from time to time. The house had no furniture. I slept on the bare floor with a bundle of law papers for a pillow and a foul-smelling horseman's cloak as a blanket."

Becker pointed. "Number thirty-eight is just down the street."

"Does anyone appear to be watching for visitors?" De Quincey asked.

"Everything looks quiet."

They opened a coach door and descended to the pavement. A cold breeze made Emily pull her coat tighter.

"This is the address from which one of my informants saw a man matching Brookline's description depart," De Quincey said. "Constable Becker, I trust that you still have your knife and your truncheon?"

"Close at hand."

"Emily, stay behind us. If we encounter difficulties, run."

"I won't leave you, Father."

"Both of you stay behind *me,*" Becker ordered.

All the houses on the street had three levels and adjoined one another. Number 38 drew attention because of its gloom.

"Fifty-two years ago, it wore the same unhappy countenance," De Quincey said. "The only difference is the windows."

"They all have bars," Emily noted.

"The bars weren't here when I knew the house. And the window on the second floor wasn't that small. It has been altered to reduce its size."

"Someone's worried about intruders," Becker said.

As in every other house, thick curtains prevented a view of the interior.

"Emily, while I go up the street and appear to beg, why don't you and Constable Becker knock on the doors to either side of this residence? Tell whoever answers that your last name is Brookline and that you're trying to find your brother, a former colonel who lives on this street but who won't give you his number. Pretend that you and he had a long-ago disagreement, that you desire a reconciliation. Request information about his welfare. Constable Becker, it might be best to fold your arms over your chest to hide the slashes on your coat."

De Quincey walked up the street and sat on a step, watching Emily and Becker speak to women who stepped outside each residence. Each of the women wore the apron and dust bonnet of a servant.

Even though De Quincey was seated, his need for laudanum forced him to keep moving his feet as if walking in place. He took a small sip from his bottle, holding his tremors at bay. The cold breeze bit his cheeks and contributed to his shaking.

A breeze tossed debris past him. He couldn't help noticing the unusual lack of activity as numbers of people either stayed indoors or else left the city.

In five minutes, Emily and Becker walked up the street to join him.

"They were reluctant to answer the door," Becker said. "If not for Emily's presence, they probably would have suspected me of being the killer."

"Brookline does live there," Emily confirmed.

De Quincey felt his pulse quicken.

"He never gave his last name, but he matches Brookline's description, and he insists on being called 'colonel,'" Becker added.

"Of course," De Quincey said. "Brookline's mother was a riverbank scavenger. He rose far beyond that. He couldn't restrain himself from demanding to be addressed by his hard-earned title."

"A distant man, one of the servants calls him," Emily continued. "There are signs that he's planning to move."

"Oh?"

"Yesterday and today, coaches took away objects wrapped in blankets."

"Indeed?"

"But why would he live in a house where you found shelter more than a half century ago?" Becker wondered.

"I hope to discover that."

De Quincey stared at his laudanum bottle, wishing he could finish it and an endless number of other bottles until he could sleep and pretend that this waking nightmare didn't exist.

"Father, this boy appears to be wearing your clothes," Emily said in confusion.

De Quincey looked where she pointed down the street.

He smiled with genuine enthusiasm. "Joey. How good to see you, my fine lad."

As the boy hurried toward them, Emily and Becker tried not to frown at the smallpox scars on his face.

"Those *are* your clothes, Father."

"I was told you wanted to see me," Joey told De Quincey. "I came here as fast as I could."

"Did you catch a glimpse of Colonel Brookline entering and leaving Lord Palmerston's mansion?"

"An hour ago when the church bells rang. A dustboy is followin' Brookline on a donkey's cart."

"And someone else is watching the mansion now that you're here?"

"Yes. But I don't think the guards'll let 'im stay in the park too long in his rags." Joey tugged at the coat De Quincey gave him. "I don't feel proper in this."

"Then you won't be disappointed if I need to exchange garments with you again?"

"Disappointed? I can't breathe in these."

"Then by all means, we shall allow you to breathe."

Five minutes later, they returned from a nearby alley, De Quincey wearing his clothes again while Joey looked comfortable in his rags.

"Constable Becker," De Quincey said. "I don't suppose you've ever —"

"Constable?" Joey asked in alarm.

"Not at the moment," Becker assured him.

"A friend," De Quincey said. "This man intends you no harm."

"That'd be a new one, a peeler meanin' me no harm."

"Becker, have you ever acquired instruction in manipulating locks?"

"Picking them, you mean?" Becker asked.

"In a word."

"I'm trained to keep locks secure, not force them."

"I feared as much. Joey, in your endeavors, have *you* learned to manipulate locks?"

"With a peeler in front of me, you want me to admit I —?"

"Mr. Becker, turn away and put your hands over your ears," Emily said, pointedly avoiding the word "constable."

"Do what?"

"To make Joey feel at ease."

Becker hesitated, then awkwardly did what Emily requested, putting his hands over his ears.

"Joey, have you ever picked a lock?" De Quincey requested.

"Once or twice," the boy admitted. "Usin' a nail."

"Then go over to that door and knock on it. Can you read numbers?"

"I learned a little."

"The number on the door is thirty-eight. Knock loudly. If people are in residence, I want them to hear you and open the door. The absence of chimney smoke on this cold day suggests that the house is unoccupied, but we need to be certain."

"What if someone does answer?"

"Beg for bread. For a penny. Anything whoever answers can spare. And while you're waiting, study the lock. Meanwhile we'll step into this alley. If someone answers, I don't wish us to be seen."

While De Quincey, Becker, and Emily waited in the alley, the sound of Joey striking the knocker on the door reached them. The sound persisted.

Two minutes later, Joey rejoined them in the alley.

"Nobody answered."

"And the lock?"

"Never saw a keyhole shaped that way. No way can I pick it with a nail. It don't even have a doorknob." Joey looked suspiciously at Becker.

"Then it appears I need to ask you to demonstrate your speciality," De Quincey said.

"But I already tried to beg and nobody answered."

"You normally beg in a particular way."

Joey began to realize what De Quincey was talking about.

"That's correct, Joey. You're an acrobat."

As DE QUINCEY, Becker, and Emily watched in the alley, Joey gripped a drainage pipe and climbed. The pipe was made of cast iron and gave his fifteen-year-old hands ample room to grip it. Sometimes he found niches where mortar between bricks had fallen away, providing a place for him to wedge the toes of his worn-out shoes. Wanting to show off to the attractive young lady, he climbed as quickly as possible, although he had another reason for climbing quickly — the December cold made his hands ache against the metal. By the time he crawled over the eaves trough and positioned himself on a pitched tile roof, he needed to blow on his fingers to return sensation to them. If anyone noticed him on the roof, he wouldn't arouse suspicion because it was common to see ragged boys on roofs, cleaning chimneys.

Soot made the tiles slippery. The breeze didn't help. Twice Joey was forced to pause and steady his nervous breathing. But at last he reached the peak of the roof, from which another slope descended, one to the front, the other to the rear of the stretch of adjoining buildings. Straddling the peak, anchoring himself in the breeze, he briefly surveyed the magnificent expanse of London. Then he focused his concentration and squirmed past ten chimneys until he came to the part of the roof that De Quincey had told him about.

"I resided here many years ago," the little man had said. "Searching for a blanket to give me warmth at night, I climbed the stairs to the top floor and found empty servants' quarters. In a closet, a small staircase led to a space beneath the pitch of the roof, and that tiny space contained only a metal hatch that provided access to the chimney. The device allowed chimney sweeps to exit the chimney after their task was accomplished. It prevented them from needing to exit on the roof, from which a number of sweeps had fallen. I remember the hatch because it was unusual for the designer of a building to care about the welfare of sweeps. You are thin enough to descend into the chimney. The hatch will no doubt be secured on the other side. But Constable, I mean, *Mr.* Becker will loan you a knife. With its blade, you should be able to pry between the chimney bricks and the hatch, lifting the swinging bolt that secures it."

"You want me to go into a bloomin' chimney?"

"Only for what I judge to be eight feet. If you cannot open the hatch, you can easily return to the top of the chimney and make your way back across the roof."

"Easily? And didn't you say sweeps fell from this roof?"

"No doubt they lacked your acrobatic skills."

"What will I get for this?"

"As I promised, food. Plenty of food. Lord Palmerston will be extremely grateful to you."

"Well, Lord Cupid weren't too grateful to *you,* judgin' from the handcuffs I first saw you in."

"Father, the boy deserves more than food," the beautiful young woman objected.

Joey enjoyed looking at her. "Believe me, miss, I won't turn my back on food."

"Would you turn your back on going to school?"

"School?"

"And receiving your food *there?*"

"Such things are possible?"

"I will do everything in my power to make it so."

"If this young lady promises something," the man who claimed not to be a constable assured Joey, "I have yet to see her not gain her way."

The woman looked at the tall man as if she wasn't sure that what he said was a compliment.

Now Joey felt proud that he had been able to count the ten chimneys. He looked toward the opposite side of the street, where the tall man nodded, confirming that Joey was at the correct chimney. The man returned to the alley.

Joey stared down the chimney and verified that there wasn't any smoke drifting up. He also determined that there weren't any obstacles and that the chimney had a standard width, allowing access. The constable's knife sheath was strapped to his left arm, where he could reach it as he descended. He took a deep breath, knowing from experience — he had been a chimney sweep four years earlier — that a cloud of soot would be dislodged when he squirmed into the chimney.

When Joey had been a sweep, his employer had forced him into the bottom of the chimney and then lit a fire under him, compelling him to climb as quickly as possible, thus allowing for the maximum number of chimneys to be cleaned each day. Joey had held a bag above him to collect the ashes and emerged from the top of the chimney with his skin and clothes totally black, coughing, weighed down by the heavy bag.

By comparison, this particular job wasn't difficult, but Joey had made a fuss anyhow, trying to learn what else he could get for his efforts, although so far he hadn't received anything. To this point, his only reward was that the little man amused him and the man's daughter had a pleasant smile and treated him kindly.

The trick was to brace his knees against one side of the chimney while he shoved his back against the other side, easing down. Unfortunately, the rough texture of the bricks would create more holes in what he wore. Trying not to breathe, he slowly descended into the cramped darkness. Soot immediately floated around him, covering his hands and face. The sharp smell stung his nostrils. He paused, let the dust settle, inhaled shallowly, and descended farther. Sunlight no longer reached him.

Unable to see, he needed to feel along the bricks in search of the metal hatch. He squirmed down farther, pressing his back harder against the bricks, but he still didn't feel the metal plate. Perhaps it had been removed in the many years since the little man had lived in this house.

Almost choking on the soot, Joey descended even farther. A portion of a brick broke away, plummeting and crashing. Joey grimaced and increased the pressure on his shoes to keep from falling. He grimaced for another reason also—if anyone was in the house, the noise would have warned that person about what he was doing.

Lungs aching, Joey slid lower. His heart raced when he touched the metal hatch. It didn't budge. With care, he removed the knife from the sheath strapped to his arm. Feeling the edges of the hatch, he identified the side that had hinges and inserted the knife on the opposite side, between the hatch and the bricks.

The knife was too thick to pass through the narrow gap.

Light-headed, Joey scraped the knife against the bricks, working to widen the gap. Forced to breathe, he felt soot irritate his throat. All the chimney sweep boys he had worked with had died from lungs filled with soot. Blind, he subdued a gagging sensation and kept scraping at the bricks as more soot covered him.

Slowly the knife penetrated the gap. He shifted the blade up, felt resistance, raised the knife with greater effort, and felt the bolt swing away. His lungs were so starved that he didn't care if someone waited for him on the other side. All he wanted was to breathe. Pushing the hatch open, he squirmed through the narrow space and sank onto the floor of a dark compartment so small that it barely had room for him.

In absolute blackness, Joey took a deep breath, then another, trying to calm the pounding of his heart.

His shoes dangled over an open space, which he discovered was a narrow stairway. Not daring to rest, he eased sightlessly down the stairs and came to a door that wouldn't open. Desperate, he felt around the doorknob but didn't feel a keyhole. Gently, he pushed at the door and heard a rattle on the other side, as if a board were positioned across the door, held in place by hooks.

Although this top part of the house was extremely cold, sweat trickled down the soot on Joey's face. He felt around the door and touched splinters where nails had been driven into the wood on the opposite sides of the door, securing the hooks that held the board. Choosing the area near the doorknob, he dug the knife into the splinters. He twisted and gouged, prying away wood, exposing the nails. Working the knife's tip harder, he created a deeper hole.

When he pushed at the door, it moved a little. He dug deeper with the knife, continuing to excavate the wood around the nails, and the next time he pushed, the door shifted enough for him to see a wedge of pale light. Now he pried at the wood with fierce resolve, and suddenly the board fell loudly.

Anyone in the house couldn't have failed to hear him. Caring only about leaving the house, he shoved the door fully open and charged into a small, empty room that was illuminated by a tiny, barred, soot-covered window. Holding the knife, ready to slash with it, he yanked open another door, saw a dim passage, and hurried downstairs. On the next level, the stairs continued, leading toward the front door.

Frantic, Joey raced down. Frowning when one of the stairs felt soft, he heard a sudden noise behind him. At the same time, something punched his back, taking his breath away. Overwhelmed by pain, he rose into the air and hurtled down the stairs.

* * *

De quincey calculated that Joey would need fifteen minutes to cross the roof, squirm down the chimney, free the hatch, and hurry downstairs to the front door. Rather than attract attention by loitering on the street in front of the house, he remained in the alley with Emily and Becker. Since none of them could afford a pocket watch, he marked the time by walking in place, counting each relentless step as he relieved his nervousness and his need for laudanum.

Becker tried to make the time seem to pass less slowly by noting, "Not far from here is Broad Street, the center of the cholera epidemic three months ago. Ryan helped a local physician, Dr. Snow, make a map of where the victims lived. The map showed that the public water pump was at the center of the contamination. Turns out a cesspit is buried next to it."

Preoccupied, Emily nodded, pretending to be fascinated by Becker's discussion of a cesspit while De Quincey kept counting his paces.

When he reached fifteen times sixty, he emerged from the alley and approached the house. It took a further minute for the three of them to arrive there, so Joey now had *sixteen* minutes in which to accomplish the task.

But the door wasn't open a few inches, the way Joey had been instructed to leave it as a sign that they could enter.

"Maybe the chimney gave him more trouble than he expected. Or else the hatch," Becker said. "Or the lock."

A typical lock in 1854 London wasn't recessed within a door. Instead, it was screwed onto a door's surface. The metal slot into which the bolt slid was attached to the doorjamb, in plain view of anyone on the inside. There wasn't a lever with which a door could be locked and unlocked on the inside. A key needed to be used. Without a key, the only way to open a locked door from the inside was to unscrew the slot attached to the doorjamb. Joey would require another few minutes to use the knife to do that.

"Yes, perhaps the lock." De Quincey couldn't bring himself to say what he was thinking.

But Emily did. "Or else Brookline is inside."

De Quincey reminded himself to breathe. "All Joey needs is a little more time," he tried to assure them.

But another minute passed—and then two.

"We're bound to be noticed, just standing here staring at the door," Becker said.

At once the door budged, only a little, so tiny a movement that De Quincey needed to ask his companions, "Do you see that? Is it real?"

"Yes, it's real, Father."

They shifted toward the steps in front of the door.

The door opened slightly more.

"Joey?" Becker asked.

A hand appeared at the edge of the door. The hand was covered with soot.

De Quincey started up the steps. "Joey?"

As the door opened wider, a figure staggered into view. Rags and face were dark with soot, except for Joey's eyes, the whites of which bulged with pain, and except for Joey's left shoulder, which was crimson with blood.

"Joey!" Emily raced up the stairs.

Entering, she grabbed the boy, holding him up, as De Quincey closed the door and Becker looked around warily, on guard against a threat.

"What's this in his shoulder?" Emily exclaimed.

As she and De Quincey lowered the boy to the floor, they were forced to set him sideways because a foot-long shaft projected from where his shoulder met his neck. The tip had barbs. The rear had feathers.

"From a crossbow," Becker said. "If he'd been taller, it would have struck him full in the back, just about where a man's heart would be."

Continuing to scan the area, Becker focused on the stairs, the middle section of which was obscured by thick shadows.

Joey moaned.

"We need to stop the bleeding!" Emily cried.

Becker crept up the side of the stairs, keeping close to the banister. His weight pressed a stair down. Something clicked under the stairs. Wary, Becker stooped and found a hole in the wood between one stair and another, a hole large enough for a crossbow to fire.

"Here," Becker said. "A trap. There are probably others. Be careful what you touch."

"He'll bleed to death," Emily said.

"You heard me mention Dr. Snow." Becker jumped to the bottom of the stairs. "He lives the next street over, on Frith Street. Ryan sent me to him on Saturday night."

Becker scooped up the boy as if he weighed nothing. "Quickly. Before Brookline comes back."

Emily rushed to open the door.

"No," De Quincey said. "I can't leave."

"What?"

"Not until I see what's here."

"But we need to take Joey to Dr. Snow!" Emily told him.

"We don't have time for this!" Becker insisted. "The boy will die!"

"Emily, go with Becker! You can help Joey more than you can help me!" De Quincey saw a knife on the floor, the one that Becker had lent Joey. He picked it up.

"Even with that knife, you don't have a chance against Brookline!" Becker insisted.

"And we don't have a chance to stop him if all three of us run to Dr. Snow. This house needs to be searched! Go! I promise I'll be there soon!"

Joey moaned in Becker's arms.

"Can't wait," Becker warned.

Emily stared at Joey, then at De Quincey.

"Emily, if you insist on staying, I'll be forced to leave to keep you from danger! What Joey did for us will be wasted!"

"There's no time!" Becker hurried down the steps, carrying the small, bleeding figure.

Emily kept staring at De Quincey. She turned toward Becker running along the street.

"I love you, Father."

She raced after Becker and the boy.

SILENCE GATHERED IN THE HOUSE. The only sound De Quincey became aware of was the fearful agitation of his heart. When he shut the door, the thick curtains in the rooms to his right and left allowed hardly any sunlight to enter. The knife in his hands didn't give him confidence. Trying to steady his tremors, he took out his laudanum bottle and drank deeply.

As the heat of the opium sank to his stomach, it intensified his senses. Shadows appeared less dense. The rattle of a carriage passing outside sounded next to him, as if the door wasn't closed. He turned toward a candle and a box of matches that he had earlier noticed on the floor against the wall. In his youth, the only way to light a candle had been by using flint and steel to deposit sparks into straw in a tinderbox. The newly invented matches, known as lucifers, still seemed unreal to him, able to produce a flame simply by being scraped against a rough surface. Early forms of matches had created a sulfurous odor of rotten eggs, a defect that was now eliminated. But when De Quincey struck the match, the distinctive rotten-egg smell of older-style matches made him pull back his head.

In a rush, he lit the candle and blew out the match.

Have I been poisoned?

Holding his breath, he waited for dizziness and nausea to afflict him. But with each long instant, his only dizziness seemed to be the consequence of fear. Gradually he inhaled and felt steadier.

Is the stench intended to warn Brookline that someone entered and used one of the matches to light a candle?

If so, the tactic was doubly effective because the candle had an odor also. The best candles, made from beeswax, exuded a fragrance while the worst, made of tallow, stank of animal fat. These candles were almost as foul-smelling as the match. Why? Brookline's income was sufficient for him to afford candles and matches without a stench. Why had he refused to acquire them?

As the candle illuminated the area around him, De Quincey's unsteady hand caused the flame to waver. He peered toward the room on the right. The last time he'd been in this house was fifty-two years earlier, but it seemed that nothing had changed. The room he entered had been as empty of furniture then as it was now. In those long-ago, despairing winter months, he had slept on the cold floor, the nervous twitching of his legs constantly waking him.

The floor was even more filthy now. Grains of soot littered it. At the far end, the soot showed round outlines where objects had sat, perhaps what the servants in the neighboring residences had noticed being removed, covered with blankets.

On guard against more traps, De Quincey returned to the passage and entered the opposite room, which a half century earlier had been an office for the mysterious man who had maintained several such offices throughout the city, constantly shifting his premises. Here the man had worked on legal documents for a few furtive hours each morning, sometimes eating pastries, the crumbs from which he'd allowed De Quincey to savor.

A straight-backed wooden chair was next to a small table on which sat a chimney lamp. A stack of books rose from the floor next to the table, books that looked unnervingly familiar.

De Quincey set down the knife, removed the glass chimney from the lamp, and lifted the lamp so that he could more easily bring the candle to the wick.

He froze as the candle's flame wavered toward the wick. The sensation was literally of freezing.

A trap, Becker had warned. *There are probably others. Be careful what you touch.*

The wick on the lamp was so new that it looked totally white.

The lamp seemed heavier than it ought to be. It didn't make the sound of coal oil sloshing in it. Nor did it have a coal-oil odor.

Carefully, De Quincey lowered the lamp onto the table. He set the candle on the floor and unscrewed the cap on the side of the lamp, opening the channel into which coal oil could be added.

Sweat oozed from his brow when he inserted his finger into the channel and touched a granular substance. Some of it stuck to his skin when he removed his finger from the channel. He saw black specks similar to those he had noticed on the floor in the opposite room.

He dropped a speck onto the candle's flame. The speck flashed in a miniature explosion.

Gunpowder.

The lamp was a bomb.

Moving as quickly as he could without extinguishing the candle, he returned to the first room, picked up a speck of the substance on the floor, and dropped it onto the flame. Again the speck flashed.

De Quincey suddenly realized that the round outlines on the dirty floor had been made by kegs, one of which had a small leak.

Gunpowder.

Urgency overcame fear as he returned to the second room and studied the unnervingly familiar books.

Sickened, he confirmed that he had written all of them. On shelves behind the chair, more books were stacked — all by him — along with countless magazines that contained articles he had written. The collection was more complete than De Quincey's own. Brookline possessed a copy of every book, magazine, and newspaper that contained De Quincey's work.

He opened the books, astonished by how tattered the pages looked from compulsive readings. Every page had underscored lines. Foul comments were written in the margins. *The little shit* appeared frequently.

The most frequent execrations were next to the numerous times De Quincey had written about Brookline's father, the genius of John Williams's murders, his brilliant butchery, the sublimity of his blood-spattered achievements.

Mocks killing and death, Brookline had written. *He needs to be shown reality.*

De Quincey's *Confessions of an English Opium-Eater* was bountifully underlined also, with exclamation marks in the margins.

How many people died from laudanum overdoses because of him? Brookline seemed to shout at the bottom of a page.

De Quincey felt nauseous.

How many thousands died in India and China because of opium? How many have I myself killed because of opium and the British East India Company?

But which of us, the Opium-Eater or I, is the greater killer? Brookline demanded in angry handwriting that obscured an entire page.

"Did all these people die in the past few days because of me?" De Quincey murmured. His words echoed in what felt like a tomb.

Now he knew why Brookline had chosen to rent this house.

In his mind, he connects me with his father and himself. To him, we're all killers, De Quincey realized.

He vomited.

The horror of his discovery was sharpened by his urgent awareness that Brookline might return at any moment. Wiping bile from his mouth, he overcame his shock and picked up the knife. Aware of his rapid breathing, he proceeded through the two remaining rooms on this floor but found nothing that appeared significant.

Staying close to the banister, avoiding the hole where the crossbow was hidden under the murky stairs, he climbed to the next floor. His footfalls on the creaky wood were magnified, increasing his tension. Four other rooms—two in front and two in back—awaited him.

One room had its door closed.

Avoiding it, he searched the other rooms and found them empty. He climbed the stairs to the small servants' quarters on the next floor. Aside from footprints made by soot—presumably Joey's—nothing was evident. The house was as abandoned as it had been fifty-two years earlier.

But what about the closed door on the middle level, the only closed room in the house?

Fearful, De Quincey descended to it. Wary of other traps, he tried the doorknob, hoping that it would be locked.

But the knob turned.

He stepped to the side and thrust the door open. If another weapon such as a crossbow was aimed at the doorway, it couldn't harm him.

Nothing happened.

He peered around the doorjamb and saw that an undraped, small, barred window added light to what was a sparsely furnished bedroom. The window was on his right, facing the street. A wardrobe stood across from him. To his left, in place of a bed, he saw a military cot.

Entering, he noticed crumpled newspapers on the floor. His right boot brushed against one, creating a papery clatter.

Inspecting the door, De Quincey saw an inside bolt.

So Brookline secures the door when he goes to bed, but even with that, he feels the need for the crumpled newspapers to warn him about intruders. Does he wake from nightmares?

Why didn't he lock the door now? To lure someone in? Where's the trap?

De Quincey proceeded toward the cot, which was of a sort that Brookline had probably used in India. A blanket and a small pillow were on it.

De Quincey looked under the cot.

The space was empty.

About to turn toward the wardrobe, he wondered if something might be hidden under the blanket, but when he cautiously raised it, he found only a sheet.

When he raised the sheet, he found dried bloodstains on the cot.

The stains were thick.

Lord in heaven, what happened here?

Uneasy, De Quincey approached the wardrobe. As he had done with the bedroom door, he stepped to the side before grasping the wardrobe's handle.

He pulled and flinched as something shot from the wardrobe, embedding itself in the wall near the doorway: a shaft from another crossbow. Sweat now soaked his underarms as he stepped from the side and faced the wardrobe's contents.

He saw a colonel's uniform. One pair of formal evening clothes. One set of gray trousers, a black waistcoat, and a black knee-long coat, the standard business clothes that respectable Londoners wore.

A shelf revealed a colonel's hat and a collapsible top hat.

A drawer revealed two pairs of underclothes, two ties, two shirts, and one pair of dress gloves.

De Quincey doubted that anyone else in Brookline's lofty position lived so austerely. The room felt like a monk's cell.

I don't dare stay any longer.

But as De Quincey stepped from the bedroom, he couldn't resist looking back and focusing on the space above the wardrobe.

The rush of his heartbeat made him feel sicker.

The wardrobe's top was much taller than *he* was. There wasn't a chair on which to stand. He set down the candle and the knife. He jumped, gripped the top of the wardrobe, and pulled himself up. His arms in pain, he looked over the top and almost let go, so startled was he by what he found.

He was staring at a three-stranded whip with dried blood on it.

He released one hand and managed to grab the whip before he dropped to the floor.

Each night, Brookline flagellated himself.

De Quincey now suspected that the malodorous match and candle weren't intended as a warning that someone had been in the house. Rather, their stench was a deliberate displeasure, just as the straight-backed wooden chair would become painful during the many hours that Brookline spent obsessively reading De Quincey's work.

A monk's cell indeed.

A monk devoted to hell.

De Quincey pulled everything off the cot so that the bloodstains were fully exposed. He dropped the whip onto them, wanting Brookline to have no doubt that this secret had been uncovered.

Despite De Quincey's urgency, he remembered to keep to the side of the stairs in case there were further traps.

At the bottom level, he studied Joey's blood on the floor. He stared at the vomit that he himself had left on the floor. Yes, Brookline would definitely know that visitors had been here.

He ran to the stack of books and tore out the page that began his *Confessions of an English Opium-Eater.* He took a pencil from the table and wrote,

The Opium-Eater came to call and regrets that you weren't at home.

He put the page on the stairs, where it would certainly be noticed. All that remained was to blow out the candle and free the bolt.

As he pulled the door open, someone towered over him.

LIKE MOST PHYSICIANS in 1854, Dr. Snow had his office in his home. Running with the boy in his arms, Becker came around a corner one street to the west and charged up the steps of the building on Frith Street to which he'd been taken on Saturday night.

Holding Joey, he fumbled with the doorknob and felt a hand surge past his, opening the door. The hand belonged to Emily, who had raced here with him, her free-moving dress giving her more speed than he believed possible for a woman.

They hurried across a vestibule and reached another door, which Emily quickly opened, allowing Becker to rush in.

Dr. Snow and a male patient looked up in surprise.

Snow was in his early forties with a thin face and dark side-whiskers that framed his narrow jawline. His eyes were intense. His hair had receded, making his forehead seem unusually high.

His patient was well dressed, middle-aged, and portly, with a full beard.

They sat on opposite sides of Snow's desk.

"What the devil?" the patient exclaimed as both men sprang to their feet.

"This boy needs help," Becker said.

"He's filthy," the patient protested.

"He's been shot with a crossbow."

"The beggar was probably trying to break into someone's home. Dr. Snow, look at the blood he's dripping on your floor."

"There's a surgeon ten streets over," Snow informed his unexpected visitors.

"The boy needs help *now*," Becker told him.

"But I'm not a surgeon any longer. I'm a *physician*."

Becker understood. Physicians stood at the top of the rigidly stratified medical world. They never touched their patients but instead listened to them describe symptoms and then recommended drugs supplied by chemists with whom the physicians had a financial arrangement. In this way, physicians did not receive money directly from their patients and were not considered to be "in trade," an activity distasteful to the upper class.

Below physicians were surgeons, who lacked social status because they dealt with all the gore that humans were subject to. Even worse than touching patients, they received money directly from the people to whom they administered. A physician was called "doctor" while a surgeon was referred to as "mister." A physician could be presented at the queen's court. A surgeon could not.

"You're telling me you won't help this boy?" Becker demanded.

The well-dressed patient reacted with shock at the idea that his physician might actually lay hands on someone, a bleeding soot-covered beggar, no less.

"What I'm telling you is, it's a job for a surgeon," Snow replied, looking disturbed as more blood dripped on the floor.

"Dr. Snow, shall I step outside and summon a constable?" the patient suggested indignantly.

"Thank you, Sir Herbert, but—"

Becker almost shouted that he *was* a constable but then realized that he couldn't say that any longer.

"You acted as a surgeon to me on Saturday night," Becker reminded him.

"You did *what?*" Sir Herbert exclaimed.

"You disinfected my wounds and closed them. Why can't you do the same for this boy?"

"You actually closed wounds?" Sir Herbert asked in dismay.

"I did it as a favor to Detective Inspector Ryan," Snow replied. "He helped me locate the source of the recent cholera epidemic. I felt I owed him a courtesy. Yes, I was a surgeon years ago, but I progressed."

"This is nonsense," Emily interrupted. "*You,*" she told Sir Herbert, "please leave."

"Pray tell on what authority do you—"

"Leave," Emily repeated, escorting the portly man to the door. "You have no purpose here. You are disruptive."

"But—"

Emily had him in the vestibule now and was opening the outside door. "If you're not careful, some of the blood from the boy will touch your clothes."

"*Blood on my clothes? Where?*"

"Good day." Emily pushed him outside and shut the door firmly. "Dr. Snow, do you still have your surgeon's instruments?" she asked as she marched back into the office.

"In that cabinet. But I have no intention of—"

"*You* might not, but *I* have every intention. Constable Becker, set the boy on this desk. Help me remove his clothing."

"You can't barge into my office and assume control," Snow told her.

Instead of paying attention to him, Emily was already tugging off Joey's filthy, blood-soaked coat.

"I assume that the first step is to clean the boy so that we can determine the extent of his injuries. Dr. Snow, where is your kitchen? We need hot water. Please instruct someone to bring it. Becker, in the meantime, help me pull the projectile from his shoulder."

"No, no, no," Snow objected. "The feathers on one end or the barbs at the other will make the wound larger."

"Then what should I do?"

"The shaft needs to be cut to remove either the feathers or the tip. Then the shaft should be cleansed with ammonia before it is pulled through the wound."

Emily freed Joey's coat and found his shirt so full of holes that she could easily tear it off. "How do I cut the shaft?"

"With a saw."

"And where is the saw? Dr. Snow, you need to be more hasty and helpful. This boy risked his life to try to stop the murderer."

"The murderer?"

"Who lives one street from you, on Greek Street."

"A street away?" Snow repeated with greater alarm.

"The murderer could kill you in your sleep, but this boy might have saved you. Now please stop repeating everything I say. We need the saw and the hot water, and . . . Yes. Good. The saw. Thank you. How do I hold it? Is this where I cut the shaft?"

"If you do it that way, you'll tear his shoulder open."

"Like this?"

"No, no, no, like *this*."

"Then for heaven's sake, show me before I make a mistake. Yes. Good. Please keep demonstrating. I'll fetch the hot water. Where's the kitchen?"

"Through that door."

"Is your wife at home?"

"Not married. Hold the boy," Snow told Becker. "He's thrashing so much I can't work on him."

When Emily returned with a clean rag and a basin of steaming water, she found Dr. Snow holding a mask over Joey's face while he turned a valve on a metal container.

Joey stopped struggling.

"Is he dead?"

"Asleep. There's no more risk to the boy than when I administered chloroform to the queen during her recent childbirth." Snow put the saw on the shaft, telling Becker, "Keep him turned on his side. Hold the shaft tightly. You need to prevent the force of the saw from moving the shaft and tearing his shoulder."

Becker used his large hands to grab the front and the rear of the shaft, steadying it.

Emily wiped blood away as Snow began sawing. The grating sound of the saw against the shaft made her cringe.

To distract herself, she asked Snow, "You truly administered chloroform to the queen?"

"To the consternation of some clergymen, who believe that according to the Bible women should suffer during childbirth." Snow pressed harder on the saw.

"The Bible says no such thing."

"It's in Genesis four sixteen. After Adam and Eve fell from grace in Eden, God banished them, telling Eve, 'In sorrow thou shalt bring forth children.'"

"Those clergymen are idiots."

"My opinion also. Almost through. There!" Snow triumphantly held up the barbed tip of the shaft. "And now to put ammonia on the shaft before I pull it out."

The door suddenly opened.

Emily looked up, surprised to see three men enter.

Father!"

Hurrying with him were Inspector Ryan and an authoritative man she didn't recognize.

"This is Police Commissioner Mayne," Ryan explained quickly. "Before I went to Scotland Yard, your father told me where he suspected Colonel Brookline had a residence. We met your father as he was leaving."

"Not that I believe Colonel Brookline is responsible for the recent murders," the commissioner made clear. "The cook who drugged the food at the prison vanished. Our constables learned that he used to be a soldier in India."

"A tattoo on the dead man at the prison established that he too used to be a soldier in India," Ryan said. "In the very same regiment. It turns out that Brookline also served in that regiment."

"Perhaps the colonel will remember the two men and be able to tell us something about their criminal relationship," the commissioner suggested. "Forgive me, young lady. I know Constable Becker, but I haven't had the pleasure of —"

"Emily De Quincey."

"Of course. Inspector Ryan speaks highly of you."

"He *does?*" Emily asked in surprise.

Ryan's cheeks became as red as the hair that peeked from his newspaperboy's cap.

"And this is the street beggar who broke into Colonel Brookline's residence?" Mayne asked.

"Surely you don't intend to arrest him," Emily intervened. "He risked his life to find the killer."

"It remains to be proven that Colonel Brookline is the killer. My intention in accompanying Inspector Ryan is to urge caution. We all need to work together, not fight with one another."

"You called him 'inspector.' Does that mean we're police officers again?" Becker asked.

"Even *I* can't countermand Lord Palmerston's orders. But unofficially you have my confidence. After Mr. De Quincey showed me the interior of the colonel's residence — an intrusion which made me feel extremely uncomfortable, by the way — I admit that I now have concerns."

"To begin with, why was Brookline storing a quantity of gunpowder in his home?" Ryan wanted to know. "And why does he abuse his body in a way too indelicate to discuss in front of Miss De Quincey?"

"I'll take your word for that," the commissioner said. "Since I refused to violate the colonel's privacy by invading his bedroom, I did not see the blood and whip that you described."

"Whip?" Emily asked.

"Truly," Ryan answered, "the subject is too delicate for —"

"Brookline flagellates himself with sufficient force to draw blood," De Quincey told her.

"Thank you, Father. My imagination might have leapt to even greater extremes."

"I fail to see how the subject has anything to do with the murders," Mayne said. "What Colonel Brookline does in his home is no concern of ours."

"That he is the son of John Williams must carry some weight against him," De Quincey insisted.

"You have only the word of an elderly woman who works in a bake-shop near the worst rookery in London. There's no proof that the woman is in fact Margaret Jewell."

"And yet Brookline's remarks in my books indicate an obsessive identification with John Williams."

"An equal obsession with *you*. None of that proves he's the killer. I instructed a constable to wait for the colonel to return to his residence and inform him that I wish to speak to him."

BROOKLINE NEVER ALLOWED a cabdriver to know where he lived. His usual method was to tell a driver to turn from Oxford Street toward Soho Square, proceed onto Greek Street, and stop a couple of streets farther south. All the while, he would study the neighborhood. If all appeared normal, he would return on foot, continuing to watch for surveillance.

Now as the cab went past number 38, Brookline leaned back in the compartment's shadows, alarmed by the presence of a constable at the steps to his door. The door was ajar. The steps had blood spatters. Brookline didn't dare show his face to peer out and see where the spatters led along the street.

Streets away, he paid the driver, descended from the cab, and varied his usual route by going around the corner and proceeding up a parallel street. There, he entered a low passageway between buildings, reached a gate, unlocked it, reached another gate, and unlocked it also. In each case, he studied the locks for signs that they had been scraped by someone manipulating them. He also examined carefully positioned grime on the edges of the gates to determine that the gates had not been disturbed.

He entered a dismal courtyard that contained a privy. Steps led down to the basement, where the kitchen was located. Its single window was barred. Its door remained locked, with no indication of having been disturbed.

Steps led up to the first floor. Here the windows were barred also. Like the front door, the back door had no knob. Brookline's uniquely shaped key fit into the lock. Again, strategically placed grime revealed no evidence that the door had been opened.

Inside, a narrow stream of light protruded into the front passage, where the front door wasn't fully closed. Indeed, that door wasn't capable of being closed—the slot for the lock's bolt had been removed from the doorjamb.

The rotten-egg odor of a match lingered in the air, as did the disagreeable smell of the tallow candle.

Blood was on the floor.

Brookline's astonishment turned to rage that his home had been violated. His impulse was to rush to learn what else had been disturbed, but years of military discipline took control. He was suddenly on a reconnoitering mission, determined not to alert the sentry outside. After moving cautiously along the passage, he shifted into the room where he kept his chair and his books.

Vomit was on the floor. The books were disarranged. One of them was open, vandalized, a page having been ripped from it.

The lamp on the table had its glass chimney removed. The cap that covered the hole into which coal oil could be poured had been removed also, indicating that someone had discovered the gunpowder inside.

Mindful of the constable outside, Brookline moved quietly to the opposite room, where the strip of light from the slightly open entrance revealed footsteps in the grains of gunpowder that one of the kegs had left on the floor. The footprints were small.

Reaching the stairs, he saw that the page torn from his book awaited him. A note had been penciled onto it: *The Opium-Eater came to call and regrets that you weren't at home.*

Brookline's rage swelled as he climbed the stairs, taking care to remain close to the banister and avoid the step that triggered the crossbow. Not that his precaution was necessary—he discovered that the crossbow had already been triggered, its shaft released, with luck into the little shit who had left the note.

My bedroom.

Mounting hurriedly to the top of the stairs, he saw that his bedroom, always closed, was now open. Entering, he found the wardrobe open also, its crossbow triggered, its shaft in the wall next to the door.

But what occupied Brookline's attention was the military cot on which he slept. Its blanket and sheet had been thrown off, exposing the dried blood on the canvas. The whip that he had hidden above the wardrobe was now on the bloodstains.

His gaze focused so intently on the cot that he felt he could see the fibers of the canvas and the dried blood that filled the area between them. In India, he had slept on an identical cot, waking from nightmares about the things he had done. He had wakened from nightmares about the things that his father had done. No matter how much punishment he inflicted on himself, he could not purge any of it from his memory.

There is no such thing as forgetting, the Opium-Eater had written.

Fury and shame overwhelmed him. He extended his arms and raised his head toward the ceiling. He opened his mouth to scream. Although no bellow emerged from his widely parted lips, the roar expanded inside him, reverberating silently, making him feel that his chest would explode from the power of the primal rage that possessed him. The veins in his forehead pounded until he expected them to burst. The sinews in his throat stretched so tautly that it seemed his quiet roar would make them snap.

The little shit.

THE LITTLE SHIT.

The constable outside was proof that the police knew about the gunpowder. How would Brookline explain things to Lord Palmerston? Nothing linked Brookline to the murders, but after tonight, there would be serious questions about why he had stored gunpowder in his home. At last, even Lord Palmerston would be compelled to consider the unimaginable.

For that eventuality, Brookline had long ago made plans. Without a transatlantic telegraph to broadcast police reports about him, he could easily escape to America. In that ever-expanding country, he could readily vanish. After all, India had taught him about disguises.

The evidence of his shame, though, could not be allowed to remain.

Brookline descended the stairs. Hearing the constable shuffle his feet beyond the gap in the door, he gathered the box of matches and the lamp that contained the gunpowder. He crept back up the stairs, reentered his bedroom, and placed the lamp next to the cot.

He drew a knife from under his coat, sliced the cot's sheet into strips, and tied one of the strips to the wick on the lamp. Next, he stretched the strip across the floor and overlapped it with another. He did the same with a third and a fourth strip, lengthening and curving them so that they fit the room.

Finally, he placed matches along the strips so that if the flame began to fail, the matches would give it fresh strength.

Brookline struck a match. Punishing himself by a deep inhale of the rotten-egg odor, he touched the match to the end of the fourth strip. As the flame moved slowly along the cloth, he stepped from the bedroom and closed the door.

Quickly he descended the stairs, proceeded to the back, and went outside. Even in the dismal courtyard, he could feel a breeze. Tonight there would not be a fog. The city would view its destruction.

He shut the courtyard gate behind him, moved along the passageway, closed another gate, and emerged onto the next street.

"Boy," he said to a beggar, one of the unfortunates who could not escape the city tonight. "Here's a shilling for extending me a favor."

"A shillin'?" The boy looked suspicious. "What do you want me to do for a whole shillin'?"

Is any of you the opium-eater?" a scruffy boy asked as De Quincey and the others hurried from Dr. Snow's building.

"Why do you want to know?" De Quincey asked.

"Yes, you'd be him. The gentleman said you was little. The gentleman paid me a shillin' to follow the blood from Thirty-eight Greek Street. Said to be quick. Said to give you a message."

"What's the message?"

"That the gentleman regrets not bein' home when you came to visit."

The air seemed to compress. De Quincey felt as if an invisible hand nudged his chest. One street away, an explosion roared, its shock wave making his ears ring. Even from a distance, the sound of falling debris was powerful.

The group rushed toward the corner. When they reached Greek Street, they gaped at where number 38 had been.

The top floors were in flames. On the middle floor, the room to the right had exploded into the street. The glass in all the other windows had been shattered. The building's brick front leaned forward, about to collapse.

The policeman who'd been on duty outside the entrance lay motionless on the street.

As Ryan and Becker ran to him, people gathered in a panic. Shouts accompanied the increasing crackle of flames. The breeze carried bitter smoke.

Frantic, Ryan and Becker tugged the fallen constable toward the opposite side of the street. The wall creaked, bricks scraping, and suddenly toppled in an enormous crash that sent debris flying in every direction.

People stumbled away. Hunched over the constable, Ryan and Becker turned their backs to the chunks of bricks and wood that clattered around them. A fire bell rang in the distance.

DOWN THE STREET, Brookline watched from an alcove as the Opium-Eater gaped at the devastation. Ryan and Becker were with him, unable to resist the impulse to rush to the fallen constable and be heroes.

Commissioner Mayne was there also. No doubt he would soon be talking to Lord Palmerston.

Brookline walked away.

THE GROUP DESCENDED quickly from a coach and faced the wax museum.

"Brookline was seen here this morning," De Quincey said.

They looked to the southeast, where the strong breeze carried the smoke from the fire on Greek Street. By the time they'd left the area, two firefighting crews were working to suppress the blaze.

"People will worry about the smoke. Rumors about the explosion will spread. The panic will worsen," De Quincey said.

The few vehicles and pedestrians on the street emphasized De Quincey's point.

Commissioner Mayne gestured toward the wax museum. "What do you hope to find *here?*"

"With everything that's on Brookline's mind, he wouldn't have come here unless this place is important to him."

De Quincey needed to knock several times on the window of the ticket booth before a woman arrived.

"Finally some customers," she said.

"Afraid not," Mayne told her, showing his police commissioner's badge.

With a look of disappointment, the woman opened the door.

"A gentleman came here earlier," De Quincey said to the woman. He described Brookline.

"Yes, he rented the exhibition for an hour. Three other gentlemen joined him. They were the only business we had today."

"Where did they go?"

The woman pointed down a passage. "The Chamber of Horrors."

The group entered a shadowy room, where they encountered two men in the midst of removing a corpse from a coffin in a graveyard. The display was so realistic that Emily drew a sharp breath.

"Burke and Hare, the resurrectionists," De Quincey commented.

Another display showed a guillotine with blood on it and the heads of two of the French Revolution's victims.

"That's Robespierre and Marie Antoinette," De Quincey said.

Abruptly he stopped at the next display, which showed corpses on a floor, their heads bashed in. A man swung a mallet toward a clerk at a counter.

"This is why Brookline came here," De Quincey said. "An effigy of John Williams in the midst of his first killings. Does he look familiar, Commissioner?"

After a moment, Mayne answered, "Good God, he resembles Brookline."

"Uncannily. Brookline can't stop obsessing about the murders his father committed." De Quincey pointed past the rope barrier toward the grotesque scene. "When he looks at that wax figure, does he imagine himself killing those people as much as he sees his father doing it?"

The commissioner frowned. "Is that an opium thought? It makes me dizzy."

"He's been making the rest of us dizzy since Saturday night," Ryan said.

"And making us have thoughts of our own," Becker added. "Such as *this* one. Brookline wouldn't have destroyed where he lives if he didn't think he was close to being exposed. He knows he doesn't have much time."

"Yes. Whatever Brookline plans to do next," De Quincey agreed, "it will happen tonight."

THE COACH STOPPED on Oxford Street, near a legless beggar who rested his stumps on a platform with wheels under it.

Ryan motioned for the beggar to approach.

Wheels squeaking, the beggar complied.

"Edward, my good man," De Quincey said from the coach, out of view of anyone who might be watching for him. "Did you receive any more reports?"

"This Colonel Brookline you're lookin' for, a boy on a dustman's pony cart followed him to the docks this mornin'."

"Which docks?"

"The boy couldn't get close enough to find out. Brookline was in a police wagon with three constables."

"Constables? A police wagon?" the commissioner repeated with concern. "I know nothing about this."

"Can you spare a shilling for this unfortunate man?" De Quincey asked.

The commissioner dropped a silver coin into Edward's cup.

"Thank you, guv! My blessin's to you!"

"Keep receiving reports, Edward!" De Quincey called as the coach moved forward.

"The docks?" Becker asked. "But there are a dozen of them."

"Given Brookline's background, I suspect only one set of docks would interest him," De Quincey replied.

"What do you mean?"

"Brookline served for twenty years in India. The comments he wrote in my books refer to all the people he killed there. Because of opium. People he killed for the British East India Company. He emphasized the company in his notes."

Ahead, two streetwalkers stood on a corner.

"Becker, please ask the driver to stop," De Quincey said.

The women looked hopeful as the coach halted.

"Doris. Melinda. How excellent to see you again."

"It's my favorite little man," Doris said, batting her eyes.

Melinda guffawed toothlessly.

"I have work for you," De Quincey said.

"Wait, aren't these the streetwalkers we questioned at Vauxhall Gardens?" Ryan asked in confusion.

"Better send for the police wagons again," De Quincey told him. "Tonight we have need of these fine ladies and their companions."

"Father, what on earth are you talking about?" Emily demanded.

16

A Sigh from the Depths

BEGINNING AT THE TOWER OF LONDON, London's docks extended east along the Thames. In the early 1800s, the city had expanded those docks until they formed the largest harbor in the world. By 1854, one third of those docks were used by the British East India Company. Ships carrying opium, tea, spices, and silk came up the Thames and entered a channel cut into the northern bank of the river, proceeding via locks to immense basins bordered by quays, one basin for imports, the other for exports. The basins were so large that two hundred and fifty vessels could anchor in them at one time.

Shortly after dark, a police wagon arrived at sturdy gates. Brookline descended from the wagon and approached a guard, who raised a lantern to Brookline's face and nodded in recognition.

"Back again?" the guard asked. Several other men stood behind him. A cold wind buffeted their coats.

"Lord Palmerston's orders."

Brookline pulled out his credentials.

"No need. I saw your badge often enough."

"His Lordship remains concerned about a rumor that someone plans to take advantage of the panic in the city and cause trouble on the docks."

The repeated reference to Lord Palmerston had considerable effect. As home secretary, Palmerston controlled security for the docks as well as for everything else within the country. As a previous foreign secretary, Palmerston was also guaranteed a position on the British East India Company's board.

"God knows, there's plenty of panic out there," the guard agreed. "Last night, a mob forced a bunch of sailors to barricade themselves in a warehouse over at Shadwell Basin. Nearly killed 'em. We can use any help His Lordship wants to send us."

The guard unblocked the gate and motioned for the driver to bring the police wagon through.

"The rumor we received concerned the opium warehouse," Brookline told him.

"Take a look. Do whatever you need to."

The wagon proceeded past the lanterns of other guards.

At the warehouse, the wagon stopped, and the three men dressed as constables climbed down. In reality, they were all former members of the same regiment in which Brookline had served in India.

The cold wind slapped waves against the wharf. Lanterns swung back and forth in the distance as guards patrolled the waterfront.

The men disguised as constables lit lanterns of their own and entered the warehouse. On three other occasions, Brookline and his companions had come here, pretending to check security, using the tall sides of the wagon to give them cover as they accomplished their real purpose. For safety, gunpowder kegs were often small—five inches across and eight inches high. In December they could easily be concealed under an arm, hidden by voluminous winter clothing.

Brookline and his companions made sure that no one else was inside the warehouse. Then they went from stack to stack of burlap-covered opium bricks, verifying that the powder kegs remained concealed within the stacks throughout the warehouse. They added others. From twenty years of experience, Brookline imagined the sickening odor of the lime with which the opium had initially been treated in India.

"I leave tonight," he told the men.

"So soon?"

"I've come under suspicion. It's time I made a strategic withdrawal."

They smiled at the military joke.

"You've done what you agreed to," Brookline continued. "Tomorrow, after the fire destroys numerous buildings, there'll be few people in the city. The banks and businesses that remain will be unprotected. Take your rewards as you find them. No one will stop you, especially when you're dressed as constables. Make sure you burn the buildings that you steal from."

"And you? What's *your* reward?"

"To begin with, the destruction of all this opium."

"And then?"

"After half of London burns, maybe the panic will become extreme enough to cause a revolution."

"You always like to talk about a revolution," one man said.

"The army's supposed to protect England, but in India, all we really did was help noblemen become richer by selling more opium. I lost count of how many people I killed because of those wretched noblemen and this damned stuff."

"So now you kill English people instead."

"Necessary casualties. The system needs to be obliterated. I like the idea that the noblemen who profited from our killing are now terrified."

"You take your revolution. We'll take the money."

"A fair trade. You won't have trouble leaving the city in the hearses you stole. Dress as funeral directors and put corpses in coffins on top of the money you confiscate. No one will interfere with you."

"The sooner we start, the better. Let's tell the guards at the gate that everything looks as it should."

"The fuses are timed for ten minutes?"

"Yes. By then, we'll be safely out of the area." The man pulled away a burlap sack, exposing a fuse between opium bricks. "Light this one. It leads to many others."

Brookline struck a match.

"Stop!" a voice ordered.

A HALF MILE AWAY, a hansom cab rattled over cobblestones, approaching Ratcliffe Highway.

Inside, Margaret Jewell became agitated as she recognized the dreary streets. "No! You didn't tell me we were coming *here!*"

"I realize this is difficult." Emily touched her arm. "We need your help."

"You can't *possibly* realize how difficult it is."

The cab turned onto Ratcliffe Highway. Normally the street would have teemed with activity. Tonight it was eerily deserted, fear having emptied it.

"Take me back! I swore I'd never look at this place again!"

"Margaret," Becker said, "your son needs to be stopped."

"That's why I went to Scotland Yard!" Even in the faint light from the streetlamps they passed, the elderly woman turned her face so that her scar didn't show.

"*You,* Margaret. *You're* the one who can stop him," Emily said.

The cab reached its destination.

Margaret looked out the window and moaned.

What she saw was the linen shop that in 1811 had been owned by Timothy Marr and where John Williams had slaughtered his first four victims.

Her voice was now so low that Emily and Becker could barely hear her. "You can't force me to go in there."

"Not there," Emily assured her. "Across the street. My father and Commissioner Mayne arrived earlier and found a place for us to wait."

She and Becker eased Margaret from the cab, turning her so that she couldn't see the shop.

The wind chilled them.

A door creaked open. Only darkness seemed beyond it.

"In here, Emily," her father's voice said.

As their eyes adjusted to the interior shadows, it became clear that the place was a grocer's shop. The smell of flour hung in the air. Packages of biscuits stood on shelves next to patent medicines.

Becker quickly shut the door and took Margaret to a chair by a counter. She kept her eyes away from the window and trembled.

De Quincey went over to her. "Margaret, I'm Emily's father."

She didn't reply.

"Thank you for coming. Your presence is immensely important."

Margaret made a sobbing sound but still did not reply.

"This gentleman is Police Commissioner Mayne. He is very grateful to you, also."

"Why did you bring me here?" Margaret demanded in anguish.

"We believe that tonight your son will do something even more terrible than his previous crimes."

"How could that be possible?"

"We believe he plans to blow up the British East India Company docks. In this breeze, the flames will almost certainly set fire to London."

"What?"

"After that, he will leave the city, perhaps forever, but not before he comes here. His obsession with his father's murders, his compulsion to revisit the past—these make me believe that he won't be able to resist seeing Marr's shop one last time."

The room became silent.

"John Williams." It was strange to hear Margaret use the full name of a man she had once loved. "God damn him. God damn me. God damn the child we created."

Even in the shadows, the scar on her cheek became visible as she turned her head and stared through the window.

"Back then, this was a boot shop. The night John Williams waited to confront Marr, he told me he stood in the shadows over here, next to this shop. He watched me leave on the punishing errand that Marr gave me. Marr claimed he wanted oysters for his family's supper. What that terrible man really wanted was to scare me by making me walk in the dark. After I disappeared down the street, John Williams entered the shop and..."

Tears trickled down Margaret's face.

"If you help us," De Quincey said, "what was set in motion forty-three years ago will finally stop."

STOP!" A VOICE ORDERED.

With the match paused near the fuse, Brookline jerked his head toward the direction of the voice. It didn't come from anywhere around him. Instead it came from *above*.

One of Brookline's companions raised his lantern. The edge of its illumination stretched faintly toward the roof, where a face appeared—Ryan's. He had hidden on top of the stacks of opium bricks.

Doors opened, the force of the wind crashing them against the outside walls.

Constables rushed in. Holding truncheons, they aimed their bull's-eye lanterns at Brookline and his companions.

Squinting from the painful glare, Brookline lit the fuse.

"No!" Ryan shouted.

The flame streamed sparks and smoke as it proceeded along the fuse, most of which was hidden under the opium bricks.

Ryan slid down a stack, his boots scraping against the burlap.

The moment he landed on the echoing wooden floor, he lunged to grab the fuse.

He never reached it. With eye-blinking speed, Brookline drew a knife and sliced Ryan's arm.

Crying out, Ryan clutched his arm and darted back.

"How many constables do you have here?" Brookline asked him.

One of Brookline's companions provided the answer. "Looks to be about a dozen."

"And a half dozen over there," Brookline's second companion added, pointing toward a group of patrolmen who entered through a farther door.

Bleeding, Ryan made another grab for the fuse, only to dodge back as Brookline swung the knife again.

"You didn't bring enough help," Brookline said.

His three companions now had knives in their hands.

The constables converged on them. But what Brookline most cared about was making certain that the fuse, sparking and smoking, disappeared into the opium stacks.

"Now," Brookline ordered.

Their movements were startlingly rapid. Before the constables could react, Brookline and his companions attacked with the skill and discipline that came from twenty years of combat in India and China. Acts that ordinary people would have been sickened to imagine didn't merit a second thought for them, so accustomed were they to violence. The apex of the British military, they were the reason the Union Jack flew over a quarter of the world.

Truncheons fell. Helmets dropped. Lanterns crashed. Cloth and skin shredded from the whistle of razor-sharp blades. Knives whipped faster than eyes could follow, a back-and-forth relentless blur. In a matter of seconds, bodies lay everywhere, men groaning, some breathing their last.

Flames rose from lamps that had fallen and broken, their coal oil mixing with blood.

"The stupid bastards believed they were equal to us," Brookline said.

"The gate will be blocked," one of his companions warned.

"We'll go over the wall and make our way by foot to the hearses," another said. "Nothing's changed. The plan will work. Compared to India, this is cake."

"It was an honor to serve with you," Brookline told them.

"And you, Colonel. I hope you get your revolution."

The roar of a shot filled the warehouse.

Brookline's three companions, who'd been hurrying toward a rear door, spun in surprise, seeing Brookline drop to his knees.

DRIPPING BLOOD, Ryan cocked the Colt navy revolver a second time and fired, killing one of the men dressed as constables. While the remaining two tried to recover from their surprise, Ryan managed to fire a third time, the large pistol kicking in his hands. The muzzle flashed, smoke rising. His bullet missed, but the blasts were so deafening that they couldn't fail to be heard from a distance. More guards would soon rush into the building.

Amid the smoke, the two uninjured men suddenly raced away, their boots thumping across the warehouse. A far door banged open, the men vanishing into the night.

Ryan watched Brookline topple from his knees and sprawl on his stomach.

"I'm told that this type of revolver is what your man used to pretend to try to assassinate Lord Palmerston," Ryan said.

Wincing from the knife wound in his arm, he approached Brookline on the floor.

"A calculated overload of gunpowder made the pistol explode without harming your man. By stopping what appeared to be an assassination attempt, you gained Palmerston's greater confidence. Meanwhile, the apparent attack on a cabinet member helped spread the panic. No misfires with *this* weapon, though. The armorer who lent this to me made sure that the powder, the bullets, and the wadding were perfectly loaded into the cylinders."

Ryan stood over Brookline's body.

"Please, don't die from the gunshot. I want to see you hang."

Abruptly Ryan felt breathless. Wincing, he stumbled backward. Brookline's sudden upward slash had been astonishingly quick.

Ryan groaned, clutched his abdomen, and lurched away, striking the opium stacks. His knees bent. He sank to a sitting position on the floor.

Brookline groped painfully to his feet, mustered strength, and walked toward him. As he drew back his knife, preparing to thrust at Ryan, shouts approached.

Ryan raised the large, heavy revolver, managed to hold it with both hands, cocked it, and again pulled the trigger.

The deafening shot missed Brookline. He stared toward the door beyond which the angry voices were louder. He watched Ryan fumble to recock the revolver.

Amid the gathering smoke, he ran.

Guards rushed into the warehouse. Shock paralyzed them as the rising flames revealed the bodies.

"Brookline and two men dressed as constables ran out that door." Ryan groaned. "They're heading toward the wall around the docks. Brookline's been wounded."

The pistol dropped from Ryan's hand, thumping on his outstretched legs.

Some of the guards raced toward the door. Others stomped on the flames.

Men rushed in with pails from the docks, throwing water on the fires.

"Gunpowder," Ryan moaned to them. "Under the opium."

"Gunpowder?"

Ryan tried to raise his voice. "The fuse is lit."

Amid smoke, Ryan gripped the stack behind him and struggled to stand. It seemed to take him forever to get on his feet. His trousers felt wet, as if he had urinated on them, and perhaps he had—but he knew that they were mostly wet from his blood.

"We need"—he coughed from the smoke—"to pull the opium bricks out and find the fuse."

"Did you say 'gunpowder'?"

Ryan yanked a burlap-wrapped package of opium from a stack, throwing it on the floor.

"And a lit fuse?" someone else asked.

Wincing, Ryan pulled another burlap package from a stack.

"Let's get the hell out of here!" a man shouted.

"The wind will"—Ryan groaned—"carry the flames to the city."

He tugged more burlap packages from the stacks. "Found it."

Dizzy, he strained to focus his vision on the sparks. "Too many. Dear God, it has spread to three other fuses."

Men rushed to join him. Packages of opium bricks flew through the air.

"I got one!" a guard yelled, cutting the tip off a burning fuse.

"Two others went into these stacks!"

Coughing, the guards hurled opium packages into aisles.

"Here!"

"This one spread to more fuses!"

"Hurry!"

"Found one!"

"Another!"

The guards raced from stack to stack, frantically pulling away packages.

Ryan found another fuse and cut off its tip. His legs wavered.

"The last one went under this stack!" someone yelled. "We'll never get to it in time!"

"Run!"

As the men charged past Ryan, someone grabbed him, shoving him toward the door. The explosion lifted him and threw him outside. He landed hard on gravel, rolling from the force of the blast. Walls disintegrated, wood and burlap and opium bricks erupting, the force flipping him, so stunning him that he barely realized he was falling off the edge of a dock.

BROOKLINE FORCED HIMSELF to ignore the pain in his chest. Working his strong legs, climbing a slope toward the base of a wall, he told himself that the wound couldn't be serious. Otherwise, he wouldn't be able to run as fast as he was. The bullet had struck the right side of his chest. He was wearing a heavy overcoat, a business coat, and a waistcoat. They had absorbed some of the force. The bullet hadn't penetrated deeply. He was certain of it.

With the wind chasing the usual fog, the light from stars and a half moon guided him. He reached the bottom of the wall and found a ladder on the ground. The British East India Company guards used it to peer over the wall and throw rocks if they had information about thieves massing out there.

His ribs hurt when he raised the ladder and clambered up, but his breathing was deep, and he told himself that the pain came from bruises. The tops of the poles that formed the wall had been sharpened, with broken glass wedged between the points. Hearing loud voices behind him, men chasing him, he gripped two of the sharpened posts and raised a boot to step on the broken glass. A point snagged on his trouser leg, tearing the cloth. As he shifted to the other side, he pushed the ladder away and heard it crash on the ground.

"What's that?" someone yelled.

He dangled from the outside of the wall. Here the distance to the ground was greater, a trench having been dug.

Something popped in his chest. He literally heard a popping sound, and at once agony surged through him. He released his hands and dropped. Although he was prepared for the shock of landing, he nonetheless gasped when his knees bent and he lost his balance, toppling sideways.

The angry voices reached the opposite side of the wall. With effort, Brookline came to his feet, ran across the ditch, and squirmed up its slope. Pain gripped his right knee when he climbed over a rail fence and reached East India Dock Road.

From his high perspective, he saw the warehouse and the ship basin. Flames showed through an open warehouse door.

Straight ahead was the vague outline of the city. He broke into an awkward run, adjusting his balance and speed to compensate for the pain in his knee.

And the pain in his chest. After something had popped in it, the pain was now deep.

The explosion knocked him to the ground. Flames and debris erupted from the warehouse, fire and smoke shooting up. His ears, which had been ringing from the numerous shots in the enclosed space of the warehouse, now rang more severely.

Only one explosion.

There should have been ten. The force of the multiple blasts should have been strong enough to level not only the warehouse, which it hadn't, but also other buildings in the area. It should have thrown so many burning chunks of wood into the air that a rain of fire would now be falling around him. The wind should have carried a fury of sparks into the city. On the northern side of East India Dock Road, buildings should be starting to burn. Ahead, roofs should be smoldering.

In pain, he saw lanterns wavering as men raced up from the docks. He reached an intersection in which five roads led to many directions. He went south, reasoning that his pursuers would not expect him to go back toward the river. A signpost told him that this was Church Street. Close by, he had killed his mother and the former soldier, then set fire to their riverfront shack.

He passed the church where he'd learned to read. A passage he'd been taught from *The Book of Common Prayer* flashed through his mind.

If we say we have no sin, we deceive ourselves, and the truth is not in us.

Wrong, Brookline thought. *I have no sin.*
Opium is the sin.
England is the sin.
The Opium-Eater is the sin.

My father is the sin.

Stumbling more than running, he reached the southern end of Church Street. Again, five streets formed an intersection, leading to various parts of the compass. Police clackers sounded alarms, but they were distant, to the north, probably on East India Dock Road. His tactic was confusing his pursuers, and this five-street intersection would confuse them even more.

He chose west, struggling along a street that he recognized from his youth: Broad Street. As the flames from the warehouse threw sparks into the wind, his heart swelled with hope that the great fire would happen.

He reached another intersection, another place to confuse his pursuers. Now Broad Street changed its name, and even without a signpost, he couldn't possibly have failed to recognize it. It was the one place in London that he knew better than any other, better than the Opium-Eater knew Oxford Street.

With a shock of recognition, he looked to his left, and even in shadows, he realized that he limped past New Gravel Lane. There, at number 81, amid pathetic shops that sold to sailors, had stood the King's Arms tavern, where his father had committed his second set of murders, cracking the heads and slitting the throats of John Williamson, his wife, and their servant.

John Williams.

John William*son*.

John Williams.

John William*son*.

Before Brookline had joined the army, the last thing he'd done was go to Marr's shop and then the King's Arms tavern. He had stepped inside each establishment. He had stood where he imagined his father had stood, where his father had killed.

When he had returned from India, to which his father had sailed many times as a merchant seaman, the first thing he had done after twenty years was to go to Marr's shop and stand inside it.

Then he had gone to the King's Arms on New Gravel Lane, but to his dismay, the tavern had no longer existed. A huge, gloomy wall now occupied that western side of the street, protecting the area where the docks had been extended.

"When did *this* happen?" he had demanded of a passerby, who looked at him with fear and hurried on.

He had rushed south to Cinnamon Street. Drenched with sweat from running, he had leaned against a lamppost with relief when he discovered that the Pear Tree boardinghouse, where his father had slept after he killed the Marrs and the Williamsons —

John Williams.

John Willam*son*.

— still existed. That first night after having returned from India, Brookline had managed to rent the same room that his father had rented. For all he knew, he had slept on the very same bed that his father had used.

Now the high wall that had replaced the King's Tavern loomed in the darkness as Brookline stumbled past it, continuing west. Sparks drifted over him. People in the neighborhood had heard the explosion, some of them braving the night to leave their dwellings and investigate. When they saw the sparks strike walls, they desperately swatted them out.

The pain in his right knee made him wince every time he put pressure on it. What tortured him, though, was his chest. Under his overcoat, his business coat, and his waistcoat, he felt liquid against his skin, and he didn't believe it was sweat from his effort. The bullet might have penetrated a little deeper than he tried to assure himself.

Passing isolated streetlamps, he counted the numbers on the buildings to his left: 55, 49, 43, 37. And there up ahead was 29 Ratcliffe Highway.

Continuing the Journal of Emily De Quincey

In the gloom of the grocer's shop, as I sat next to Margaret, holding her aged hands, I heard Father poking among objects on the shelves. With a murmur of triumph, he uncorked a bottle and drank from it.

"If that's wine, I'd enjoy a sip to ward off the chill," Commissioner Mayne said.

"It isn't wine," Father told him.

"Then what is it?"

"Medicine."

"*Medicine?*"

"*Laudanum,*" Becker explained.

"*Dear heaven,*" Commissioner Mayne said.

The air seemed to tighten. I both felt and heard something rumble to the east. The window vibrated.

"*What was* that?" Margaret exclaimed.

"*An explosion,*" Becker answered.

Margaret jumped to her feet, about to rush to the door.

"*No.*" I blocked her way. "*We mustn't be seen.*"

"*Ryan failed,*" the commissioner said.

"*Perhaps not,*" Father replied. "*In the house on Greek Street, the floor had several impressions from gunpowder kegs, but we heard only one explosion.*"

"*One explosion might be enough.*"

Becker concealed himself beside the window, peering out. "*Sparks in the sky,*" he reported. "*Blowing from the east. But perhaps not enough to ignite the citywide fire that I assume Brookline intended.*"

"*It would take only a few strong blazes,*" Mayne noted. "*This wind would spread the flames quickly.*"

I felt Margaret sobbing next to me as the wind blew dust past the window.

"*De Quincey, perhaps you're wrong that he'll come here,*" the commissioner suggested. "*There'll be a lot of commotion at the docks. Brookline will be under pressure to leave the area.*"

"*There is no such thing as forgetting,*" Father emphasized. "*Brookline is a creature obsessed about his past. He might not know that he intends to return here, but I have no doubt that if he is able, he will come to what used to be Marr's shop.*"

"*'He might not know that he intends to return here'?*" Mayne frowned. "*What are you talking about?*"

"*Another thought to make you dizzy,*" Becker answered. "*Mr. De Quincey persuaded me that sometimes we do things without knowing why.*"

"*Such as why I allowed you to convince me to spend the night here when I could be helping to organize the hunt,*" the commissioner said.

The shop became silent again, except for the occasional sound of Father uncorking the laudanum bottle and drinking from it.

"I need to leave," Mayne finally declared. "Lord Palmerston will demand my resignation if he learns I'm associating with you rather than attending to my duties."

"It's imperative that you stay," Father insisted in the darkness. "Lord Palmerston won't believe us, but he'll listen to you."

"He might not listen. Remember, I'll be asking him to turn against his chief of security, the man who supposedly saved his life yesterday."

"Father," I said, "someone is outside."

The shop became eerily still.

Beyond the window, a figure had materialized, a tall man who stood with his back to us, studying what used to be Marr's shop.

"Where John Williams stood forty-three years ago," Margaret moaned. "He watched me shut the door and go down the dark street."

I kept my hands on Margaret's arms, restraining her from sudden motion, as our group shifted toward the window.

With his back to us, the tall man's silhouette moved into the middle of the street. He limped. His hands were raised to the right side of his chest, as if he were injured.

"Have you prepared yourself, Margaret?" Father asked.

"I had a lifetime to prepare myself."

Beyond the window, the tall man leaned to the right, pain seeming to make him favor that side.

Even though I saw the man only from behind, the intensity with which he stared at what had been Marr's shop was palpable.

To the east, police clackers sounded.

The man cocked his head in their direction, bracing himself to depart.

Father opened the door, calling out, "John Williams?"

The man spun toward the door.

"Is it you, John Williams?" Father asked.

"Who speaks to me?" Moonlight revealed dark liquid glistening on the right side of the man's coat.

"John Williams, yes, I'd recognize you anywhere."

"You confuse me with someone else."

"Impossible."

Down the street, from darkness between lampposts, a woman called, "John Williams!"

Another voice joined hers. "John Williams!"

And another. "John Williams!"

"Who are you?" the figure demanded.

In the opposite direction, a woman yelled, "John Williamson!"

And others. "John Williamson!"

The cries of the women shifted back and forth, alternating names.

"John Williams!"

"John Williamson!"

Abruptly all the voices changed. As one, the women shrieked, "The son of John Williams! You're the son of John Williams!"

Brookline broke into an urgent limp, heading to the west, toward the Tower of London, the demarcation between the wretchedness of the East End and the better part of the city.

But at once he lurched to a halt as a line of constables appeared, filling the street from one side to the other, walking toward him, aiming their lanterns. Father had instructed them to stay in hiding until the women began their chorus.

Brookline pivoted in the opposite direction, and there a line of constables appeared also, from one side of the street to the other. They, too, aimed their lanterns as they walked toward him, trapping him.

"John Williams! John Williamson! The son of John Williams!" the women shouted.

Unnervingly, the voices stopped.

The constables stopped also. The only movement was the wind.

Within the dark shop, Father turned toward Margaret. "Do you remember what we require of you?"

"How can I possibly forget? Step away. I have things to say to my son."

I released Margaret's arms.

She walked through the shadowy doorway.

I followed. Knowing that Margaret would not have been there if I hadn't insisted, I felt a grave obligation to help her in any way I could.

"Robert?" she called.

Brookline spun toward her, on guard.

"Robert?" she repeated, appearing on the street.

"Who calls me that?"

"Your mother."

Brookline stepped back, as though the wind had pushed him.

"No. My mother died a long time ago. In a fire."

"Samuel died." Margaret walked slowly toward him, each footfall communicating her emotional agony. "But I survived."

Brookline took another step back. "This is a deceit."

"Despite my wound, I managed to crawl away."

"You are lying."

"The fire burned my face. Can you see the scar, Robert? Here on my left cheek. Every day, the scar reminds me of the puke that was John Williams and the filth that he and I brought into the world. Every day I pray for God's hand to come down and crush me."

"Don't call me 'filth'!"

"I wish I had never been born so that I could never have given birth to you."

"You're not my mother. No mother could speak to a son that way."

"Who else would know that you tortured animals under the docks?"

"No."

"You tied their paws to stakes and put muzzles over their jaws."

"A child doesn't know what he does or why he does it. I made amends. The world will be better because of me."

Margaret stepped closer. "By killing?"

"For twenty years in India, my orders were to kill. I was given promotions and medals for acts that would have caused me to be hanged here in England. Don't talk to me about killing. Killing is wrong only if you look at it in a particular way."

"You have lost your reason."

"Then England has lost its reason!"

"What about the five people you slaughtered on Saturday night, two of them women and two of them children?"

"I admit to killing no one on Saturday night. But I killed many women and children in India and was praised. My commanders said it

was necessary for the empire. They really meant that it was necessary for rich men to become richer because of the opium trade."

"And what about the people you slaughtered on Monday night? They had nothing to do with the opium trade."

"I admit to killing no one on Monday night either. But if five or eleven or even hundreds die to save millions from lifelong misery, those casualties are heroes. If you are truly my mother, you can tell me how much you and I and Samuel managed to earn each day, you as a mud-lark searching the riverbank for chunks of coal, Samuel and I collecting ashes?"

"All of us? If we were lucky? Two shillings a day." Margaret had almost reached him.

"Perhaps fourteen shillings a week. Not even a pound. Not enough to eat properly and live in a room without rats. When I returned from India, I received sixteen hundred *pounds from a landowner who wanted to be an officer in the army. Did you know, Mother, that most officers in the military don't earn their rank? They purchase it from a retiring officer. And this idiot landowner was happy to pay me sixteen hundred pounds to take my place as a colonel. Sixteen hundred pounds for being a killer. If you are indeed my mother, you can tell me what I received at the church every Sunday when I went there to learn to read."*

"A biscuit."

"Until then, I was lucky to taste the crumbs *of a biscuit. When I worked for the dustman, collecting ashes from the houses of the rich, I saw things I never dreamed existed. Some homes had eight and ten rooms, any of which was larger than the shack that you and I and Samuel were forced to share. I saw splendid clothing, so new and expensive that I thought I must be dreaming. I saw more food consumed in one day than the three of us managed to find in a week. How many millions in England suffer the way you and I did, Mother? When I look at Lord Palmerston and his wealthy, powerful, arrogant friends, when I see their greed and their indifference to the poor, I feel a rage that it takes all my effort to keep under control."*

"But you didn't control it."

Margaret reached him.

Determined to help in every possible way, I remained behind her. A cold shock swept through me as Margaret suddenly raised her fists and struck her son. Too short to reach his face, she directed her blows toward his chest. Right, left, right, left. The solid thumps of the impacts were surprising, given that they came from an elderly woman. In a frenzy, she kept striking him. As her fists hammered, the effort brought such forceful breaths from her mouth that I feared she would collapse.

Brookline showed no pain, even when she pounded at his wound. Despite the injury that slicked his coat with blood, his only reaction was to stand straighter. His arms at his sides, he merely braced himself and absorbed his mother's blows.

I ran to her, desperate to tug her away before Brookline might harm her.

Instead he grabbed me. With his arm around my throat, I dangled against his chest, struggling to breathe. At once he dropped me to my feet, appearing to demonstrate that he could have easily injured me if he desired.

Again, I tugged to get Margaret away from him. Becker was suddenly next to me. Seeing that Brookline no longer threatened me, Becker gripped Margaret's other arm, but despite both our efforts, she continued flailing at her son.

"I see the heroic constable is here," Brookline noted. "Maybe you too will one day receive medals, Becker, but I assure you the medals will come faster if you kill people."

The old woman kept struggling as we dragged her toward the grocer's shop.

"Don't claim you kill for the wretches who live here!" Margaret screamed. "Tonight you almost murdered them!"

"If the revolution came, their children would be better for it," Brookline insisted. "They would thank me."

"You're filth!" Spit flew from Margaret's lips.

"Men like Lord Palmerston are the filth. The quicker they and their way of life are exterminated, the sooner this country will be free of suffering."

"Colonel," Father yelled, "thank you for not harming my daughter."

Turning, I saw Father emerge from the shop.

"Who's there?" Brookline demanded. "The Opium-Eater?"

Father showed himself in the moonlight. "Despite my gratitude, I'm afraid I must object that you're not being entirely truthful with us."

"You little shit," Brookline said.

"I am thin, not little."

"Everything is a joke to you. Opium. Violence. It all has the same amusement to you. 'If once a man indulges in murder, very soon he comes to think little of robbing,'" Brookline quoted with contempt, "'and from robbing he comes next to drinking and Sabbath-breaking, and from that to incivility and procrastination. Once begin upon this downward path, you never know where you are to stop. Many a man has dated his ruin to some murder or other that perhaps he thought little of at the time.'"

"You flatter me by quoting my work so accurately."

"You are the true filth to which my mother referred. Your praise of opium and violence caused far more deaths than those for which I admit to being responsible."

In the distance, the alarm bells of fire wagons filled the night. Father glanced in that direction.

I followed his gaze. To the east I saw a glow above where I had been told the British East India Company docks were located. Sparks rose from the glow. The wind sped the sparks across the sky, propelling them toward me, like a swarm of fiery insects. But the grotesque fireworks kept fading as they neared me, extinguished by the wind as much as blown by it.

When I looked again at Father, he was a step closer to Brookline.

"I assure you, Colonel, that neither opium nor violence amuses me. Every day for the past fifty years, I have regretted the terrible moment when I first swallowed laudanum for my facial pains. As for violence, I write about it compulsively and with apparent humor because it horrifies me. Long ago I stared a mad dog in the face. The terrifying intensity in his eyes above the froth in his mouth so hypnotized me that I was unable to turn away."

"You compare me to a mad dog?" Brookline drew a knife.

"Not at all. A mad dog knows nothing of what it does. You, on the other hand, are extremely aware of what you do, even though you aren't aware of why you do it."

"You don't make sense. The opium has addled your mind."

"To the contrary, it makes my mind clear."

In the distance, the alarm bells of the fire wagons gained in number and strength.

"The sparks are receding," Father noted. "The crisis is under control. You failed, Colonel, and if I may point out, you are standing in a large pool of blood. Should we send for a surgeon?"

"I have endured worse injuries."

"To your body or to your mind?"

"My mind? Do you insult me again?"

When Brookline made a threatening motion toward Father, Becker stepped protectively forward, ready with his truncheon.

"Constable," Brookline warned, "even in my compromised condition, do you honestly think that you are a match for me? You might be stronger at the moment, but I have one quality that you lack entirely."

"And what would that be?" Becker demanded.

"The willingness to inflict death without hesitation. Examine your soul. Are you prepared to cause as much damage to me as I am prepared, without pause or regret, to inflict upon you?"

Becker didn't reply.

"You might wish to defend the Opium-Eater, God knows why, or the woman who calls herself my mother, or the Opium-Eater's daughter," Brookline said. "But nobility is not sufficient. You do not have the temperament or the training to be the kind of artist that England made me. Ryan already learned that lesson."

"Ryan?" Becker asked quickly. "What about him?"

"His bullet is in me. But he did not have the resolve to finish what he began. I showed him what he lacked."

"You showed him what? Where is he?"

"The last time I saw him, he was sprawled in his blood, devoting his attention to keeping his insides where they belong."

"You . . . !"

"*Becker!*" *Father shouted as the constable seemed about to attack Brookline.* "*That's what he wants! He's baiting you! Don't you understand him yet? To kill, he needs a motive he can justify!*"

Becker froze.

"*Very smart,*" *Brookline said.* "*The little shit saved your life.*"

"*Colonel, the pool of blood at your feet is spreading. Are you sure you do not wish us to send for a surgeon?*"

"*I suspect that a surgeon would not be of help.*" *Brookline wavered.*

"*Instead of hanging yourself, as your father did, you choose to commit suicide by bleeding to death?*"

"*The consequences of combat are honorable.*"

"*Given the amount of blood that you are losing, the two of us do not have much time to arrive at the truth. Why do you flagellate yourself, Colonel?*"

"*You dare talk of such things when women are present?*"

"*They are about to hear worse. Answer my question. Why do you flagellate yourself?*"

"*You are a sneak.*"

"*I agree. Invading your bedroom was contemptible. Why do you—*"

"*To punish myself for all the people I killed.*"

"*Do you punish yourself for killing the former soldier with whom you and your mother lived? Do you punish yourself for attempting to kill your mother?*"

"*It was a horrid thing to do. I was a child. I was confused and did not realize what I was doing.*"

"*Do you punish yourself for all the people you killed in India because of the opium trade?*"

"*I have nightmares about them.*"

"*Perhaps a better word is 'dreams.'*"

"*Dreams?*"

"*Of a particular sort.*"

"*I don't understand.*"

"*You know the type I mean. Despite our differences, we are both men and understand the consequences of certain dreams. We don't need to embarrass the ladies by being explicit.*"

I was indeed embarrassed. Disturbingly so. This was a rare instance in which Father's comments made heat rise to my cheeks.

"Did you flagellate yourself after you killed those five people on Saturday night?"

"As penance."

"Did you flagellate yourself after you killed those eight people in the tavern on Monday night and the three people in the surgeon's house?"

"To atone."

"I saw more than bloodstains on the cot in your bedroom."

Despite the wind and the bells of fire wagons in the distance, the street became unnaturally silent.

"My bedroom?" Brookline asked.

"You flagellate yourself to complete the arousal that killing stimulates in you. The evidence of that arousal was on your cot."

Brookline's bellow so startled me that I took a step backward, as if I were being attacked.

His roar reverberated toward the constables who waited in a line three shops away on each side of him. His cry of anguish rose to the sky, where the stars and a half moon impassively received it.

His head was thrown back. His mouth gaped. His arms stretched toward the heavens.

Slowly, his cry diminished. As he lowered his arms and head, his shoulders heaved with a profound exhale that might have been a sob. One of Father's books is called Suspiria de Profundis, *a sigh from the depths. That was what I heard: the most racking sigh that I imagined could ever come from the depths of a human being.*

Brookline turned away. In a daze, he shuffled along the street, trailing blood.

Father kept pace with him. "You kill because you enjoy it. Everything else is a lie that an alien part of you repeated until you believed it."

The line of constables who waited in that direction stepped toward Brookline as he approached. They prepared to secure him with handcuffs.

"Shackles are not required," Father told them. "He doesn't intend to escape. It's obvious where he is going. Let him proceed."

They parted, allowing him through but staying with him.

The streetwalkers whose help Father had enlisted emerged from hiding places along the street. Their haggard features and windblown rags reminded me of drawings of banshees.

"Doris!" Father called. "Melinda! Is this the man who promised you an additional sovereign?"

"He dressed different and wore a yellowish beard, but he's the same size, and I'd recognize his voice anywhere," Doris responded.

"Colonel, does your concern for the poor extend to paying these kind ladies the additional fee that you promised them for antagonizing me at Vauxhall Gardens?"

Brookline stumbled on, staring at something far beyond the shadowy street. Margaret and I followed. So did Becker and Commissioner Mayne. So did the constables and the streetwalkers, who kept pace with Brookline.

Father walked directly behind him.

"Colonel, what happened to your concern for the poor? If you have any honor, you will keep your promise to these ladies."

Staring straight ahead, Brookline fumbled in his coat and pulled out his pockets, dropping coins onto the cobblestones. Their copper, silver, and gold made different metallic sounds as they landed and rolled.

The streetwalkers raced for the coins, fighting for them.

With his outturned pockets blown by the wind, Brookline reached a signpost that said Cannon Street. He staggered to the north past dismal buildings that seemed about to collapse. The constables and the rest of us stayed with him.

"What about Ann?" Father asked. "Do you have information about her?"

"Who?"

"Ann! You brought me to London, claiming you had information about her!"

"For all I know, the slut died from consumption after you abandoned her."

"I didn't abandon her! Tell me! Do you have anything at all to report?"

"How could a prostitute with consumption have possibly survived? For most of your life, she's been rotting in a pauper's grave. You're a fool."

I was close enough to see the emptiness that seized Father's face. The last vestige of his youth slipped away. His skin shrank around his cheeks. His eyes receded with hopelessness. A moan escaped him — or perhaps it was a sob, rising from the depths of his broken heart.

A wretched-looking woman stepped from a decaying structure and stared in fear at us. A sickly thin man appeared behind her.

Speechless, they followed Brookline, seeming to sense what was happening.

Other pathetic men and women emerged from bleak doorways, frowned at Brookline, and joined the horrid procession.

Soon dozens of people were with us, then a hundred, then two hundred, their footsteps scraping on the cobblestones.

Brookline reached a large intersection. A sign on a wall said Cable Street. Abruptly I remembered something that Father had written. Chilled, I understood that Brookline had taken the route by which his father's body had been brought here forty-three years earlier.

The procession halted as Brookline wavered toward the middle of the crossroads. The lanterns of the constables illuminated him. He scanned the crowd that filled the intersection, although his faraway gaze made it seem that he couldn't see us.

Again he exhaled an immense sigh from his depths.

He fumbled to pull something from beneath his coat.

"Stay back!" Becker warned us. "It might be a weapon!"

Brookline's knees bent. His tall body didn't drop as much as it collapsed. He landed face downward on the stones.

He trembled, then lay still.

Hushed, the crowd stepped forward, surrounding him at a careful distance.

"Cannon and Cable streets," Commissioner Mayne said. "Somewhere under this crossroads, under these paving stones, John Williams is buried."

"Not somewhere," Father told him. "Here. I'm certain Brookline knew the exact spot where his father's bones rest."

"Emily and Margaret, look away." Becker stooped warily to turn Brookline onto his back.

But we didn't turn away. Normal emotions had deserted me. I was so numbed that I didn't flinch or feel nauseous when I saw the knife that Brookline had pulled from beneath his coat and slid between his ribs when he landed.

As when Brookline had wailed toward the sky, his mouth was open in anguish.

"He was already dying, and yet he felt the compulsion to use the knife. It's not precisely a stake through his heart," Father said. *"But I imagine Brookline intended it to be the same as what ultimately happened to his father. Margaret, I'm sorry."*

"He was dead to me a long time ago," the elderly woman replied. *"There's no need to feel sorry about that. But for what he did because of my weakness, God pity me."*

"A man can find within himself, in a separate chamber of his mind, a separate alien nature," Father said, echoing something he had written. *"But what if that alien nature contradicts his own, fights with it, and confounds what he once thought to be the inviolable sanctuary of his soul?"*

"Can you do without me?" Becker asked abruptly, glancing from Father and the commissioner toward Margaret and me.

"We are safe now. Go!" I urged.

Becker broke into a run, hurrying through the crowd, racing toward the glow on the dark horizon.

FLAMES CRACKLED. Horses reared in terror. The din of bells summoned more help as men lay on the docks, stretching over the side to fill pails with water. They handed the pails to a line that led toward the warehouse. In a rush, another line brought empty pails back. Hoses went from the water to fire wagons, where men furiously worked the pumps and other men directed a spray toward the warehouse.

In the chaos, Becker charged toward a constable. "Where's Detective Inspector Ryan?"

"Don't know him."

In the reflection of flames, Becker sprinted toward another constable. "I'm looking for Detective Inspector Ryan!"

"Haven't seen him."

Breathless from his rush to the docks, Becker looked around frantically.

"Did you say you were looking for Ryan?" a guard asked.

"Yes!"

"He was with those constables who were killed," the guard reported.

"Ryan's *dead*?"

"I don't know." The guard needed to raise his voice to be heard above the shouts and the roar of the fire. "He was stabbed."

"Stabbed?"

"I helped him from the warehouse before it blew up. It tossed us through the air. I never saw him after that."

"Where? Show me where the blast threw you!"

"Over there!"

The guard indicated a gravel area. No one was there.

Becker strained to look in every direction. "Ryan! For God's sake, where are you?" He stopped a man hurrying by. "Do you know where the injured were taken?"

"There! To the spice warehouse!"

The man pointed toward a building near the burning warehouse.

Becker ran to it.

The living and the dead were positioned on blankets. Becker rushed to each of them, searching their faces, wiping soot from them.

Desperate, he ran back to the opium warehouse. Through the flames, he saw where a doorway had been blown apart. Anyone coming through it would have been lifted by the explosion and—

Becker followed a line from the doorway toward the section of gravel that the guard had indicated. He found blood. He followed it to the wood of the dock. The blood went over the side.

"Ryan!"

Kneeling, Becker stared down toward the greasy water. Despite the speed with which his heart pounded, it nonetheless seemed to stop when he saw a figure half submerged, right arm snagged on a loop of rope.

"Help me!" Becker yelled. "For God's sake, someone help!"

A constable heard and raced toward him.

"I'm a policeman!" Becker shouted. "That's Detective Inspector Ryan down there!"

Becker pulled his overcoat off with such urgency that several buttons popped. He yanked off his boots and jumped.

The water was painfully, shockingly cold. Plunging into it, Becker felt the cold only briefly. In seconds, numbness spread through him. His hands shook as he grabbed a rope that the constable dropped to him. He tied the rope under Ryan's arms and motioned for the constable, who'd been joined by another man, to pull Ryan up.

But as Ryan was lifted from the water, the reflection of the flames showed the terrible slash in his abdomen.

Becker almost gagged but stifled the urge and yelled, "Stop! He's been cut! We're separating the wound!"

The constables eased Ryan back into the water. Becker, whose tenant-farming father had insisted he learn to swim before he could fish from a river that flowed near the farm, gripped Ryan with one arm and pulled at the water with the other, forcing his way along the dock. His water-soaked clothes weighed him down, but he gripped a piling and pushed beyond it. He grabbed at more water, fighting toward a walkway that stretched down from the dock.

There, the constables waited, helping to lift Ryan from the water.

"He's dead," one of them murmured.

"No!" Becker said. "He can't be! I won't let him be!"

"Look at the gash in his stomach," the other constable said, not even bothering to note the slice in Ryan's left arm.

"I think he moved," Becker said.

"I want him to," one of the constables said, "but it's just the flames playing tricks."

"He did! His lips! I saw them move!"

Becker leaned close, straining to hear what Ryan said.

The other constables leaned close also.

"Snow," Ryan murmured.

"The poor man's hallucinating. He thinks it's snowing."

"That's not the snow he means! Help me lift him! Help me take him to Dr. Snow!"

WILL INSPECTOR RYAN survive his wounds?" Lord Palmerston asked.

For the second time in two nights, De Quincey, Emily, and Becker stood in the ballroom of Lord Palmerston's mansion. Commissioner Mayne had been summoned also.

Dawn paled the darkness beyond the windows. But Palmerston was dressed as if for business, wearing his customary gray slacks, black waistcoat, and black coat, the hem of which descended to his knees. His heavy frame continued to give him authority, as did his thick, long, brown-dyed sideburns that emphasized his powerful eyes.

"Dr. Snow is cautiously optimistic, Your Lordship," Becker explained. "The doctor says that under usual circumstances, Ryan would have bled to death, but apparently the cold water did something to his body—reduced the blood flow is how I understood it. The doctor disinfected the wounds and closed them. Now it's a matter of waiting to see if Ryan's body can heal itself."

"Where is Ryan now?"

"Resting at Dr. Snow's residence until he can be transported to a hospital," Becker replied. "Ryan had sufficient strength to warn us about the men who helped Brookline. They were arrested, trying to leave the city in hearses that Ryan heard them talk about. The men were dressed as undertakers and had money they stole hidden under corpses in coffins."

"Commissioner Mayne, send a constable to Dr. Snow and tell him that I want Ryan brought here instead of to a hospital."

"Your Lordship is very generous."

Lord Palmerston nodded. "When Ryan is well enough to converse, I'll have an opportunity to learn further details about what happened. During last night's confrontation, did Brookline say anything about me?"

"About Your Lordship? I, uh…"

"Answer my question, Commissioner."

"He did in fact speak about you."

"In what specific words?" Palmerston's gaze suggested that the conversation had entered dangerous territory.

"With Your Lordship's forgiveness…"

"Get on with it."

"He said that you and your… I beg your indulgence… what he called your wealthy, powerful, arrogant friends were greedy and indifferent to the poor."

"And?"

"That is all, Your Lordship."

"Nothing about politics?"

"No, Your Lordship. Is there something specific that occupies your concern?"

"Brookline was privy to numerous confidential discussions. It would be unfortunate if he had broadcast their contents." Palmerston's eyes relaxed. He changed the subject. "Becker, you're shivering."

"The water was very cold, Your Lordship."

"Will it make you feel warmer if, with Commissioner Mayne's approval, I promote you to the rank of detective?"

Becker looked as if he didn't believe he'd heard correctly. "Detective?"

"Stand before the fire." Palmerston motioned to a nearby servant. "Bring Detective Becker dry clothes and a blanket. Hot tea for everyone."

The servant departed.

"De Quincey," Palmerston asked, "why are you walking in place? Your face shines with sweat."

"With Your Lordship's forgiveness…" De Quincey pulled a bottle from his coat and swallowed from it.

Palmerston looked horrified. "Is that…?"

"My medicine."

"You're pathetic."

"Quite so, Your Lordship."

"Aren't you worried about ruining your health?"

"After a half century of laudanum, my health was ruined long ago, Your Lordship."

"And aren't you ashamed of setting such a poor example to your daughter?"

"On the contrary, I set an excellent example. Emily's daily experience with me teaches her never to touch a drop of this evil substance."

Palmerston, whose riches came largely from the opium trade, considered the word "evil" in reference to the drug. Briefly his eyes hardened again.

"Yes, well, I summoned all of you so that I might do something that a man in my position almost never does—admit a mistake. You have my regret that I misjudged Brookline and misjudged *you*. If there is anything I can do to express my gratitude for your help, you need only ask."

"My daughter and I find ourselves without lodgings, Your Lordship," De Quincey said promptly.

Palmerston was surprised by the quick response.

"Colonel Brookline arranged for our previous accommodations," De Quincey elaborated, "but the association is so disagreeable that I'm afraid neither my daughter nor I could sleep peacefully under that roof."

Palmerston made a calculated decision. "The two of you shall remain here under my protection. Perhaps you'll think of something else that Colonel Brookline said about me. If there's nothing further..."

"Actually, Your Lordship..." Emily, who'd been silent, stepped forward.

"Yes, Miss De Quincey?" Palmerston looked uneasy, as if sensing what was about to happen.

"An undertaker needs to be paid sixteen pounds for funeral expenses involving the first set of victims."

"Funeral expenses?"

"In addition, my father made promises to a group of beggars on Oxford Street. For their considerable help, they were guaranteed an abundance of food throughout the next year."

"Beggars? Food?"

"I myself promised one of them—a boy with acrobatic capabilities who was wounded—that his tuition and board would be paid at a commendable school."

"Tuition? Board?"

"Also, I promised a group of privately employed ladies that they would be taken to a farm where they could become healthy in clean air, growing vegetables."

"Privately employed ladies?"

"Prostitutes, Your Lordship," Emily explained.

"Detective Becker, is this young woman always so forthcoming?"

"I'm pleased to say that she is, Your Lordship."

Emily concealed a smile, but not enough so that the new detective failed to notice it, concealing his own smile.

"I grant your requests on one condition," Palmerston pronounced. "An exceeding number of newspaper reporters wish to speak to all of you. You shall make clear that all the efforts to save the city were coordinated through my office and that I myself personally directed the unmasking of Colonel Brookline."

Ryan lay on a bed in a servant's room in the mansion's attic.

Emily tried not to show how alarmed she was by his pallor. De Quincey and Becker stood on the other side of the bed.

"Dr. Snow told me that your wounds do not appear to be infected," Emily assured him, hoping that her brightness didn't sound forced.

Ryan's eyelids flickered. Slowly he focused on his visitors.

"Are you in pain?" Emily asked.

"No," Ryan managed to say. "Dr. Snow gave me laudanum."

"Be careful not to become habituated," De Quincey cautioned.

"I would laugh," Ryan murmured, "but it might tear my stitches."

"Ah, I detect a smile," Emily said victoriously.

"Despite the circumstances, I admit I enjoyed meeting you and your father, Miss De Quincey."

"If that is intended as a good-bye, it is premature. You have not seen the last of Father and me. Rather than return to debt collectors in Edinburgh, we plan to stay in London a while longer."

Ryan considered her statement and nodded, surprising her. "Good. London will be more exciting for your presence."

Emily felt warmth in her cheeks. "Excitement turned out to be a dubious experience. Father and I look forward to the humdrum of resuming his discussions with booksellers and magazine writers."

"Surely you can spend your time to better advantage," Ryan found the strength to say. "London has greater attractions than magazine writers."

"Yes, I heard so much about the famed Crystal Palace that I am eager to see it," Emily enthused. "A glass structure so tall that full-grown elm trees decorate its interior."

"It is indeed a marvel. After the Great Exhibition three years ago, it was disassembled at Hyde Park and rebuilt at Sydenham Hill."

"I volunteered to escort Emily and her father there," Becker said happily.

"How thoughtful," Ryan muttered. "I would have been pleased to volunteer as well."

"Your convalescence frustrates you, I am sure," Emily noted. "That is another reason Father and I decided to stay in London."

"Another reason?"

"Dr. Snow has obligations that prevent him from visiting you as often as he would prefer. He taught me to administer treatment to you in his absence."

"Since we are not related, the intimacy might be uncomfortable for you, Miss De Quincey. I fear I will be a burden."

"Nonsense. Given what Florence Nightingale has accomplished for nursing in the Crimean War, it's obvious that an injury has greater priority than false modesty. Women will soon have a profession to pursue besides being a servant, a shopgirl, or a governess."

"One thing I have learned from my experience with you is to appreciate new thoughts. I shall be grateful for the attention, Miss De Quincey."

"Please call me 'Emily.' Detective Becker learned to do that. After everything that we have been through together, why do you insist on being formal?"

"*Detective* Becker?" Ryan looked at him, puzzled.

"My stature has risen," Becker explained. "I owe it to the opportunity you gave me and look forward to many more adventures together."

"I believe I have experienced sufficient adventures." Ryan's eyelids began to droop.

"Weariness makes you say that," Emily decided. "You and Detective Becker are men of action if I ever saw them. We shall let you sleep. But in your hazy condition, perhaps I can persuade you to tell me your first name."

Ryan hesitated. "Sean."

"And what is *my* name?"

"Miss..."

"Please try again."

"Your name is Emily."

"Very good." She looked at Becker. "And what is *your* first name?"

Becker hesitated also. "Joseph."

"Splendid."

Emily looked from one man to the other. Becker seemed only a little older than her twenty-one years, a tall, strapping, handsome fellow with solid manners, and a slight scar on his chin that somehow made him more attractive. In contrast, Ryan was almost twice her age, theoretically too old to be considered as anything but at best a brother, and yet the lines of experience in his face made him oddly pleasing to look at, not to mention that his confidence and even his gruffness were appealing.

What strange thoughts, she told herself, but as Emily did with all new concepts, she refused to suppress them.

"Sean and Joseph." She touched their hands. "I believe we can finally declare that we are friends."

"There is no such thing as forgetting," De Quincey said with a smile. "But for a change, this is *one* circumstance I shall happily always remember."

POSTSCRIPT

In 1886, SEVENTY-FIVE YEARS after the Ratcliffe Highway murders, employees of a gas company tore up the paving stones at the intersection of Cannon and Cable streets to dig a trench for a pipe. Six feet down, in the middle of the crossroads, they found a skeleton with a stake through its left rib cage. At first, the workmen suspected that they had discovered evidence of a long-ago murder, but a police investigation determined that the skeleton belonged to John Williams, a suspected killer who had hanged himself before he could be declared guilty of brutal slayings that had paralyzed London and all of England three quarters of a century earlier. People walked away with arm bones, leg bones, and ribs as souvenirs. The owner of a tavern at Cannon and Cable streets displayed the skull on a shelf behind the bar.

No one knows what became of it.

AFTERWORD

Adventures with the Opium-Eater

FOR TWO YEARS, I lived in 1854 London. Charles Darwin prompted me to do it, or at least a movie about him did. It's called *Creation,* and it dramatizes Darwin's struggle to complete *On the Origin of Species.* If you're a Christian fundamentalist, you probably wish that his struggle had persisted. Darwin's wife certainly did. She believed that his theory of evolution was blasphemous and urged him not to continue. Meanwhile he suffered from extreme guilt because he might have been indirectly responsible for the death of his favorite daughter, having sanctioned medical treatment— hydrotherapy—that possibly aggravated her lingering illness.

These multiple pressures made Darwin chronically sick with headaches, heart palpitations, and stomach problems, rendering him barely able to function. But here's the point. Darwin wasn't aware of his guilt, both about the death of his daughter and about how his research was harming his relationship with his wife. We post-Freudians understand the link between the mind and the body, but Darwin's persistent health problems were a medical mystery in Victorian England of the 1850s.

The turning point of the film occurs when a friend visits Darwin and tells him, "Charles, people like De Quincey believe we're influenced by thoughts and emotions we don't know we have."

Thoughts and emotions we don't know we have? Sure sounds like Freud, but Freud's theories about the subconscious weren't published until the 1890s, forty years after Darwin's crisis. In fact, De Quincey's theories about what he called the separate chambers of our minds (he invented the term "sub-conscious") were initially developed in the 1820s, *seventy* years before Freud.

Something in me came to attention. De Quincey? I remembered a long-ago course in nineteenth-century English literature in which a professor mentioned Thomas De Quincey not as a precursor of Freud but as a notorious drug abuser, the first to have written about that forbidden subject, in his scandalous *Confessions of an English Opium-Eater.* The professor referred to De Quincey dismissively as a footnote in literature and went on to praise the usual greatest hits of the Romantic and Victorian eras.

Curiosity compelled me to go to the bookshelf on which, like a pack rat, I still kept my undergraduate textbooks. Given what the professor of my youth had said, I wasn't surprised that De Quincey was scantily represented: ten pages in a thousand-page anthology. What did surprise me was that while only a portion of one of his essays, "The Mail-Coach," was included, those few pages were the opposite of what my professor had led me to expect. They were spellbinding.

With rare vividness, De Quincey described riding next to a mail-coach driver as their vehicle hurtled along a dark road. They both fell asleep. Waking, De Quincey saw a shadow approaching him. The shadow became a carriage speeding around a curve, a man driving, a woman listening to something he was telling her. De Quincey tried to waken the mail coach's driver, without success. The carriage sped closer. De Quincey struggled to take the reins from the driver, again without success. The carriage raced nearer. The massive size of the coach left no doubt that a collision would destroy the carriage and its occupants. At the last moment, De Quincey roused the driver, who gasped at the danger and turned the coach enough that it only grazed the carriage and yet caused sufficient damage that the woman, aware of how close she came to dying, opened her mouth in a silent scream.

That resembles a scene from a thriller, but in actuality it's part of an essay about the English mail-coach system, which (I found out later when I acquired a full text) expands into a discussion about the subconscious and the nature of dreams.

I was hooked. I bought a copy of *Confessions of an English Opium-Eater.* Reading that 1821 memoir, I felt that the little gentleman was speaking directly to me as he recalled the death of his father and the abuse he suffered because of his indifferent mother and his four guardians. His escape from school, his winter on the cruel streets of London, his relationship with his beloved Ann, their tragic parting, his first experience with laudanum...De Quincey's description of these events gripped me.

I learned that he created a further sensation with his essay "On Murder Considered as One of the Fine Arts," the third installment of which was the most blood-soaked true-crime narrative written until that time, describing at length the notorious Ratcliffe Highway multiple murders that terrorized London and all of England years earlier, in 1811. *It's as if he was actually there,* I thought. And that's when the idea for *Murder as a Fine Art* came to me. The third installment of that essay was published in 1854. De Quincey was living in Edinburgh at the time. But what if someone lured him to London, promising news about Ann? What if that person used the third installment of the "Murder" essay as an instruction manual, replicating the original Ratcliffe Highway killings? What if De Quincey became the suspect? What if...?

Seldom have plot elements fallen so swiftly into place for me. But as every novelist knows, the plot's the easy part. What matters is how the story is handled, and in this case, the task was huge. Some historical fiction is often little more than costume drama, with modern dialogue and attitudes.

What I had in mind was something more immersive. Before I wrote the first sentence, I wanted to become an expert in De Quincey, as if I were writing a doctoral dissertation about him. To support his wife and eight children as well as his laudanum habit, he wrote an impressive number of essays, memoirs, book reviews, translations, and stories. His collected works amount to thousands of pages. Like a Method actor absorbing a role, I read those pages again and again, each time finding new insights. I decided that wherever possible, I would adapt De Quincey's prose into the text and especially his dialogue, channeling him. As his American publisher noted, De Quincey "talked with an eloquence I had not heard surpassed. It seemed as if it were sinful not to take down his wonderful sentences."

Then I needed to learn about De Quincey's life and all the events that he hadn't written about in his memoirs. In that regard I was immeasurably helped by Robert Morrison's biography *The English Opium-Eater*. Professor Morrison and I eventually struck up an e-mail friendship, during which I learned even more. *Murder as a Fine Art* is dedicated to him, as it is to another De Quincey biographer, Grevel Lindop, whose *The Opium-Eater* also proved to be extremely informative.

Next, I needed to learn about 1854 London, to the point that I convinced myself I was actually there. What were the streets made of? What sort of money did people carry? How heavy were their clothes? What were the ingredients of an ordinary meal? How did people bathe?

For two years I traveled into the past, reading nothing that wasn't related to that time and place. Among numerous books, the following were especially revealing: Richard D. Altick's *Victorian People and Ideas,* Heather Creaton's edition of *Victorian Diaries: The Daily Lives of Victorian Men and Women,* Orlando Figes's *The Crimean War,* Judith Flanders's *Inside the Victorian Home,* Alison Gernsheim's *Victorian and Edwardian Fashion: A Photographic Survey,* Gillian Gill's *We Two: Victoria and Albert,* Henry Mayhew's *London Labour and the London Poor,* Sally Mitchell's *Daily Life in Victorian England,* Liza Picard's *Victorian London,* Daniel Pool's *What Jane Austen Ate and Charles Dickens Knew,* Lytton Strachey's *Queen Victoria,* Judith Summers's *Soho: A History of London's Most Colourful Neighborhood,* Kate Summerscale's *The Suspicions of Mr. Whicher: A Shocking Murder and the Undoing of a Great Victorian Detective,* F.M.L. Thompson's *The Rise of Respectable Society: A Social History of Victorian Britain 1830–1900,* and J. J. Tobias's *Crime and Police in England 1700–1900.* Gregory Dart's essay "Chamber of Horrors" in *Thomas De Quincey: New Theoretical and Critical Directions* (edited by Robert Morrison and Daniel Sanjiv Roberts) was also helpful.

Some books deserve special mention. The best account of London's 1854 cholera outbreak is Steven Johnson's *The Ghost Map: The Story of*

London's Most Terrifying Epidemic, which describes Dr. John Snow's desperate search for the source of the disease. Snow had considerable help from clergyman Henry Whitehead. Unfortunately my narrative had no room for Reverend Whitehead, so I am pleased at last to mention him.

The most complete account of the Ratcliffe Highway killings is *The Maul and the Pear Tree,* by noted mystery author P. D. James and T. A. Critchley. One element that this fascinating book doesn't discuss is the curious similarity of names between John Williams, the accused killer, and John Williamson, one of the victims. The first time I read that John Williams killed John Williamson, I thought it was a typographical error. The 1811 court transcripts don't draw attention to the similarity. Only G. K. Chesterton (a century after the slayings) thought the almost identical names worthy of comment: "A man named Williams does quite accidentally murder a man named Williamson. It sounds like a sort of infanticide." Because De Quincey pioneered theories about the subconscious, I decided that not only infanticide but also patricide and a host of other psychoanalytic topics would figure prominently in my re-creation of the original murders.

I studied London maps of the period. The layout of Coldbath Fields Prison is based on a contemporary diagram, as is the layout of the British East India docks and Vauxhall Gardens. I learned a new vocabulary, employing words that have long since fallen out of use: dustman, mudlark, dipper, dollymop, linen lifter, rookery, costermonger, and many others.

The only fiction I read belonged to the mid-Victorian period, especially works by Charles Dickens, Anthony Trollope, and Wilkie Collins, who provided minute details about what characters ate and wore and so on. Collins's fame came a few years after De Quincey with *The Woman in White* in 1860 and *The Moonstone* in 1868, but he has strong relevance to De Quincey, for while Collins is often credited with being the inventor of the sensation novel, De Quincey's persistent topics of drug abuse and murder anticipated the sensation mania, qualifying him as a major influence on the genre. Collins acknowledges as much in *The Moonstone* when his characters explicitly discuss De Quincey's *Confessions of an English Opium-Eater,* which provides a clue to the solution of the mystery.

De Quincey also influenced Edgar Allan Poe, who in turn influenced Sir Arthur Conan Doyle's creation of Sherlock Holmes, so to a degree De Quincey also contributed to the invention of both the mystery genre and its most famous detective.

Murder as a Fine Art is my version of a nineteenth-century novel. Although modern novels almost never use the third-person omniscient viewpoint, nineteenth-century novels favored it, allowing an objective narrator to step forward and provide information. I found that device to be helpful in explaining aspects of Victorian life that modern readers would otherwise have found as baffling as a culture in an alien universe. I ignored another modern convention by mixing viewpoints and inserting sections from a first-person journal, a frequent device in sensation novels. By returning to the nineteenth century, I felt liberated to use more ways to tell a story.

Despite my lengthy research, I sometimes differed from the record. For example, Emily would not have referred to De Quincey as "Father" but would instead have called him "Pa*pa*," with the emphasis on the second syllable. In an early draft, I used the historically accurate "Pa*pa*," but it made Emily sound juvenile, and I abandoned the device in favor of "Father." Similarly, on occasion I condensed some of De Quincey's quotations and combined a few events in his life.

For plot reasons, I was forced to include a deliberate historical error. I'm aware that by 1854 Dr. Snow had moved from Soho's 54 Frith Street and resided at 18 Sackville Street in the nearby district of Mayfair. But the proximity of Frith Street to where teenage De Quincey had lived in the empty house on Greek Street (only a block away) was too convenient to be ignored. I finally decided that Snow's Sackville address was undergoing renovations, requiring him to return to his previous Frith Street address.

Otherwise, *Murder as a Fine Art* is as historically accurate as I could make it. For two years, I had the pleasure of living in 1854 London. I hope that you, too, enjoyed the adventure.

ACKNOWLEDGMENTS

As always, I'm grateful for the friendship and guidance of Jane Dystel and Miriam Goderich along with the other good folks at Dystel & Goderich Literary Management, especially Lauren E. Abramo and Rachel Stout.

I'm also indebted to the splendid team at Mulholland Books/Little, Brown, particularly (in alphabetical order) Judith Clain, Theresa Giacopasi, Deborah Jacobs, Josh Kendall, Wes Miller, Miriam Parker, Michael Pietsch, John Schoenfelder, Ruth Tross (in the UK), and Tracy Williams. Copyeditors and proofreaders are my last line of defense; in this case I'm grateful to William Drennan and Peggy Leith Anderson, respectively.

One of the pleasures of doing research is that I have the opportunity to become friends (sometimes only through e-mail) with people who are generous enough to teach me about my subject. One of those I already mentioned: biographer Robert Morrison (*The English Opium-Eater: A Biography of Thomas De Quincey*). A world-class scholar of Romantic and Victorian literature, Robert is a professor at Queen's University in Kingston, Ontario. He graciously read the manuscript of *Murder as a Fine Art* and advised me about the fine points of De Quincey's life. He also sent me copies of hard-to-find De Quincey documents as well as scholarly articles that I hadn't been able to locate.

Jeff Cowton at the Wordsworth Trust (Dove Cottage, Grasmere, the UK) was helpful in providing a photograph of Thomas De Quincey and

.net, along with terrific additional artwork by Tomislav Tikulin.

My good friend Barbara Peters, owner of the Poisoned Pen bookstore
in Scottsdale, Arizona, provided immeasurable encouragement when I
told her that I was traveling to 1854 London, a departure that neither of
us could ever have expected.

My wife, Donna, gave her usual excellent advice as my first reader. I
appreciate her decades of patience as each day for several hours I become a
hermit.

ABOUT THE AUTHOR

David Morrell was born in Kitchener, Ontario, Canada. As a teenager he became a fan of the classic television series *Route 66,* about two young men in a Corvette convertible traveling the United States in search of themselves. Stirling Silliphant's scripts for that series were an unusual blend of action and ideas, so impressing Morrell that he decided to become a writer.

The work of another writer (Hemingway scholar Philip Young) prompted Morrell to move to the United States, where he studied with Young at the Pennsylvania State University and received his MA and PhD in American literature. There he also met the esteemed science fiction author William Tenn (real name Philip Klass), who taught Morrell the basics of fiction writing. The result was *First Blood,* a groundbreaking novel about a returned Vietnam veteran suffering from post-traumatic stress disorder who comes into conflict with a small-town police chief and fights his own version of the Vietnam War.

That "father" of modern action novels was published in 1972, while Morrell was a professor in the English department at the University of Iowa. He taught there from 1970 to 1986, simultaneously writing other novels, many of them international best sellers, including the classic spy trilogy *The Brotherhood of the Rose* (the basis for a top-rated NBC miniseries that premiered after a Super Bowl), *The Fraternity of the Stone,* and *The League of Night and Fog.*

Eventually wearying of two professions, Morrell gave up his academic tenure in order to write full time. Shortly afterward, his fifteen-year-old son, Matthew, was diagnosed with a rare form of bone cancer and died in 1987, a loss that haunts not only Morrell's life but also his work, as in his memoir about Matthew, *Fireflies,* and his novel *Desperate Measures,* whose main character lost a son.

"The mild-mannered professor with the bloody-minded visions," as one reviewer called him, Morrell is the author of more than thirty works, including such high-action thrillers as *The Naked Edge, Creepers,* and *The Spy Who Came for Christmas* (set in Santa Fe, New Mexico, where he lives). His writing book, *The Successful Novelist,* analyzes what he has learned during his four decades as an author.

Morrell is an Edgar, Anthony, and Macavity nominee as well as a three-time recipient of the distinguished Stoker Award from the Horror Writers Association. The International Thriller Writers organization gave him its prestigious career-achievement Thriller Master Award. His work has been translated into twenty-six languages.

To send him an e-mail, please go to the contact page at his website, www.davidmorrell.net.

Reading Group Guide

Murder as a
Fine Art

DAVID MORRELL

A conversation between
David Morrell and Robert Morrison

Following is a discussion between novelist David Morrell and Robert Morrison — author of *The English Opium Eater: A Biography of Thomas De Quincey* and Queen's National Scholar and professor of nineteenth-century British literature, Queen's University, Kingston, Ontario — about *Murder as a Fine Art.*

> **Robert Morrison:** I love the idea behind *Murder as a Fine Art.* John Williams commits a series of sensational killings in 1811. Thomas De Quincey writes his most powerful essay about the killings in 1854. Somebody reads De Quincey on Williams and decides to produce his own version of the killings, far exceeding them in terror. How did this idea come to you?

> **David Morrell:** Robert, coming from a De Quincey scholar, your enthusiasm means a lot to me. I studied De Quincey years ago when I was an undergraduate English student. My professor treated him as a footnote in 1800s literature, giving him importance only because De Quincey was the first to write about drug addiction in his notorious *Confessions of an English Opium-Eater.* I forgot about him until I happened to watch a movie about Charles Darwin, *Creation,*

which dramatizes the nervous breakdown Darwin suffered while writing *On the Origin of Species*. In the movie, someone says to Darwin, "You know, Charles, people such as De Quincey believe that we're controlled by elements in our mind that we're not aware of."

RM: It sounds like Freud.

DM: Yes. But Freud didn't publish until half a century later. In fact, because De Quincey invented the word *subconscious,* Freud may have been influenced by him. Anyway, I took down my old college textbook, started reading De Quincey, and became spellbound. I read more and more of his work. Then I got to his blood-soaked essay about the terrifying Ratcliffe Highway murders, "On Murder Considered as One of the Fine Arts." The idea came to me that someone would read the essay and, for complicated reasons, replicate the murders on a more horrifying scale. De Quincey, the Opium-Eater who was obsessed with murder, would then be the logical suspect. You wrote a terrific biography about De Quincey, *The English Opium-Eater.* What caused your own interest in this brilliant author?

RM: I first heard of De Quincey many years ago when I was a graduate student at Oxford. My tutor was Jonathan Wordsworth, the great-great-great-nephew of the poet.

DM: What an experience *that* must have been.

RM: For one of my tutorial assignments, Jonathan asked me to read De Quincey's *Confessions.* I had no idea what to expect, and certainly no idea that I was going to spend the next thirty years hooked on him. Of course I found the drugs and addiction part of the narrative very interesting. But what really grabbed me was how well De Quincey wrote.

He could be, by turns, humorous, conversational, elaborate, or impassioned. And this great ability as a stylist made it possible for him to chart his experience with remarkable depth and energy. After that, and like you, I just kept reading. One of the wonderful things about *Murder as a Fine Art* is how vividly it brings De Quincey to life, and how compellingly it exploits his fascination with dreams, violence, memory, and addiction. It's not only a superb thriller, but it also packs an intellectual punch. How did you bring these two elements together so successfully?

DM: A reviewer once called me "the mild-mannered professor with the bloody-minded visions."

RM: Ha!

DM: Yes, it makes me laugh too. I was a literature professor for many years, one of several things that you and I have in common. When I was in college, I worked in factories to pay my tuition. Some of my fellow workers read thrillers during their breaks, and I started wondering if it was possible to write a thriller that would appeal to two kinds of readers—those in my factory life and those in my college life. The former wanted an exciting story to distract them from their jobs, and the latter wanted a story to have what literature professors call subtext. From the start, with *First Blood,* I followed that approach, but with De Quincey, I felt like I'd struck the mother lode. On the one hand, he writes in blood-soaked detail about the Ratcliffe Highway murders. On the other hand, he layers the killings with amazingly complex perceptions. The two elements—visceral and intellectual—came together. Your biography of De Quincey was a big help to me. Did you have any scholarly adventures as you researched it, any discoveries and revelations?

RM: Writing the biography was definitely an adventure. As you're aware, the most well-known modern derivative of opium is heroin, and while working on the book I had long discussions with two heroin addicts, one of whom was still using, and another of whom was in his third recovery. I asked them to read the sections in the biography where I talk specifically about De Quincey and drugs, and their comments really gave me a much better understanding of what it is like to live with opiates. They also helped me to realize that De Quincey must have been an alcoholic as well as an opium addict, for he ingested opium as "laudanum" (opium dissolved in alcohol), which means that he was consuming vast quantities of both substances.

DM: Vast quantities indeed. At the peak of his addiction, De Quincey drank sixteen ounces of laudanum each day. The alcohol alone would have affected him, not to mention the opium. Yet somehow he was able to write some of the most brilliant prose of the 1800s.

RM: My biggest adventure in writing the biography came six days after I finished it, when I was casually leafing through a London bookseller's catalog and saw the following item for sale: "119 Autograph Letters by De Quincey's Three Daughters: A Significant New Source for the Author's Life." David, I fell out of my chair. A "new source"? I had finished my biography less than a week earlier, and it was already out of date! Needless to say, I phoned my publisher, hollered "Stop the presses," flew to London two days later, and then had the exhilarating experience of reading through the 119 letters.

DM: It sounds like a scene from a literary thriller. Your heart must have been pounding.

RM: The letters gave me all sorts of new information about De Quincey and led me to revise the biography in twenty-one places, most noticeably when it came to De Quincey's relationship with his three daughters, Margaret, Florence, and Emily. In *Murder as a Fine Art,* Emily De Quincey is of pivotal importance. What intrigued you about her? How and why did you make her such a vital part of the action?

DM: When I decided to bring De Quincey to 1854 London, I needed to give him a companion.

RM: Your own version of Dr. Watson to Sherlock Holmes.

DM: The comparison is apt. De Quincey inspired Edgar Allan Poe, who in turn inspired Sir Arthur Conan Doyle to create Sherlock Holmes, so when I chose De Quincey as the hero of this thriller, I was definitely thinking about the origins of the detective genre. Anyway, one of De Quincey's daughters was the likely candidate. Margaret and Florence had established their own families by then, so that left Emily, who was twenty-one and offered all sorts of possibilities.

RM: Because not much is known about her?

DM: Exactly. With De Quincey, I needed to be scrupulously loyal to the facts, but with Emily, I had more latitude. De Quincey used his children to help him evade his numerous debt collectors. They would sneak over fences, through holes in walls and windows, bringing food and writing supplies to wherever he was hiding. Then they would take his manuscripts to his publishers in the same clandestine way and sneak money back to him. After he took a small amount of money for his basic needs, he told the children to deliver the rest to their mother.

RM: So you had evidence that Emily was street-smart and athletic — all those fences and windows.

DM: I was reading between the lines of your biography of him. His daughters grew up in an intellectual household and had independent attitudes because of the radical-thinking people he knew. Thus in my novel Emily became not only De Quincey's spy but also a delightfully outspoken woman whose advanced ideas make people in the novel gape. As one example, Emily refuses to wear the awkward thirty-seven-pound hooped dresses of the period and instead prefers a loose dress with trousers underneath, a garment known as a bloomer dress that was named after an early feminist named Amelia Bloomer. She constantly outsmarts constables, undertakers, and even England's home secretary. I always smiled when I wrote a scene that Emily dominated. It occurs to me that we're in a long-overdue De Quincey renaissance. Tell me about the various De Quincey publications that you're editing.

RM: A renaissance indeed. It's gratifying to think that we're part of it. *Murder as a Fine Art* will reach a wide audience and play a major role in furthering interest in De Quincey's life and writings. On my side, my new edition of *Confessions of an English Opium-Eater* was recently published by Oxford University Press. I'm really excited about it. I thought I knew the *Confessions* pretty well, and yet when I sat down to edit his memoir, I discovered all sorts of things that I hadn't noticed before, especially in the magnificent dream sequence at the end. Right now, I'm working on a much longer selection of De Quincey that will be published in the 21st-Century Oxford Authors series. The edition will contain all of De Quincey's finest work, including his great essays on murder and his articles about his friends Wordsworth,

Coleridge, and other literary stars of the time. I think of it as equivalent to a *De Quincey's Greatest Hits* album.

DM: De Quincey was so cool that if he were alive today, I think he'd approve of the metaphor. His prose can be so vivid that sometimes I think he *is* still alive. I read his thousands of pages so often that after a while I felt that I was channeling him. One of my own adventures in writing *Murder as a Fine Art* was the chance to become friends with you and to share our enthusiasm for all things De Quincey. Thanks, Robert.

This interview first appeared on mulhollandbooks.com, April 2013.

Worlds Colliding

My name is David Morrell.

I write thrillers.

On occasion, people are puzzled when they learn that I also have a PhD in American literature from Penn State and that I was a full professor at the University of Iowa, where I taught Hawthorne, Melville, Henry James, and Edith Wharton.

For me, the two worlds blend perfectly. In my youth, I earned the money for my undergraduate tuition by working twelve-hour night shifts in factories. In one memorable task, I made fenders for automobiles, shredding several pairs of thick leather gloves during each shift as I handled razor-sharp sheets of metal. When I was transferred to another area of the factory, the man who replaced me lost both his hands in the fender-molding machine.

I noticed that, even though the workers had the glazed look of zombies, they read books during their lunch hour. When I looked closer, I discovered that every book was a thriller. The excitement of the plots took the laborers away from the terrible tedium of their lives.

One morning, after my factory shift ended, I drove to the nearby university, where I was scheduled to meet with my adviser about the requirements for finishing my BA studies. During that drive, I had an epiphany. I had already made the decision to become a writer, and I had no doubt that I wanted to write thrillers. After all, they had given me a psychological escape when I was a child and family arguments so frightened me that I frequently slept under my bed. I knew that the kind of stories that had been my salvation would be the kind of stories I would write.

But how would I do it?

My epiphany came in this form. Struck by the contrast between the factory I had left and the university I approached, I wondered if it was possible to write thrillers that satisfied two different types of readers at the same time: those eager for distraction, and those who wanted the kinds of themes and techniques that I was accustomed to in university literature courses. A thriller — by definition — must be thrilling. Could it accomplish that primary goal and simultaneously have other purposes? I was reminded of illustrations that seem to depict one thing when observed from a particular angle and then depict something else when seen from a different perspective.

Back in 1915, Van Wyck Brooks, a famous analyst of American culture, deplored the use of "highbrow" and "lowbrow" as labels that critics used to categorize fiction. Brooks condemned both extremes and suggested that there weren't inferior forms of fiction, only inferior practitioners. In his view, it was possible for popular fiction to have serious intentions without ever sacrificing entertainment appeal and narrative drive.

That became my goal. The letters I get from readers that most gratify me are of two different types. In one, readers thank me for distracting them from the harsh reality of fires, car accidents, lost jobs, divorces, serious medical problems, and similar calamities. In the second kind of letter, readers tell me that, when they reread my books, themes and techniques that weren't obvious on first reading suddenly emerge from the background, with the result that the books become different with a later reading.

This shifting nature of reality, depending on the angle from which we perceive it, is one of my favorite themes. My novel *Murder as a Fine Art* takes place in 1854 London. Its main character, Thomas De Quincey, uses the theories of the German philosopher Immanuel Kant ("Does reality exist objectively or only in our minds?") to solve a series of mass killings that imitate the infamous Ratcliffe Highway murders of forty-three years earlier.

Call me schizophrenic — or the sum of my contradictions. All these years after I left the factory where I worked and drove toward the university where I studied, I continue to be two separate people when I write, with two different kinds of readers in my imagination.

This essay first appeared on mulhollandbooks.com, November 2011.

Questions and topics for discussion

1. Thomas De Quincey, the protagonist of *Murder as a Fine Art,* is based on a person of historical record, a writer popular in the 1800s. What do you think the novel says about De Quincey? What does the novel convey specifically about addiction, given De Quincey's dependence on laudanum, a medicinal form of opium that was once commonplace in English households?

2. What did you think of De Quincey's daughter Emily? How would you describe her relationship with her father, and would you care for him in the same way if you were in her shoes? What does *Murder as a Fine Art* reveal about gender roles in Victorian society and how they might or might not have been in a state of flux?

3. David Morrell researched the period and setting of his novel in great detail. What about the novel's depiction of Victorian society most surprised you? What do you think the novel tells us about class mobility and social stratification?

4. What literary works do you think influenced Morrell the most in the writing of *Murder as a Fine Art*? Did the writing style or characters remind you of the style or the characters of another author's work in particular or any other novel in Morrell's body of work?

5. Who did you think might be responsible for the killings in *Murder as a Fine Art* leading up to the novel's central revelation? Were you surprised at the killer's identity? How did you react when the secret was revealed?

6. Were you familiar with Thomas De Quincey before reading *Murder as a Fine Art*? What, if anything, did Morrell's novel teach you about the writer or his work? Will you be picking up anything written by Thomas De Quincey after reading Morrell's novel, and if so, what?

7. What do you think the novel's depiction of criminality and of its two central members of the police force, Detective Inspector Ryan and Constable Becker, says about the law enforcement of the time?

8. *Murder as a Fine Art* ends with the hint of romantic potential between Emily De Quincey and either Detective Inspector Ryan or Constable Becker. Which suitor do you think would be a better match for Emily and why?

MULHOLLAND BOOKS

You won't be able to put down these Mulholland Books.

Visit mulhollandbooks.com for
your daily suspense fiction fix.

Download the FREE Mulholland Books app.